*And the only noise is the tape and the slightly
flat singing of a man trying to dwell slightly less
on his day, his year and his less-than-ideal
handling of relationships.*

Penguin Books

BACHELOR KISSES

Nick Earls is the author of four books, including the best-selling novels *Zigzag Street* and *Bachelor Kisses*. His work has been published internationally and also in translation. *Zigzag Street* won a Betty Trask Award in the UK in 1998, and is currently being developed into a feature film. His earlier works include the award-winning young-adult novel *After January* and *Passion*, a collection of short stories that was equal runner-up in the 1993 Steele Rudd Australian Short Story Award.

Nick Earls graduated in Medicine from the University of Queensland in 1986, and is still not quite sure how he ended up with an honours degree. He lives in Brisbane.

BACHELOR KISSES

NICK EARLS

Penguin Books

If you would like to write to Nick Earls,
his email address is nickearls@peg.apc.org

Penguin Books Australia Ltd
487 Maroondah Highway, PO Box 257
Ringwood, Victoria 3134, Australia
Penguin Books Ltd
Harmondsworth, Middlesex, England
Viking Penguin, A Division of Penguin Books USA Inc.
375 Hudson Street, New York, New York 10014, USA
Penguin Books Canada Limited
10 Alcorn Avenue, Toronto, Ontario, Canada M4V 3B2
Penguin Books (NZ) Ltd
Cnr Rosedale and Airborne Roads, Albany, Auckland, New Zealand
Penguin Books (South Africa) (Pty) Ltd
4 Pallinghurst Road, Parktown 2193, South Africa

First published by Penguin Books Australia Ltd, 1998

1 3 5 7 9 10 8 6 4 2

Design by Jo Hunt, Penguin Design Studio
Typeset in 9.5/12.25 pt Sabon by Post Pre-press Group
Printed and bound in Australia by Australian Print Group,
Maryborough, Victoria

National Library of Australia
Cataloguing-in-Publication data:

Earls, Nick, 1963–.
Bachelor kisses.

ISBN 0 14 026963 0.

I. Title.

A823.3

1

Rick will wake in half an hour or so. He will wake slowly, uncoil the stiff morning grumpiness from his body and shuffle round the corner to the Cat and Fiddle shops where he will buy the *Sunday Mail* and croissants. Jen will sleep late.

I heard a man in her room as I left the house, a man's breathing, the usual kind of man's breathing that comes from her room. The breathing of a man who has played too much rugby union, has too much bone in the front part of his head, has had his nose pushed back into his paranasal sinuses too many times and grunts and snuffles his way through slow, dumb dreams of rucks and mauls and things that might have been. Where does she find these men?

To approach it from another angle entirely, why do I stereotype them? What do I get out of dismissing as prehensile every man who finds his way into her bed? Sure, they're all big across the shoulders. Sure, they all seem to have their eyes set a little further back under the fronts of their skulls than most of us. And if some of them were even slightly less hensile, they'd be grooming Jen affectionately for fleas. But most of them are functional, or at least able to handle things like uni, jobs and routine social interaction as well as anyone else. Perhaps, as the most adjacent representative of small-shouldered men, I take it as some slight that her taste directs her only to men of size.

1

Perhaps I'm spending too much time in psychiatry. Perhaps I should leave Jen's head alone and work on my own. Perhaps I should be getting my mind onto the day ahead of me.

It's seven-fifty a.m. It's a dazzling late-summer Sunday and I should still be in bed. In bed with the day sneaking in through the venetians. My mind should be on nothing more complicated than rolling over to face away from the sun. I should have thirty minutes' more sleep before Rick beats on my door on his way to the toilet, says *Wakey, wakey, hands off snakey* in an accent he fondly imagines is German.

Not today though. Today is the one Sunday in six when I'm on the road at seven-fifty a.m., crossing town to be surgical DMO, Duty Medical Officer for the hospital's surgical wards, half of its four-hundred-and-fifty beds. Since I'm the psychiatry resident this, superficially at least, doesn't make a lot of sense, but it's how the roster works. Rostering is, after all, only rarely an activity for clever people. Rostering is probably what Jen's rugby boys do when their knees go.

And DMO Sundays are such crap that I wear my best clothes. My black pointed side-lacing shoes, my black jeans that taper at the ankles, my bright white shirt that fits like a spinnaker, my thin green, silver-and-black swirly tie. My favourite clothes (not that I believe in the idea of favourite clothes).

Today they're not saving me. Already I'm desperate for the day to end, even though it won't end for sixteen hours and ten minutes. And there will be moments during those sixteen hours and ten minutes (and this is only the first of them) when I'll be desperate enough that I'll be wanting 1989 to end, just so I don't have to do sixteen-hour DMO shifts any more. Even though I don't know what I'll be doing instead.

2

I turn up the volume of the car stereo because I know the next song on the tape is The Go Betweens' 'Bachelor Kisses'. I sing along, and I know every word now. Someone I once went out with happened to have quite an attachment to The Go Betweens, and happened to have left the tape in my car at the time we broke up. And it wasn't one of those break-ups where you can go over a couple of days later (or in fact ever) and say, Here's the tape you left in my car. I'm sure the realisation of this is mutual. She's never called me to ask for it back.

So the Sunday morning sleeping-in suburbs pass like a backdrop, just below and beyond the freeway's edge, and the only noise is the tape and the slightly flat singing of a man trying to dwell slightly less on his day, his year and his less-than-ideal handling of relationships, trying to pretend that he could stay on the freeway, sing along to this song eighteen times and get out of the car at the beach.

The hospital is in sight before the second chorus. Mount Stevens General and its old, red brick wards and eternal prefab temporary buildings, its 1970s grey multi-storey block and the tall chimney of the incinerator. Birds arguing in the poinciana tree that hangs over the car park as 'Bachelor Kisses' cuts out on its second time through.

The night resident is sitting in the Quarters in a brown, vinyl-covered armchair, slumped down in the chair with his feet on the pile of old magazines that litter the coffee table, drinking a cup of tea and watching 'Rage'.

He jumps when I call out to him, and his pager starts to slide off his lap but he catches it without spilling any tea.

Are you surgical? he says.

Yeah.

Okay. Well, it's really not bad if you're surgical. There's a guy in Four C who came in yesterday with a gut obstruction, but it looks like it's settling just with a nasogastric

3

tube and nil-by-mouth. There's another one there with a post-op fever. Blood cultures are ordered, so you might get some results back. There's an old guy, a really old guy, in Two C with a ruptured aneurism, and the plan is to go easy on that. The family knows he's not for resusc. He'll probably go some time today. Zavattaro his name is, something like that, Zava something. Anyway, the ward'll let you know. And there's a mad old girl in Seven, Mrs Dyson, just your sort of thing, had a total hip replacement and was discharged on Thursday, I think. She came back in yesterday, totally crazy.

So why is that surgical?

She had a total hip replacement.

Days ago. Days ago. She went out, she came back. She's confusion for investigation now, she's general medical. It's not her hip that's gone crazy. How is she back in orthopaedic?

He laughs, which he can do since it's not his problem. *Very slick work by the med reg on call, I imagine.*

And I can imagine it, too. I can imagine the medical registrar on call, the indignation on finding out that the call was about a patient who'd been admitted under a surgical unit some time this century. I can imagine the med reg browbeating the admitting resident with a list of possible operative complications that could be causing this presentation. And the resident calling the surgical registrar and saying *Mrs Dyson's back,* selling the story in some necessarily surgical way. Till midnight then, mad Mrs Dyson is one of mine.

I call the switchboard to tell the operator I'm here and I decide to do a pre-emptive round of the wards to see what I'm in for. I start in Four C, the top of the multistorey, picking up a pen and listing my tasks on the back of a pathology order form. Wandering from ward to ward accumulating several hours of tasks in a spirit of studied magnanimity.

Studied magnanimity is the way to go, I worked that out last year. Most people like me here. I want to keep it that way.

There are two good ways not to be liked as a resident. The first, which is both faster and easier, is to resent openly any call from a member of the nursing staff that is likely to lead to work. The second is to handle personal relationships with nursing staff injudiciously. The obvious trap (obvious now, anyway) is that efforts to avoid the first error may be rewarded with opportunities to commit the second. Today I'm focussing on avoiding error number one, telling myself these people have to call me, it's their job. Even if, for at least the first twelve of the next sixteen hours, they will keep wanting me to do more than I possibly can.

I have ten admissions – a moderately bad load, but half of them are for the same thing. Today, when almost everyone else in town isn't doing this, I'll be talking to old men about passing tubes up their penises to bore out their prostates. Old men who won't ask questions when I invite them to, who will spend the rest of the day in pyjamas, becoming patients, vaguely apprehensive but looking forward to the time when they might enjoy once again the urinary stream of early middle age.

In Seven, Mrs Dyson has chewed through her IV line. I ask her why but she can't quite put her finger on it. She sits there with her small body slowly sliding down into her pink nightie and her mouth crowded with a set of teeth that were surely made for a much larger head, and the bitten-through line seems as much a mystery to her as it does to the rest of us. As though the teeth did it themselves. But looking at her teeth, that does seem at least

5

possible. I'm sure they're the teeth of a much bigger, much nastier person than Mrs Dyson, out to do harm and using her as an alibi.

But Mrs Dyson, I say to her. These tubes are tough. You can't just chew through them on a whim. This takes commitment.

To which she says, *Thank you, doctor,* and smiles a smile from which she seems so dissociated it's as though she's merely standing near it, rather than arranging it voluntarily on her own face.

I resite the line and I ask her how her hip is.

She says, *Yes, doctor.*

I'm sure that even Mrs Dyson, who is aware of very little, is aware that she should no longer be an orthopaedic patient.

This time she keeps the teeth, I tell the nurse when we're out of the room. Next time, I'm not so sure.

The morning keeps me more than busy. I'm most of the way through my second-last prostate admission when a cardiac arrest in Four A is called over the PA system.

Naturally I'm on One, three flights of stairs away. I tell the patient I'll leave him to his lunch and we'll finish off later. The double-beep arrest signal sounds on my pager as I reach the stairwell and the Code call crunches again through the static of the PA, sounding, as it usually does, like Paul Hogan with a mouthful of gingernut biscuit.

Code Blue, Ward Four A, Code Blue.

Bed six, a nurse says to me when I open the door to the fourth floor.

I follow the crash trolley in. Marco Cassimatis is already there. He must be today's medical DMO. I ask him what the story is as two nurses pass a board under the patient to give us something to push against while we're resuscitating.

Okay. Eighty-two-year-old man, long history of coronary artery disease including several infarcts, admitted a week or so ago with a dense right-sided hemiplegia. Neurologically stable. Eating lunch a few minutes ago. Well, not eating, propped up here having some mashed pumpkin spooned into his mouth, and he just went flat.

What?

That's the story.

Okay. Take the head. Get the suction onto any residual pumpkin, get the bag and mask going and get some oxygen into him, see if you can pass a tube. You okay with that?

Yeah.

A nurse automatically moves to the chest to do the compressions.

Okay. I want to try and get a line in. Could we also get the drugs ready, and the defib? He's peripherally shut down, so I'll do a femoral line. And let's get an ECG as soon as we can.

I find the femoral vein from memory and connect the line up. The emergency drug pack rolls out along the patient's shins. On the ECG the baseline wanders, but there's nothing else.

Marco, tube in?

No.

Okay, skip it. Someone else take the bag. Marco, you happy to defib?

Sure. Three hundred? He takes the defibrillator paddles.

Three hundred's fine. Whenever you're ready.

Okay then. He takes a deep breath, and pauses. *The red button, I press the red button?*

Yeah.

Okay. Clear please.

We stand back. He presses the red button, scrunching his eyes up as though it might detonate something. The

7

patient jolts, the ECG spikes and then flattens again. We go back to work, another burst of resusc activity, and some adrenaline from me up the femoral vein. *Clear please* twice more from Marco, two more defibs, each without a hint of success.

The med reg arrives. *What's happening?*

Not much. Eighty-two, dense hemiplegia, multiple MIs previously. His ECG's been flat throughout. No response. He's been defibbed three times.

Why are we here?

I guess there's no indication in the file that we shouldn't be, so someone called it.

This man's not an ICU candidate.

The vigour is fading from our attempt. This is the code that underlies the Code: not an ICU candidate, not suitable for Intensive Care. Meaning, we shouldn't be doing this at all, since anyone who survives an arrest is transferred to Intensive Care. Expensive Intensive Care, where beds need to be kept for people whose long-term outlook justifies it. And eighty-two years old with a paralysed right side and very little remaining heart muscle doesn't exactly suggest a good long-term outlook.

The ECG continues to signal a relentless bright line, uncomplicated by cardiac activity, and the bag keeps squirting oxygen down into the lungs. The nurse working the chest keeps pushing, keeps counting to five. I hold the next drug ampoule in my hand, but I'm waiting.

Waiting for Marlon to call it. The outcome's been obvious the whole time, but he has to call it. As the med reg on duty, only he can end the Code Blue.

He draws in and lets out a long breath and frowns, watching the body for a couple of seconds as though something might change. As though the patient isn't visibly, comprehensively, unfortunately dead.

Beats me, he says. *Let's pull the pin. Which one of you is on medically?* He looks at the two of us and Marco nods. *You happy to write it up then?*

Yeah.

All right. Well, back to the books, I guess. And as he turns to leave he looks at his watch, almost as an afterthought. *Twelve-ten? Twelve-ten okay by everyone?*

Sure, Marco says, and notes it in the file as the time of demise.

The nursing staff start to clear up, calmly, slowly. Marco takes almost half a page of the patient's file to write up the arrest.

Twelve-ten'd be a good time for lunch, I tell him. Everyone will have heard the Code and they'll leave us alone for at least another twenty minutes.

I've got a lot of things to do.

In which case, if you don't have lunch now you won't get it at all.

Marco, almost at the end of his second month as an intern, still has a lot to work out. He's still slightly charged after the arrest, still desperate to do good, to press the red button. Still hovering, not ready to walk.

It's incredible how much can change in a year. How much has changed in me in the year since I was in his position. How much you get used to, how quickly you get used to it. How easy it gets to find the red button, push it a few times, do the job. Walk away when it's done. Make time for lunch.

You turn up hopeful and unbearably naive and fairly scared of it all, and the second years seem like such veterans. By the time I graduated, I'd watched three surgical procedures and assisted in one in an almost superfluous capacity. I think I stood for forty-five minutes tucked behind the surgeon's left elbow holding a very small retractor. I was such a part of the action that I never found out what I was retracting. Any passing creature with an opposable thumb could have done my job. I stayed very still, maintained a consistent grip on the instrument, hid behind the surgeon's green-gowned elbow and was slowly intoxicated by his aftershave. Afterwards he asked me what I thought and I said, Great, but only because I couldn't say, Surely that wasn't Old Spice?

I think I had also done two pap smears, put in four drips and delivered one baby, but it was the woman's sixth and it delivered itself. Showed me the top of its head and then slopped out of there at high speed with the midwife shouting for me to catch it, as though I was planning to turn away and let it bungee-jump.

Like most of us, I focussed very effectively on being a competent med student, but I wasn't any more involved than I had to be. I learned a great many lists that served me well in exams. Like most of us, I hadn't found the time to address the idea of being a competent practitioner.

Like Marco, I suspect, I came here on my first day reluctant to order Panadol for a headache without consulting my registrar. (Panadol, sister? Do we have liver function tests on this patient? Have we excluded an intracranial haemorrhage? Meningitis?)

At seven that first morning, after a night of almost no sleep, I sat in front of the 'Today' show in bad clothes, unable to hold down any breakfast other than a large glass of Fanta.

At seven forty-five a.m. I was having my photo taken, the off-white ghost of a mug shot that is part of the name tag I still wear, though it's now bent slightly out of shape and the word Intern has a piece of surgical tape stuck over it, with RMO written on it in elegant Old English script by the RN with whom I am presently involved. I am, of course, entitled to a new name tag now that my designation has changed, but the 1989 name tags are pale blue and I've explained to Admin that this is incompatible with most of my wardrobe. They did, though, make me remove the other piece of tape Penny had put on there. The one that replaced Dr J. Marshall with Jon-boy. I didn't fight them on that.

Marco and I take our trays and load them as high as we can, since DMO lunches are free.

'Clear please' with the defib was a nice touch, I tell him when we're sitting down. A lot of people forget politeness when they're busy.

Thank you. Nice of you to notice.

I've just managed to fill my mouth with overcooked fish and chips when I hear Penny's voice behind me. *I thought we were having lunch together, Jon,* she says as she and two other RNs from her ward come from the servery with trays. *I thought you were going to call me mid-morning so we could make a time for lunch.*

Penny does not look pleased. She sits down next to me. Marco looks out the window.

There was the Code Blue, I tell her.

Yeah, at about quarter to twelve. What about before then?

I was busy. It's been very busy today. Ten admissions. We always knew it might not work out. This looked like my only chance for lunch, and I figured by now you'd know which lunch you were on. So I thought I'd either see you here if you were on twelve or twelve-thirty, or we wouldn't be able to get the chance anyway.

She looks down at the table, pushes a chip around her plate with her fork.

Dinner's still on, isn't it? Tonight? I was going to make you dinner, remember?

11

Sure. Sure it's still on, barring emergencies. What sort of time?

Seven? Seven-thirty?

Seven-thirty'd be good.

Okay.

She seems content with this, or at least prepared to accept it.

Things started with Penny at the haematology ward Christmas party, which now seems quite a while ago. I'd finished my haematology term by then and I was in respiratory. I was in her ward on a DMO shift, and someone said to me *Hey, are you coming to our Christmas party?* So I did. The party was at a cheap Chinese restaurant at West End and I went back with a few other people to the Nurses' Quarters for coffee afterwards. One by one, people left.

Sometime after midnight, when I was more than slightly drunk and it was just the two of us, Penny said, *So how about a game of Scrabble?* To which I said something pretty awful like, It's not really my game. I'm more a Nude Twister man myself. And she said, *Okay.* And we took it from there.

The real problem with this, apart from my Nude Twister line, which completely appals me, is that I misunderstood her Scrabble invitation. I took it to be a deeply and admirably ironic way of pointing out the awkwardness of these moments, while communicating to me a certain interest. This, drunk as I was, was all factored in to my reply. It wasn't until days later that I worked out that she really liked Scrabble, and that irony was beyond her.

But by then it was on. I really wasn't having a good time in respiratory, and there was no reason not to be going out with her. Other than the expectations it might lead to. Has led to. Ten weeks later, we do everything together. Ten weeks later, I get told off for forgetting lunch. And I'm not even sure if I forgot, or if I just wanted to forget, to show her some slackness. Ease back a little.

Mr Zavattaro dies at three-fifteen.

The ward pages me and when I call the sister says, *Oh hello pet. It's Jean, Jean Tillman,* as though there might be several sisters in the ward, all called Jean, who might call me pet and speak in a Scottish accent. *I'm just calling about Mr Zavattaro. Did Bruce tell you about Mr Zavattaro when you came on this morning?*

Yeah.

Okay. Well, whenever you get the chance then. No hurry. Family's all here.

I might as well come now. I've got nothing drastically urgent happening.

Lovely. I'll see you soon then.

The family, right in the midst of despair, treats my appearance in the wake of the substantial Sister Tillman as though it's somehow important, as though it matters at all. They break the circle they've made round the bed, and they let me in. Quiet, watching me.

Mr Zavattaro is pale in a waxen way, not a living way. I sit beside him. I am to examine him rigorously now for signs of life before declaring them gone. There are many things to check before I can prove Mr Zavattaro is dead.

I hold his cool hand, clammy with the last escape of sweat. I watch his face, his chest. There is no moving, no breathing. He has not shaved today. I put my hand on his forehead and, with my thumb, I lower an eyelid just enough to see a post-mortem pupil that does nothing when the light comes in. I shut it, but in a way more like tidiness than finality, like straightening a collar.

Outside the room a trolley rattles past. I hear Jean's

13

voice saying something, some mild telling-off, and then I hear her thumping an errant carpet tile back into place, swearing at it quietly but firmly, saying something about *people breaking their necks on these damn things*.

Still the family holds back, stands near but looms over me like a breaking wave. As though there's some verdict to deliver here. Some pronouncement to make.

He looks very peaceful now, I tell them. And I make eye contact with a woman who might be his daughter, and she nods. I'll leave you with him, I tell them. And if there's anything you need, just let one of us know. Okay?

Thanks, the woman says.

In the doctor's office I make my file note. HR 0, BP 0, HS X, BS X, Pupils F&D. Shorthand. No detectable heart rate or blood pressure, no detectable heart sounds or breath sounds, pupils fixed and dilated.

He looks very peaceful now.

One way or another, I think I am defined by my crappy lines. Some of them I get to use several times. He looks very peaceful now. I know when I'm going to say it. I know it's a line. But it helps me slip in and out without adding to the harm, without tossing the poor man's body around and saying at the end, Yep, he's dead. That's my justification for it. So I concentrate hard on the performance, less on the examination. And I write what I'm supposed to in the file. It's the best I can do. With practice, it's the best I've come up with.

And as long as I come out with the right line and deliver it with conviction, I'll be okay. A lapse in concentration and a drunken invitation to the Zavattaro family to participate in a spot of Nude Twister might not have gone down well.

Jean Tillman comes in. *Now pet, usual question,* she says, grinning because she always does. Showing almost

14

all her teeth in a way that could give mad old ladies bad ideas about how to treat their IV lines. *Is there a post-mortem?*

I don't think so. Not as far as I'm concerned anyway. The cause of death's pretty clear.

So do we put it down as Denied?

Whatever. Whatever you want. I'll trust you.

Lovely. How's it going today? Keeping you busy?

Yeah. Busy as usual.

Haven't seen you for a while. Where are you at the moment?

Psych.

Is that by chance or by design?

Design. I think. I'll see.

I would've thought you were too sane for psych, 'cause you're quite a normal boy, really.

I'm actually just good at hiding it. What's going on in my head is floridly bizarre most of the time.

Oh, okay. You'll be fine then.

With this she proves that at least some members of her profession have a grasp of irony. Of course, irony in a forty-five-year-old unflappable sturdily built lesbian weekend charge sister is no help in my relationship with a straight twenty-two-year-old who loves me for my crazy sense of humour. Which she doesn't actually understand. I do imagine, though, that Jean could be a formidable force on the plastic playing field, should she ever take up Nude Twister.

On the way to a fever in Seven I pass the library, and Marlon de Lisle's outside strolling along and cracking his knuckles.

How's it going? he says, probably only to let me know that he's seen me and won't collide with me as we pass in the hall.

Fine. Nearly halfway through this glorious day. How about you?

Study. Study and more study. But it's got to be done. He covers a yawn with his chunkily ringed left hand.

When are you sitting?

June. That's the plan, anyway. So I should get back to it.

It's strange watching Marlon subjected to study, getting ready for an exam. It's so normal, so average. It's strange to see him here on a Sunday, but maybe he only organised it thinking that it would make him put in library time. Marlon is a hospital legend. Actually he is *the* hospital legend. If they came up with a job and called it Hospital Legend, no-one else would apply, since they'd all be sure it would go to Marlon. He is about forty, and came to medicine late. He is tall and broad-shouldered and handsome in a way that suggests he's almost tired of it. He wears black shirts and gold rings and never wears a tie. He owns a six-seater plane, and rumour has it that once, a long time ago, Marlon played keyboards for Pink Floyd.

Apparently he was a major session player in the early seventies in London and New York, and he worked with the biggest. Uncredited appearances on some of the landmark albums of the time and occasionally filling in for people live. The live stuff was usually with smaller acts, but not always. Sometimes maybe it was stadiums. Certainly if the Floyd story is true. But he's such a legend that he never mentions it. He's such a legend that I think he's not even sure of my name, and I only respect him more for it.

The consultants treat Marlon as one of them, because they'd actually like him to be. It seems wrong that Marlon should have to sit an exam. It seems so strange that he's here on a Sunday that I can only believe he asked to be.

Long after the fever in Seven and the next couple of drips and numerous other minor calls, after the shortness of breath in Three C and the discovery, once she'd spat them down her nightie a couple of times, that Mrs Dyson's teeth do in fact belong to someone else at her nursing home, I'm back with one of my prostate admissions who has gone into acute obstruction. I'm passing a catheter as gently as possible, when I realise I'm getting hungry. And I really don't want to go to the Nurses' Quarters for dinner with Penny.

I realise I'd rather eat in the hospital dining room. Hospital food. By myself.

As I'm inflating the balloon at the end of the catheter and the urine is running out briskly and the patient is saying *God that's good, you don't know how good that is,* I'm realising that this is a very bad sign. Hospital food, by universal tradition, sets the benchmark in diabolical, and Penny loves to cook and does it well.

Seven-thirty is approaching. Most of the tasks on my current piece of paper are crossed out. I hang around in Two C for a while checking a patient, working out a new insulin order. I review a toe that has been stubbed on a toilet, and I decide it doesn't need an X-ray. I okay two Panadol in someone who has a headache and was inadvertently written up only for pethidine after an abdominal operation on Friday. I am now enormously comfortable with the prescription of Panadol, in all but a very small number of circumstances.

I am almost ten minutes late for dinner.

I guess you were busy, Penny says.

Yeah. You know how it gets.

It's hot in the Nurses' Quarters, still hot everywhere outside the airconditioned multistorey wing. Hot and humid, with the sun set an hour ago and the fan in the corner not doing much, just making noise.

Fettuccine marinara, she says. *I made the fettuccine this afternoon.*

She drops it in boiling water and it seems to cook in seconds. The marinara sauce is simmering, and it smells great. She's set a table. Put a gingham tablecloth over the old Nurses Quarters' coffee table, a loaf of fresh crusty bread in a basket in the middle.

She hands me a glass of mineral water and says, *We should toast.*

To fresh crusty bread, I say, and clink her glass. To fettuccine made this afternoon, and an end to DMO Sundays.

We sit cross-legged on the floor. My beeper goes off.

Shit, she says. *Don't go unless it's urgent. They can wait twenty minutes if it's not urgent.*

I call the ward.

Hi, the RN says. *It's just a guy who's got a cannula in, just a bung in a forearm vein. He's not getting any fluids through it. We have to keep it going till tomorrow, and it's blocked. He's a few days post-op and he's fine, apart from a bit of normal wound pain where he's had the rib spreaders, so if you could come up and resite it some time, that'd be great.*

Okay. Okay, I'll come now.

Whenever.

I'll see you soon.

That doesn't sound good, Penny says when I put down the phone.

Chest pain.

Shit. What am I doing, going out with a resident? What about dinner?

Well, maybe if you could just keep mine and I'll come back as soon as I can. We can always give it thirty seconds in the microwave. I don't think we can do much more than that. Go ahead and eat yours, though. I don't know how long I'll be.

Okay.

It's only then that she actually starts to look as though she's upset, rather than mildly irritated. This stalls me at the top of the stairs, but I can't deal with it now. Not now that I've said I'm on my way to a chest pain.

I didn't want her make dinner for me. DMO Sundays are always chopped to bits by calls. I didn't want her to, but she wanted to because she knows how I hate DMO Sundays. She wanted to make it more bearable. I've tried to tell her that nothing can save DMO Sundays, not even my favourite clothes, and that I'm probably better left alone. But that's not the way she operates. Alone, from Penny's perspective, is surely a worse option than anything. I couldn't possibly prefer being left alone.

By the time I get to the ward I'm sufficiently distracted that I almost ask where the guy with chest pain is.

Everything's already set up in the patient's room. The tourniquet, the dressing pack open with the prep solution already poured, the cannula, the brown rubber bung to stick in it once it's in place. The job's done in a few minutes.

So how's it looking here at the moment? I ask the sister when we're back at the Nurses' Station.

Tonight? Quiet. So far, at least. Hopefully we won't have to bother you too much.

Back in the Quarters, Penny has covered both of our plates with Glad Wrap. She gives them each thirty seconds in the microwave. We sit down again at the gingham-covered coffee table. I'm hungry now, so I eat quickly.

How is it? she says.

Oh, good. Really good.

It was probably better half an hour ago.

Twenty minutes. I wasn't gone more than twenty minutes.

She says *Hmmm,* watches me. Watches me eating like a

19

pig, an ungrateful pig as she slowly winds a ribbon of fettuccine onto her fork. Watches me as though she's suffering, enduring some slow but tolerable pain in front of the marinara pig. As though she'll keep suffering the pain and say nothing.

What? What's wrong?

I don't know.

You don't know?

I don't know. But something's not right. You don't want to be with me today, do you? You don't want to be here eating this.

I'm DMO.

Yeah, right.

I'm on duty. I've got responsibilities.

That's not what I mean. You know that's not what I mean.

So what do you mean?

You're so distracted, so disinterested.

Uninterested.

What?

Uninterested. Disinterested means impartial. You wanted to say I was uninterested, not disinterested.

What? How can you do this?

Do what?

This. All of this. This correcting. How . . .

What do you want? This is the way I am. This is me. If that's not working for you . . .

What do you mean?

I mean, this is the way I am. If it's not right for you, if you need something different . . .

My beeper goes off.

What are you saying?

Nothing.

Nothing?

Nothing.

So what's happening? What's happening with us?

Nothing. Nothing's happening with us. I'm DMO. I'm eating dinner.

I'm eating dinner, and I'm eating it in an ugly way, eating it like a brute, eating it like someone who badly needs to be broken up with.

Why are you being like this? Why are you being so distant?

Why do you want me to change?

I don't want you to change. This isn't making sense. Fuck. I've had just about enough of this. I've really had just about enough of you and your moods. I just don't understand you.

A tear rolls down her cheek but only I seem to notice. She's talking. Telling me it's not working. My beeper goes off again. And she's telling me there's so much good in this relationship but there's so much crap, and she just can't take it any more. That she doesn't want it to go this way, but she can't take it any more.

I'm looking at her here in close-up, watching this more than listening. Looking at her right in the pores as we're breaking up, saying to myself this has to be. I don't love you. I never will. Thank god we're breaking up. But saying none of this to her, just letting her talk, letting her get it all out. Letting her end it all now and blame it on me, since I couldn't see how to begin the conversation where I end it with her. And whatever she says to me, I don't dispute a word of it.

She says I hardly even seem to be in the relationship. She says I just don't seem to care about what happens to us. She calls me a shit, and that's fine. I probably am.

I'm sorry, I tell her when she's finished. I'm sorry all this has happened. I'm sorry if I'm not right for you, since I'm obviously not.

It's not that.

It is that. I've got to go. I've got calls. I'm sorry.

So am I, she says, and she's still sitting at the coffee table, facing away from me as I'm walking out, her uneaten dinner in front of her. She puts down her fork.

I know I got two calls in there, but my beeper has no memory so I've lost the first one. The second is easy and I sort it out over the phone from the Residents' Quarters. It's twenty minutes before the first ward pages me again. Twenty minutes of nothing but waiting, flicking through the newspaper, flicking through the beginnings of three Sunday night movies. Trying not to get involved in one since I could be called away at any time.

From where I'm sitting in front of the TV I can see the light on in Penny's room.

Two C pages. I explain that I lost the earlier call and the sister says, *Oh yeah, been napping, have we?* On my way back into the hospital I pick up a packet of barbecue chips at the vending machine. The corridors are empty now, with visitors gone and no patients on the move for tests or procedures. Just the echoes of my feet on the scuffed lino, following the blue line round to the lifts.

I'm a free man. Extracted from my relationship with Penny like a bad tooth, something she had to get rid of. It's better to do it that way, better to be quite unlovable and then no longer required. Better for her, when I know I couldn't give her what she wanted. All along I could tell. She was slipping easily into some level of commitment. We never talked about it, but it's where we gravitated. Where she wanted to be. And just not going to work for me.

The barbecue chips are finished before I'm out of the lift at the second floor. The Two C call is easy. The evening winds down. After eleven the wards keep things for the night resident unless they're urgent or someone doesn't know the etiquette. At eleven forty-five, I make my habitual end-of-shift toilet visit.

I sit there, killing the last bit of time of my sixteen hours as DMO, daring someone to call an arrest. Thinking, you can't get me now. You've had me for fifteen hours and forty-five minutes, but I'm taking fifteen minutes back. Shitting on your time, not on mine. The pettiest possible protest against DMO Sundays, but it's all I've got.

I hear a car door shutting. Feet on gravel and then the stone steps. I know I'm in the clear.

The night resident's hair is still wet, slicked down across his head as though he's just stepped from the shower after trying to catch a few hours' sleep. He's leaning against the pool table, flipping the end of his stethoscope into his hand so that the diaphragm hits his open palm with a pop. Doing this repeatedly as though he'll do it a thousand times tonight and never know. A habit. Walking along the empty corridors. Pop, pop, pop. Darkened wards. Pop, pop. Nurses' Stations with the mad nurses who only work nights. Pop.

How are things? he says.

Fine. Nothing special happening. Haven't seen Marco for a while though, so maybe there's more happening medically. Surgically things should be okay. We had a woman who chewed through her IV line earlier.

Chewed through her IV line. That's pretty impressive.

Yeah. She had someone else's teeth in though, so we've confiscated them. Hers won't arrive till tomorrow so she shouldn't give you any trouble.

My car smells like the aftershave Penny gave me for Christmas. 'Bachelor Kisses' starts when I turn the key, jumps in loud and surprises me. I turn it down. There's no traffic on the way home and I'm back in Toowong, back in Bayliss Street, parking in front of the house, in about ten minutes.

The others are in bed. There are sometimes messages on the kitchen table for me after a weekend DMO shift, but tonight there are none. An empty pizza box, two dirty plates, one on top of the other as though this means they've cleaned up.

I move quietly about the house, clean my teeth, drop my clothes on the floor in the corner of my room, lie on my bed with the ceiling fan blowing warm air over me.

Another Sunday gone, another DMO Sunday I'll never have to do again. Six more this year, maybe seven. Maybe no more after that, depending on where I end up.

I don't sleep well. I don't go to sleep easily after days like this, as though I still have some responsibilities.

Rick is cleaning his sinuses out. Standing in the shower grunting old mucus out of his sinuses, yesterday's mucus, stalagmites, stalactites. How can one person make so much mucus overnight? It's as though someone's pumping it up there just to piss him off.

In the kitchen, on the other side of a flimsy wall, I am applying creamed honey to toast with less and less enthusiasm.

The kitchen is a bigger mess than usual, as though they tried to make something yesterday. Hardened cheese gratings on the brown laminate table, a chunky green substance coating the blender, a crusty daub of something that looks like tomato paste on the side of the toaster, though this is partly disguised by the grain. The toaster, like much of the kitchen, both laminated surfaces and appliances, has the timber-look of a past era.

We are the owners of brown goods, but not yet the owners of white goods. Every appliance we own has arrived as a consequence of a parental upgrade. The TV, the fan-heater, the stereo and even the toaster were all bought at a time when the timber look was inexplicably big.

Things could be worse. Rick once moved into a shared flat that had previously been rented by soldiers and everything, walls, fridge, appliances, bath and toilet (inside and out), was painted a very stolen shade of khaki. Rick even maintains that it had its advantages, claiming that the toilet never needed to be cleaned more often than monthly. And using it became known as touching up the camouflage. Women never visited the flat. At least, not more than once. Rick doesn't know why.

Jon-boy, he says, emerging from the steamy bathroom with his sinuses empty and resonant and a faded green towel draped around him. *Back from the war.*

Looks like the war was in the kitchen.

Nachos, he says. *Lunch yesterday. We made nachos.*

And then bought a pizza in the evening.

It was a multicultural day.

And the green shit in the blender?

Guacamole. We made the nachos el grande. Very special nachos, senor. Nachos and light beers and little sleeps in the afternoon. Siesta.

I had multicultural too, I tell him. I had north of England for lunch, fish and chips. And marinara for dinner, fettuccine marinara.

They do marinara there now? I should eat at your hospital.

That was Penny.

Always looking after you. Looking after her boy.

Yeah.

I watch the 'Today' show with the volume low. I can hear Jen talking in her sleep behind the partition, muttering away to herself as though she's both sides of a foreign conversation. Rick's enthusiasm for accents is doing her no good.

When does she start this morning? I ask him when he comes out of his room.

Who knows. Bloody uni students. Never get a decent day's work out of them.

Rick, I think, would do almost anything to pretend he hadn't graduated, so he could be a student again.

On the way into town he sits in the passenger seat in one of his series of wide-lapelled, worn-slightly-shiny, unspectacular suits and a mood heavy with the relentlessness of morning, with Monday, with the first of five consecutive workdays after nachos *el grande*.

I don't know how many suits he has, since I can't tell them apart. I don't know how many ties he has either, but that's only because he has so many. His ties are very wide, distinctive, absurdly colourful and all a hundred per cent silk. He buys a tie whenever he's grumpy, and they cost eighty dollars a time. He has many ties and little money. My ties are polyester and cost less than eighty dollars in total. I am cautious with expenditure, and I hope that ties are not the only way to happiness.

On bad days, days when the purchase of a tie can be all that gets him through, Rick can only cope with my ties by telling himself they have to be very washable because of their inevitable contact with bodily fluids. I'm not sure that he really understands what I do with my day.

We loop off the freeway and into the city and he's just in the middle of telling me he should have done more with his weekend, when he has to get out. And somehow not one of the several dozen Yogi bears dancing on his tie seems to make him any happier at the moment. But maybe I'm wrong. Maybe Yogi will get him through today and I'm only being so negative because I wore my favourite clothes yesterday, and every other ensemble this week can be no more than second best.

Soon I'm on the freeway again, and Mount Stevens appears all too quickly.

I park, I walk in. And it's as though I never left. I clip my pager onto my belt and my name tag onto my pocket. My name tag, with Penny's careful calligraphy. I can see her hand holding the pen for each neat stroke, I can see her wanting to do this for me. I wonder how she is today.

She was looking for something that I couldn't give, and really it's as simple as that. That's why last night had to happen. She was looking for someone else, but no-one outlasted me at the Christmas party. And just as I'm about to regret the Nude Twister line again, I remember correcting *disinterested* last night. A correction that comes all the way from my English teacher in grade ten, and I think I even used his line about impartial. At least I didn't go on with, *A cricket umpire, for example, should be disinterested but certainly not uninterested.* That would perhaps have been overkill. Some conversations, though not many, are not improved by a cricket reference. To be fair to my English teacher, I think he had a different agenda in mind, and I'm sure at least some of the class found the cricket umpire example helpful.

And it's better if she's angry with me, probably. Clear that it's my fault it went wrong.

In psych there's nothing new. Same smell of stale

smoke, same abundance of hanging around. Someone actually goes to the trouble of telling me nothing happened on the weekend, but perhaps they're just making conversation. I'm asked about my DMO shift, something they view almost the way Rick does, as though it's nastily exotic, as though I'm back from the war. They talk about the multistorey as though it's quite a different world.

When the other RNs are out dispensing morning medication or cajoling patients into shifting from their beds or the kitchen onto the verandah to do a crossword on the blackboard, Glen, the charge nurse, says, *Word is that you and Sister Frew are no longer a going concern.*

Word doesn't waste any time then, does it?

Last night, they say, he goes on, as though he's telling me some sly story about someone else, someone we both know but don't necessarily like. *And she's suggesting you're not quite the nice young man you seemed to be.*

Behind him I can see the blackboard through the window. They've solved one across, and they're moving onto two down.

Haven't been playing up, have we? Glen says, as though my life might be much more interesting than it is.

No. Nothing like that. Maybe I'm just not a nice young man.

She said you were so bad in a relationship, your own mother's probably dumped you by now.

Wow. That's pretty impressive. Ten weeks we were together and she didn't come out with one line like that.

Behind him, debate rages over two down. I go through the medication sheets and rewrite the several that are due to expire. Glen, finally accepting that the end of my relationship with Penny isn't interesting at all, starts sorting through files for the ward round.

Is Johnno here yet? he says when he has them in a pile.

28

I don't know. I'll go and check.

From the back steps I can see that his motorbike is in his parking spot. Gil Johnson is the proud owner of perhaps Australia's last surviving Honda 100, though it's changed considerably since it left the factory. Bit by bit, all its tubing has perished and been replaced by hospital IV lines and it now has a saddle and panniers made in the Occupational Therapy Department by grateful patients. This might be fine if the panniers didn't have the face of a Cheyenne brave burnt erratically into one side with poker-work and a mounted pony express rider scorched equally erratically into the other.

Johnno, never too sure whether any act of generosity is being used to mock him, took this in his stride. Accepted the gift with appropriate gratitude, fitted it to his bike and kept it there. I asked him about it once, a couple of weeks ago when a patient gave me a monogrammed leather key ring (the only thing I've got that's monogrammed D.J.M. for Doctor Jonathan Marshall), and I wasn't sure how to deal with it. *Mainly,* he said, *you should feel bad for the cow. That it died for so little. Other than that you should always tell yourself it's the thought that counts, and if it looks as though it's actually worth something you should try to make them take it back. But don't worry. It's highly unlikely to look as though it's worth something.*

And I think he almost likes it as his bike becomes more of a shambles with the passage of time, made up more of add-ons and off-cuts than anything Honda had in mind. I can't imagine what he'll do when he needs parts that the hospital doesn't stock, or that patients can't make. It's the only vehicle he's ever owned.

It's not easy to know what he thinks of himself on there, what kind of figure he imagines he cuts in the city traffic. Johnno, Honda 100 whining under the weight of

29

over-worked leather, goggles over his ice-blue eyes on wet days, army surplus overalls zipped up to his black beard, khaki plastic raincoat with its hood tapering to a point. Johnno, grappling with genius and melancholy and the selfish perversity of traffic. A cross between Biggles and a druid, individual enough that he was once stopped and searched by police, and then accused of stealing the brief-case and wallet of the Director of Psychiatry of Mount Stevens General.

You are what you drive, he said to me one wet day of discontent as he dismounted next to Simon Dubois's bur-gundy BMW, mud up his boots and flecked up his overalls and across the bug-eyed divergent gaze of the stoic Cheyenne brave. *You are what you fucking drive, aren't you?*

Simon Dubois would, I'm sure, agree. Red socks, silk shirts, burgundy BMW. All very Simon Dubois, a man too easily defined by his badges. I wonder what Dubois thinks sometimes, as he parks in the staff psychiatrist's spot, next to the director's Honda 100. Presses the button on the CD player to turn off Mahler's Second, eases himself out of the climate control, checks his cufflinks and walks into the cinnamon carpet-tiled corridor of Ward Nine.

Johnno's round begins. Johnno sits behind his desk and the patients are brought in, one at a time. I sit next to Glen and I write the notes. The registrars stay for half the round each, just their own patients, but I'm here for the whole thing. All the depression, the detoxing alcoholics, the occa-sional schizophrenics, the placement problems that would have gone general medical if the psych registrar hadn't buckled. The old people with failing brains and nowhere to go, who should be headed off at the pass, swerved into a quiet corner of a general medical ward with an emphatic, *I can see no evidence of a treatable psychiatric condition in this patient* from the psych registrar while the patient is still in Casualty. But it's not like that, and the med regs are tough. They take nothing they don't absolutely have to.

During the round I pick up the usual handful of minor complaints. Constipation, a sore throat, a tough old toenail requiring a podiatry consult (a nothing job that will take a file entry, a form and at least a couple of phone calls). In psych, the resident handles the mundane medical issues, does the medical parts of the admissions, orders tests, writes things up. This leaves the registrars to handle the psychiatry. The enthusiastic resident can choose to take this on with occasional patients. This increases the chances of getting another psych term, and it's more interesting than constipation, sore throats and working out which podiatrist is assigned to Ward Nine. Of course, there's always the danger that you can overplay it, and end up on track to be a psychiatrist before you know it.

Have we got journal club today? Johnno says at the end of the round as we walk down to the tearoom.

Journal club. A term widely applied to any gathering where one person tells a few others about an article. I think it must be an American idea that this is somehow a club. We sit in the tearoom eating the daily packet of Arnott's Family Assorted that Glen orders for the patients (but that the patients never find out about), drinking tea or instant coffee from polystyrene cups while Helen Reid, the senior registrar, goes through sixteen photocopied pages about drug treatment of attention deficit disorder, reading out the bits she's marked with a green highlighter pen. The casual observer would, I suspect, fail to notice a club occurring at this point.

The members of the nursing staff who were stuck in the tearoom when we convened are really beginning to regret it. Glen is staring past Helen's head at the wall, gnawing

31

on the paddle-pop stick he's used to stir his tea until it splinters and wedges behind a molar. I'm starting to glaze over myself when a buzz of wordless static comes over the PA and we double-beep with a cardiac arrest somewhere in the multistorey. We hit our mute buttons and Helen goes on without a pause.

Today, it's someone else's problem.

When I graduated I think I had the idea that when an arrest was called people would run from all over the hospital. Of course, in even a relatively small hospital this would mean dozens of medical staff all trying to push in to have their turn. So a cardiac arrest, which we initially thought was the biggest, most medical thing that could happen, is soon something you wouldn't leave your lunch for. There's no point being the fourth person at an arrest, let alone the fortieth. If it's in the immediate vicinity you go. If you're the cardiology registrar you go. Otherwise there's no point.

Not that there's necessarily an overwhelming amount of point anyway. Cardiac Arrest Misunderstanding Number Two. Yesterday's was, unfortunately, typical. I used to have the naive assumption that these things worked out, at least most of the time. Otherwise why would they have invented the gear, devised protocols? I took the first few failures personally (I had, after all, travelled great distances to be involved), before it was explained to me that inpatient arrests, in the best of hands, have a long-term survival rate of several per cent. Why was this never made clear to us at uni?

My current failure-to-success ratio of forty-one to zero is therefore only a couple of wins short of average. I could pick up that kind of slack on one good day.

Yesterday was not the good day in question, and only sent my stats out past forty zip, but that's okay. The problem, as usual, was the material. These arrests are not chance events. This is another thing I didn't think through in six years of uni. Often when a heart stops it's a sign that life has come to its close, not a signal that a person's chest needs jumping on. So it's fine to give it your best shot, but there's no point in letting the outcome have any bearing on your self-esteem. I've seen some really determined, technically immaculate Code Blues carried out on patients who were never going to make it, and eventually you work out that you can't do better than that. You can't do more than get everything right and do your best to see your zero per cent success rate in context.

Helen has sent me into this. Just when I should have been thinking of drug side effects, questions to ask, her drone has sent my brain flat-lining and I've missed most of what she's said.

Who's next week? Johnno says when the questions are mercifully, predictably few. *Was it you, Jon? The astronaut article?*

The astronaut article. The large-mouthed resident with the poor judgement pays for his sarcasm.

Johnno presented last week, and I noticed that the article that followed his in the journal was about astronauts' biological changes with space flight. While questioning its value, I may have made some flippant remarks about astronauts and rectal temperature probes, so everyone thought it would be interesting if I discussed the article critically at journal club. I guess it's just that kind of crazy club.

Johnno times his *Let's adjourn* to coincide perfectly with the rattle of approaching meal trolleys, and goes into the kitchen to plunder. He selects the lasagne and sits in the tearoom, eating it quickly as though he's at boarding school, stopping only momentarily between mouthfuls to complain about the quality.

What got to me most on my first day of psych was that everyone treated this as normal. On some days it's even brought to him and he doesn't have to leave the tearoom. I wondered if patients were missing out, but Glen orders extra every day and just puts *Day patients* on the form. So every day Johnno eats lunch for nothing.

Not that he would have the slightest difficulty paying for it. There is no evidence that he spends money on anything, and there was a time when he was, very temporarily, worth over a million because of his gold shares. He knows this because he added it up, just slightly retrospectively when the shares were worth nothing after the crash of '87. He decided that that was okay, probably for the best. That he'd grown used to a life of chronic dysthymia, and wealth would give him nowhere to go. Loss of wealth was something he could accommodate far more easily.

It was around this time that he became Director of Psychiatry, having been a psychiatrist for only three or four years. He did most of his training here and is now viewed as a hospital fixture. He'd perhaps like to be viewed as something more exciting, but Hospital Legend's already gone, and he accepts this, like almost everything else, as his lot. Not that he doesn't have aspects of the legendary about him. Years after a notorious succession of short-term relationships with members of staff, he somehow remains single and yearned for in several departments. And a source of lasting discontent in others.

There's a lot to unravel about Johnno, a lot more than mad-bearded, lunch-stealing melancholy. Fatalism and parsimony, a ramshackle motorbike, a gift for the saxophone, a fondness for jazz, an unlikely trail of broken hearts, and

34

probably more still. It must take years to accumulate these credentials, to become ready to be Director of Psychiatry.

My current tally of three relationships with members of staff, now all complete (though none with any ease), is no match for his. Nor is my caution with money, though I'm not bad with that either.

While I may have played some role in the untidy demise of the three relationships, I blame the tightness of my wallet sphincter on my parents and they, being born in England in the 1930s, can probably put it down to the war. *I had to walk fourteen miles through snow to school in a pair of old hand-me-down boots when I was a lad,* et cetera. I've never been sure what this demonstrates. While I was certainly glad that I didn't have to walk fourteen miles through snow to school, I didn't often feel that I was indulging myself by catching a train to the Valley and then a council bus to East Brisbane. And at no stage, on looking out the window of these luxuriously appointed vehicles, did I see anyone clomping along in their hand-me-downs battling the deep snows of winter and getting to school by the proper means.

I go to the library and I find the astronaut article and make the obligatory ten copies so anyone who's interested can read it through in advance. Which I'm hoping they don't. The less they know about this when I talk, the better.

I read through the article myself for the first time, resisting the temptation to cover it with green highlighter pen surprisingly easily. I realise that my undergraduate training has prepared me quite poorly for astronaut medicine. I'm a long way short of faking it next Monday, and faking it is usually one of my best things. With a more regular article I could demonstrate the appropriate level of interest after one careful read and maybe twenty minutes checking a few points. With astronaut medicine I could be here a while.

So how much do I want another psych term? That's the question. If I can be moderately impressive, if I can look somewhat interested, that could really help put me back in psych later in the year. I might even have some time relieving the registrars when they go on holiday.

Psych. Finishing by five-thirty p.m. almost every day. Saturday mornings off every week. There's no other term like that. Most terms you put in a few hours every Saturday morning, doing a round of all your patients before leaving them to the DMOs. In two-resident terms you can work alternate Saturday mornings, but the only two-resident term I've done was respiratory, and the other resident was sick for most of it.

Real weekends. Two consecutive days off, two weekends out of three. That's worth some library time.

So, *The circadian rhythms of astronauts in orbital and non-orbital flight (physiological, biochemical and hormonal, various), some rhythms noted to free-run in zero gravity, possible zeitgebers considered, comparison with hibernation in animals.*

This is looking bad. I am already not at one with this article. I am going to come to grief on the key words before I understand a thing. Circadian rhythms, I recall from physiology, are simply the twenty-four-hour cycles of various things in the body, like sleeping and waking. I hope. Free-running is, I assume, loss of that twenty-four-hour rhythm. Something either finding its own rhythm, or having no rhythm at all. *Zeitgeber*, from my grade-ten German, should be 'time giver'. Which in this context, I suppose, means an external cue for the timing of rhythms.

Grade ten is proving surprisingly useful to me at the moment. What's next, I wonder? A practical application for calculus, an opportunity to advance myself through quoting the poetry of William Butler Yeats? Has anyone ever had one of those? If either of these explained the *comparison with hibernating animals* aspect of the article I'd be grateful, but I'm not getting my hopes up. But somewhere in the *comparison* may be something persuasive enough for the astronauts to consent to continuous rectal monitoring, so I decide to start by finding a few articles on the physiology of hibernation. And then I decide that that's enough for one day.

After lunch I phone the Podiatry Department twice, but the phone rings out. I admit a profoundly depressed man who's come in through Outpatients and I play table tennis with a detoxing alcoholic. I beat him 21–17, but he is a little shaky. I leave right on five p.m., having put in a couple of hours of looking busy, talking to people, taking an interest, making copious file notes.

When I get home, Jen has moved her desk to her open French doors and she's sitting in her men's flannel pyjamas, a book face down in front of her. Sitting watching the street, watching nothing happen, begging for distraction, her legs crossed at the ankles, the soles of her perfectly arched feet facing out.

Why don't I have feet like that? How do I end up with flat slabs of feet that are slightly different sizes while someone like Jen gets a perfect pair and, I'm sure, has no appreciation of them?

This thesis is really shitting me off, she says in a heartfelt moan, as though she's suffered all day.

But you've only started.

I know. It's a bad sign, isn't it? A very bad sign. I've cleaned the kitchen, though, and shampooed my hair. Isn't it shiny? Want to kick a ball around?

It's a bit hot.

She gives me a look. *I need to go out.*

I'm a bit tired.

A worse look. *I stayed home all day. Every minute of the day to work on my thesis, and now I need to go out.*

Okay, okay.

She shuts the French doors to change. She and her thesis are obviously not friends today.

When we moved in the agent said that the room with French doors could be good on hot summer nights. Good for a man, since a man could safely leave the doors open. So Jen took it. The room has subsequently been good, and then very bad, for many men.

I didn't do well in the room deal. Jen claimed the room with the French doors since it needed to have its gender bias reversed, and Rick claimed the master bedroom since he found the house. Leaving me with two much smaller rooms, known as 'the hutches'. Apparently they were children's bedrooms when the house was built in 1911. Clearly this was a time when children stayed very small, owned not more than one change of clothes and slept standing up. The hutches, as rooms go, are not big.

So I keep my clothes in one and my bed in another. I tried to convince myself this was by choice, minimalism, my double bed with its slim rim of room around it. I put it to Rick that it made some kind of statement and he agreed. He suggested the statement went something like, *Face it son, you got shafted.* And with a small clock radio and a slender black bedside lamp, the room does look marginally overfurnished.

Jen bounces the ball in the corridor till I emerge from my dressing room. She is wearing rugby shorts and her thin, tight white T-shirt with 'Die Pervert Die' in small black letters over her right breast.

I am surprised, continually surprised, that so many men don't realise she's not to be messed with. Don't consider for a moment that they might have to deal with far more than just the excellent view from the front. Like the captain of the *Titanic* said, *Hey, nice icebergs,* but the bit that does you harm you never see. Sure, she might know how to push out the front of a T-shirt, she might seem as though her life revolves around beer and big-shouldered boys, but she's not to be underestimated.

We walk along the driveway of the Serbian Orthodox Church Hall and we climb the fence into Wests Rugby Union Club. She kicks the ball with feeling, like someone whose frustrating day necessitates it. I hope we're not going to have a year of this.

Rick's at home when we get back. He shows me his new tie. Who decided that Snow White and five of her dwarves would be good on a tie?

I ask him which dwarves got dropped and he says *Grumpy and Sneezy are round the back, look,* and flips the tie over.

You've got a big cartoon thing happening at the moment, haven't you?

And you wouldn't believe how many cartoons are out there. I would've got Betty Boop but they'd sold out.

Life is really full of possibilities for you, isn't it?

Hey, Betty's a favourite. You know that. I wouldn't buy just anything with a cartoon on it.

Jen arranges to have a drink with friends and Rick and I, not unpredictably, go to the Sunny Garden, the shabby, dimly lit (and gardenless) Chinese restaurant that's become a Monday night regular.

What'll it be? he says, flipping over the pages of the menu and trying not to make eye contact with the trussed-up lobster in the adjacent tank. *Feeling adventurous tonight?*

Did you have a very bad day today?

Very bad, very bad.

And tonight you want to live. You want to go crazy. You want to break the mould. You want to say no to Mongolian lamb.

Damn right I do.

Keno?

Not tonight. Tonight, a totally new strategy. We will ask for a Chinese person's recommendation.

Could be risky.

Keno's risky. Remember Number 97?

Sunny Garden Keno requires participants to order based only on the last two digits of the number plate of a passing car chosen at random. It's how we found Number 34, Kun Po chicken, now one of our regulars. It's also how we discovered that Number 97 is Large Steamed Rice. It took some work to convince the staff that what we wanted was steamed rice for two, plus Number 97, but we insisted. *In a lot of countries this is probably what people have to eat every day,* Rick said, as though there could be an upside, as though we were making a gesture. *Just the rice. We should be grateful.* As he drizzled soy sauce across it, and tried to effect some kind of UNICEF-aware look.

The woman who comes to the table tonight speaks little English. Rick thinks this is a good thing. He asks what her favourite is and she says *Double-cooked pork. Very nice, very soft.*

When it arrives, it is immediately apparent that the part of the pig used for double-cooked pork is that part that is external to the part we would usually eat. It is warm pan-browned back fat, held together in strips by the overlying skin, still with an occasional authentic bristle.

Good choice, Rick, I tell him. No visible meat at all. You first, I insist. Very nice, very soft. I want you to remember that. While we have teeth, we never order very soft again.

They don't waste the pig, do they? he says philosophically.

These bits of the pig they could turn into soap and wallets without wasting them. Not everything has to be a meal.

He eats a bowl of rice and soy sauce, and then tentatively picks up a wobbling piece of back fat with his chopsticks.

Have I got one without hair? he says, as though this will make it okay.

No.

He's still looking at it, still daring himself to eat it when one of the other staff comes up and asks if everything's all right.

Fine, Rick says. *Fine. Just eating our double-cooked pork.* Wobbling it round between his chopsticks, trying to look as though he does it all the time.

Not a lot of Australians order the double-cooked pork.

Really?

It's more a Chinese dish. If you wanted, if you've changed your mind, I could maybe take it away and give you something more Australians like. Mongolian lamb maybe?

Rick hesitates for only a moment before giving in, and the waiter takes the plate away, grinning.

I feel so culturally inadequate. We go to a Chinese restaurant and we order something Chinese people actually eat and we have to send it back.

You were a bit multiculturally confident after yesterday, weren't you? Nachos for lunch, pizza for dinner. I think you thought you were ready for the world.

Hubris. Vanity. And I'm sure Mongolian lamb's bull-shit. I bet in Mongolia they toss the red meat to the pigs and double cook the fat till it's very nice, very soft. Mongolian lamb. I'm sure it's just a con.

In Mongolian restaurants they probably sell it as Australian lamb. Who knows what they get up to. I read somewhere that in Mongolian wrestling there's a guy whose only job is to hold the pillbox hat of the wrestler during the fight. So who knows what they do with lamb.

Some days, Rick says, *some days I think I could be that guy. Just at the edge of the action, holding the hat and figuring that's as close as I'm going to get.*

The Mongolian lamb arrives and things are comfortably familiar again.

How's Penny? he says.

That's a good question. Or in fact a bad question. I was going to tell you about Penny.

What do you mean? There's nothing wrong, is there?

Not as such.

No. You didn't.

I might've. These things happen. Okay, last night we reached a point of discontinuity.

I can't believe it.

What can't you believe?

I can't believe you didn't tell me this morning. Over breakfast. On the way into the city. Did you forget? I liked this one. We were getting to know her. We didn't mind her at all. Sure she was a screamer, but, you know, you can't hold that against a girl. It did, at times, make the loneliness in my room a little more poignant, but I've got to accept that. What did she do? What did she do to you?

Nothing.

It was the toothbrush, wasn't it? I knew when she told you she'd got you your own toothbrush to keep at the

*Nurses' Quarters, I knew she was history. I assume you've
lined up the next one.*

You have a very poor understanding of the way I oper-
ate. You're far too cynical. There's no *next one*. I just
happened to realise that the time had come. That our
expectations for the relationship were no longer compati-
ble. But don't think it was easy.

*What's that? A pang of conscience? It must be easy
now, all the practice you've had.*

He's still suffering on Penny's behalf in the car on the
way home.

*How does this happen? Do you have no respect for
these women?*

Of course I have no respect for them. They're interested
in me. How could I possibly respect that?

Bingo is raging in the Serbian Orthodox Church Hall.

Rick says he'll make coffee and goes into the kitchen,
still shaking his head about the Penny issue. Conceptually,
he's just not across it. He can't understand how, once
you've got one, you might even think about letting go.

He is not great with women. His approach is not only
unsophisticated, it's barely an approach. He seems to follow the idea that if you spend the maximum possible time
with a girl, at some point genital juxtaposition will seem
inevitable to her. And he thinks this will be assisted by
ludicrous cartoon ties. As though the first time he gets to
say *Grumpy and Sneezy are round the back, look,* to a
girl, he's done his bit and the rest is up to her.

Last year we had a club, not a good club, but a club.
Better than journal club, but not by much. The Recon-
stituted Virgins Club. There were two prerequisites for
membership. You had to have had sex. And you had to
have not had sex for a long time. Minimum qualifying
period a year, and Rick and I made it easily.

I lost my virginity at nineteen in fairly unimpressive circumstances. I was at a party, drinking quickly and just becoming aware of my rapidly filling bladder while in a conversation with a girl I didn't know particularly well, another med student. Suddenly she seemed to think I'd suggested we might have sex now, something I'd not knowingly suggested to anyone at that point of my life, and she was saying, *Well, okay, I could be persuaded* and being drunkenly, messily seductive and tugging at my jeans. I thought about it, I thought about saying no because of my bladder, but then I figured it probably wouldn't take long and this was a chance that wasn't likely to come my way all the time. I was right on both counts. Several minutes later I was to begin a fairly bad run of involuntary celibacy that only came to an end when I discovered my status had changed after graduating.

Rick does his cause no good by having two loss of virginity stories, which come out at different times. The first involves a caravan at Bribie Island when he was eighteen, the second a uni ball at nineteen. This does make us wonder if he should be barred from club membership through failure to comply with rule one, First lose your virginity.

Rick started out a hopeless romantic, blew his uni days in the pursuit of one girl (though he doesn't seem to have worked this out yet), and is now therefore a slightly more hopeless romantic, perplexed and paralysed by the practicalities, living in hope that he'll be swept off his feet.

When he was seventeen he spent most of the holiday between school and uni in desperate love with a girl who worked at the London Roast at the local shopping centre. He and a friend went there almost every day. Between visits, Rick would compose poems for her, commit them to memory and transcribe them onto paper serviettes while eating his ham, cheese and tomato toasted sandwich. And when she cleared the table, the serviette would be there on the plate, poem up, waiting for her. She never said a word.

Last summer, five years later, a female of more than passing interest gave him a mango. He talked for days about the bits that were stuck between his teeth, as though this was some kind of relationship. But he said nothing to her. He planted the stone in the backyard. Thirteen months have passed, still no mango tree.

He confronts the girl problem with attempts to re-invent himself. Recently he bought a book that told him he needed a plan. It told him that he should make a list of his goals for the next five years. It told him to find a quiet place, free his mind from the shackles of everyday thoughts and be open to inspiration. He told me he realised this was a stupid approach when he sat gazing out the window, deshackling, and the HB pencil in his hand began to write the words, *Watch more TV.*

Last year, at a similar crisis point, he decided he should learn French. He paid for a course at Alliance Francaise and went several times. He learned to say, My name is Richard, and he learned our phone number, and then he seemed to stop going. He kept rehearsing the phone number though, and his big intro, and saying he'd probably go back next week. For weeks he was proud of his phone number in French, until we asked him to say it just a few too many times.

Perhaps he'd thought it was enough, name and phone number, the only edge he'd need over the monolingual masses if he happened to bump into a devastatingly attractive French woman who spoke no English. Or perhaps he knew he'd never be French enough, and he'd have to make girls want him some other way. Ties maybe.

Coffee, he says, and passes me my cup.

I want to tell him now that no-one ever had sex with

anyone on account of a tie, but I don't think he's ready to hear it.

Jen's still on the loose, he says. *You know what that means. Someone's in danger tonight.* He sips the coffee. *How is it, how is it that tonight the two of us will retire to our rooms completely without company and for me it's a lifestyle, the norm, and for you it's a moment's aberration? You're probably just days away from luring some nice, sensitive, vulnerable girl in there until her time comes to be trashed.*

While you're just a thin tongue-and-groove wall away, pumping the skin piston with Ms Kleenex? They don't know what they're missing, spunk.

Could the next one not be a screamer? That's all I ask.

Come on. It's me on their bones. It's perfectly appropriate to scream.

3

Wednesday is the ward outing. This is not some sophisticated strategy aimed at the gradual re-introduction of the dysfunctional to society. It is simply one of many attempts to come up with an activity other than smoking, watching TV and eating, but it's hard to maintain interest.

It's not as though a great many things aren't tried. Bingo is appropriately passive for some, bores others and occasionally provokes conspiracy theories among the paranoid. Table tennis is great for a few, somewhat embarrassing (but briefly seductive) for a few more and completely out of the question for most.

The Craft Room at the OT Department goes in and out of favour. Art, woodwork, macramé, but particularly leatherwork. Sometimes they're all into it, every patient who moves and can muster an attention span. Sometimes it's as though the ward has been overrun by a roaming band of leatherworkers, as they roll back in for lunch brandishing their stubby holders, drink coasters, key rings, neatly tooled pictures of Jesus (rarely a good prognostic sign), orthopaedic devices to support injuries they'd like to have. Belts were big last Christmas, and most staff members ended up with at least a couple with ridiculously overblown western motifs. Glen got one with an optional holster.

The leathering of Johnno's bike was undoubtedly the biggest undertaking, but one patient came close to matching it when he made his own lederhosen.

There was no reason for this, no reason other than opportunity. He never explained it, but he spent a month on the job and then he wore them every day. Every day for six weeks in December and January. Creaking around in his leather shorts as though we were all doing it. And it certainly aroused interest in the ward, with at least two other patients in the developmental stages of their own lederhosen when it was found that both he and his hosen had a very unattractive fungal infestation in the groin area.

There are, of course, lower-level craft activities for the less able. Beads, for example. Conceptually simple perhaps, but by no means immune to uncommon interpretation. One patient who became a little too attached to one of the members of the nursing staff made her a necklace of wooden beads seventy-eight metres long. The OT hadn't wanted to stop him, since he'd never been enthusiastic about anything before, and whenever she asked what he was doing he told her it was a surprise. And no-one's sure if he simply couldn't grasp the idea of joining the ends together to finish it, or if he wanted it to reach from the Craft Room to the ward before he gave it to her, or if he just wanted to make it really, really good.

Today, while they're out and the ward is quiet, I'm indulging my own temporary new hobby, my journal club task. I'm in the library, telling myself to read whatever hibernation articles are available, preparing myself to compare what I find with astronaut physiology, though not with much confidence. Telling myself there must be some sensible connection between furry animals and astronaut rectums, something beyond the conjecture that the isolation of space does strange things to a person's judgement.

The library is more crowded than I'd like. Visiting specialists flipping through journals. A bunch of students tapping each other's reflexes, killing time before tutes, swapping names of patients with obscure cardiac murmurs. Marlon de Lisle, head down in study. As I'm walking back to my seat I'm aware that these people all find what they're doing inherently acceptable, while I'm carrying a pile of articles about furry animals sleeping. This, I realise, is not something I would find easy to explain, even without mentioning the rectums of astronauts. Particularly to Marlon de Lisle who, I suspect, is way too legendary to have to give a passing thought to furry animals sleeping.

Hibernation. The hamster seems to be the mammal of choice. I make a few notes, start putting some thoughts together.

The hamster
The hamster, like many mammals, has a circannual rhythm; a rhythm based on the seasons. It breeds at

a particular time of year, stores food at a particular time of year, hibernates. In hibernation, in darkness and abstinence and far from arousal, its rhythms can free-run, set their own pace. Some of its circadian rhythms, away from the imposition of night and day, drift out of rhythm. The rhythms of waking and sleeping, activity and inactivity, hunger and satiety. The rhythms of metabolism, body temperature, sex hormones, other hormones. All of these change, and some lose rhythm completely. This is brought about by the shortening of days, a signal to alter habits, prepare, go to ground. This can be reproduced in labs, provoked by a change to winter day lengths. Food intake decreases, stored energy is mobilised, gonads regress, the hamster withdraws. Hibernation, even when it hasn't prepared. Maintained by darkness. Reversible with a single burst of light.

So where is this taking me? What's the hibernation connection in the astronaut article? Are the astronauts somehow out of season? Losing circadian fluctuations of light/dark and temperature, like hamsters in a hole? Having their regular *zeitgebers* interfered with, like lab rodents?

And there's a lot of work on gonads in these hamster articles. Metabolism and gonads. A surprising amount on gonadal regression and sex hormones. I'd never really thought of this with hibernation, but I guess if you're asleep for months your gonads aren't your most essential body parts.

I wonder if someone discussed this with the astronauts. *We've just worked out that space flight might be something like hibernation, so you understand that you may be coming back with a little more room in your shorts?*

I can still see Johnno, laughing his wheezy, almost silent laugh, rocking back in his chair as I made the remark about astronauts and rectal temperature probes, and then saying, *Why? Why don't you tell us why? Take this article and tell us what it was they said to the astronauts that made the astronauts say, Sure I'll stick that up my arse. Give me that butt wire. Let me do my bit for humanity.*

Clearly I'm a very valued member of the psych team.

Rick declares kitty to be in surplus when I get home. This is a negotiated right, the trade-off I made for the others to agree that we would each pay twenty dollars more than the rent every fortnight so bills wouldn't take us by surprise. This entitles Rick and Jen to call for a night of cocktails on any occasion when we're more than sixty dollars up and no big bills are known to be due.

Tonight is such a night. Rick waves the Quality Street tin in front of me, encouraging me to listen to the rustle of notes. *Big surplus,* he says. *Cocktails tonight.*

They only make you sad, I tell him, but he won't be talked out of it.

We go to the Royal Exchange bottle shop and buy Cointreau, Tia Maria and Bailey's, and we pick up four litres of vanilla ice cream at the Night Owl at Auchenflower.

Jen says, almost as an aside and just for the purposes of catering, *I've got a guy coming over.* As though he might come or he might not, no big deal.

So, Rick says, unprepared to accept Jen's deliberate nonchalance as any signal to leave well alone, *tell us more.*

His name is Sam.

Does he play rugby?

Yes. Sometimes. Maybe.

Where does she get these guys? Is there some facility that provides them for her? They certainly always seem to be returned when they should still be under warranty.

I met him on Monday, she says, deciding to get it out of the way. *Monday night when you guys were Sunny Gardening. Well, I've met him before once or twice, but he was going out with someone then. And now he's not. As of last weekend.*

Anything to do with you?

Nothing to do with me. She found someone else and it came to a fairly sticky end.

So you're going for road kill now, Rick says.

He was in a relationship as recently as Saturday, and that's more than some of us can claim.

Rick has no comeback to that. Rick would kill to be road kill, but at the moment he'd have to fall under the wheels of his own vehicle.

Sam knocks softly at the door when he arrives.

I'm looking for Jenny Beckett. Have I got the right place?

He has just a hint of the haunted look of the recently trashed, the brittle uncertainty of being out in different company, and so quickly. But maybe I'm reading too much into this and it's just reticence, just him.

He's less reticent after a couple of cocktails. Much less reticent after a couple more. Saying, *Check this out* and pouring a layer of Tia Maria and a layer of Cointreau, sucking Bailey's up into an empty pen and releasing it into the middle. And the Bailey's hangs there in suspension, like a small dense cloud. *Test-tube Baby.*

Rick is impressed and makes one himself. He studies it from all angles, turning the glass slowly, fascinated by the complex morphology of the milky creature in the middle of the liquor.

It's got little arms, he says. *Two little arms.* Jen asks if it's a boy or a girl and Rick looks closer. *That bit's in the Tia Maria. It's hard to tell.* He keeps looking. *I can't drink it now. You know I can never drink this.* He rests his head on the table. *It'd stick in my throat. It'd be all lumpy, like a foetus.*

Rick has suddenly found himself on a short journey to a bad place. We tell him we'll leave his foetus alone, for nine months, if that's what he wants. And when it's his baby we'll treat it well.

I want a baby, he says, so we make him a Burning Beaver to take his mind from this deep, obscure pain, but he gets the timing wrong and it costs him eyelashes.

The Burning Beaver is a creation of my sister's. My sister is in London acting, and tradition therefore dictates that she should make cocktails for a living when the acting doesn't pay. She is a co-inventor of the Burning Beaver, the most dangerous cocktail on Fulham Road, a particularly incendiary combination into which the middle finger (preferably of the non-dominant hand) is dipped, lit and turned outwards in a defiant gesture while the cocktail is consumed as quickly as possible.

How my sister came up with this I'm not sure. Cocktails, I thought, were to be savoured, to give some lingering over-priced kind of pleasure. The Beaver seems to be the antithesis of this, the only cocktail that appeals because of its genuine physical danger. Maybe it's not unlike the man who worked out he could only reach orgasm by dousing his groin in lighter fluid, igniting his pubic hair and plunging into a bath. I must admit, if I was having trouble getting my shot away, it wouldn't be the first therapy I'd think of. But then, I'm probably just approaching this from within the confines of a rigid medical model.

Rick gives the middle finger of his non-dominant hand a few minutes under the cold tap, and says he wonders how his eyelashes got involved at all.

The need to sleep is starting to overwhelm me. Usually this is preceded by a good half hour when I think I'm the funniest man in the world, but somehow I missed that tonight. Even Sam's flagging as I creep off to bed. Jen, of course, isn't. Jen is looking bored with our inability to keep up.

Maybe this is what she's going through with men. An endless search for someone who can match her drink for drink, and she's assuming it's more likely to be someone of large mass. Sam's effort is slipping rapidly into the 'Could do better' category, and they don't often come back from there.

Last year, Jen worked at Expo '88 in one of the least popular pavilions. It was rated two platypuses out of a possible five, and in the spirit of Expo generosity there were no one-platypus pavilions. Working there was so unstimulating she and a friend used to stand at opposite sides of the exhibit and throw their shoes to each other. After most shifts she went to the Munich Festhaus which, unlike her pavilion, was packed day and night. For the entire duration of Expo the Festhaus sold more beer than any pub in Queensland, and a great deal of it to men who were buying it for Jen, hoping to loosen her inhibitions. This, of course, was a two-fold tactical error. Jen could outdrink every one of them, and hadn't had an inhibition in her life.

Rick loved the Festhaus too, but never lasted long. But that's okay, neither did I. Once he'd had four beers and chicken-danced till he could chicken-dance no more, we'd walk home along the Coronation Drive bike path, the happy drunk and the maudlin drunk, crapping on to each other like some Shakespearean light relief.

Whenever he's drunk he seems to wonder what will become of him. Once he found himself in a cab after a work function, explaining to the cabbie that he was only drunk because he didn't get to eat more than a single little salmon hors d'oeuvre. The cabbie, just as conversation, told him he'd heard about some kids becoming sick after eating some fish that was off, and Rick cried all the way home, thinking he was going to die and working out he just wasn't ready for that yet.

He recently told me he'd realised that, when it came, his death would be far less interesting than this. A lapse in concentration, death by inattention. Crossing the road while contemplating the purchase of a tie, perhaps, something like that.

4

At the end of Thursday's ward round I present the new patient, the depressed man I admitted earlier in the week. When I've finished, Johnno starts talking through particular details in the history.

He gets to the vegetative features of depression, the physical features that are often part of a major depressive illness. I check the list I made in the file when I did the admission, to see if I missed anything.

Early morning waking
Diurnal variation – feels worse in the morning
No energy – feels like staying in bed all day
Loss of appetite

Constipated
Weight loss – 5 kg
Loss of libido
Psychomotor retardation ++

Any more of this and he could be a hamster.

He could be a hamster. He could be hibernating. When you write it in point form it looks like the same phenomenon, but described in different languages. Hibernation and the vegetative features of depression. Much more interesting than astronauts.

Diurnal and circadian are effectively synonyms. Psychomotor retardation just means a slowing down of thought and movement. Extreme psychomotor retardation produces stupor.

There is a loss of rhythms here. Sleep–wake cycle, hunger–satiety cycle, rhythms losing their usual clarity. But when we think of them as symptoms, we don't think of them as rhythms.

Naturally, this takes me back to the library. I'm getting to like the library. It's quiet, hassle-free and it doesn't stink of·years of old smoke. All it really needs to make it perfect is a few other activities.

The hibernation–depression thing isn't new. The connection has been made, but years ago. People who think like Freud and Jung, but couldn't know the biochemistry.

I turn, as I did at. uni, to *Excerpta Medica*. The best thing about *Excerpta Medica* is that it's better than they ever meant it to be. Each volume contains thousands of journal article abstracts about studies conducted all over the world, with an index and key words at the back. The interested party is supposed to go to the index, check the key words, check the abstracts and then leave *Excerpta Medica* to locate and read the article. The problem with this is that the abstracts are great. There is no incentive to find the article at all, to mess up clear thinking with a detailed discussion of study design, subject selection, unfathomable statistical methods.

I completed several assignments at uni by doing nothing more than lining up bits of information from *Excerpta Medica* in the right order. The boldest of them had one hundred and thirty-eight references, all totally second-hand.

I treat the process like uni. I follow various lines of thought, I write notes on scraps of paper. I put the scraps in piles where things seem to fit together. Something unlikely seems to emerge when I sort through.

Hibernation

I need to focus on the common things, the things common to hibernating animals and humans. Not the hibernation itself. The biochemistry, the physiology of the slowed-down state. I follow the hormones. Thyroxine from the thyroid gland since it controls metabolism. Cortisol from the adrenal gland since it's involved in arousal. Sex hormones and others. But the one that keeps coming up is a hormone I've hardly heard of before. The hormone of the pineal gland, melatonin.

More than any other, it seems to be the hormone of hibernation, the hormone of day and night. It seems to be melatonin that's associated with changes in body weight, fur, and gonad size in hamsters. In the lab, these changes occur with a winter light pattern only if the melatonin levels fall into line.

In some species, melatonin free-runs in continuous darkness and in hibernation. Sudden light exposure then leads to immediate suppression of melatonin levels, followed by restoration of circadian melatonin rhythm. This seems to correlate with an end to hibernation.

Melatonin in humans

Humans too have melatonin, though it has long been thought to have no significant role. Melatonin in humans can be measured directly in plasma, rising to a peak during the night and becoming almost absent during the day. Once it is metabolised it can also be measured in the urine, as six-sulphatoxy melatonin.

While the total daily urine six-sulphatoxy melatonin output is stable over the year, the time of the nocturnal plasma melatonin peak varies ninety minutes between summer and winter.

In most normal human volunteers, nocturnal melatonin production can be suppressed by night-time light exposure. Perhaps this is analogous to the exposure of hibernating hamsters to light.

Melatonin is closely related to serotonin. Made by converting serotonin in two simple steps. A role for serotonin in depression has long been the subject of hypotheses and research. The Monoamine Theory proposes that depression may be due to reduced levels of serotonin at receptor sites in the brain.

Seasonal affective disorder

A sub-population of people with depressive illnesses are noted to undergo seasonal exacerbations. Specifically, recurrent depression in winter. This has been called seasonal affective disorder. Some of these people suffer recurrent major depression with vegetative features, the biological features of hibernation. Some have responded well to bright light exposure.

So here in the shadow of one of the big biological depression theories of our time is a closely related hormone, linked to hibernation, light and the seasons. An old model linking depression and hibernation. A small group of people who allow another link to be made, between depression and the seasons, cure and light.

Is melatonin actively involved? Could the hormone of hibernation be the hormone of depression? Causing the physical symptoms of major depression and perhaps even the change in mood? Could phototherapy in seasonal affective disorder be the *zeitgeber* that restores normal melatonin levels, and brings the depression to an end? Could this be how antidepressants work?

I'm getting ahead of myself. Sitting here, a rank amateur with three piles of notes, ideas free-running somewhat dangerously. I could find myself next Monday reporting on my short walk down a blind alley, ending with a cage of hamsters somewhere in Prague, baffled by the lights. And if I start suggesting rectal probes and checking our depressed patients' gonads, no-one's concerns will be allayed.

I wonder if anyone's tried to add it up this way yet. To speculate that serotonin was close, but not quite there. Not quite the right monoamine for the Monoamine Theory.

For one dangerous moment I want to tell someone, but the person nearest me is Marlon de Lisle and he's caught in the mantra of *Harrison's Principles of Internal Medicine*, murmuring some list over and over in the aisle seat of row three, cracking knuckles, tapping the top of his head in what might be six–eight time. All of these very clear leave-me-alone signals, very clear don't-bug-me-with-a-crazy-theory-now signals. Not that I think crazy theories would be greatly to his liking at any time.

I don't even tell Rick when we're on the way to Coles for late-night shopping. I want to say, Hey, I've got this theory, but it's not really a theory yet, and it's already too messy to discuss in the aisles of Coles. It's still in bits, *Excerpta Medica* bits.

Besides, I have to pay close attention to him when our shared funds are at stake. In any kind of shop he shows no judgement at all, and happily buys the most expensive-looking item in any particular category, assuming it will be better. I have to do the maths in my head comparing brands (dollars per kilogram, cents per toilet roll), and sometimes I have to be firm.

Within seconds of my mind wandering just slightly onto melatonin, he's fondling the honey jar that becomes a drinking glass, even though it costs more and we have thirty-eight drinking glasses at home. I persuade him to put it back, and I tell him I will not be won over by the excellent fit of the handle, or his lively but poorly constructed attempt at a German drinking song.

We load the groceries into the car and go across the road to Kwali for chicken satay and beef rendang. Our standard Thursday night. Sitting at the window looking down at the shoppers moving in and out of Toowong Village, probably the same shoppers, week after week. Observing this rhythm, this seven-day cycle. Not unlike hamsters, really. With the possible exception of fluctuating gonad size. Or maybe not.

5

The Mount Stevens buck's ritual is horribly, horribly standard.

Shane Sandercock, one of the surgical registrars, is getting married. He should therefore be very scared about Friday and all it will bring. Earlier in the week we got fliers in our pigeon holes, telling us the buck's festivities would begin on Friday lunchtime at the Federal Hotel, followed by drinks in the Residents' Quarters after work.

The text of this is so bare it could, to the outsider, be open to misinterpretation. But the Fed is no place for anyone seeking a polite fisherman's basket around lunchtime on Friday. Friday lunchtime in the back bar of the Fed is The Naked Lunch – Five Babes for Five Bucks, and drinks in the Quarters after work is far worse.

The Fed is just down the road from the hospital, easily within beeper range, and unless you have a good excuse you're expected to be there. I hardly know Shane Sandercock, but that's not the issue. I don't have a ward round, I'm not in theatre, I am a male member of the resident medical staff and saying that I was planning to be in the library reading about hamsters just wouldn't do.

The woman on the door has straggly, bleached-blonde hair and wide shapeless arms and says *Five bucks* and sticks her hand out without taking her eyes off the racing on the wall-mounted TV screen.

The room is crowded. I join the buck's enclave in the usual place and I buy a light beer. This is my limit, one light beer, the limit for most of us, other than the buck.

We're all standing round drinking our beers slowly,

standing there in our name tags and our cheap, styleless clothes, gorging on chips and the endless supply of cocktail sausages that is part of the package, part of the great five-buck deal. Again I wonder if this is done with any irony at all. We'll let you watch a parade of vigorous female nudity, but you have to eat phallic symbols as you're doing it. Cocktail sausages dipped in tomato sauce. Tantalised and disempowered all for one five-dollar note.

But Freud is not at this Naked Lunch, any more than William S. Burroughs. Freud will be ignored and Burroughs ripped off by this. And I bet this isn't the only strip show in the world where the name of the book was felt to be just right for one o'clock on Fridays. And there are probably more than a few people who, if you told them *The Naked Lunch* was the name of a novel by Burroughs, would assume that it was subtitled 'Five Babes for Five Bucks'.

The buck, as tradition dictates, gets rapidly smashed. We all put in a few dollars and ask for as many Head Fuckers as it'll cover. They bring us eight on a tray. Eight Heinekens, each with a shot of Tequila. Shane's head is fucked before the show, so everything's going to plan so far. Soon it'll be babes, babes, babes, all in a blur for him, and then he'll be back in the hospital, placed somewhere out of harm's way while the other surgical staff cover for him. It's all about planning. You can do anything you like as long as you plan, as long as your patients are covered. A blind eye will be turned.

The room lights, already low, go out. A spotlight comes up on the small stage. The music begins. 'Eye of the Tiger'.

A woman in mock leopard skin comes on cracking a whip. She raunches around making leopard noises, leopard faces as the music pumps. How hard would it have been to get mock tiger skin, I wonder, and actually fit in with the song? Clearly I'm missing the point. She rubs the whip up and down her leopard front and then cracks it overhead, as though to keep back the baying masses.

The baying masses who, as she piece by piece eases herself from the big cat, are standing silently, staring straight ahead with the appropriate kind of fascinated indifference.

The buck, meanwhile, has slid easily past indifference and is reaching across the table, gripping on tight to his seventh Head Fucker, going, *Yeah, yeah* as though he's having the time of his life. She drops her mock-leopard bikini top and squeezes her breasts, works them as though she's being milked. Shane pounds the table with his fist, waves his Head Fucker in the air, shouts, *Yeah, yeah*. I hope his wife-to-be is up for this sort of stuff. It seems important to him.

I can't accept that I could ever be only a handful of Head Fuckers away from this point. Slumped over a table quietly shellacking my pants, and getting married in eight days.

The last triangle of the mock leopard is flicked aside, and it's just a girl and a whip up there now, a girl rubbing the whip across her naked abdomen as she writhes through the final chorus. Tantalising her vagina with the whip handle, and then tut-tutting with a waggle of a long-nailed finger, as though it's too early in the day. Too early in the day to be passing a whip up oneself.

And then, just as it looks like she might do it, the song stops, the stage snaps into darkness, she scurries off.

The ward, as arranged, pages me at five past one, while our eyes are getting used to the dim light between acts. I look down at my pager, swear with the appropriate level of intensity, shake my head like a man defeated and go for the door.

Hang on, doc, the bleached-blonde woman says. *You've*

hardly got your money's worth. And she fetches me six cocktail sausages and a glob of sauce on a paper plate.

Thanks.

I just picked up a quinella at Rose Hill, she tells me, in a way that suggests I might be interested. *Quinella,* she says. *Rose Hill. The races. The gee gees.* Nodding, moving her eyebrows up and down, making it clear it's a good thing.

Behind us the skin show grinds on. The next act is a schoolgirl, about to be very, very naughty. I can't see how Shane can last four more babes without orgasm. And, if going back to the hospital seriously overloaded with Heineken and Tequila sounds bad, wobbling round heavy with Head Fuckers having just come in your pants is surely much, much worse.

As I run across the road, the sausages roll around on the plate, buffeting against the thick paper rim and sludging into the sauce. The plate has balloons on it – red, blue and yellow balloons and the words 'Party!!! Party!!! Party!!!'

I swirl a sausage round in the sauce like a finger painter and I bite the end. It's cold. She's given me a plate of cold sausages. I drop it into the bin inside the gates and I decide to go to the hospital shop for some Cool Mints to take the hint of beer from my breath. Blowing beer breath over a detoxing alcoholic as I whip his butt at table tennis later this afternoon would be more than a little insensitive.

What is it that I don't love about The Naked Lunch? What am I looking for? Intimacy?

The shop is run by a group called the Hospital Auxiliary, which used to be called the Ladies' Auxiliary. These are the Pink Ladies, the impossibly good-hearted volunteers who serve trad food and comfort. Three cold pikelets in Glad Wrap, fifty cents. Cup of warm sweet tea (for the treatment of shock), sixty cents. I think they are a world-wide phenomenon. In 'Days of Our Lives', which I used to watch regularly when I was at uni, they were called Candy Stripers. I'm not sure, but I think this may be even more demeaning than Pink Ladies.

Marco Cassimatis is in the shop buying some sand-wiches and an apple. I haven't seen him since we DMO'd together on Sunday. He looks around and I ask him how he's going.

Oh, hi. Good. Not at Shane's buck's thing then?

I got paged. Between Babes One and Two. What about you?

Busy. Lots of things on. You know. Do you know where the bereavement clerk is?

Do I know where the bereavement clerk is? No-one knows where the bereavement clerk is like I do. Come with me.

He peels open the plastic wrapping round his sand-wiches and takes a bite. *It's different, isn't it, when you know them?*

You know one of the strippers at the Fed? I've never known a stripper.

No, not a stripper. The bereavement clerk thing, I mean. A patient. It's different when you know them.

Oh, right, yeah. What do you mean? This isn't, you know, your next-door neighbour or anything?

He laughs. *No. My next-door neighbour's a deadshit. He'll probably live forever. This was just someone I'd got used to, someone who'd been in for a couple of weeks. A nice guy, you know.*

Sure. Yeah. I know what you mean. You see him every day, you get to call him Jack, he bites the big one.

And it's not like Sunday. Not like a Code Blue on some-one you've never met who hasn't got a chance. It's different when you've seen them pink.

Yeah. It is. So you haven't done this paperwork before?
No. What's the deal?

It sucks. You'll be a while. Lots of paper. But that's why there's a bereavement clerk, just to hand you the right bits and tell you what to do. There are two tricks to it. One is to get the right spin on the cause of death, or the Death Cert bounces back and you have to do it again. The general rule is no abbreviations, no acronyms and blame it on the biggest disease they've got, unless there's a good reason not to. The other issue is the post-mortem. What's the story with a post-mortem on this guy?
I don't know.

Did you ask the family about a post-mortem?
No. I couldn't. I mean, it didn't cross my mind. The cause of death was clear, so I just didn't think about it. So what do I do? It's not like I can call them back now and say, you know, By the way, how about it?

That's fine. You just put 'Denied'.
Denied.

Yeah. You raised it with them. They asked you why. They asked you if there was any doubt about the cause of death. You said no, and you told them this is a teaching hospital. They said they'd really rather not. Denied.
I say that now? To the bereavement clerk?

You say that now, yes. And she'll ask you to remember to document it in the file next time.
Okay.

The door is open. Sharon Gale, the bereavement clerk, is at her desk.

Jonathan Marshall, she says. *It's been ages. You've really mended your wicked ways.*

Thanks, Shaz. Thanks a heap. I've missed you too.

And this, she says and glances at a sheet of paper in front of her, *this must be Doctor Cassimatis.*

Got it in one. Marco, this is Sharon Gale. Sharon will be your guide through the paper labyrinth that awaits you.

It's not that bad, she says fussily and holds up a handful of sheets of paper that looks bad enough to me. *Besides, I'm sure it's not a labyrinth to you any more.* She turns to Marco. *Doctor Marshall had a lot of practice while he was in respiratory. He actually got into the habit of visiting me on the way in in the mornings before going to the ward.* Marco laughs, thinking this is a joke. Which it isn't. *Not a very high post-mortem rate, though,* she goes on. *But that's a small quibble, really. Great with the paperwork. Anyway, take a seat, take a seat.*

She fusses him into the hard wooden chair in front of her desk. As I'm heading out the door I hear her say *So, do we get a post-mortem on this man?*

I go to the Quarters, empty now with everyone over at the Fed or in the wards. I hit a few balls on the pool table, and then I decide to put in some time at Galaxion. I tug the paperclip hanging out of the coin slot and rack myself up a few free games. The rule, since one of the anaesthetic registrars rewired it and put the paperclip in place, is that you put in twenty cents any week you play, and if you play a lot you put in forty cents. The paperclip vanishes the morning of the routine quarterly service, and the technician finds just enough in the coin box to justify the machine's continued presence.

After a couple of games I'm back in the groove, blowing away aliens in large numbers.

My low post-mortem rate was a problem in respiratory. I think I may have been personally responsible for bringing the hospital's post-mortem percentage down to an all-time low last December. And this isn't paranoia. No-one was in a stronger position to influence the stats than me and, while we all got pigeon-holed about it, I was the only one who received a personal invitation to discuss the matter with the Medical Superintendent. The Dud. Doctor Frank Dudgeon.

He approached it from his usual well-meaning but woolly perspective. Leaned back in his chair, put his hands together as though prayer wasn't out of the question and complimented me on my work. Told me how happy everyone was with my work in respiratory. That I was doing good work, very good work, and I should feel good about that. And when it came to the paperwork, he'd looked through it, and it was good too.

Always good and clear with the cause of death, he said. *I've got no qualms about that. And my goodness you've had a lot of cancer up there lately, haven't you? I just wonder, I just wonder about the post-mortem side of things. What do you think's happening, Jon? We're just not getting enough. I thought we might take a look at that. Just a few broad brushstrokes perhaps. This is how it looks to me. Our pathology registrars, you may not know, have a certain quota to fill. They have to perform a certain number of post-mortem examinations before they can be admitted to the College of Pathologists. And this is a teaching hospital. People know that when they're admitted. This is, if you like, part of their contract with the hospital. Not that we'd ever approach it that way. And I know I can rely on you to handle these things with tact, but perhaps if families could be made aware that they were doing something for the greater good . . .*

After this I felt I knew exactly how the Dud would be when approaching his children's sex education. Offering them his broad brushstrokes, his pauses for contemplation, his hands, folding and unfolding in and out of shapes like origami sub-titles.

There's an admission waiting for me in the ward, but other than that the afternoon is the usual steady Ward Nine series of bits and pieces, minor complaints, medication sheets, tests to organise, test results to check, table tennis.

Shane Sandercock's buck's night begins at the bar in the Quarters at five-thirty.

Shane has metabolised some of the alcohol of lunchtime and is talking enthusiastically about the show. *Did you see those tits?* he's saying, as though anyone might not have. *Did you see those tits?*

After an hour I'm still on my first light beer, a dozen pizzas have arrived and we've been here long enough to establish clearly that there are three groups of people in the room. A small number who actually like Shane and are matching him drink for drink, talking loudly and already walking the less well-attached parts of their pizza topping into the carpet without knowing it. A large number who are still on their first or second light beer, looking bored, looking as though the outside world will soon be offering them something better to do, but not soon enough. And the usual half-dozen who are pissed because they are nei-ther sleeping nor working.

Like anything else, the RMOs' bar buck's night has an etiquette to it. For close friends of the buck this is only the beginning, and the night will not end until he's trouserless and chained to something in a very public place with his genitals bathed in maple syrup and a sign next to him say-ing, 'Last chance girls'. Most of us, though, know we only have to stay until the Black Widow.

For several hundred dollars the Black Widow comes

and dances exotically in the vicinity of the face of the smashed groom-to-be, divests herself of her shiny black costume bit by shiny bit, squirms her naked buttocks around on his lap, instruments herself wickedly, takes him into another room and, we believe, fucks him.

At least, she leads him back five minutes later with his eyes rattling around in his head as though she's shooting craps with them, his shirt hanging out, his fly undone. And legend has it that one buck came back with his penis flopped through his fly and smears of black lipstick on his shaft.

There's also a story about the buck's night of a gynae reg two or three years ago, when hospital gear was smuggled in and the Widow dealt with herself severely with an extra-large duck-billed speculum. As someone said, *If only we'd had a swizzle stick handy she could have done her own pap smear.*

On the other hand, maybe it was as you'd expect, and only the orthopaedic and gynae regs went all the way and actually fucked the Black Widow, and the others squirmed out of it, or feigned excessive drunkenness.

She arrives, and Shane reacts with a kind of horrified excitement. His friends push him forward and into a chair, and then smartly step well back. The buck is offered like a sacrifice, the ceremony begins.

I'm near the back of the room, so I can't see much. I can see her looking menacing with a Richardson retractor, holding it by the blade so that its long steel handle is vertical, and then I get the idea that she's making him hold it in his lap while she lowers herself onto it and humps up and down. When she leads him out of the room, retractor round his neck like a shepherd's crook, I hear his voice, an urgent flash of reality. *Danni'll kill me.* And they're gone.

I go out onto the balcony for another piece of pizza, and Marco Cassimatis is doing the same.

Great show, huh, he says.

As always.

You know, if I got married I'd tell no-one around here.

Wise man. How'd you go with Sharon earlier?

Fine. Yeah. No big deal.

What you said, seeing them pink, it's right, isn't it? The first person I ever saw alive and then dead was a patient here last year. It freaked me out a bit, you know? I probably should have got more involved at uni and got it over with then. I had a couple close together and it was strange. When I'd be here till midnight on a DMO shift I'd get home and I'd park the car and I'd hear the wind in the trees and nothing from the house and just for a second, for a second, I'd wonder if everyone else in the house had died while I was out. I'd seen them pink, and I could see them grey, 'cause I'd seen that now, that transition. Crazy, really. It passes pretty quickly, fortunately. Not that you have to do it my way. I think the housemate aspect was pretty much my own aberration, but, you know, you get used to it. You realise you can only do what you can. Some terms are like that.

I guess.

They are. I started last year with general surgery and orthopaedics and things were really pretty good. Busy, but good from the point of view of people being discharged vertical and not passed through Sharon Gale's office. I finished the year with haematology and respiratory and it was complete carnage, but that's just the way it goes. It's those units.

Marco says *Yeah,* but I can see he's a way short of coming to terms with this. I want to tell him that that's okay, but I've probably already said more than enough.

I think we all hoped that we got the death thing out of the way in anatomy, years ago, second-year uni. The staff were good. They said some people didn't cope when they first walked into the dissecting lab and the bodies, the cadavers, were lined up in clear plastic bags on steel tables.

Everyone in my group coped. We called our cadaver Flora, because her substantial amount of body fat was by then more like margarine. But Flora wasn't like knowing someone. She was always like some strange model of a person, old, ugly, firmed up with formalin. And due to a body shortage we only got a sixth of her each. I scored her left leg, and a half-share of her abdomen.

Jen's on her way out when I get home.

Out for a bit of a dance, she says, and she throws her keys under a bush and leaves with only a twenty-dollar note and her driver's licence, in case she's asked for ID.

The impressive thing is that, while she's often too drunk to find the keys when she gets home, she almost always still has twenty dollars.

6

I'm woken in the morning by the rhythmic clang of steel on concrete. It enters my dream as the Black Widow standing over me, enormous, humping something industrial-sized and pounding Shane Sandercock like a bug, looking round with eight red eyes to see who's next.

It's the neighbour doing weights. Gavin, the bristle-headed, big-all-over abattoir shift worker who lives next door with his mum and dad, pumps large amounts of iron, clangs and grunts far too early in the day for my liking. My sleep-ins are prized, and Gavin pile-drives them out of me almost every weekend, even though he does his weights as quietly as possible. With Gavin though, nothing is small. He does his weights then takes his alsatian for a run, jogs like a boxer, skips at high speed when he gets home. Fries up a breakfast and sings the way a rusty wire caresses a pane of glass. Drinks ten beers on their back deck in the afternoon, smokes half a packet of Winfield reds and reads old yellow-edged westerns aloud, including the bullet noises.

At night, I can hear his father snoring in bed, breathing, even. That's how close the houses are. Only in prison is there more pressure for orgasm to be silent.

Gavin, when he found out that Jen was in her honours year of a degree in English literature, said that he'd noticed a while back that there was a competition for unpublished novels by writers under thirty-five, and he was planning to have a crack at it. He'd seen the entry form when he was putting down newspaper for the dog's bowl. He reckoned that the closest an Australian had come to writing a great western novel was Colleen McCullough's *The Thorn Birds*, and it hadn't been too great. He figured her main mistake had been to set it in Australia. He was thinking more about cattle rustling in Wyoming, not that he'd ever been to Wyoming, but jeez, he'd read a few books by now. The big problem, he said as he sketched the synopsis to her over the fence, was the 'Gavin' thing. *I reckon the judges might not think that's western enough, so I thought I might enter as Tex. Tex McClune. Figure that'd be about right,* he said, and ground the butt of his cigarette into the fence railing, easing the last of the smoke out through his clenched teeth.

And he promised to give Jen a look at the manuscript before he sent it in, said he wouldn't mind getting her opinion. Somehow Jen couldn't tell him she wasn't an aficionado of the western. She couldn't tell him that her thesis was on a comparison of the depictions of women in English fiction by female and male writers of the early nineteenth century. She couldn't do anything but live in fear of the sound of typewriter keys tap-tapping away next door, sending bullets through the clean clear Wyoming skies, recounting the deeds of bad men, and rough justice.

The neighbours on the other side have revealed no such ambitions. They are French, and Emil works in the nearby patisserie. While Rick's decision to learn French was apparently independent of this (I think he had hoped it was the language of elegance, worldliness and love), he now wishes he hadn't told them, feeling that they have every right to take his reckless disregard for his paid-up Alliance Francaise course as a slight on their culture. On several occasions when he's heard them talking he's wanted to go over and apologise, to tell them he regards them and their culture highly, and the fault is his own. He is a peculiar man, but a man of honour nonetheless.

The neighbour's cat, Jean-Paul (after Belmondo), considers our place part of his territory. He is black and slinks around, always guarded and guilty, with his face fixed in a sneer as a consequence of some old accident. One morning late last year I woke after a big night to find him drinking water from a glass next to my bed. Lapping at the water with his crooked mouth and purring his raspy purr with his face right in mine. I briefly thought I was in hell.

Next door the sound of iron on concrete goes on.

Until I saw the Richardson retractor waved around last night, I'd wondered if the duck-billed speculum story had been just a hospital myth. I can't imagine what it was like for Shane, drunk but keenly aware that he was the centre of attention, trying not to spin out. And looking down into his lap to see that he was fucking a spider woman with eight sparkling inches of steel.

73

What is it with male black widow spiders? Don't they know? Do they not think it's even slightly suspicious that all their male friends are virgins, that no-one brags about sexual exploits down at the black widow boys' club? And what about sex education? Who does that with black widow boys? Their mothers, sending their sons to certain deaths? Or do they work it out themselves? *Hey, I think I'm going to take this weenie little obscure part of me and rush up behind her and see if there's anything I can think of to do with it when I get there.* Or do they know, and they just can't fight it? Or do they think, maybe if I'm quick I'll be okay (now that's a pretty male outlook), maybe I can beat this thing? Or, maybe I'll be so good she won't want to kill me.

Rick knocks on my door.

We go down the road to the Cat and Fiddle shops. We buy the *Australian* and the *Courier-Mail*. In the bakery Rick buys three croissants and I ask for a loaf of this morning's white bread, not sliced.

It's too hot to slice, the woman says, not for the first time.

I'm not sure what point she's making and on the way home I tell Rick it's beginning to piss me off.

You just don't see the parentheses, he says. *She's actually saying it's too hot to slice, anyway. The anyway is just understood.*

No. She's not saying that at all. It's the tone. You're not paying attention to the tone. She's saying it's too hot to slice, fuckwit. It's the fuckwit that's understood. And that's what I don't get.

Maybe her daughter's a nurse at Mount Stevens.

What did you bring me? Jen says when we get home.

We weren't sure how many we were having from your room, Rick tells her.

Just the one.

Sam been terminated, has he? I ask her.

Sam was never a starter. He was at the Underground last night, but he was being very dull. So we talked.

That's twice in one week for him. Trashed twice in one week.

I never led him to have any expectations.

After breakfast, she goes off in her T-shirt and shorts to her Saturday morning job, working in the team that cleans the Toowong Village offices. Jen is their shiny surface specialist, and there are plenty of shiny surfaces. Like villages the world over presumably, all chrome and pastel pink, travelators and muzak.

So now we're all between relationships. But some of us, I guess, are more between than others.

So do you reckon Sam had expectations? Rick says.

Sure. They all have expectations. But Jen's an expert by now. I'm sure it was as quick and as clean and as painless as possible.

After the ward round we go down to the staff room for journal club. I have at least enough notes to look good, though the word hamster does appear a little more often than I'd like.

Both registrars are here today, Helen Reid and Dean Kruger, and several members of the nursing staff. Simon Dubois is not, as journal club clashes with his outpatients. This has never seemed to trouble him. Johnno goes to the biscuit packet and takes out three of the four Monte Carlos. Three of the four, and quite carefully, as though by leaving one he's not being greedy, giving us all a chance.

And today's question, he says, pretending to a credibility that someone with a beard full of Monte Carlo crumbs just can't have, *is, Why do astronauts wear butt wires? Doctor Jonathan Marshall has the answer. Over to you, Jon.*

I talk through the article. Most of them have a copy in front of them but my guess is that few of them have read it. I talk about space flight as an opportunity to study rhythms. I admit that at first I didn't quite see why this was worth putting anything in your rectum. I talk about circadian rhythms and circannual rhythms. Hibernation and its parallels with the vegetative features of depression. Seasonal affective disorder and light. Melatonin and light and hibernation. Melatonin and serotonin.

So what are you suggesting? Johnno says.

I'm just saying that, with a lot of attention having been focussed on serotonin, and the idea that depression might be a serotonin-deficient state, but with no conclusive evidence that I'm aware of, it might be worth having a close look at melatonin, to see what turns up. Just in case serotonin's association is because it's a precursor to melatonin. That could be why it's cropped up a few times, but nothing categorical's been established.

There's been a lot of work done though, Dean Kruger says, frowning, his copy of the article rolled up into a tube and tapping against his thigh without any rhythm, circadian or otherwise. *A lot of people think serotonin's it.*

And maybe they're right. But maybe they aren't. Maybe they're just close.

And the depression and hibernation thing isn't new.

No, I didn't say it was new. I just find it interesting from a biochemical perspective.

I realise as I'm saying this that I hadn't expected that at any time in my life I would describe anything as interesting from a biochemical perspective.

You said, have a close look at melatonin and see what turns up, Johnno says.

Yeah.

How would you do that?

Well, okay. I guess what you'd be looking at is devising something that could show whether or not melatonin is a marker for depression, or at least some subgroup of people with depression. To see if you could measure a change in melatonin levels in people who were depressed. To see maybe if a change in melatonin levels correlated with any clinical features, biological features probably.

So who would you use? Who would you measure?

People with major depression, and a matched group of normals, non-depressed. And I guess you'd think about trying to divide the depressed patients up into those that seemed more biological, and those that seemed more reactive, or didn't have vegetative features.

So you would use, maybe, the Beck Depression Inventory? Something like that?

Yeah. Any scale that would differentiate, really.

And what are you looking for? Deficiency?

Maybe. I don't know. Maybe a change in rhythm, but that's more subtle. That'd be harder to measure.

But possible, if you wanted to.

Sure. I guess so. People do it all the time.

One tough question and I'm done for here. I've never heard of the Beck Depression Inventory for a start, and there's only so long my faking skills can cover me. Just as I think he's about to test me out way too seriously, just as I think my fragile theory is about to crumple and my journal club debut will be remembered only for my brazen ignorance (*Our last resident seemed to turn something about astronauts' bottoms into a preposterous theory on depression, so do be careful your first time at journal club*), the unmistakable rattle of lunch trolleys can be heard, approaching from Ward Ten.

So, Johnno says, *in conclusion, is all this worth a rectal probe?*

Personally? My rectum's a very private place. But I'm no astronaut. You could measure my melatonin level any time, though. For that, I'd have nothing but respect.

And now, unless anyone has anything compelling to raise, we might leave Doctor Marshall's rectum, and his more than competent probing, and move on to lunch. Nothing is raised. Everyone's happy to leave my rectum alone. Johnno turns to Glen and says, *What've we got today?*

Chicken à la king.

Really? Something bad always happens with the chicken à la king. There must be something else.

He goes into the kitchen to check the trolley to see if there's a plate of sandwiches anyone's too out of it to eat. I'm walking past on my way to lunch when he calls out to me.

This melatonin thing. Do you want to look into it more and give us an update in a couple of weeks? When it's your turn next.

Sure.

As in, Sure, make me commit to next time while I'm still tense about this time. But what else can I say?

And in the meantime, I'm getting the bad feeling that I've got the choice of chicken à la king or buying my own lunch today. I really don't like it when I have to buy my own lunch.

So how much do you hate the chicken à la king?

It's not good.

Looks like it's the Pink Ladies then.

I can't believe it's right to pay for that stuff. You could make it at home.

Feel free to bring your own pikelets.

Let's go. Let's just go before I change my mind.

It seems that we're going to the Pink Ladies together, the two of us, as though if he tries to go himself he won't last the distance. On the way there he says, *So, do you think that if melatonin was a marker for depression, it would normalise when the depression was treated, or is it chronically abnormal in people who are predisposed to depression?*

That's a good question.

So what's your answer? Based on what you've read so far, what do you think?

Does it depend on the mechanism? Maybe the abnormal levels are directly involved with the clinical episode, in which case you should see them normalising with treatment, I guess. On the other hand, if depression, and this is kind of a different way of looking at it, maybe, if depression is fundamentally a disorder of circadian rhythms, then perhaps people prone to it have some inherent instability of those rhythms. The extreme version of this, I guess, is if you said, instead of saying a person had depression and vegetative symptoms, that the person had a primary circadian disturbance, one of the features of which is depressed mood. Which, if anything, validates the way depressed people can present. The way they can present with sleep disturbance or weight loss, and we end up diagnosing them with depression.

You don't mind this, do you?

Nothing's shot it down yet. Please, if I'm making a dick of myself, don't waste any time waiting to come in and save me.

He doesn't say anything. He laughs, but he doesn't say anything. And he doesn't save me. We get to the Pink Ladies, and it's only now I realise I've never seen him away from the ward before.

Wow, bought food, he says as the money passes from his hand to the Pink Lady's and he looks at the wrapped-up salad sandwiches, the wrapped-up lamington. *So what happens now? I'm not at all familiar with bought food. How do we handle this?*

According to hospital etiquette, bought food is generally eaten in the Quarters.

I thought hospital etiquette was that we stayed up in Nine.

See? This only contributes to misunderstandings. There are dozens of RMOs who have no contact with psych. They look on psych as an opportunity to slough any patient who's medically stable and vaguely strange or unhappy.

I think they used to do that with the residents back in my day.

Hey, it's not all bad. There's a lot to be said for being medically stable.

Is there? Medically stable is the curse of my family. Three of my grandparents lived to their nineties.

Frank Dudgeon happens to be on his way out of the Quarters as we get there. He visits only occasionally, and does so like a minor member of the royal family, offering us each a small piece of jolly, pointless conversation before busying himself away.

Gil, he says to Johnno, hailing him breezily. *Don't see you down here too much.*

I'm down here all the time Frank, Johnno protests. *Someone's got to show these youngsters how to play pool. Besides, I get sick of eating the patients' lunches every day.*

The Dud of course laughs at this, knowing there must be a joke in there somewhere. The Dud never actually gets jokes that aren't his own, but he can recognise the mechanics of joke delivery and laugh on cue.

And you, Jonathan, he says, *you're in Ward Nine right now, aren't you? How are you finding it? You had it number one on your form for this year, didn't you?*

Yeah. It's good. It's interesting stuff.

Interesting stuff. Good. That's what I like to hear. And he leans towards Johnno and, still in tedious minor member of the royal family mode, says, *And what do you think, Gil, picking up the tricks of the trade, is he?*

Sure. What would it be so far today, Jon? A few admissions, ward round, and then there was that new hypothesis for the cause of depression. That wasn't bad.

Cause of depression? The Dud takes it. Why did I know he'd take it? Why do people have to bait him?

Someone's got to work out what's causing it. And Jon's already got a few ideas about how he'd test his theory. Better watch him, Frank. He could run rings around a few of us.

So why was it chicken à la king today, I'm wondering? Why the fuck was it chicken à la king and not something Johnno likes, something that would have kept him in Nine?

I didn't know you were interested in research, Jonathan.

It's just an idea. We have journal club on Mondays and it's just to do with an article I presented today.

The Dud clicks his fingers noiselessly and gives me one of those I've-just-had-a-brilliant-idea faces. This scares me, and with some justification.

You're aware, I assume, of the Hospital Ethics Committee. The committee that oversees and approves any research to be done in the hospital.

81

I say yes, since it's the only appropriate way of saying no that I can think of at the moment.

We're supposed to have an RMO representative, and we haven't got one this year yet. I'm sure you'd have a lot to offer. It's not an enormous imposition. Five-thirty, third Monday of the month. A good stepping stone for someone with an interest in research. You could come on board for the March meeting, in two weeks. What do you think, Gil?

Oh, I'd look on it as good for the profile of the Psych Department. How we're viewed in the hospital at large. I think we can get a bit isolated up there in Nine. I'd welcome the chance for something like this.

Done, says the Dud, and shakes my hand. *You'll get a copy of the material to be dealt with at the meeting in about a week.*

And then he's gone, and Johnno's practically eating his own lips to avoid laughing till the Dud's across the road and in the multistorey.

It's not safe letting you out of Nine, is it?

It was just, you know, a bit of positive feedback. I had no idea of the potential consequences. I was thinking, maybe, another psych term. If you wanted it. And he laughs his wheezy laugh until he makes almost no sound at all. He just manages to say the words *Ethics Committee,* and then he actually slaps his thigh. *It was just his approach. As though he was your dad and I was your cricket coach and he was asking me about your outswinger. He provoked me. Sorry.*

No, that's fine. I like ethics. It's one of several things I like. I like drinking in the company of friends, reading people's research projects on weekends, staying back late on Mondays and girls. I've been struggling with a couple of those, so you've been a big help.

From what I hear we should try to find you a girl next.
What? With all my committee work? Where would I find the time to service a girl's needs at the moment?

And then of course there's the hypothesis. Now that you're the big research hope of the Psych Department. Depression's a pretty major part of our business and, like I said to Frank, someone's got to work it out. Hard to find room for girls in there, but as a resident you've got certain responsibilities. I'm sure you're aware of that.

Bearing in mind the complete absence of girl news, it's the hypothesis (such as it is) that I find myself telling Rick about in the Sunny Garden. That and my great Ethics Committee opportunity.

So you had lunch together? he says. *You and the Director of Psychiatry had lunch together? Where did he take you?*

He didn't take me anywhere. There's nowhere he could take me, and it wasn't really like that. We went to the Pink Ladies. The Hospital Auxiliary. We were just in the ward and he said he didn't want the patients' lunch today.

He normally takes a patient's lunch? Any particular patient?

No, there's an extra one ordered for him, an extra lunch. But he didn't want it today. So we went to the Pink Ladies and he bought himself sandwiches and a lamington.

I'm not getting this. I'm not getting this Pink Lady shit at all. You watched the guy buy a lamington. I don't get what it means. For me, if one of the partners thought I had prospects, he would discuss it over lunch somewhere nice. With wine. If I had occasion to watch him buy a lamington it would, on the other hand, mean very little.

Johnno never buys food. He never leaves the ward.

And this is the guy who's encouraging you? The guy who likes your theory?

I didn't say he liked my theory necessarily, but he didn't shoot it down. I've got to look into it more and do an update in a few weeks. And we'll see what happens then. See if the theory's still intact. It's always possible I could look pretty dumb with this. I mean, I am fearfully ignorant, really, and hypothesising recklessly based on a very small amount of information. But, you know, I like the idea. I like the theory. And I think the concept of putting in some completely legitimate library time pursuing a theory is a good deal more appealing than a lot of my other options.

Okay, so assuming this is fine, and assuming he's a lot less like Dustin Hoffman in Rain Man *than he sounds, why hasn't someone thought of it before?*

That is a very good question. And another possibility that causes me more than a little concern. Maybe someone's done it and I just haven't found it in writing yet. Maybe there's something really, really bad about the idea. Maybe Johnno even knows, but he's letting me find it for myself, making this some kind of very unwelcome, undeclared learning experience. Things were looking pretty comfortable in psych till this. So much better than last year.

Maybe you were just a bit too keen. Maybe you just did something that got his attention, and he misunderstood and thought research was your thing.

No, I think it's environmental. I think my mistake was that I didn't realise how little I'd have to do to be impressive. I didn't realise that just having an idea could lead to such consequences. I should have worked out the ward better. Johnno, eccentric, gifted, melancholy, but perhaps a deep-seated unsatisfied need to nurture. Or maybe to be nurtured. One way or another, a man negotiating a difficult relationship with the breast. Dubois doesn't give a fuck, not really. And the registrars. Helen's already decided she'll do kids, so this is her last year of adult psychiatry. She's doing her time really. And Dean Kruger's just a bit thick. I must have looked like such a high-flier in there. Shit. How could I not have worked it out in time?

The victim of your own genius, yet again.

And I really thought I'd been keeping my genius under control for some time now.

You can't help yourself. Genius will out. And here it is, 1989's Mokable Rocket.

I realise when he says this that it has been a while since the Mokable Rocket. Maybe twenty years. I should have grown into my genius by now. I should have moved past the prodigy phase to be a comfortable, settled, mid-career genius. Like Einstein, getting the photoelectric effect out of the way early, nailing the Nobel Prize and moving on to the big things, relativity.

The Mokable Rocket certainly got my hopes up. I designed it at the age of five, around the time of the first lunar landing. I was working on the assumption that NASA had the moon covered, and that the real work lay beyond. The real work needed the Mokable Rocket. Amazingly, it turned out to be possible to capture one of the most bewildering leaps of science on a single sheet of Quarto paper, using nothing more than a few different coloured pencils.

My father sent the design to Edward de Bono. And Edward de Bono sent a card in reply, complimenting me. For years I assumed he was one of our friends. For years I also assumed he was something to do with Bonio-brand dog biscuits, but I now realise that's unlikely.

It worries me that my genius mind might work this way.

It worries me that I might have a fondness for connecting things for the most inappropriate of reasons.

This is my parents' fault. They, with the unwitting assistance of Edward de Bono, made me realise I was a genius, and they encouraged my interest in rocket science. Rocket science was, of course, big at the time, but it came into our home when my mother bought Pyrex cookware. She unpacked it from the box and said to me, *This is the same material they use to make the nose cones of rockets, so they don't burn up on re-entry.* And from her it might have just been an aside, but it's in my mind like a sacred moment, a revelation. In my mind she lifts it from the box slowly, in awe, this thing that has been to space and back, and she lets me touch it, its cool white sides magically spared as it tore through the atmosphere, completely spared, as though it's new.

I watched it in the oven the first couple of times, but nothing particularly special seemed to happen. I think I'd hoped that it might struggle slightly, glow at the edges at least, since our oven was so hot I wasn't allowed near it without an adult. I realised then that, if our oven challenged it so little, re-entry must be hell. I probably needed one of these up the front of any future rocket I designed.

Naturally I told everyone at school that my mother had just bought the front part of a rocket to cook in. They asked me which rocket, and I said I thought it was probably Apollo Nine, Eight or Nine. They were, as expected, impressed, particularly when I told them most of the astronauts were friends of ours, and sometimes came round to tea. Along with Mister de Bono the scientist, the one who invented the dog biscuit, which he'd really invented for use in deep space travel, but was trialing in dogs first. Our dogs, since we were friends of his. And the fact that the Russians had sent a dog into space shortly before they'd sent Yuri Gagarin was only seen to make this claim irrefutable.

And I can see myself now, in the sandpit, shovelling with my small blue plastic shovel, telling them that there just might be a causative link between the obscure hormone melatonin and depression.

Rick's early inventions were, though more earthbound, no less respectable than the Mokable Rocket. Rick is the inventor of the Balsa Car. Balsa was the material of the era since it was light, workable and allowed you to use the most dangerous instrument in your repertoire – the Stanley knife. In its later design stages his Balsa Car was to have a lawnmower engine, but he never quite got the clutch worked out.

Had we met earlier and collaborated, it's hard to see any limit to the possibilities. The obvious start, but obviously only the start, would be a Balsa Mokable Rocket, with a Pyrex casserole dish up front, heating up just enough on re-entry to emit the classic homecoming fragrance of my mother's burgundy beef. Letting the astronauts know they were back, letting them know that months of Astro-Bonios and tubes of condensed milk were about to end, letting them know that their loved ones were just a splash-down away. Of course, at that stage no-one had done the work that could have let them know that, by the time they came to celebrate their achievement, their gonads might be very small.

And as I contemplate the Mokable Rocket and its failure so far to influence deep space travel to the extent I had hoped, I can tell myself that these quiet periods happen to the best of us. Rick's Balsa Car is still on the drawing board. And at least I didn't wander around my school grounds mapping out the best BMX and go-kart racing tracks. At least I didn't work out where the tunnels should go for Brisbane to have an underground urban transit system.

But I did, at the age of twelve, want the school to have a parliament, so that decisions could be made by our own elected representatives. I did instigate the plan to speak only German at lunchtime (abandoned after half an hour when we all got tired of me asking Warwick Clark one slow question after another about a bicycle he didn't have).

And I was the founder of the satirical journal *Marshall's Weekly*, which I wrote, edited and, with the endorsement of my English teacher, roneoed myself in the staff room and sold at a small and undisclosed profit. Its first edition ran to eight pages, its second to four, its third ran late and its fourth was indefinitely postponed.

My English teacher handled it well, telling me there was no problem with the content, but that perhaps *Weekly* had been a little ambitious.

Thank you for the splendid design by your five-year-old son. I like its elemental simplicity and confidence, both of which so easily get lost later on.

So says Edward de Bono in the card to my father, mailed from Cambridge twenty years ago with a 4d stamp. The message is typed, and E de Bono is signed in black ink with some flair.

And he's right. I've lost it. I don't even know what mokable means any more, except that it's something very useful. This is it. A warning from the great lateral thinker that went unheeded.

The elemental simplicity, the confidence, my laterality. All of them lost years ago, my horizons closed in, shaped in around the obvious.

By fifteen I was no longer a lateral thinker. This is how it looks now. But the loss of the lateral had started earlier, and I didn't even know it. Already at twelve, in the scholarship exam, I had plagiarised stories for both creative writing exercises, and won a half-scholarship. The same year I sat the national maths competition for the first time and it baffled me, completely. It asked for the lateral. I strapped on the blinkers. I had memorised pi to twenty places and it did me no good at all.

And I think the collapse of *Marshall's Weekly* at fourteen was the end of me. I'd put the lateral on the line there, without even knowing it. So by fifteen I was longitudinal, a follower of the straight line, the line of least resistance, all the way to medicine at uni, to Mount Stevens.

I went from being a visionary designer for whom deep space was only the start, to being a consistent near high-flier, in the most unimaginative of ways. And when the car battery ads came on TV, with the cartoon cowboy doing his bit to save the couple stalled across the train lines, I became the Reliable Marshall. I don't remember a great deal of hollering for me, but I can remember being the Reliable Marshall for my last couple of years at school. Even then it didn't appeal to me. Even then it seemed like some solid-citizen name. Not the name of someone even slightly interesting. Not the name of someone who would attract girls. And now, I realise, not the name of someone who could design anything anywhere near as mokable as a Mokable Rocket.

And, my god, was I reliable. I didn't miss a beat.

I cruised along just below the best of them, getting slightly less glamorous versions of the same results. So I could pick what I wanted at uni, and I thought medicine'd be interesting. And I kept being the tediously Reliable Marshall, and I graduated bottom honours student in my year. I didn't fail gloriously and join a band. I didn't take a year off to live with a dark-eyed woman in Portugal who spoke no English. I didn't come close to a university medal. Minimum time, minimum fuss. And here I am.

It occurs to me that I am the least lateral person in my whole family. My parents are in Europe right now. They have train passes, and they only occasionally have destinations. My mother is an entomologist, with a particular interest in the fruit fly *Drosophila melanogaster*. Next month she is giving a paper in London, at the university where she studied as an undergraduate. In the 1950s she was a successful amateur racing driver. She still drives an MG midget, and argues with police about speeding tickets on a regular basis. (*So how should you drive an MG then? Slowly?* As though it's preposterous.) She keeps being required by law to attend defensive driving classes. She refused to let me have her car while they're away, because she thinks I'm not up to the double declutching.

My father is said, in our family and perhaps far further afield, to have been the first person to transport semen across an international border (or at least the first person to do so using an esky). To be specific, Denmark to UK, pigs, early 1960s. This should not be taken to indicate an abiding interest in the semen of other animals. It is nowhere near that specific. This is just an indication of his interest in the new, the lateral, the possibility. And it managed to fit in somewhere between service as an officer in the Royal Naval Volunteer Reserve and a career as a management consultant, culminating in the again somewhat lateral step of a PhD in information technology last year.

It was never easy at school when we had to talk about what our parents did. I had to say that I didn't know what my father did, but that my mother had a job to do with flies. This was not well received, nor at all understood. While our knowledge of the world may not have been sophisticated, we all thought we had a good idea of the jobs out there, and none of them centred on flies. And if I didn't even know what my father did, his job was probably stranger.

This must have distressed me somewhat, because I can remember a tearful conversation with my father about it one evening in my first or second year of school. He said, *Next time, just say I'm a management consultant,* and he made me practise it until we were both quite confident that the problem was solved. So I said it next time, proudly and clearly, Management consultant. And the teacher said, *Now Jonathan, please tell everyone what a management consultant does,* and I told them. A management consultant captains a mine sweeper and breeds pigs.

With my father's various interests and my mother's involvement with flies, the closest my class could come to fitting this in with their Happy Families understanding of occupations was that my father was an Odd Job Man and my mother was a Bin Man. These were both highly regarded, the former because it was thought to involve large amounts of sawing and hammering and other desirable activities, the latter because it was believed that the collectors of garbage got first pick of the loot and were paid as well.

My sister doesn't help. She only ever followed a wobbly version of a straight line at the best of times, and then she broke it. She trained as a kindergarten teacher, and now she's acting in London. Acting and scorching the fingers off pissed English people with Burning Beaver cocktails. She has the attic room in a house that she shares with Jocasta, who spends most of her time under a pyramid in a trance-like search for eternal youth, and Naomi, a dietitian who is thin and pale and grows cress on every available horizontal surface, struggling through a life made up only of grazing, tiredness and a battle with numerous nutritional deficiencies.

My sister believes that it's reasonable that she made her agent haggle for Special Skills money because she rode a bike in a building society ad. My sister was blown up on 'The Bill' four times in one afternoon.

We used to collect empty toilet rolls for her kindergarten children to use in some artistic practice, and it's hard to get out of the habit, once you persuade yourself that they're worth keeping. And the more we have, the more we can't throw them away. As though a kindergarten teacher might come to our door one day and say, *You don't happen to have thirty or forty empty toilet rolls lying around, do you?* The sound in our toilet is so muffled by empty toilet rolls it could be a recording studio. Not that there's ever a lot of sound in our toilet. I'm just assuming.

I put the Edward de Bono card back in my expanding file. My parents gave me the file when I moved out, so I could handle my own affairs. It contains everything about me that I might need, and more, documentation to prove that I was born, that I was vaccinated, that I can duck-dive in water over own height to recover a brick.

It's quite a mixture, and M typifies it, containing only letters from the Medical Board notifying me of my provisional and then full registration, and the card from Edward de Bono (presumably filed under M for mokable). Not many M things really.

So why did the lateral become so risky for me? I couldn't walk out of my room now, hold up an A4 page and say, I just designed this. It's a Mokable Rocket. But when I was five I could. I did. I was fearless then. Perhaps not a finisher, but fearless.

And now I'm far too concerned about looking dumb, about exposing my ignorance, I guess. Ignorance that this has been around for years, ignorance of its terminal flaws, whatever. And afraid to be seen to be ignorant when it's much better to be seen to be moderately well-informed, cynical, smart enough not to take risks like this. That's the kind of resident I've been trying to be, and it seems quite out of character for that kind of resident to be excited by an idea.

But I don't want to let the idea go. And I have agreed to look into it and report back in a few weeks, so I've got a chance to sort this out. To find out what I need to, and deliver it all in the appropriate cautiously motivated style of journal club.

And if this takes me nowhere, that's fine. If it's a bad idea or an old idea or a completely impractical idea, that's fine too. At least I'll know. And I can summarise competently and back away.

9

More library time, then.

I go down there when the ward excursion is on. The librarian greets me by name and says, *We've seen a bit of you in the last week or so.*

She asks me what I'm doing and within seconds she's telling me how exciting it sounds and making me fill in article request forms, as though there's a problem with my *Excerpta Medica* method.

There is something of a pattern to this. Has she been talking to the Dud? Should I keep my theories private from now on, and only emerge from Nine when I've finished the work, come up with all the proof I need and had the article accepted by the *New England Journal of Medicine*? Why didn't I go to a hospital where they treat you like shit and you can be anonymous for years? There are plenty of those.

I had already decided to go for background today, to leave article abstracts from the last two years alone, find a big book or two and actually develop some understanding of what I'm dealing with, how these rhythms work. My theory (as if I need another theory right now) is that some of the better hypotheses are thought up by people who actually know what they're talking about, and there must be a certain level of comfort in being one of them.

Clocks

The human body is controlled by a series of internal clocks. These clocks, through continual reference to each other and to outside stimuli, keep the human routine as long as the day. Without light and other external influences, the average human day would be a little over twenty-five hours long. This explains why we sleep in on weekends, and why Monday mornings always arrive too early. It also explains why flying west across meridians of longitude (thereby lengthening days) is easier to accommodate than flying east.

It is clear that these clocks, or oscillators, have an

effect on melatonin synthesis. The body can maintain a melatonin rhythm in prolonged darkness. Artificial darkness during daytime does not trick the body into an artificial melatonin peak. Normal melatonin production begins several hours after dark onset, and decreases several hours before light onset. It is not, therefore, simply switched on by darkness and off by light.

It may, in fact, be controlled by two oscillators, each keeping its own time and responding to its own range of signals, one turning melatonin production on and the other turning it off.

These two clocks are almost certainly in the part of the brain known as the suprachiasmatic nucleus of the hypothalamus (SCN). One has a longer spontaneous interval than the other, and together they affect many things, switch many things on, and then off again. Melatonin takes them into account, but doesn't synchronise with either of them. It is also influenced, but not controlled, by the timing of light–dark exposure averaged over the past one to two weeks.

Evolution, exaptation

The biological origins of melatonin may relate to a role in vision, since there is a clear and direct neuronal connection between the retina and the SCN. The higher levels of melatonin at night suggest a role in the perception of visual input at low levels of light.

Day-to-day mammalian survival depends on timing, seeking food at the right time, shelter at the right time, sleep at the right time. Day and night, light and the absence of light, can be critical for this timing. The difference between day and night is largely visual, known directly only to the eyes and not to the rest of the body. Not to the appetite, not to the centres that control wakefulness and sleep.

To feed, to wake, to sleep efficiently and safely, the internal systems of the body need a means of reliably differentiating between day and night. The body's most reliable internal indicator of night is melatonin. Melatonin therefore became a signal of night through this ability to create a biological print of night upon the chemistry of the body. It consequently became co-opted as a timer of certain circadian and circannual rhythms. This has been referred to as exaptation, a character evolved for another use, but co-opted for its current role.

So why is it all this complex? I imagine it must be for the sake of flexibility. This is why we can't build a human yet, why robots can do so few things each. These rhythms must work in a way that allows us to make sense of most things, most days, but stops us being so rigid that we can't adapt to others. So there is not one clock. There are numerous clocks maybe, all watching each other, watching the world, filtering everything as though it's a signal and calibrating, calibrating, calibrating.

Captain Cook carried two chronometers, knowing that one of them lost time while the other gained it. I remember that from a poem (Grade Ten English comes through again?).

At six-thirty every weekday morning my alarm goes, plays music, wakes me. But it's the roughest clock in the world. If it were a real clock, a biological clock, it wouldn't wake me on Monday until it had sent other signals that gave me enough REM sleep, switched on my appetite to peak twenty minutes later, got everything lined up and then woke me at six-thirty. It wouldn't just barge in with noise, and stand back while every part of me struggles to fit into line, fit into Monday coming far too early, cutting off the end of Sunday night.

But my alarm and Captain Cook's chronometers couldn't change with the light, couldn't read the signs in the internal world and the external world. And maybe that's depression, the mechanism underlying depression. Maybe some people's clocks aren't as good as others, don't calibrate as efficiently, let things slide.

On Friday the library calls me. A couple of weeks ago I couldn't have guessed that I was so close to this point in life. Out of a relationship for ten days, no prospects of a new one, and the library calling me. Soon I'll be finding long white coats irresistible, shopping for a pocket protector and wandering Kierkegaard-like through the hospital gardens, my head humming with reckless theories.

Three articles have arrived. Complete articles, with all the parts I don't understand, the sampling, the stats.

These were easy, the librarian says when I get there. *Just in the uni Central Med Library. The interstate ones won't be here till next week. I hope that's okay.*

I tell her it's fine, no hurry. And once I get over the concern that my theory has now gone national, I realise that these are just the articles I need.

Melatonin and depression

1 There is a statistical association between seasonal variations in daylight duration and changes in rates of depression and suicide. Some depressed patients studied were found to have reduced total nocturnal secretion levels of thyroid stimulating hormone and melatonin.

2 In three of five patients with depression, the peak

97

plasma melatonin concentration was reduced and occurred later than usual. All eight non-depressed controls had normal melatonin rhythms.

3 Five of eight patients with depression, or a predis-position to depression, were found to have a lower nocturnal melatonin peak. Three also had a dis-turbed twenty-four-hour cortisol rhythm.

I keep thinking, which patients? Which three, which five, which some? I can't find any subclassification of the depressed people. Changes are noted in some patients but not in others, and the differences are lost in the statistics.

Perhaps this is where biology comes in. Perhaps it's the patients with biological disturbances (which we recognise as vegetative features of depression) who have the changes, and the ones without who don't. But the articles don't show this separation being made. No-one seems to have thought that they might be dealing with two differ-ent groups of depressed people.

Right at the moment I'm going to be very frustrated if someone doesn't look into this, if it slips away because something so simple wasn't done and the evidence is left to say only that a relationship couldn't be clearly established. For me, this theory's been around for days already and no-one's tested it.

I go back to the ward with the articles. Johnno's lunch-ing, sitting in the tearoom with a patient's meal tray on his knees, scooping up spoonfuls of a pink wobbly dessert.

You wouldn't believe this, I say to him, and I know I'm waving the articles like one of our less stable patients, but it's the mood I'm in.

What? The spoon hovers below his mouth. The pink lump on it wobbles. *What wouldn't I believe?*

This is what I've got. Several articles showing abnormal

melatonin rhythms in some depressed patients, but they don't say which. There's no selection, not any that I can see.

So what should you be seeing? Still not quite with me.

Something that really understands rhythms, that makes a distinction. That says, these depressed people are chronobiologically disturbed, while these other depressed people are just unhappy. If they did that, it might stick. You might really see the pattern. You might end up with something that achieved statistical significance, and couldn't be dismissed.

Is there any overlap? Are you saying there's endogenous depression and reactive depression, and nothing in between?

No. While I think there may be two basic types, bio-logical and non-biological, chronobiologically disturbed versus reactively unhappy, I think they can interact. I think all of these things interact, feed off each other, influence each other, set themselves by each other. And that means overlaps can occur. And it spoils all that clarity, but I don't think it spoils the model. I don't think it spoils the idea. I think it's possible that people with a primary rhythm disturbance feel depressed, and at the other end of the spectrum we know that a lot of people who are reactively unhappy don't have vegetative features. But I think some people who are reactively unhappy might have vegetative features because their rhythms drift out of line when the unhappiness affects their eating and their sleeping and things like that. Affects some cyclical things and then unmasks an inherent instability.

So what would it take? What would it take to show this? What's the first thing you'd do?

The same thing as everybody else. Get a few depressed people and test them, with the difference being that I'd focus on dividing them up. I'd want to see if, at the two ends of the spectrum, melatonin changed with one group and not the other. That's the first thing I'd do.

He's looking at me seriously now, thoughtfully. He puts down the spoon and hands me the tray. He goes to the phone, flicks through the hospital directory that hangs beneath it on a string, calls the Dud, asks if we can visit.

Do you want to do this? he says, timing it perfectly so that the question's slightly too late.

It's kind of surreal, the walk to the Dud's office, all the biochem in my head. I've been spending too much time in the library. My mother always warned me about that. My mother, who always says that her best work is done with old fruit, while someone else does the literature review.

I'm wondering if I've missed something. I'm wondering what Johnno really thinks of this, what's going on in his mind.

I want to laugh on the way down there. I've made this idea up, made it up out of almost nothing and now I'm going to have to follow it through. I want to tell him it'd be okay if we went back to the ward now. I want to tell him that, looking back on it, I'm even a little embarrassed that Edward de Bono got to see the Mokable Rocket.

We go past the multistorey and the facts, the lines I've lifted from abstracts and the bits from books, are swirling in my head, as though they're all trying to get out first.

And the Dud goes for it, and suddenly he's full of ideas. Me getting it down on paper, getting the feel of the Ethics Committee and coming up with something that'll work. Getting biochem on board, linking up with endocrine, looking at government funding possibilities. Flicking these ideas around as though he's the dealer at a sharp blackjack table. All fast hands and bug eyes and bustle, and quite unlike himself.

And I'm saying that, of course, it'll need time to develop it. I'll need more time in psych where I can get feedback, more time in the library.

And I suppose you'll be lining up for the psych training program next year, he says as he takes the roster from his drawer. *Let's see. We've got the resident on rotation from Greenslopes down for psych next.*

So that should be fine, I tell him. They've got no gynae at Greenslopes, so my gynae term would be a good swap. He'd probably be keen for my gynae term, he or she.

He, he says. *It's a he. Yes, I don't see any problem with that.* And he's rubbing out our names, swapping us round.

So I've managed another ten weeks in Nine. I've managed to hear my theory spout out of me again, as though it's the real thing.

What do I want from this? It's like a game, a dare, as though I'm daring myself to come out with this stuff, to provoke people into taking me by the hand and leading me out of the multistorey wing, as though I can't make it myself. As though I want to swap one role-play for another, competent RMO for psych research hero.

I feel like a juggler, but more like a person standing under half a dozen falling balls, not sure if he's a juggler or not. Not sure if he mightn't just be some kid, remembering a picture he once drew, a rocket, a more certain time than this.

10

At home it's a different rhythm we have to deal with this weekend. The rhythm involving the growing and shortening of grass. Luckily this fits in around Rick's already established non-optional fortnightly family laundry activity. This should be a good thing, driving off with two weeks of dirty shirts and coming back with clean shirts and a mower, but it's not that straightforward.

Rick has an interesting relationship with his mother. She plays him out on a certain length of umbilical cord, and insists on the right to wind him back in at will. Even his tokens of independence are negotiated, and continually re-negotiated. His relationship with his mother is constructed of so many negotiated compromises that I'm sure they each have to write them down and keep a copy, just to have any chance of remembering where things stand.

His mother says he's no good with shirts, so she does his shirts. He does his underwear, loads of underwear. What does he do to his underwear that it needs changing so often? Is this just his mother again, or something even more worrying? He also looks after his hankies, and I know what he does to those. Hankies pegged up by the handful, by the dozen. Victims of his problematic sinuses.

Polyps like a bunch of grapes, he loves saying, claiming it's a quote from his ENT surgeon. *Big, plump, juicy grapes just ripe for picking.* It's amazing how he can talk with such enthusiasm about having his nasal passages 'reamed out', but try to explain any other surgical interference with the human body and he hits the ground with minimal provocation, as though he's just discovered he's totally boneless.

His mother, I think, chooses wisely when she decides to control him through the laundering of his shirts, and not his hankies.

So his hankies hang in rag-edged off-white clumps from the Hills Hoist, as though signalling some less than note-worthy surrender as Rick loads his laundry bag into the back of his car and sets off across town.

I can't believe you get to do all your own laundry, he said to me once. *You lucky bastard. I'm fine with shirts, you know. As good as anybody.*

Before we moved into Bayliss Street he was temporarily between houses and back with his parents. When he left to move in here, his mother said he could only ever live with them again if he remembered to pick up his towel from the bathroom floor. The way he remembered it, he always had.

He is a man controlled by his mother, his allergies and a destiny that has so far not been kind to him. Laundry brings these all together. His mother stakes her claim and his allergies necessitate large numbers of hankies, but it's the rest of it he doesn't see.

His fretting about allergies leads him to do his smalls with yellow gloves, yellow rubber gloves. Special elbow-length yellow rubber gloves.

Where does he get these from, some veterinary supplier? And are they to protect him from his hankies and his underpants, or the chemicals he uses to clean them (which would have to be pretty serious chemicals)? But the real problem is the gloves themselves, the elbow-length yellow rubber gloves that he leaves draped over his laundry basket. Folded over each other and half full of air, floppy, nasty hands hanging over the edge of his laundry basket all week, as though they're waiting for something.

How does he ever expect a girl to be willing to enter the room when the first thing she sees from the door is the gloves, and the second is his Porky Pig doona cover? From the doorway, this is not good. From the doorway, if you're operating on the premise of normal guy, normal sex, the long, waiting gloves and the Porky Pig doona must at least make you wonder. Neither of these is a symbol of a conventionally desirable man, and the combination only deepens the uncertainty. I don't think many women have stood at Rick's door thinking, *This is just what I want. A guy who's into cartoons and rubber.*

But he has no idea. He has no idea of signals. In the company of women he signals ambivalence and fear, and no-one ever decided to have sex with anyone on account of ambivalence and fear. Well almost no-one, surely.

His mother made him the doona cover, from children's curtain material. And doesn't it just say, *No-one's having sex with* my *boy*? You'd have to bring a girl home drunk and late at night and come up with some good reason for keeping the lights off before you'd be likely to pork under the pig. And how would she feel when she woke in the morning, dry mouthed and desperately trying to piece together the night before, and saw the biggest, happiest Porky Pig imaginable unfolding across her knees?

His mother probably bought him the gloves as well. She keeps him her prisoner, and he doesn't even know.

Today, once the next fortnight's pressed blue shirts are in his wardrobe and we've each done our share of the mowing, we go across the road to the fete at the Serbian Orthodox Church Hall.

It's a little less Serbian than we were hoping for, but maybe fluoro, padded coathangers and decoupage cross international boundaries. Anywhere there are magazines and tedium, some loser's invented decoupage (and worked out it's perfect for livening up the dull underside of the toilet seat).

Jen buys a pot plant that, by Rick's next laundry day, will have died a brown and crispy death through inattention. Rick gets a large bag of fudge, chocolate fudge, and we all sit on the back steps eating it and looking out across the newly shortened grass of our scrappy backyard.

Jen's going out tonight, drinking with friends. Which might, or might not, mean that there's a boy involved. And it's starting to sink in that I'm at least dateless, if not yet desperate. There were moments in the week, library moments, when I forgot this in the romance of theorising, but maybe it's something I should try to remedy.

Sure I had a lot of bad years, a lot of lonely pig-doona-style loser years, but since I graduated things have been different, and I've usually had a contingency plan when a liaison has reached its necessary end.

Any more fudge and I'll throw up, Rick says, groaning and leaning back against the steps, looking at me upside down. *Want to go to the movies, Jon-boy?*

Fudge and a movie in one day? If only we were showing girls such a good time.

I'd love to buy a girl fudge. Do you know how much I'd love to buy a girl fudge?

11

On Monday morning journal club is cancelled. Dean Kruger says he's not ready to present the post-traumatic stress disorder article he's been reading. He says he's been too busy seeing patients. Whether or not this is any kind of hint, any kind of comment on my growing relationship with the library and shrinking presence in the ward, I decide I should stay in Nine for the day, and be seen to be the resident.

But I can't shake my melatonin complex completely. Mid-afternoon I admit a depressed man, a self-absorbed, depressed man whose self-absorption is no match for my present enthusiasm for depression. I admit him so thoroughly I think he gets bored. I have just enough insight left to accept that he is here as a patient and not for a lecture on chronobiological disturbances, and I let him go. And I don't mention melatonin once. I don't say a word about circadian rhythms, and I don't even suggest checking his gonad size.

How would you do that most effectively, anyway? The hamsters gave them up for science, but I don't think that'd get through the Ethics Committee. With men you could use a set of rings, like umpires do to check the shape of a cricket ball. Or perhaps Archimedes' principle, by making them lower their pants and dangle their scrotums into a bucket of water and seeing how much liquid was displaced. And having some formula where you subtracted volume of scrotal tissue and divided by two.

I remember a tutorial when I saw a set of plastic testes on a chain, a little like rosary beads, but starting bigger and increasing in size, with the volume of each written on its side. But this takes skill, and it's not exactly direct. It is, however, less subjective than the surgery tutor we once had who said that his technique was to examine the patient's testes with his right hand while keeping his left hand deep in his own pocket, giving him some idea of normal. One of the female students said, *It must be hell examining prostates*, but he just didn't get it. The joke he got, the idea of slipping digits up two rectums at the same time, and one of them his own, but not the irony. It's probably no surprise that there still aren't a lot of female surgeons.

I'd first found out about rectal examinations a couple of years before this, and I have to admit it came as something of a shock. It was one of those hopefully rare occasions when you just don't believe what you're hearing. Where you think, I'm being set up here, taken for a ride. It was a tutorial in anatomy, fairly early on at uni when I'd never had cause to contemplate the prostate, or anything else that can be felt by a finger in a rectum. I guess if anyone had asked me I would've figured there'd be a machine that would check things like that.

The tutor brought out sketches, sketches of human finger, up human anus, feeling human prostate. I stayed totally quiet, in case my friends had put him up to it, but slowly I had to come to terms with the fact that it was real. That in just the next few years this would be expected of me. Human finger (mine), human anus (someone else's), sage opinion regarding possible pathology, while squirming the digit around in there, checking everything out. Any idea of medicine as a glamorous profession evaporated that same afternoon.

The other thing I couldn't believe when I heard about it was periods, menstruation. When I found out that regular women went through something that insane every few weeks, it totally blew me away. I was nine or ten at the time. I couldn't think straight for days. I believe in menstruation now, but I can't help thinking, surely there's a better way.

On Tuesday I'm DMO again. The first call comes just after four when I should still be calmly ensconced in psych, flipping through a sheaf of test results or syringing an ear or playing table tennis. Kelly McLean, a student nurse I remember from my time in respiratory, calls me from Four C about someone who needs four o'clock IV antibiotics and has a drip that's tissued while the resident and registrar are both in theatre.

I'm sorry to hassle you so early, she says when I get up there.

It's fine. No problem. I mean, sure, I might be busy being very important elsewhere, but it's no big deal.

As long as you don't mind being important here for a couple of minutes.

Well, I do have eight hours to kill before I go home. What's the story with the patient?

She's due for gentamicin. She's in with a ruptured diverticulum. She had an abscess drained a couple of days ago. She's picking up with the antibiotics now. And her veins aren't good. Tissue paper. So I'm told.

Oh great. And I do put in so many drips up in pysch.

We go into the treatment room to get the trolley set up and she says, *So, haven't you noticed my uniform's changed?*

And she's standing on her toes, reaching up into a high cupboard for a box of syringes, her long blonde hair held in a red ribbon, her white uniform riding up above her knees.

Hey, yeah. It's an RN's uniform. No more mauve. No more of that unseemly student nurse thing.

Yeah, she says, stepping back with the box in her hands. *Much more seemly, don't you think?*

Much more.

And she's showing me her new-found seemliness as though it's important to her, important to have shed the unforgivably unappealing mauve student nurses' uniform with its big mauve collar and its lilac belt. Seemly never came easy in those uniforms.

Nice white shoes too, I tell her. With shoes like those you could own real estate on the Gold Coast.

Thanks a lot. She laughs, and punches me in the arm. It's been a long time since a girl punched me in the arm.

All this glamorous white-uniformed new-found seemliness, and you go around hitting people?

Just keeping you in line.

I'd love to be out of line. I'm way too in line for my own good.

Come and do this drip for me. Do what you're told.

The patient isn't looking forward to it. She has bruises over both arms from numerous past attempts to site a line, and a bandage on her right hand where the tissued drip has just been removed. I try the left, putting a tourniquet on and getting her to pump her hand. Somewhere, through the paper-thin skin and among the old bruises, I feel something that seems like a vein. And I get into it first time. Kelly connects the line up and it runs.

Well, he made that look easy, didn't he? she says to the patient as she starts to wrap a crepe bandage around her forearm.

I go back to Nine, since I do actually have one or two mundane tasks to attend to before five. And even as I'm driving body-temperature water into the ear that needed syringing, I'm thinking that there had to have been something good about respiratory, and maybe it was Kelly McLean. Of course, at the time it seemed like Penny, but that was really just a hangover from haematology, and a poorly judged remark about Nude Twister.

Kelly McLean in her new white uniform, her new white shoes, her long legs. This girl was built for Twister.

Those student nurse uniforms must be bad. Kelly is fine, thinking about it now, thinking about her standing on her toes reaching up into that cupboard. Reaching way, way across the Twister field to put her left hand on red. Contorting impossibly, but every inch a champion. I'd go some distance to watch her play, even fully clothed. Even if both of us were fully clothed. Fuck it, with the slightest excuse I think I'd go back to Four C right now to watch her take a syringe out of a cupboard. Is this the sound of lonely hormones stirring? Kelly and her *Much more seemly, don't you think?*

And I do think. I keep thinking about it and I trash some poor bastard's vein in another ward when I'm resiting his drip. Feeling the full vein, rocking it round under my fingers, my mind pleasingly and completely distracted, thinking calves, thinking seemly, driving the cannula through the vein without effort, into it and then through it, right out the other side.

Punch in the arm. *Do what you're told.* Why do I like that? Why do I respond to being treated like a naughty boy?

I'm waiting for Four C to call me again. I can't believe things are so good up there that they've got no need to call me. Every other surgical ward seems happy to call me for the crappiest of reasons. Hours pass, two hours maybe of the crappiest of reasons, two hours of clomping around lino corridors and carpet-tiled wards going through the motions with my mind elsewhere. So call me, call me, call me. Call me and let me watch you reach into the high cupboard. Call me for no good reason and let me watch you talk to me. Be seemly and confident, and don't let me get away with a thing.

Other calls. Other calls. Other wards, other small tasks, one after another. Dinner alone. Half-warm beef stroganoff on a lump of rice. I can't believe people pay for this.

Seven, someone with a falling urine output, Three C (just beneath Four C) a post-op fever.

Finally Four C, I get the call. I phone, and I'm just thinking about what I'm going to say to her, just ready to pick up where we left off, when someone else answers.

110

I've got this guy who's acutely short of breath, she says.

And I'm thinking, Fine, but what about Kelly McLean? I can't believe all her patients are totally well. I get to the ward and she seems to be away at dinner. I manage to spend a while looking through the file, talking to the relevant RN, hanging round the Nurses' Station ready to be noticed. People come and go but Kelly isn't one of them.

I visit the guy with the shortness of breath, run through the usual list of possibilities. With his longstanding heart failure it seems obvious, but I keep telling myself, Don't fall for it. If it's something else don't miss it. And stop thinking of girls, just for a second. Once I'm sure it is his heart failure I write him up for 40 mg of Lasix and I go back to the doctor's office to make an entry in the file.

Kelly's in the treatment room, preparing a trolley as though she's about to put up a drip. I think I've just missed the reach for the syringe box. Is this all my life is? Glimpses of flesh? I'm sorry, Kelly, but above the knees I've already forgotten you?

I was going to call you, she says. *That drip, that impressive first-time drip that you did for me before . . .*

Don't. Don't make me go in there again. I'm sure it's the last vein she's got.

She shrugs. *You don't know how much I've fiddled with it, how much I nursed it along to get that gentamicin into her. How temperamental it was, right up to the time when it blocked completely. I've tried everything, but it's history. Anyway, she thought you were lovely. This'll be fine.*

And it's bad. Of course it's bad. Of course it's not fine. I couldn't get impressively lucky twice in a row. And soon the woman's lying stoically with her arms out to the sides with my puncture wounds in several places. It'd be like acupuncture, if it wasn't so like crucifixion. And her veins, her obvious veins, are already blocked, and the first couple

111

of spidery little veins I try that aren't blow when the needle tip touches them. Finally I get something tiny into a vein on the back of one hand, and it seems to run.

You realise, of course, Kelly says to her, *that you have to keep this hand in a fist until you leave hospital. In a fist, on this pillow and no moving.*

I won't even breathe, love, the woman says as Kelly fixes her hand to an arm board. *Trust me.*

I've worked up a sweat doing this. Kelly starts to tidy up and I tell her I'm going to write up the other thing, the shortness of breath, and I go back to the doctor's office.

It's such a confidence game, cannulation. You and the opaque skin and the deceptive moving target of the vein, somewhere in there. You blow a few and you live in fear. You expect to blow the next one. For a while you just don't feel good about veins. Then you get a few right, and every vein seems big and fat and easy. You hear the interns talking about the trouble they're having with IV lines and you can't understand it.

I hadn't wanted to do that in front of Kelly. If I'd had the choice of which side of me to show her, I wouldn't have picked the sweaty, incompetent side. Not that I think I had to prove myself to her through my ability to cannulate, but I don't think I'm looking my best when I'm demonstrating a profound inability to cannulate, an ability only to make a patient old woman gnash her dentures as I puncture her skin again and again.

Kelly comes to the door and looks embarrassed for me.

That was so bad, I say to her. So bad. What did she do to deserve that? I hate it when that happens.

Yeah.

I hear that tonight's night resident is really good with matters of intravenous access, just in case you need to know. In case the worst happens.

It's okay.

I couldn't face her again after that. And she thought I was lovely. You should never have told me that.

Yeah. It's running fine now. Just another thing . . .

No. No, I can't go near a vein again just yet. All that stuff about falling off your bike and getting right back on again, I never believed that. I stopped riding my bike when I was seven. Don't make me.

She looks around, as though she's checking for something, and then she looks back at me.

Could you forget about veins? she says. *Just for a moment?*

Sure. For the rest of my life, if that's okay.

Good. Well, this is actually something completely unrelated. She walks into the room, leans against the edge of the desk, looks down at me, looks past my shoulder as though there's something important happening in the bin in the far corner. *It's, I don't know how you'll feel about this, and however you feel is okay, it's just an idea. So, you know, if it's not an option that's fine.*

Mmmm.

And she goes a little pink and tucks a stray strand of hair over her ear.

It's the grad ball this Friday. Graduating nurses ball. And it could be fun, you know?

Yeah. I'm sure it could.

And a few of us, we didn't have people to take and we all decided we'd be tough and go along without partners, but now all the others have gone and found someone and . . . Oh, I'm sorry, that sounds very bad. It sounds as though I'm about to invite you just because I'm totally desperate. Could we forget that I said that bit, that bit about no partners? I actually, well, I might have asked you anyway. It crossed my mind last week even, last week when I heard that you and Penny . . . And she's quite flushed now, digging this small, neat hole of embarrassment. Coiling a loose strand of hair around her index finger. Coiling and uncoiling. Coiling and uncoiling. *It's only three days' notice. I'd understand if you were busy.*

I think I'm not. That is, if this is an invitation.

Yeah.

Good. Okay. I'm in. I am DMO on Saturday though, so, you know, midnight and I'm a pumpkin.

Fine, that's fine. You're coming then?

Sure. I'm coming. I'd like to come.

Good. She smiles, and her cheeks choose a slightly different shade of pink for this, but still a shade of pink nonetheless. *Well, I've got medication that I should be giving, and I'm sure you've got plenty to do.* And she clears her throat and goes.

Probably just before the point where she would have filled me in on all the necessary details.

And then it's just me and the file. Me and a few notes justifying Lasix, showing what I did to rule things out, all that time ago with the man who was short of breath. I dump the file on the empty Nurses' Station desk and I walk past the room where Kelly's tipping tablets into a paper cup, but she's looking the other way, saying, *We'll just get these into you and then you can pop off to sleep.* And a crumbly but jovial old person's voice is offering something in reply. Kelly laughs.

And then I'm in the stairwell, taking the stairs two at a time, singing 'Bachelor Kisses' loudly, shamelessly, tunelessly, damning The Go Betweens to hell with this bad singing, but that's okay.

So here I am, suddenly in this life made up of blabbing about blow jobs and romancing the hormone of darkness.

12

I get home and I want to tell people.

I want to tell people, but I don't. There's not much to tell, and I'd only be telling them to hear myself say it. A girl asked me to a ball. Sixteen days I'm out there, and word gets around and a girl asks me to a ball. And a pretty reasonable sort of girl, too. A girl with calves, seemliness and an admirable tolerance of a person's sweaty, incompetent side. I'm not sure Rick needs to hear all that.

Besides, they're in bed. It's the middle of the night.

There's a note under my door, Rick's writing, *I'll be cooking tomorrow night.*

I wonder how he persuaded Jen this was a good idea. I guess I'll have to eat a lot for lunch. And what's he doing with the note? Warning me?

I open the window and lie down on the bed. Next door's snoring sounds as clear as always.

And Kelly manages to go from self-assured, which I like, to horribly shy and insecure, which I think I also like. To go from cool, bossy, fixing me with those eyes and sending me to work, to the incredible physiological overload of asking me to the ball. No eye contact (unless she was in fact asking the bin in the corner, and I misunderstood) and her face blotching up with the risk of asking, blotching red like the British Empire on an old map of the world.

In the car in the morning Rick says, *Dinner, tonight. You'll be home?*

Sure.

Good. I'm going to do a quiche. There's someone I'm thinking I might ask round to dinner and I thought I might do quiche. Quiche Lorraine. So I thought I'd practise.

I see.

I've got a recipe.

Good. And someone you might ask round to dinner.

It's a possibility. It's just a possibility.

Come on. There's more. Give me some background.

She's in another section of the firm. First-year articles.

So you know her already.

Not really. She's a QUT graduate. I've just done some work with her section. And I hear she's had this on-again, off-again thing going, and it's now totally off. And she said Hello *to me in the lift yesterday.*

She said *Hello* to you in the lift?

Yeah. It's not a friendly firm, you know. Hello is big. You don't just get in and hello everybody. There's an agenda with hello, I think that's understood.

So does everyone else know it's on between the two of you, now that you've been publicly helloed?

I guess so. And it was an encouraging Hello. *It was like she'd thought about it, you know?*

Not just one of those Hi situations in a lift, where you're unavoidably face to face and you have to Hi before breaking off contact and maneuvering round to get your back to the wall.

Exactly. That's exactly what this wasn't like. This was a Hello, *and it was mine. Just wait.*

Rick, I think, demonstrates that the line between optimism and desperation can be a fine one, a thread even. And I can see him, going geographically blotchy at the *Hello*, offering only a small *Hi* back, regretting it later. Thinking about it and planning to signal his intentions with quiche. But what intention does quiche signal? *I've got very long rubber gloves. I've got a Porky Pig doona. I've got a quiche with your name on it, babe. How do you like me so far?*

When I get the chance, when I'm in an empty room with a phone, I call Four C. The ward secretary answers and I tell her I'm just calling to check up on a patient I saw last night, but I can't remember the name.

I think it was Kelly McLean who called me to see her, I tell her. She'd probably remember who it was. Is she around at the moment?

She should be. I'll just go and find her. The phone thumps down onto the desk and I can hear her saying, *Anyone seen Kelly McLean?* Her voice drifting off as she walks further from the phone and then back in again as she's saying, *It's just Doctor Marshall, calling about a woman he came to see last night. A woman you got him to see.*

Hi, Kelly says. *That woman with the drip, is it? That you're calling about?*

No, not that I hope the drip isn't running beautifully. Friday night, I'm not sure that you actually told me any of the details.

Oh, how embarrassing. She laughs. I can hear the colours again over the phone, red moving to colonise her face. *It's still okay, then?*

It's still great. I just need a few details. When and where, that sort of thing.

I can hear noise around her, people talking.

The drip is doing fine, and it should come out about seven, she says, slowly and carefully, as though English mightn't be my first language.

What?

119

The drip should come out about seven p.m.

What is this? 'Hogan's Heroes'?

It's a ward round. I have to go on a ward round now. Everyone's here.

So seven p.m. Is that what you're telling me? Seven p.m. Friday?

That's right.

Good. Okay, where?

There is a pause, no answer. I can almost hear her trying to encode something, wanting me to guess.

Don't you hate those open questions?

Yes.

Okay. You live at the Quarters?

Yes.

So I'll pick you up, do you want me to pick you up?

That'd be good.

Seven at the Quarters?

Great.

I'll be in disguise of course. One of the early Tudor kings, I think.

Good, she says, and laughs. Just a short laugh and then she says, *Bye,* and she's gone, off on her ward round.

Leaving me thinking about the laugh, probably finding almost as much in it as Rick can in a hello, so I should be less critical.

I struggle to remind myself of this later, as the house fills with quiche smells and Rick rattles around the kitchen like a man concussed by a flour bomb, dusted and smudged with a range of ingredients, his recipe fearfully compromised by his tendency to short-cut, pieces of spare pastry drooping from the edges of the table and, inexplicably, from the backs of chairs like Dali clocks.

I might need them, he says. *I might need them. You never know.*

And he circles the brown laminex table, fiddling with things in case they might help him, pushing the scattered flour into little piles, as though this somehow constitutes tidying up, flapping the door of the oven open repeatedly and prodding his quiche with a bamboo skewer.

We leave him alone and he flaps and prods, flaps and prods, tidies the flour piles, clears his sinuses. Thinks briefly about pursuing this and indulging his enthusiasm for allergy, but the urgency of the moment is upon him. The quiche is ready.

It seems to bend when he tries to cut it. This is not, as far as I understood, a sought-after quality in a quiche.

And, as one might have expected, it's like chewing a shock absorber. It's as though sorbothane now comes with a crust, and hints of diced ham. He should have cut it in the shape of a shoe, rather than pie slices. That way we might have had some warning.

Jen sits at the other end of the table, makes weary eye contact, devotes her muscular effort instead to her jaw. She swallows a large lump and takes a drink. The phone rings.

Rick goes to answer it and it soon becomes apparent that it's his mother. *No it's fine, well, not bad for a first try . . . No, I think they like it . . . It's maybe slightly on the firm side, but . . . A while, I didn't time it. Not specifically. How long should it have been in there?*

I got invited to the nurses' grad ball last night, I tell Jen. The ball for the student nurses who've just finished their training.

Is this, like, a date invite, or just a thing everyone goes to?

I don't know. I don't think it's a thing everyone goes to.

Date invite then.

Possibly.

What is it about you? I mean, don't get me wrong, but what is it that makes you this chick magnet?

Supply and demand probably. Market forces. We've got maybe thirty RMOs, two-thirds of them male, half of them married and several of the remaining number are either gay or overtly undesirable. I only get there by exclusion. And do you think it's easy being a chick magnet? You think I chose this for myself? There's a lot of pressure involved. It's not something to be taken lightly.

What? You'd rather be Mr Pig Doona? You'd rather pin your hopes on this? She bounces her knife on the quiche.

Rick comes back into the room.

That was just my mother, he says, shaking his head. *Calling to see how it was going. Don't feel neglected, just because your mothers don't call when you cook.*

He eats another mouthful.

It's slightly, um, he says, hoping he can negotiate a description. *Slightly more solid than I had in mind. I didn't want it to fall apart. I didn't want it to be all eggy and sloppy. I know how people don't like that in a quiche.*

Yeah, I don't like those ones, Jen says. *Those eggy, sloppy ones.*

Good. That's what I wanted to avoid.

I want to tell him now, I want to take him aside and tell him now, don't ever cook this quiche again. Not to get a girl, not even well into a relationship. This is a quiche with ramifications. Sure, it could help stop wear and tear on weight-bearing joints, but that doesn't make it food.

Rick and I have both tried to impress girls with cooking, and it's rarely gone well. Since my sister gave me a wok I've been better. Before then I had six recipes, all of which involved crushed Weetbix. Certainly this now looks limited from a tactical point of view, but you can only work with what you've got. And what I had was Poor Knights of Windsor, an unwelcome hangover from my Anglo heritage, bread dipped in egg, coated in crushed cereal and fried. So my next five recipes involved crushed cereal and frying. One of them was a carbonara sauce.

Then I got the wok, and I figured that in the several thousand years the Chinese have had to perfect wokking, they've never succeeded in making crushed Weetbix a popular ingredient, and that should be good enough for me.

13

Friday night is the first time I've gone to the Nurses' Quarters since I went the marinara bastard and backed out of things with Penny nearly three weeks ago. I should have planned this better.

We, we should have planned this better, Kelly and me. It's not just my plan. Kelly standing there on the fringe of the ward round talking about an old woman's gentamicin as though this was making some arrangement. I had to keep it simple. Quarters, seven.

Quarters, Penny. Penny could be in there. Penny could be walking down the stairs right now as I'm walking along the path.

But just as I'm thinking this, walking along and listening to my feet on the concrete as though feet have some sense of destiny, I see Penny in the distance. Beyond the Quarters, getting into a car, a man's car. He's holding the door open for her and I'm just close enough to hear her laugh. She gets in. He shuts the door, goes round to his side. They drive away.

So Penny is not in the Quarters. Penny will not be driven into a grief-stricken rage by my arrival. Penny is dressed up for going out and she's laughing with a man now. I can't believe she's with a guy who opened the door for her. I can't believe she laughed then. I can't believe she doesn't know that that door shit went out years ago, that she deserves better. How very 1950s.

But not my concern.

My feet proceed along the concrete, any pretence to a sense of destiny now gone, sounding like my regular feet, or at least my favourite, black, pointed, side-lacing shoes. Rick was against this, not in favour of my favourite shoes as part of this ensemble.

You have no sense of style, he said, as though I'd ever suggested I did.

Then he had to admit that we both owned dinner suits bought in op shops specifically for trashing at uni balls, and that we haven't yet upgraded. He does, though, have a far more impressive range of bow ties with cartoon motifs, and he couldn't understand why I'd opt for basic black.

Don't you want to make a statement?

And I wanted to say, You really have no idea why people have sex with people, do you? But I didn't.

I'm in the small foyer area of the Nurses' Quarters when I realise I don't know which room is Kelly's. I'm just settling in to some quality loitering, toying with my cuff-links (Rick's cufflinks, at his insistence, chunky and ugly though they are), watching two birds argue in one of the poinciana trees, trying not to clear my throat obsession-ally, when I hear a rustle of fabric at the top of the stairs.

I turn round. Kelly's there, in a scarlet dress, a scarlet

dress that's holding pretty closely to her curves. She looks good, she looks very good. And nothing about her rustles. It's her far less attractive friend in the exuberant student-nurse-mauve number who rustles, even just standing still, folds of mauve, metres and metres of superfluous mauve busying themselves against each other as they settle.

At uni, that would have been my date. The girl whose dress looks like a larger version of the kind that very misguided people use to fancy-up their toilet brushes (probably to complement the decoupage on the underside of the seat). Bo Peep, sheepless. And still she would have made it clear from the start that sex was out of the question.

Kelly says, *Hi. Can we take Jo? Her partner's going to meet her there.*

Sure.

She looks at me, looks at the stairs, doesn't move.

Um, I'm not sure I can get down on these heels.

So we should hold the ball up there?

She takes her shoes off and walks down with them in her hand. Next to her, Bo Peep does fine, but who could guess what kind of shoes she's got on under there?

So much for the grand entrance, Kelly says, standing next to me, her mouth scarlet to match her dress, her breasts cupped neatly, swelling almost out of the dress as she draws in a sigh, receding as she lets it go.

I want to see her dance in this dress. I want to see her mouth do special things. I want to make her breathe deeply.

It was just fine, as entrances go, I tell her, going to some effort to calm the adrenaline rush. Trust me.

I made the dress myself. Do you think it's a bit too red?

No. No. I think it's just about red enough.

And she keeps walking barefoot, all the way to the car, almost as tall as me, her shoes still in her hand.

And, courageously, she does dance. Still barefoot, since she can't dance in the shoes either, and they stay under her chair all night.

We go outside for some air. She says *for some air* and we go out to the balcony.

We're standing close, close and leaning on a railing just above the street and I'm probably about to make a move when she says, *So what made you do medicine?*

I don't know, really. Maybe it just seemed like a good idea at the time.

So it's not a family thing then?

No. My parents are just a couple of peculiar English people with no medical background whatsoever.

At this point I don't mention the pig semen and my father's adventures of the early sixties.

You don't sound English.

I'm as English as socks and sandals. Why, underneath this shirt I'm wearing a good British vest and I'm hanging out for a pint of best bitter. We came here when I was eight. My father is so English he plays billiards fanatically, snooker if persuaded and he refers to pool as the American game. He refers to my house as digs. I am in digs.

What does that mean, exactly?

Exactly? There's no exactly about digs. It's just one of those things. One of those terms that your English parents use, that you never understand, and that you hope they avoid when outside the confines of the family. They're in Europe at the moment, doing some strange middle-aged British kind of backpacking.

She laughs. *They sound great.*

Oh, they are. It's just that they're almost completely out of control.

So who should be controlling them?

They should be controlling themselves. Parents should

be entirely predictable, dull even. And don't look at me like that. Don't tell me control means nothing to you. You don't even let other people make your clothes.

There's a problem with the dress? she says, giving just a hint of a heave with her chest, I think. I think a hint of a heave, but maybe just breathing.

The dress. I don't think there's any problem with the dress, but I guess that depends on what you had in mind. Did you ever see *Who Framed Roger Rabbit*? Jessica, I think it was, the nightclub singer. Very sultry. Very sultry. She had a dress just like yours, a red dress, just like yours. And perhaps, in fact almost certainly, she's the only cartoon character that ever assumed a sexual dimension with me. And I'd never expected that a cartoon could do that, or a rabbit, so it's a pretty powerful effect.

It must be. I've never felt that way about a cartoon, she says. *Except maybe Elmer Fudd, but maybe that's not the same. He'd be my favourite, though.*

Yeah, but I think every woman feels something for Elmer Fudd, deep down. And I've got a friend, a housemate, who is driven to uncontrollable heights of desire by the merest glimpse of Betty Boop. But I'm not like that. I'm just not that easy. It takes a lot to get me. Jessica Rabbit, she got me. Do you know what I'm saying? Do you sing?

She laughs. *Not at all. Not a note.*

That's okay. In fact, that's probably a lot less important than I thought. Let's be realistic. It's excellent that you aren't a rabbit. It's also handy that you aren't a cartoon. It'd be completely unreasonable if I expected you to sing.

This time she just says, *Mmmm,* with the laugh from before easing back into a smile. Her mouth opens, just slightly. I move forward and she moves too, tilts her head a little and then our mouths are together, my arms are around her, my hands on her warm back.

Um, it's time for the presentations, someone's voice says quite near us. Jo, her Bo Peep friend.

Kelly breaks away, says *Okay* matter-of-factly, goes red, looks at the ground, bites her lip. She looks at me again. *Better go inside.*

There are speeches, uninteresting, well-intentioned speeches, and in the middle of one of them Kelly leans forward and says, just into my ear, *I don't want to be here.* But we stay till midnight, till the speeches are over and the presentations made and all the graduating nurses have held hands in a circle while the band has played 'Auld Lang Syne'.

Let's get out of here, Kelly says as soon as the circle has broken and she's hugged everyone she should. *Take me home.*

And in the car she says, *Are you still DMO tomorrow?*

You mean I could have changed my mind about it in the last couple of days?

And I'm working the night out, thinking we'll be at the hospital by twelve-thirty and I have to be back around eight. Thinking that I want to go in with her, I want to go to her room. I want to go, but I can't stay. Not more than a couple of hours. How would a couple of hours be?

We park outside the hospital.

Well, this is it, she says. *Thanks. Thanks for coming.*

And she leans over, kisses me as though it might not be it, slowly. Draws back only slightly and we kiss again. I turn around to face her, move towards her until most of my weight is on the handbrake. This is not comfortable, but I can live with it. Then I'm kissing her neck and she's biting mine. Her hand is in my shirt. I'm kissing her breasts, the tops of her breasts, slipping the left shoulder of her scarlet dress aside and moving further down with my mouth, and I'm watching the glow of the streetlight on her breast, her whole breast. I take her nipple in my mouth and she makes a noise and digs her finger nails into my leg. And then she lifts my head, looks into my eyes, kisses me on the mouth.

I should go, she says. *You should go.*

And my hand is on her breast and her hand is on my hand, but not moving it away. Just holding it there.

I've swapped to a late tomorrow. So I guess I might see you. Since you're DMO.

Yeah.

And she adjusts her dress, as though the disarray is something she's just noticed, and she kisses me like I'm her great aunt, and then again, half-properly as though she's making up for it.

I've got to go.

And she does.

14

I get up too late to have breakfast at home, so I just shower and go to the hospital.

I make toast and tea in the Residents' Quarters and I sit reading the paper. Gazing at the paper and, I have to admit, contemplating Kelly's dimly-lit left breast.

For more than two hours nothing happens. Nothing is what should happen, since everyone should be in the hospital doing the Saturday morning round of their patients, but I have to be here in case anyone else isn't.

I play pool, I sort through the last few days' junk in my pigeon hole. One by one, people come in to report, telling me they're leaving early since they've seen everyone, if that's okay. Briefing me about any potential action. Telling me about post-op complications, unexplained fevers, results due to come in, someone who's not for resusc and going downhill.

And I'm thinking of Kelly most of the morning, the taste of her mouth, her skin, even as I'm fiddling with the edges of people's nasty wounds, resiting drips without flare. Ticking off jobs, minutes, hours. Kelly, down in the Nurses' Quarters probably, sleeping late. Or out buying groceries. Or sitting round with her friends talking about the ball.

She must start work with a handover at about two-thirty. I'm in Four C once around five but I don't see her, and I don't see her at dinner. The ward pages again just after seven. This time it's her.

Four C, Sister McLean.

Hi. It's Jon.

Hi. How are you?

Good. I'm fine. How about you?

Fine. Pause. *I've actually got a guy with a fever.*

Okay. I'm just writing something up in Two C, so it might be easiest if I come up now. I don't have anything else that's particularly urgent.

This isn't urgent. But now would be fine.

I run up the stairs, but I can still sing while I'm doing it. Long after I leave here I'll probably associate Go Betweens songs with the drive to and from DMO shifts and with stairwells.

Kelly's waiting, standing in the Nurses' Station, leaning against the desk with the patient's file held in front of her, up against her, her arms folded across it. She hands it to me. She smells good, smells like last night, and I didn't even notice it last night.

He's seventy-six, just over twenty-four hours post-op after an elective subtotal gastrectomy. He's got a fever of thirty-eight seven, she says, looking at my left shoulder. *In place he has an IDC, a nasogastric on suction and an IV running eighth-hourly. Wound looks okay, no complaints abdominally, bowels haven't moved, fluid balance is okay, IV site looks okay. He's not great with the deep breathing and he's got a background of COAD.*

All right. Are you coming with me?

Yeah. She leads the way into the darkened room and says *Mr Schmidt, this is Doctor Marshall.* And she turns the small bed-head light on, illuminating the relevant bits of Mr Schmidt but not dazzling him with glare.

I talk to him, I check his chest and his abdomen. I move round to Kelly's side of the bed to check his abdominal and nasogastric drainage and his urine bag. She kneels down on the floor and moves them so I can look at them, tilts the urine bag round as I kneel too.

This is when we make eye contact.

Eye contact down near the floor. Eye contact with Mr Schmidt's frothy stomach contents sucking away near us, sucking gently down into the collecting chamber next to his bed. Eye contact right next to Mr Schmidt's urine bag, with his volume nudging 200 mL. Close and kneeling down here in the dim light among fluids. Our faces inches apart.

And I think we're both briefly fearful that I'm about to make some move down here near Mr Schmidt's urine bag. Nurse and doctor going the pash as Mr Schmidt breaks the two-hundred-mil barrier, grappling on the carpet tiles and extracting saliva in a way Mr Schmidt, with his nasogastric tube on suction, can only envy.

Two hundred, Kelly says. *Nearly. Since four o'clock.*

And the moment is gone. Her hand is on the urine bag,

tilting the thirty-eight-point-seven-degree urine my way, showing me 200 mL, near enough.

Okay.

And I tell Mr Schmidt I don't think there's anything to get too worried about, but we'll do a few tests just in case.

I take blood for cultures and go back to the Nurses' Station desk to do the paperwork. Kelly stands next to me.

So what's happening?

Good question. Let's do the septic things and see how he goes. Could we get the DMO to review him if he goes off or if he spikes another fever? In case something decides to declare itself.

Sure. And if he's fine, we get him reviewed when results come in?

Yeah.

You finish at twelve?

Yeah.

She nods.

An old man walks slowly towards us, shuffles towards us in loose pyjamas trundling his drip stand along beside him.

I can't sleep, sister, he says, completely without the aid of teeth.

It's just after seven o'clock, Kelly tells him.

Oh. So I have to wait then. I can't have my tablet now?

Not yet. If you have it now you'll wake too early.

Oh. Can I have it soon?

In a little while.

He nods, turns, starts on the slow journey back to his room. Kelly turns back to me.

I'll see you later, maybe.

Yeah.

And she goes after the old man, runs four or five steps to catch him.

Let's see if we can find something for you to do, she says as she takes his arm. *You're looking bored to me.*

And as they turn the corner she looks round, waves over the stoop of his back with her free hand, keeps talking.

I go down to Three C and get hassled about taking my time.

Things come up, I tell them. You know how it is.

At eleven-thirty I'm in the Residents' Quarters, playing pool with the medical DMO. At eleven forty-five, Kelly walks in the side door, still in her uniform.

The American game, she says, and the medical DMO stops, steps back from the table as though he's not sure what this means, not sure if it mightn't mean two men, a woman and pool apparatus, not sure how he should feel about that.

The phone rings. *I'll get it,* he says quickly and crosses the room, picks it up, faces the other way and gets involved in a detailed discussion designed only to displace responsibility for fifteen minutes and pass whatever it is to the night resident.

Kelly picks up the cue and pots the three and then the six.

They're both my balls, I tell her, feeling disempowered.

She aims for the black and misses, hits it way too hard and sends it skidding across the table bouncing from cushion to cushion. *I want to get out of here.*

The night resident arrives and I miss my ritual toilet visit, but tonight it doesn't seem a big deal.

Kelly comes with me to my car, gets in as though we've planned this. And then we're cruising along the near-empty freeway at eighty and she's not saying much and I'm wondering what she's got in mind, wondering why this seems so different to last night.

Bad luck about the black, I say to her.

133

Yeah.

And we park outside the house, move silently on the path, up the wooden stairs, along the corridor to my room. In the dark she takes my hand, and when I open my door there's moonlight coming in the window, lighting my bed and its understated black-and-white doona cover. I'm so glad it's not the pig. Her arms are round my neck and then she's biting my ear as I'm trying to shut the door quietly, fumbling with the handle, banging the door into the frame.

And now that she's not holding an old man's warm urine there's no doubting her enthusiasm. I hope she washed her hands, just for a moment as the hand that may or may not be the one that cupped the urine bag slips down into my pants, I hope she washed it. I want to ask her, but sometimes you've just got to go with the assumption.

And I'm lying on the bed, and her uniform is white in the moonlight as she kneels over me, her skirt bunched around the tops of her thighs. And she's pushing her hair back, pushing it out of the way and unzipping my favourite black DMO jeans, pulling them open, showing my firm but unexceptional penis to the too-bright moon. Taking it in her hand, drawing her hand up and down it smoothly, firmly, faster. Faster.

Bending down, and I feel her lips on the shaft, see her open mouth going down and taking it in, all of it, working it in and out, her tongue rasping up against it. And my hands are on her head now, twisting her hair and my eyes are squeezed tight and starting to see stars and I'm thinking, Don't come, don't come, imagining a series of sports stars and TV presenters and authority figures from my past, my grade-ten English teacher even, all staring me down, looking right into my eyes and saying, calmly but firmly, *Don't come, Jon.* But it's getting almost out of my control, and theirs.

I think, I say to her in a quick breath out (just as William Butler Yeats is failing to work the line, *Don't come, Jon,* into 'The Lake Isle of Inisfree'), I think I can't hold on much longer.

That's okay. Pausing only briefly, and then right back to it.

That's okay? You mean . . .

Yeah, yeah.

So in one last big breath I put Yeats from my mind, everything from my mind, and I let go, and my hands feel her throat swallowing, swallowing, swallowing. My head flops back onto the pillow and the moon is in my eyes. I drop my left arm and my elbow whacks into the wall, makes the wall shake. In the next room, Rick snuffles, but doesn't wake.

Kelly lies down beside me.

I thought you might like that.

You were right.

No-one's done that to you before, have they?

No. Not like that.

Good, she says.

And she kisses my cheek, kisses my cheek with a strange mixture of smells. Some perfume, my sweat, the strange smell of her breath.

She's awake just after six. *Fuck, I've got an early.* Sitting up next to me on the edge of the bed putting her shoes on saying, *Fuck, fuck.*

Do you want me to drive you?

No. No, there's no need. Could you call me a cab?

Are you sure?

Yeah. I'm sure. Just call me the cab.

So I leave the room in yesterday's shirt and I phone her a cab, and then she's beside me, straightening out her messed-up uniform, whispering that she'll wait outside, moving to kiss me quickly but then holding it a little longer, gone, shutting the door silently behind her.

And I'm left there in only my shirt, standing next to the phone, thinking, I hope you've got other uniforms, thinking, Don't you even want to rinse or something?

I lie on my bed, watching dawn happen up in the sky above my window, listening to the settled rhythm of snoring from next door. I lie on the spot where Kelly was lying, and it's still warm.

And I realise that there were at least *three* things I couldn't believe when I first heard about them. Periods, per rectum examination, and women swallowing that stuff. And this is so much better than either of the other two.

I have clearly been moving in the wrong circles. For several years I moved in no circles at all (for several years I suspect no-one gave my genitalia a thought), but even when things picked up there was nothing like this. Why is it that I had to stick my finger up so many anuses before this happened even once?

This question still unresolved, I sleep.

Rick thumps on my door at eight-thirty on his way to the toilet, says *Vakey, vakey, hands off schnakey,* shuffles by like an old man steering an uncooperative drip stand.

Next door, weights clang on concrete. The neighbourhood proceeds to treat this like any other Sunday morning.

I put on some shorts and go out into the lounge room. I can hear Rick rummaging round in the drug-free samples in the bathroom, talking to himself. And just as I'm getting the urge to run back into my bedroom and examine my penis in daylight to see if it looks the same, he comes back into the house.

Hey Jon-boy, he says. *How was the DMO biz yesterday?*
Pretty standard, really.

And what was that in the night? You must have been working away at high speed, the way you hit the wall when your hand slipped off it.

Jen comes out of her room, wearing a baggy T-shirt and shorts and stretching, saying, *Noisy, noisy boys.*

Breakfast time, Rick tells her. *Shoes on, Jennifer.*

Today the bakery is selling off croissants by the bagful, so we buy two and end up getting maybe a dozen. And Rick's talking away and Jen's dismissing last night's date as *pretty pointless, really,* and I'm thinking I can't believe what's happened to me since I last saw them, since they inspected me before my departure for the ball on Friday night and gave me a Pass Conceded because they didn't go for the shoes. I can't begin to tell them about my last night.

So is there follow-up with this one? Rick asks as he's tearing a croissant apart and daubing it with strawberry jam. *Was this just a ball date, or could she be the next of her ilk to acquaint themselves with your ugly bits?*

Could be. Who knows?

You haven't, have you? he says, sensing something, keen to be appalled at the speed at which things might move.

Haven't what?

You haven't already serenaded her with the pink penny whistle of love, have you? You haven't already rubbed uglies?

Give me time.

So you will. You would, given the chance. At a moment's notice, given the chance.

Well, sure, but . . .

He shakes his head. *I've seen people treat hand towels with more respect. I've seen dogs rub themselves against trees with more respect. I hope she's awful. Is she awful?*

You'd like her, I tell him. You would. And I'm planning to be nice to her. She has a number of fine qualities. And she's got a cartoon thing happening, so you'd like her for that alone. You should have seen her on Friday. Just like Jessica Rabbit, from *Who Framed Roger Rabbit*. The sultry nightclub singer.

What? Oh, Jesus. Really? She was pretty hot.

And I told her. I told her she reminded me of Jessica Rabbit.

You didn't, Jen says. *You couldn't have. That's such crap. That is just the worst win-on in history. No-one ever wins on to anyone by likening them to a cartoon.*

It seemed to work all right. It seemed to set me up for a bit of a squeeze. No-one seemed to complain. She said she had a bit of a thing for Elmer Fudd.

Elmer Fudd, Jen says, and she's thinking about it. *Well, sure, but that's like a nurturing thing. No-one draws your nurturing side out like Elmer Fudd. I mean, if you were talking physical, you'd probably be looking more at Roger Ramjet maybe.*

Sure. Square jaw, hero of our nation. Obvious really. See, I get that, but Elmer Fudd. I wasn't ready for Elmer Fudd.

Pretty impressive, though, Rick says. *A little obtuse, but impressive nonetheless. And she looks like Jessica Rabbit too?*

Sure. Well, in Friday night's dress.

I'm going to feel very uncomfortable on the other side of the wall from someone like that. I'm going to have to sleep with the ear plugs in or I could get pretty depressed.

Hey, I don't want you to feel excluded by this. I have told her about you, you know, in the cartoon context.

Really?

Yeah. I've told her about you and Betty Boop.

Those eyes. She's really in need of something.

You're very nurturing too, aren't you? Jen says. *Very sensitive, really. This is like girls and Elmer. You really want to care for her. This is why you're not wasting yourself on one pointless fling after another.*

No. No, *fuck it. I'm out there. I want her. I want to root Betty Boop.* He stalls at this point. Stalls for a moment and then puts his tracksuit top over his head. *I can't believe I said that.*

That's okay, Rick, Jen says in a soothing social worker's voice. *You've got to let these things out. I think we should get some people to come in and hug you now.*

He says nothing. Fumbles round for a piece of croissant, posts it up under the tracksuit top to his mouth. *Thank you. Thank you, that would be good.*

16

On Monday, the first day of the new term, Dean Kruger presents his article on post-traumatic stress disorder. He talks about arousal and cortisol levels, and when it's time for questions I ask if they measured melatonin.

Not everyone measures melatonin. They were looking at the stress response. Cortisol probably seemed like a sensible choice at the time.

But it didn't actually show anything.

That doesn't mean it wasn't the thing to measure. There's an address at the end of the article if you want to write to them and tell them they fucked up and they should have measured melatonin. Anyway, maybe we could get back to the psychiatry and away from the endocrinology. Maybe the inconclusive cortisol results show we shouldn't require everything to be measurable, to have some blood test.

I take it from his response that my fairly innocent question did not impress.

So, Dean, Johnno says, *how would you compare PTSD as a syndrome with battle fatigue and war neurosis? Are they the same thing, with the nomenclature changing with the times, or do you see any clear differences?*

And Dean screws up his face, as though this is part of being taken seriously, and he's thinking hard. Today it hardly matters to me, and Dean can be as anti-biological as he likes. Kelly will be working an early, seven to three, up in Four C. Out beyond Dean and his face, past the patients smoking on the verandah, over the garden beds and the road and four storeys up. I can see the windows of Four C from here, tinted dark, letting nothing through.

She pages me from the Nurses' Quarters just after three, and I call her back from one of the consulting rooms.

I was going to call you earlier, I tell her. But I thought it might be indiscreet.

That's fine. I just wondered if I'd done something wrong. If there was a problem the other night.

No. No, not at all. I just figured I can't keep phoning Four C asking for you to give me updates about patients whose names I can't remember. And I would have called you at the Quarters but I suspect not everyone likes me there.

So do I get to see you today?

Yeah, that'd be good. I've got an Ethics Committee meeting at five-thirty.

You're on the Ethics Committee?

It's a long story. And I don't understand it myself. Anyway, I've got stuff to read for that beforehand.

Oh.

But look, I'll take it to the library and read it in the next hour or so. And then maybe I could see you before I go to the meeting. Five o'clock, some time like that.

Dean opens the door. *Oh, sorry, are you . . . ?*

I nod and he steps outside, pulling the door quietly shut behind him.

Got to go, I tell Kelly, and I call him back in.

Just getting some collateral history on someone.

Yeah, that's fine. Look, I've got my psychotherapy case due at three-thirty, and we usually use this room.

Sure, I'll get out of your way.

There's an admission waiting for me, other crappy tasks. Johnno choosing now to ask how it's all going, to say he's been thinking about it and we should arrange a meeting with Joan Shand, the head of biochemical pathology.

By five past five I haven't looked at my Ethics Committee bundle. I have a choice. I go to the Nurses' Quarters. Clearly I'm great Ethics Committee material.

Do you want coffee? Kelly says.

No.

We go to her room and she shuts the door. She pulls her T-shirt off, leads my head down to her uncovered chest with both hands. The T-shirt drops to the floor. The Elmer Fudd T-shirt, I'm only aware of the design now that it's off, Elmer in his little car. Does this girl really like Elmer Fudd?

Then we're on her bed, lying on her bed and she's taking my shirt off, undoing my tie and tossing it onto the floor.

141

And I can't tell her now that I never actually undo ties. I just loosen them to move them on and off. Once they're knotted, they're knotted, in my drawer knotted and looped over my head when their turn comes. And this isn't the time for that, and I'm thinking I haven't actually tied a tie for a couple of years, and her tongue is in my mouth. And then I'm on top of her, her hands on my shoulders, her legs wrapped around mine.

And it's five twenty-five. Five twenty-five. I can see the clock next to her bed and I have to go.

I wash my face, fix the tie, and she says, *Call me, I'm on days off now.* And I get to the meeting just on time, smelling of sweat and, I'm sure, smelling of Kelly. I can smell her all over me, taste her in my mouth. I'm introduced to people, one of the hospital chaplains, community representatives, a pregnant thirtyish lawyer from the Health Department. Reeking of sweat and girl and bad judgement, checking all the time that my shirt's tucked in, that my trousers are arranged in a way that keeps my feelings to myself.

How can I concentrate? How can I impress even slightly when my mind is so elsewhere and I'm hopelessly underprepared?

I try to look like I'm there to listen, but the Dud keeps asking for my input. One of the senior consultants leaves the room for his project to be discussed, and someone whose name I forget turns to me and says, *What do you think of this, Jon, the practicalities of this, from the patient's position?*

And I've paid just enough attention to cover it, following the old tutorial rule of coming up with one small thing to say, and making it very specific so they think you're on top of everything (while ninety-five per cent of the time you're rocking back in your chair imagining a girl clambering all over your front).

I rock forward in my chair.

I've just got one small thing, I tell them, picking up the consent form. This says *various tests on the blood*, and they're having some standard blood tests, but they're also having an arterial line put in and I don't really think that's covered by *various tests on the blood*. A blood sample from a vein and putting in an arterial line are very different from the patient's perspective, and maybe that should be made clear.

What's the difference? the lawyer says.

The arterial line's more painful, a bigger deal. And it undoubtedly needs more expertise. I couldn't do it.

So that should be in the consent form? Something that makes the discomfort clear and requires the expertise. Makes it clear that they're consenting to having it done only by someone specifically trained to do it.

When we've talked this through the consultant is called back in, and he listens to the Dud's summary.

Yes, yes, I can see that concern, he says. *We've probably just developed the draft consent form from one we've used for something else, but I can see that it's reasonable to point that out. We could even specify that, while there is some discomfort, it will be done under local anaesthetic.*

This goes down well, and he takes a fountain pen from his jacket and changes the wording of the form in front of everyone.

On the way out of the boardroom at the end of the meeting the Dud says, *Good work,* and gives me a bit of a nod. *You've got a feel for this sort of thing, haven't you?*

And I should say to him, Well, actually, all I'm thinking about at the moment is whether or not I should go back to the Quarters and pash one of the nurses, but I don't.

And I don't go back. I go home, and still I'm telling no-one, still I'm working this out.

The next day I'm in the library again, still working it out but also looking at the measuring aspect of melatonin, listening to the ever-present Marlon de Lisle cracking his knuckles, watching his ongoing struggle with *Harrison's Principles of Internal Medicine*.

Other than the librarian, no-one comes here as often as the two of us, I'm sure of it. His resident must work very hard. This is probably all part of the Hospital Legend deal, consultants demanding little of you, giving you space to study, your resident working like a dog without a word of complaint. And while one of my consultants might be indulging me, I don't think I've quite got the deal Marlon has. I can still fit in all my own work, keep most people happy. And I'm sure Marlon doesn't even have to think that way.

What does he think? Does he ever think of Pink Floyd, of where he might be? How could he sit there day after day in the aisle seat of row three staring at that book, without almost every minute dreaming of playing stadiums, bigger worlds than this? Brisbane, Mount Stevens, gastro.

Not that it's a bad world. In my part of it things are looking pretty good, if a little unreal. The comfort of psych, relatively infrequent visits to the multistorey, something to fill the gap left by the mothballing of the Mokable Rocket, Kelly. Kelly and the ease of her company and her great attitude to body parts.

Even the Ethics Committee wasn't a problem. I was expecting that I'd be out of my depth. I was expecting everyone else's projects to be really impressive, in a totally different league, but at the end of it my plans seemed, if anything, more feasible than before.

And I don't think it's as crude as melatonin deficiency. I think rhythm is too important. So today my attention is directed to this, to how melatonin might exert its effects. I have five articles (or, in fact, two articles and three abstracts) that deal with this.

The melatonin signal

Working from the understanding that plasma melatonin levels act as a signal for other bodily changes, the question arises as to what the basis of the signal is. Properties that could act as a signal include the total amount of melatonin secreted, the duration of nocturnal secretion, the amplitude of the nocturnal peak and the phase relationship of the peak to the light–dark cycle (or physical rhythms). Since all mammalian species have prominent circadian rhythmicity of melatonin levels, it is likely that rhythm has a bearing on action.

1 In measuring circadian rhythms of melatonin, cortisol and electrolytes in humans in summer and winter, it appears that the phasing of the melatonin rhythm is of prime importance in its role as a signal.
2 In voles, the administration of lithium (used as a mood stabiliser in humans, particularly those with bipolar affective disorder) increased and altered the timing of the early morning melatonin peak, but had no effect on total nocturnal melatonin production.

Treatment implications

Since the timing of the melatonin cycle seems to be important in determining the action of melatonin as a signal, two issues regarding treatment emerge. Treatment may succeed through its effects on the timing of the melatonin rhythm, and the timing of the treatment itself may be important in its action.

1 A study of eight patients with seasonal affective

disorder demonstrated an improvement following regular treatment with one hour of bright artificial light in the morning, but not in the evening. This was noted to coincide with an advance in the phasing of nocturnal melatonin production.

2 The administration of bright morning light to a group of healthy Antarctic workers led to a marked advance in the timing of melatonin secretion, but no change in mood.

3 In hamsters, melatonin levels are more significantly influenced by the timing of dawn, rather than dusk.

Again, I have just a few pieces of information, but it seems clear that timing is very important. Timing is, after all, what melatonin is about, and any study that fails to acknowledge that will perhaps find nothing. Morning light seems to be one thing that flicks the switch that starts melatonin production, that calibrates the clock that times a dramatic melatonin rise fifteen hours or so later, if the endogenous rhythm has started to wander, is looking for bearings. And surely the mood of the Antarctic workers didn't change because they weren't depressed.

But what emerges, not only from these five articles but from everything I've read, is more than this, more than an understanding of signals. What emerges is a pattern. People are dealing with this in different ways, mainly two different ways. Some groups are looking very closely at rhythms and only occasionally at the treatment of small subgroups of depression, while those focussing on orthodox depression treatments are measuring twenty-four-hour totals, or melatonin levels two hours after treatment, or at nine in the morning. I think they're getting it wrong. They aren't finding patterns, they aren't finding changes, but surely they're measuring the wrong things.

I make a few notes, and I add the new articles to the growing pile in the second consulting room.

I call Kelly and I invite her over to dinner tomorrow night, since Rick and Jen will both be out, and she says *Sure, that'd be good. I don't have a car though, so could I maybe just go with you after work and then catch a cab back here?*

It's six o'clock when I get home, and it's getting dark. It occurs to me that it's the autumn equinox. All over the hemisphere people with seasonal affective disorder are probably getting that sinking feeling again. Rick's in the kitchen. I smell coffee. I hear singing, 'Love Me Tender', quite like Elvis.

Any left in that for me, Mr Presley? I ask him when I walk in and see him pouring his coffee into a mug.

No problem, Jon-boy.

You still going out tomorrow night?

Certainly. I'm not paying, so I'm definitely going. It's not every day people you don't like get admitted as solicitors and invite you to drink copious amounts of alcohol at their expense. Besides, I want to watch them. I want to watch them closely and I want to see that life gets better the moment you're admitted. I want to see that all this is worthwhile.

Do you think you might be setting yourself up for disappointment?

What's disappointment to me? Of course I'm setting myself up for disappointment. I'm very comfortable with disappointment.

So when will it go till, the drinks?

Who knows. Fairly late, I suppose. Why? Got something happening?

He has a nose for this. For a man who seems completely taken with his own melancholy and minor ailments, he notices the merest hint of gossip when it's about.

I might have someone coming over.

It's that nurse, isn't it?

What do you mean?

That ball nurse.

A ball nurse, that could be handy.

That nurse who took you to the ball, it's her, isn't it?

Easy, fella. You're like a hound with the scent of fox.
Her name is Kelly. She will be dining here tomorrow night,
while you and Jennifer are decidedly elsewhere.

*Dining, he says. Dining. They don't get dined easily, do
they?*

They get dined. Dining is nothing.

*Come on. This is more than just a ball date now. She'll
have expectations.*

I've done nothing to give her expectations.

*But they get them, don't they? They get them from
somewhere. What is it with you and nurses, anyway?*

It's what's available. I spend my days with nurses and
patients, and nurses seem to be the ethical option. I am on
the Ethics Committee, remember.

*And I'm sure there are a few nurses who'd have a thing
or two to say about that. I'm sure there are a few nurses
who mistakenly get the idea that they're more than what's
available.*

What's wrong with making the most of what's available? It's like you and your hands. Anyway, this'd only be
the third, and there are hundreds of them at the hospital.
I am a bit selective.

*Fourth. It'd be at least the fourth. You've got to count
that one whose father was a carpenter, even if it embar-
rasses you. It still counts.*

Fourth then, okay. But what's with this counting? And
where's my coffee?

I was outflanked by the carpenter. His daughter moved

out of home right after we started going out. And while she and her mother moved boxes into the flat she was renting, he made me help him build a double bed for her in the master bedroom. He carried two-thirds of the timber up the stairs in one go, as though it weighed nothing, and I struggled behind him dragging my third, snagging on the carpet, marking the wall.

He had a belt full of tools, and hard carpenter hands that knew just what to do and made me look clumsy, almost useless. And when we were done he patted the obviously sturdy pine planks with one of his hard hands and said, *They can take something, these slats. They can take some bloody heavy sleeping, mate.*

And it worked of course. I ended the relationship. I couldn't have sex in that bed, not with his hard hands all over it, always there, and my spindly ineptitude.

Wednesday's ward excursion is a bus trip to Bribie Island.

Glen, since he's the charge nurse, doesn't go, but he says he's happy staying behind anyway. There's nothing easier to manage than an almost empty ward.

I ask him what made them pick Bribie, and he shrugs.

So they can smoke on a beach, I suppose.

The only problem with this Wednesday is that the kitchen loses Glen's Day Patients meal order, subtracts the number of packed lunches from the number of beds occupied and gets the catering exactly right. Johnno misses out.

I'm not going to the Pink Ladies, he says to me. *I have*

a philosophical objection to paying for home food. Fuck it, let's just go totally crazy. Let's go out, like people with normal jobs. Glen, we're going out.

So we go to the front bar of the Fed, the two of us. Rick wouldn't understand this choice, but then he has no feel for the neighbourhood. He's not to know that it's the only eating place within beeper range that has carpet. At least it's not like the back bar of the Fed, not a sleaze-pit where grotty old men tumesce at lunchtimes.

The front bar is the Federal Hotel's concession to the requirements of the more refined customer. It's the place the grotty old men bring grotty old women they are trying to impress. I imagine them going home half full of beer and cask moselle, peeling away the seersucker, dropping the teeth in water, friction-burning their vast, dimply buttocks on the crocheted bedspread. I stop imagining this as soon as possible.

Wednesday lunchtime is All You Can Eat, and Johnno pays. *I said totally crazy, remember? If I'm going to pay for one lunch I might as well go all the way and pay for two.*

This is it. This is what Rick was talking about, the lunch where you have prospects. This is where I have to impress, where I have to get it just right, where I have to stay calm, and know a lot about melatonin. So do I want to be a psych registrar? Do I want to be a psychiatrist? Is that the same question? How do I handle this?

So, Johnno says. *So,* and if he mentions my future, I'm ready. If he mentions melatonin, I'm ready too. *What's this about the student nurses' grad ball last Friday night?*

What?

My future: psych sounds good, but let's see how the next few months go. Melatonin: timing's the thing. This is what I was ready for. Voles, lithium.

The ball. I hear you were there, he's saying, smiling. *With a nurse from one of the surgical wards.*

Yeah. Kelly McLean, Four C. How did you know?

I thought you'd sacrificed the pleasures of the flesh for your interest in research.

You said I should try both. And I've got some great stuff on melatonin in the last few days.

Not bad in the flesh department either, from what I hear.

What? What do you hear?

It's a hospital. There are no secrets in hospitals. Just flesh and big mouths.

What? What did you say?

He shrugs. Grins. Knowingly maybe.

No, I can't believe it. No-one was even there. You know, don't you?

He nods, almost sympathetically, tries not to smile, shrugs again.

I can't believe it. I can't believe you could know. There I was, in the privacy of my own home. I mean, sure my elbow hit the wall, but I'd never met a girl who swallowed before. How could you know?

He jolts. Coughs and gags on the water that was halfway down his pharynx. He tries hard to move it along but he laughs, and it comes out his nose.

It is apparent that I have misjudged the situation, his understanding of events. I thought we'd be talking about something else. He caught me off-guard. I'm telling the Director of Psychiatry I just got a blow job, and I don't think that's good. I thought our relationship was entering a new phase. This wasn't the phase I thought it was entering. Johnno blows his nose, and is then able to laugh out loud.

You didn't know, did you?

He shakes his head. *I knew you'd been to the ball. Someone from Four C told Glen. That was all I knew. That was what I thought I meant by the no secrets, big mouths bit.*

Not much, really.

Practically nothing, it turns out. He laughs again. *This is much better. Your elbow hit the wall?*

Yeah. It was a big moment. I can't even account for the other three limbs.

He laughs again. Slaps his thigh. It's a habit I hate. It's so unnecessary, so attention-seeking. And today he only stops it so he can wave his elbow around, while rolling his eyes back in his head. I hope someone thinks he's having a fit. I hope they shove a padded spoon in his mouth, good and hard.

It's all right, he says when he's finally had enough of this unappealing mime. *Your secret's safe with me. Anyway, people do that sort of thing all the time.*

Not to me, they don't. And I really don't want to stop them by blabbing about it.

You know, it's interesting, he says, drifting along his own tangent and ignoring my concerns, *phenomenologically. There are communities where this kind of activity is almost ubiquitous.*

I think I've been in the other communities till now.

Demographically I think the odds are pretty high anywhere north of Townsville, and in Sydney it goes without saying. And most major metropolitan hospitals too, of course. He pauses, contemplates. *All major metropolitan hospitals.*

This is what they never tell you at orientation.

I think it's just assumed. A sort of unwritten policy. I can't think of anyone I've liaised with here who didn't.

And I gather that'd be a few by now, and not just nurses either. At least I limit the damage.

It was usually their idea.

Admin staff, an RMO or two, and there's one physio who still can't hear your name without getting upset. And it was always their idea?

No, it was usually their idea. And a domestic. You left out Mrs Liebowitz, but that's another story. Everyone leaves out Mrs Liebowitz. You would never have seen her. She's down the back of the kitchen. She cleans out the big pots. Mrs Liebowitz was awesome.

That's five different categories of staff members. What do you think this is, a pentathlon? My whole life, all I got was a few nurses and one blow job.

You're still young. Anyway, why I mentioned the ball, and this sounds very anti-climactic now, why I mentioned it is that I was telling the person with whom I am presently associated about your melatonin work and she said we should have you over to dinner. So I was thinking, maybe you had someone you'd like to bring. Maybe you had a friend with a mouth, you know?

A friend with a mouth. That doesn't sound wise right at the moment.

I'll be the soul of discretion. I'm not the one who's gone shooting off at the mouth about it.

Thanks very much. And could we never mention mouths again?

My lips are sealed. Dinner then? Saturday?

And it's all of this that I have to get out of my head when I meet Kelly at six. All but the dinner invite. I have to pretend I had a kind of mentoring melatonin-related lunch that progressed calmly to a suggestion of dinner, without any digression concerning the oral event.

She's talking away, chatting like she's glad to see me.

I think I like her. I want to tell her right now that I've only told one person about the oral event, and I think he can keep it quiet, so everything's okay. But somehow I don't think it would be okay. Kelly, I always think honesty's the best policy, don't you? Well, just so you know, in case it gets back to you, I've only told one person about the oral event, and it was a complete accident. Not the event, which was brilliant, the telling. It just slipped out. I misunderstood something. I wasn't concentrating. One of those things, you know? Happens all the time.

I'm not feeling good about this.

You've had a difficult day, haven't you? Kelly says as we're sitting in traffic.

What do you mean?

You're distracted, like something's bothering you.

No. I must be tired.

It's all right if something's bothering you. Is there some problem with a patient?

No. I don't have any problems with patients.

I've seen you with patients. I was in the ward when you did respiratory, remember. But that was back when I was in mauve, and you didn't notice me.

As opposed to in white or red? And anyway, it was you who made me notice you when you'd moved on from the mauve. You reached up into a cupboard seductively when I was at a very impressionable point, just sixteen days out of a relationship. And you showed off the white look, declared yourself seemly, asked me to the ball.

Seemly, she says. *Is seemly still okay with you?*

It's great. I'm sure it's one of my favourite things at the moment.

That and a particular event I'm concentrating really hard on not mentioning.

Soon we're in the kitchen at home and I'm chopping for

a stir-fry and Kelly's sitting on the edge of the bench drinking wine. Sitting with her legs crossed at the ankles and no shoes.

This is nice, she says. *Much more private than the Quarters. So how late do you think your housemates'll be?*

Late.

Good.

How are you with garlic?

Fine. I like garlic.

Good, me too.

It comes through, you know.

What, you've smelled garlic on my breath before?

I breathe into my hand and smell it. No garlic, surely.

No, in bodily fluids.

Oh, yeah. I've noticed it in sweat. And once, when I was a student, and this is pretty bizarre, I delivered a garlic-smelling baby from a woman who'd eaten a lot of it.

And in men. You can notice it in men.

In men? Why, because they sweat more?

No, no. She shakes her head. *I mean the taste.*

Oh, okay. Really?

And it's the way she says taste that makes it clear what she means. And I'm thinking, Play it cool. Pretend that you're so calm about the whole issue you don't talk about it all the time. So calm it'd be fine if she did it several times a day.

You can notice it? Can you notice other things? Like Vegemite, or anything?

Vegemite. She laughs. *Why? Do you eat a lot of Vegemite?*

No. No more than most people. You didn't notice any . . . No, I don't want to know. What I meant was, different things. Can you notice different things? Vegemite was just an example of something strong. I could have said peppermint.

All men taste different. Most taste sort of grassy, though.

Grassy? I wonder why. And how do you get grassy? How do you know what grassy tastes like?

Well, okay, it's an assumption.

Grassy? That's just not special, is it?

I don't think it's done for the taste, she says, moving in next to me, putting her arms around me while I'm flipping things around in the wok.

And I can see her now, her face down there, replaying the oral event. Surfacing while my limbs flail against various parts of the house in unbridled ecstasy, and she's reporting, *Pizza, supreme, no anchovies,* speculating about what I might have had for lunch. And what kind of sample size has she got to compare it with? Has she done enough of this to achieve statistical significance? Not that I can talk. I haven't exactly given my affections cautiously, and the numbers are starting to add up. I should be less judgemental.

This could make my hand shaky while I'm wokking, you know, I tell her. All this grass business.

She seems to take this as some lame kind of dare, and moves one hand round to the front of my pants and starts rubbing.

It doesn't do to involve yourself with a man's penis this close to a naked flame. Didn't your mother tell you anything?

My hand twitches and flips a couple of mushrooms up into the extractor fan. I wonder if I should go for the phone now. Johnno, she's got my dick in her hand. Just thought you should know.

She laughs and steps back. *Can I get plates out, or anything?*

Yeah. Plates'd be good.

We eat at the dining table, and then adjourn to the lounge room.

So, are we going to let people know? she says.

Well, I don't think that's a problem.

(This is my big chance. Come clean, come clean. I don't come clean. I'm no fool.)

My guess is that, since we were at a function together in the company of quite a few hospital staff, they'll be assuming there's something happening anyway. Who knows what they'll be assuming, but my guess is they'll be assuming something. That's what they do, whether there's anything happening or not. So I don't think this is our little secret.

Outside, a car stops, then drives off. A body falls up the front steps. Rick says, *Fuck,* as though the steps have treated him unreasonably. There's a good deal of key fumbling and he stumbles through the door and into his room. Just as I assume that's the end of him for the evening, he lurches into the lounge room, craning his head back and shining a big yellow Eveready Dolphin torch up his nose and saying, *Are they back yet? I think they might be back. Oh, hi, excuse me.* Frantically checking Kelly out at the same time as blinding himself. *I think they're back, Jon-boy.*

And he leans over me, his flared nostrils glowing pink with the light right up them, polyps as invisible as ever. I bet Rick had an imaginary friend when he was a kid.

No, they're fine, I tell him. Well, as good as usual. Don't worry. Take drugs and don't worry.

Good on ya, he says and clomps back down the hallway, torch still pointing into his face, dancing the broad shadow of his troubled head across the lounge-room ceiling, right until he shuts his door. He hits the bed hard, perhaps even landing on the torch. Immediately, he begins the snuffly breathing of sleep.

Don't worry, I tell Kelly. He thinks birds nest in his nose. He's quite mad.

Did you meet him through work? she says, in a way that almost makes me think she's serious.

He's harmless, that's what I've got to keep telling myself. And it's a sort of altruistic thing, having him here. The bird issue only crops up when he drinks. Something to do with a traumatic incident in his childhood. But he's much better now.

He won't be coming out again, will he?

Did you hear that impact? No-one hits a mattress that hard and comes out again. Forget about him.

I'd still be more comfortable if we weren't out here in the lounge room.

I'm not often good with cues, but this one I get. We put music on, to drown out a neighbourhood of rowdy night breathing and the noises of a drunk man being tossed by cruel dreams among the dissembled parts of a yellow Eveready Dolphin. We go into my room. I open the window and the breeze is cool tonight.

Kelly kneels on the bed, reaches a hand out to me when I come towards her, smiles, I think, when our faces are close.

No naked flames, she says, undoing my belt.

And I unbutton her jeans, slide them down, feel her thighs under my hands. She takes off her shirt and bra and lowers her breasts to my face and keeps massaging my penis with her hand. We roll over, she draws me on top of her and things go quickly and she helps me with the condom, moves her hands to my buttocks, pushes against me and against me with a slow circling rhythm, breathing with it and pushing. And I'm getting closer, holding back, holding myself on the brink as I watch her open mouth going, *Aah, aah, aah,* with each push and then, *Yes, yes.*

Later, when I shed the condom and we're lying there facing each other she says, *Saturday night . . .*

Yeah?

I didn't know what to do. I mean, I didn't know what I wanted to do. How far I wanted things to get then.

What do you mean?

I didn't know if I was ready for, well, tonight. I thought about it, between then and now, and I decided I was.

Is there a problem?

No. I'm not making sense. I'm tired. This isn't making sense. It's just that, I live in the Quarters, and, it's none of my business, but, you and Penny Frew . . .

Some things just don't work out. It's as simple as that.

Okay. Sorry, it's not my business. Can I stay? I know I said I'd catch a cab home but can I stay now and get a lift back to the hospital with you in the morning?

Of course. What? You think I'm going to send you home now? You think I don't want you to stay?

No. But . . . She shakes her head. *I'm glad you want me to stay.*

And she sleeps, her head on my pillow. I pull the doona up over her bare shoulders.

Hours later, I'm jerked awake by the thump of something landing on the window sill. I look up and see the black shape of a cat, Jean-Paul.

How the fuck do you do that? I say to him, just at a whisper. Where could you possibly be jumping from to end up there?

He jumps down next to me, purring as though he's been impressive. He notices Kelly, her hair, the waves of her blonde hair across the pillow and he flicks a few strands with his paw, thinks about pouncing, in case there's a game to be had. But then he decides not to bother and he sits on her hair instead, curls up and sleeps.

18

We're a strange threesome in the car on the way into town.

I can't believe you let a cat sleep on my head, Kelly says.

Rick, pale and rough-edged in the back, catches my eye in the rear-view mirror, mouths, *What?* and gives me a look that suggests he thinks I've involved myself with a mad woman. This could become challenging, each of them thinking the other insane.

Perhaps this evening I should tell him it's just a figure of speech. Or perhaps I should tell him a cat slept on her head, but he'd only think he was slipping further behind in his grasp of contemporary sexual repertoire.

Now, let me see, you get the girl, right? And then you get the cat, and you put it on her head? Okay. You wait till it falls asleep. And then what?

Well, Rick, this is where you need the strawberry jam, the wallpaper paste and the bicycle clips. And you've got to move fast. Cats are light sleepers.

I don't think he'd ever talk to girls again.

Kelly says I should drop her off near the Nurses' Quarters. She shakes her hair, passes her fingers through it as though she's combing out any last signs of cat, and last night. I double park.

Saturday then, she says. *The Gil Johnson dinner.*

Yeah.

I think I've got a late on Sunday. I've got a crazy roster at the moment.

Do you want to stay after dinner then. At my place?

Yeah. That'd be good. She smiles, takes my face in both hands, kisses my mouth.

I'll come and get you. Seven, if that's okay.

Yeah.

I drive around to the less busy streets near psych and I park.

I concentrate poorly in the Dubois round, less in the library after when I should be focussing on the biochem, getting ready for the Joan Shand meeting.

Joan Shand is not someone you just chat to. She really knows her biochemical pathology, and can't understand anyone who doesn't. As the head of her division, she spoke to us as part of our intern orientation, and her clear lack of enthusiasm for unnecessary investigation was memorable.

You can order anything you like, she said. *You just have to be able to justify it to me if I call you.*

And she took the time to give each one of us a steely glare to emphasise what this meant. Steely glare, steel grey hair, steel-framed glasses. More cold steel than a bayonet charge. And she did call, she wasn't kidding. And she always handled it nicely, as long as she could tell you were scared.

But the Joan Shand melatonin meeting is a little too distant to scare me enough today. And last night is too close to get out of my head, a clutter of conversations, incidents, Kelly. Kelly and her interesting hierarchy of intimacy. I want to say to the librarian, or anyone who might get this, I want to say, Look, just put the melatonin aside for a moment, Imelda, and tell me about intimacy, give me the girl perspective, let me get this hierarchy thing straight.

Saturday, Kelly wasn't sure about sex, but swallowing fifty million of my sperm was fine. And then she thought about it and decided she was ready. Decided. What does that mean? How is it unilateral? What signal did I give that any decision could be based on? Did she like the taste? I have no idea what I had for lunch last Saturday.

And I can't believe anything from the hospital dining room could have a favourable influence on my semen.

Perhaps on Saturday she felt better being in control, giving it but not taking much back, putting nothing much at risk. And Penny Frew. What's Penny got to do with this? What's she saying?

I get home and Rick's there already, back from work earlier than usual, still looking somewhat shattered and poking a reluctant soluble aspirin around in a glass of water.

Hey, he says. *Hey.* And gives his eyebrows a couple of meaningful lifts as though they're lever-operated. *Very nice, very soft.*

And I'm worried that he's about to come up with some reference to double-cooked pork, but he pulls up short, snuffles some mucus aside, swigs down the aspirin, burps and then hiccups incessantly for at least twenty minutes and says, *Surprise me, fuck you, surprise me. Isn't that what you do for someone with hiccups?*

19

I had a guy die on me today, Kelly says, the first thing she says when she steps into the car on Saturday night. *A week post-subtotal gastrectomy. He was doing all right, too, picking up well after it.*

What happened?

He just said he thought he was going to throw up and

before I got back with a bowl he was bringing up blood everywhere, like everywhere. We got the DMO and she called the registrar and lined up a theatre and a cross match, but he coded before getting out of the ward. Just there on the trolley, waiting for the lifts. I moved his head to start clearing his airway and I knocked the bowl onto the floor. So my white shoes aren't as white as they used to be.

Bad scene.

Yeah, and it was just then when the lift doors opened, and it was people coming to visit one of the other patients. Imagine that. Welcome to the ward, can I help you? Just visiting? Well if it's anyone but Mr Schmidt please proceed to the left. And don't mind us.

That's quite impressively bad.

He was a nice guy, too. Didn't I get you to see him? When you were DMO last Saturday. He would have had his gastrectomy the day before.

Maybe. A guy with a fever? Did he have a post-op fever?

Yeah, that's him.

This wasn't anything to do with that, was it?

He had fluctuating fevers over the course of the week, but no-one ever worked out what was going on. Could it all be related?

I don't know. Maybe, maybe not. I don't know.

No-one knew.

And Kelly obviously had a week of conversations with the recuperating Mr Schmidt, and I can't even remember his face. Just his urine. His urine bag and Kelly's face next to it, her pupils dilating down there below the light. Her face close to mine.

So after all that it's good to be out of there, she says. *Anyway, I haven't even said hello properly yet. I just launched into my shitty day, I'm sorry.* We're at a red light so she leans across and kisses me and says, *It's good to see you. Let's have fun.*

There's jazz playing when we get to Johnno's place at Red Hill. Jazz I don't know, but then I don't know jazz so I shouldn't be surprised. Johnno comes to the door when we knock and he leads us through to the kitchen and introduces us to Suzanne, who is singing along to the music more than competently. It transpires that this is because she is a jazz singer.

We met through work, she says after she's poured us drinks. *We were in a combo. I was singing and Johnno was on sax. About a year or so ago.*

Suzanne must be twenty-something, mid-twenties, so not much different in age from me. She's tall and thin and blonde, each of them in quite a self-assured way.

So you met through work as well, she says when she finds out Kelly's a nurse. *The three of you aren't in the same ward, are you?*

No, Kelly says. *I'm in a surgical ward.*

That must be pretty gruesome.

Not usually.

And for a moment she thinks about Mr Schmidt. I can see it. I can see her watching the blood tumble down across her new white shoes.

So what made you pick psychiatry, Jon? Suzanne is saying.

It looked interesting, I suppose.

And the thing you're doing with melanomas? How does that fit in?

I'm sorry?

Melanomas. The research you're doing.

164

Um, that's melatonin, Johnno says over his shoulder. *It's a different thing.*

Oh, I thought you said melanoma. You mustn't have explained it to me very clearly. So what's melatonin?

It's a hormone. We think the levels of it might change in people with depression.

So nothing to do with skin things? Not at all?

Well, no, not really. Not in humans.

Well, it's pretty silly that they have such similar names, then, isn't it?

I'm about to serve, Johnno says. *Could you get things ready?*

Suzanne sets the table and Johnno places the turkey at the head of it and carves.

Now, Kelly, meat. How much would you like? And he glances at her, glances at me. *I'd guess a good-sized piece, but tell me if I'm wrong.*

Medium-sized would be fine, thanks.

And can I tempt you with a sausage? Two perhaps? Or would that be pushing you a little too close to protein overload?

One'd be good, she says, smiling, thinking him merely strange and generous, not getting the over-the-top innuendo that I really wish would go away. *They do look big.*

Just the right size, Johnno says. *Just the right size.* Pronging the biggest he can find with a fork and dropping it onto her plate. *And you, Jon, what do you like?*

I'll have the same, thanks.

He hands me the plate, smiling. Gives just a flicker of elbow. For a man whose lips are sealed, he's not exactly trying hard.

He opens a bottle of wine and says, *I saw this in a bottle shop today. It's French. It was marked down, so I thought I'd give it a go.*

Suzanne tries it. *It's different, isn't it? It's nice, but it's different.*

Johnno tastes it too. *Yeah, it is. I can't quite work out how I'd describe it though.*

Sort of, well, grassy tasting, she says.

Kelly chokes on her sausage.

How do you know what grassy tastes like? Johnno says, this time in complete innocence, and I really wish he hadn't.

Suzanne laughs. *I suppose I'm going on what I think grassy would be like.*

So, what drew you to jazz? I ask her, wanting grassiness to go away, wanting any safe topic and caring not at all that I sound like an SBS arts reporter.

She tries to explain what kind of jazz she likes, but it's beyond me. The whole idea that there need to be different kinds of jazz is beyond me. Isn't jazz simply about giving middle-aged people ownership of something they think is cool? Wouldn't one kind be enough?

She goes and puts on a new CD and comes back and says, *See what I mean?*

Yeah. Yeah, I think so.

I seem to be answering yes a lot when the answer's no lately. I'm really not good with conflict.

I honestly don't know much about music, I tell her.

Apart from The Go Betweens, Kelly says. *They're very popular in your car at the moment.*

And deservedly so. But I'm just a listener. I've never played anything myself. One of my housemates has been in a few bands, particularly at uni. He was trying to get a band together at one stage last year. He even had some really dumb name. I think he thought of the name and then decided he liked it so much he should get a band together just so he could use it.

And it's only when I actually hear it coming out of my mouth, when it's just too late to pull it back, cover up, that I realise that trying to fit in with small talk has its own dangers. And this is not a good time to be saying Joe Blob and the Spoonerisms.

Johnno looks aghast, chokes on his wine. Coughs, and buries his head in his napkin. Coughing and gagging and laughing and occasionally pausing while trying very hard to think about something else, and to breathe.

Are you all right? Suzanne says.

He nods, takes the napkin from his face, dabs a trickle of wine that's coming from one nostril. *Something must have gone down the wrong way.*

I don't get it, Kelly says. *I don't get the name. What is it? Some uni thing?*

Post-grad thing for you, wasn't it, Jon? Johnno says, and grits his teeth.

Yeah. Do you know anything about post modernism?

She says *No.*

Well, it's a reference to that.

One of the great philosophers of our time, Johnno adds helpfully. *Come and pick a CD, Jon.*

He leads me from the kitchen, takes a seat in the lounge room and doubles up laughing, as quietly as possible. His mouth gaping, his eyes wide, a final dribble of wine issuing from his nose. He manages to say *post modernism,* but it's a struggle.

I can only shake my head.

You just can't stop yourself, can you?

I think I must have some deep self-destructive urge.

Or an unshakable fascination with blow jobs.

Maybe both.

Could I just ask, as a favour, that you check in future to see if I'm drinking at the time? I mean, your interest in

post modernism is entirely reasonable, but I've washed my
sinuses out twice in one week now.

Yeah, sorry about that. I can't believe I might have got
away with it. How could she not know about spoonerisms?

Just be grateful.

Suzanne's probably explaining it to her right now.

That's pretty unlikely.

We go back into the kitchen.

I thought you were going to pick a new CD, Suzanne
says.

I couldn't make up my mind.

In the car on the way back to Bayliss Street Kelly says,
*I have to admit I just didn't get that Joe Blob and the
Spoons line.*

No. I'm not sure I do myself. But I knew Johnno would.
He's very well read. Apparently it's quite funny.

*If you've studied more post modernism than we have,
obviously.*

Yeah.

*Your housemate could explain it though, couldn't he? It
was his band.*

Yeah, but I wouldn't mention it. The band really didn't
work out. It's not something he likes to talk about. It
makes him tense, and he's not good when he's tense. So,
please, don't ever bring it up.

No. Sure.

20

Mr Schmidt's fever fluctuated all week, and no-one got to the bottom of it, not just me.

The sky is totally blue and it's nearly eight. I hope Rick has the judgement not to knock on my door today with his Teutonic allusions to masturbation.

Kelly wakes, half-wakes and her body's warm when she moves on top of me, her hair messed everywhere.

You should let a cat sleep on that, I tell her. Cats are tidy.

She kisses my mouth, my neck, my chest, lower, looking up with bleary-eyed half-smiles and saying not a word. She comes upon my penis like an early bird, pecks at it, catches it in her mouth. And she tucks her hair aside and I see her lips, I watch myself moving in and out of her mouth.

The doona slides onto the floor, and the sheet and she's kneeling in the vee made by my uncovered legs, her eyes closed, a strand of hair slipping free, her head rocking rhythmically and without any sense of hurry. My back is arching with this, involuntarily, and I sit up, sit with my knees bent, cradling her head, leaning over her, kissing her on her back, as though that gives her some kind of affection in return.

I lie back down, fighting the inclination to groan out loud.

And it's just as I'm leaning back that I see three painters, sitting on top of the roof next door but not painting. Applauding when they see that I've noticed them, punching the air, as if I need encouragement. I can even see their faces. Now I do groan. It's not the same groan.

I reach back and shut the blinds, but it's no good. Kelly looks up, I point to the window, lift the edge of the blind and she goes, *Oh, fuck*. My penis flops like a filleted finger and her head hits the pillow next to mine. She puts her hands on her face, goes red as the empire, and then laughs. *Well, I can't go on, but I don't think you're giving me much to work with anyway.*

And she pulls the sheet up and over her head, and she groans, too. *I can't believe . . . I can't believe . . .*

What's their problem? Why the fuck are they working on a Sunday? Isn't there some law?

Probably. So go out there and enforce it. Make a citizen's arrest.

The applause takes a while to die down. Who needs to tell people about the oral event, when you can just show them?

We've lived here over a year and I've never seen anyone on the roof next door. The moment something interesting happens in my room, I'm playing to an audience of three painters. Three burly men with thick, black turned-down moustaches, laughing and showing me almost a hundred white teeth. Like Pancho Villa and his gang, riding north of the border to wreak havoc, take in a blow job or two, surge gloriously back across the Rio Grande.

I hear Rick creak his way out of bed.

Might as well get up, I say to Kelly. Shall we get up?

We're in the lounge room when Rick emerges in an over-sized Astro Boy T-shirt and red tracksuit pants, his hair looking as though Jean-Paul chose his head as a pillow last night.

Looking beautiful this morning, I say to him.

Why thanks, Jon-boy. Nice of you to notice. And then he looks at Kelly, wonders about drawing her into this, Kelly with her impressively out-of-control case of bed hair.

He tries to make eye contact with her, can't, says *Hi* to her shirt-front instead, realises he has just greeted breasts and quickly looks back at me and pretends she's not there. He's really not good with girls. *Are we going to the shops?*

Sure. Is Jen home?

No. He sighs. *It's just us. All these Sunday morning shop responsibilities and she's shirking them again. Out there sinning somewhere. So let's do it. Let's go.*

This is a ritual thing, I tell Kelly. A weekend morning ritual. You don't mind being part of a ritual?

What kind of ritual?

The goat's out the back, Rick says, and he seems to have made a quick recovery from his particularly gutless *Hi.*

Normally, it's a goat ritual, I explain. But Rick's forgetting it's the last Sunday in the month. The last Sunday in the month is always a croissant and newspaper ritual. More laid back.

But I just bled the goat.

You'd better not have.

What's happening with the goat? Kelly says, not sure she really wants to know.

Nothing. Today nothing. It's the last Sunday in the month. Today it's croissants and newspaper.

And what happens with them?

I'm sorry? The croissants you eat, the newspaper you read.

Okay, I can do that.

Rick goes to put his shoes on and Kelly says, *Am I wrong, or was that more post modernism?*

Yeah, something like that. There was no goat. You knew there was no goat?

I was pretty sure there was no goat, but I haven't got all this worked out yet.

171

On the way to the shops Rick says, *What was all that clapping about next door earlier?*

They've got painters there. And I think there was some European soccer final on the radio, or something. Maybe someone scored. Or maybe someone nearly scored, and the painters were going for the other side.

Kelly glares at me. She gets this one. It obviously wasn't post-modern enough.

Croissants are again being sold for two dollars a bag.

So how many croissants do I get for two dollars? I ask the woman, conversationally, as though some kind of amnesty would be good today, since I'm with a girl.

A bagful, she says. *They're being sold by the bag today.*

I really don't like her. We communicate at such cross-purposes. If only we had somewhere else in the neighbourhood that sold croissants, since I think they're an essential part of Rick's weekend. As though it's beginning days with croissants that tells him he doesn't have to suit-up in grey and slightly shiny, pick a tie from his bewildering collection, grump his way to the passenger seat of my car.

Today he's dressed to get the most out of Sunday. Sunday, but without the goat. Today it's just one of his many I-am-not-a-lawyer ensembles. Astro Boy T-shirt, red tracksuit pants, green thongs, Top Gun reflecto sunnies as he flaps his way along the street, deep in thought. A man of some style, and perplexing, untapped substance.

So what do you do, Rick? Kelly says when we're back at home eating breakfast, sitting in the back room, Rick with his sunnies still on, but probably mystified by the dark. He's a slow waker.

He looks at her, looks at her with his inscrutable fly's eyes each mirroring the row of windows, and he says, *Nothing. I do almost nothing.*

Rick, I don't think it was being asked at quite that level.

I tell Kelly his ambition is to be an enigma, but at present he's only a lawyer.

I'd love to be an enigma, he says. *Enigmas are so alluring.* He sighs. *So you're a nurse, aren't you?* And the simple juxtaposition doesn't make nursing sound good, even though I don't think this was his intention.

Yeah, Kelly says, sounding only slightly uncertain about admitting to nursing in this context.

What sort of thing are you doing at the moment?

He's trying hard here, probably for my sake. Even though Kelly isn't at all enigmatic.

Surgical. General surgical. Four C.

Four C. Four C. I remember Four C. It's been a while since you knocked anyone off in Four C, hasn't it Jon-boy?

I never knocked anyone off in Four C. Four C was good for me. Apart from yesterday, possibly. I might have played a role in a knocking-off yesterday.

You managed to kill someone and you weren't even there? You managed to kill a surgical patient and you're not even doing a surgical term? Jon-boy, these are strong powers, please think about using them for good.

If you mean what I think you mean, Kelly says, *that was really nothing to do with you.*

I did see him.

A week ago. When it could have been a regular post-op fever. Plenty of people saw him since. And we still don't know if the fever had anything to do with it.

So what happened? Rick says.

You want to know?

I want to know.

You don't want to know.

It's too late. It's Kelly's story and she's telling it, but only the ending, just as Rick's realising he doesn't want to know.

So there he was hurling blood everywhere, she's saying,

173

and then I tipped a bowl of it all over myself. All down my legs and into my shoes. And you wouldn't believe how sticky it gets when it clots in your shoes. It's all clingy and squelchy. It's foul.

Oh, really? Rick says, as almost his entire blood volume diverts to his feet, turning his lips white. *I thought this was a fever story.* He grips the sides of the seat and waits for the image to leave.

As if you could bleed a goat, I say to him.

I could. I could bleed a goat. For a ritual. It's a different mindset.

Kelly leaves mid-morning.

She's got a strong stomach, that girl, Rick says.

What do you mean?

Well, all of that blood business. What did you think I meant? What are you making her swallow?

There is a hint of a pause, which I end by saying, Nothing, a little too quickly.

The pause is bad. The Nothing is bad. It was one of those times when I should have laughed and gone along with the allusion. It was just Rick, just talk. He knows nothing, knew nothing. The elbow, the painters, nothing. It's as though I can't help myself.

What? You haven't. She doesn't. And there's nothing else I can say, since she has, does. *She does. You make stuff and she swallows it. Oh god. In this house. Just a thin wall away from the loneliest place this side of the fucking Antarctic, there's this blonde chick and she's got your dick in her mouth.* And he moans through his gnashed teeth and paces up and down the corridor. *And I don't even get a peck on the cheek. And you're lying back fucking gobjobbing it, rooting the arse off dozens of them.*

I've never been comfortable with that expression. And we've established that it's more like four of them.

He gnashes, he moans. *What am I supposed to do?*

Use your imagination, I guess.

My imagination? There's only so many times you can do that, without actually meeting Christie Brinkley. You reach a point where you need to go forward, where you'd at least like to know her opinion on a few things. Where you'd kill for just a few minutes of actual conversation.

Conversation's good. Some people even start off that way. But even that's a two-step thing. First you meet them, then you have a conversation. You should try it.

Right, so it's a meeting problem. Whereas you have a workplace very conducive to meetings, he's saying, as though he's working something out, something important. Something that means that a life well short of his expectations isn't his fault. Something that's allowing him to miss the point entirely. *And how's Kelly with the conversation part? She didn't seem very lateral. I mean, she seemed nice, but not very lateral, not very like you and me and Mr de Bono.*

Rick, it might be hard for you to get used to the idea that I'm having sex with someone who isn't like you, but you might just have to adjust. And I know she's not particularly lateral. Not everyone has to be lateral. I mean, lateral is one of your most attractive features, in its own way, but it's kind of like airconditioning in a car. It's an optional extra, and it doesn't come cheap.

Airconditioning's practically essential in a car in this climate.

Power-steering. Lateral is like power-steering. In a small car. You get what I'm saying? Optional extra. Great, justifiably highly regarded, but an optional extra. Maybe you should think about this. Maybe you're expecting a little too much. Maybe there aren't many women you meet who'll knock you over with lateral straight up.

I'd settle for irony.

Yeah. Yeah, I'd settle for irony too, but sometimes there's not even much of that. And Kelly's fine. I don't think she's adjusting to you easily, but wait till you get to know her. She's great.

We're going to get to know her?

Yeah, you're going to get to know her. You might get to know her. I just have to try very hard not to tell people about the specifics of our relationship. If it gets back to her that I'm blabbing, things mightn't go so well.

Understood. My lips are sealed.

Thank you. Nothing more about mouth parts, okay?

Okay.

So let's do something. I think we've got to stop you thinking about Christie and power-steering, all of that. How about a kick of the football?

Sure, let's really give the painters something to cheer about.

Let's go to the park. There's more space there.

At the park we position ourselves on either side of the multicoloured steamroller and kick the ball over the top.

What is it that allows Kelly to make Rick look so abstract, and Rick to make Kelly look so concrete, leaving me in the middle, like an interpreter? Kelly wondering if everything she doesn't understand is explained away by post modernism, and Rick wondering if everything he doesn't understand about Kelly is explained away by her swallowing.

I'm taking every one, Rick's disembodied voice shouts from behind the steamroller as he drops another.

Good on ya, Ricky, I shout back.

No-one calls me that.

Everyone calls you that.

Damn. I bet no-one ever fucked a Ricky.

That's what we're all thinking.

I mean someone called Ricky. I bet the name Ricky doesn't get people a lot of action, he says, in case clarification is necessary.

When we get home there's a note on the door. *I'm here but I'm napping. J.*

Creeping home in the daylight hours once again, Rick says. *What will her mother think?*

Napping sounds good. I tell Rick I might get into some of that myself, and I stand at the fridge eating enough leftovers and bits of other things to total lunch.

Rick sits down in front of a big block of cheese and a box of biscuits.

Fuck you all. Nothing ever happens to me at night. I am so totally, totally awake now. Was I up at all hours copping the lube job of the century? No. I was sleeping. What a fucking loser. What is it even like? I don't even know what it's like.

It's like being a thickshake.

And before he asks, as he is very likely to, what flavour thickshake, I tell him it's my turn to nap now.

I sleep right away and for a couple of dreamless hours, until I'm woken by Rick sitting on the end of my bed, saying, *I'm bored, I'm bored* many, many times, dripping away at me with this whinging *I'm bored* until I'm awake.

Watch TV, I tell him.

I'm bored.

Call Christie Brinkley.

I'm bored.

Call Betty Boop.

I'm bored.

Bleed the goat.

I'm bored.

177

Jen's door creaks open and I can hear her bare feet walking along the corridor.

I'm bored with my thesis, she says.

I'm bored, Rick joins in, almost by instinct now.

She looks at him, not getting this, not realising how important boredom is to him at the moment.

We thought you were napping.

First napping, then reading. She climbs onto my bed, sits with her back to the wall.

So what were you up to last night?

Oh, out, you know. So now I've got this problem.

What problem?

Two guys. A choice. Why can't they come along one at a time?

When did guys ever do anything convenient?

Exactly. So what do I do? What do I do? Choice is so distasteful. The selection criteria are so diffuse.

You're kidding. I thought it was mainly to do with shoulders.

Mainly, but when they're equal on shoulders it's not easy. What do I do? Toss a coin?

Well, you've got to pick one, Rick says. *Otherwise, you know, there's the risk of ending up like that dog in that Roman poem. The one who found two bones and died of starvation because he couldn't choose between them.*

Roman poem? I didn't know you read Roman poetry. Who wrote that?

Yeah, Rick, who wrote it?

I'm not sure. Virgil maybe? I think it was Virgil.

Virgil. One of his bucolics?

Yeah. Yeah, I think so.

Or was it Devo, Rick? Could you perhaps be referring to the Devo song 'Freedom of Choice', from a somewhat later era?

It's possible. He knows I've got him. *But it mentioned this poem. This particular ancient Roman . . .*

You're giving me advice from Devo now? Jen says. *Devo? This is how important my life is to you? What? Doesn't Kylie Minogue have anything on this topic?*

I bet she does, you know.

Jen leaves the room, comes back with a twenty-cent piece, tosses it, catches it and slaps it down onto the back of her hand.

Fuck, she says. *I wanted the other one. What am I going to do?*

Rick lies back across the bed, stares at the ceiling. *I think people should pay more attention to Devo,* he says. *I think people dismiss them because of their pointy heads, and that's just wrong.*

21

On the way to our meeting with Joan Shand, Johnno says, *So, did you get any more spoonerising after Saturday night?*

You don't want to know. You just don't want to know. Joe Blob is a dangerous man indeed, and that's all I'm saying.

A trolley passes us, on the way to theatre with a nurse escort. Not Kelly. How could anyone not know what a spoonerism is? How could Kelly not know that? Suzanne not know that? Does this not trouble Johnno, not even a little? I want to stop him and ask him, here in the corridor and regardless of the passing traffic. What are we doing? They don't even know what a spoonerism is. Doesn't this tell you something?

But I've gone through that with Rick, the other side of it. Not everyone has to be . . . Not everyone has to know . . . And then he goes to the other extreme, and again over-simplifies. I can tell, but I don't raise it. There is more to this than sex and spoonerisms, surely, hopefully. Not that I have a problem with either sex or spoonerisms.

Well, Suzanne liked you, he says. *She was a bit disappointed about melatonin. I think she had a couple of pigmented skin lesions she wanted to have checked, but other than that she liked you.*

She seemed to know a lot about jazz. How long's she been singing?

Forever really, I suppose. Professionally for a few years, since she finished studying.

What did she study?

Jazz.

You can actually study jazz?

Yeah. It's an associate diploma. She finished about four years ago. She's twenty-four now, which makes her the second-oldest person I've ever been involved with.

Is that including Mrs Liebowitz?

I don't tend to think of that as involved. Just a single night of magic.

Joan Shand is in her office, waiting for us. On the desk in front of her are photocopies of a couple of articles and a large textbook open at a page with a diagram of the melatonin metabolic pathway. This is good. Good, because it means she's taking this seriously, good because it means this might be the only subject in the world of bio-chemistry where I'm not miles behind her. I am still, of course, far from relaxed.

She smiles. *Hello Jonathan, Gil. Take a seat.* This is more literal than she intends, the part of the small room not occupied by Doctor Shand and her desk being taken up by a single wooden chair. She looks at it as though it is embarrassing her, and she presses a button on her desk intercom and says, *Stool please, Esme.*

Patient's name? a younger woman's voice says.

Laboratory stool.

What is this? Some routine they're developing? Johnno's mouth opens to laugh, but he holds it back just in time.

A woman in a white coat comes to the door, suppressing a grin and carrying a lab stool. This, clearly, is my seat. I perch on its edge, my back against the filing cabinet and Joan Shand looks at Johnno. *Tell me a bit about what you have in mind.*

He turns to me. *Jon?*

By now there is an outline of the project in my head, so at least the start of this is easy. She listens, her arms folded across her chest, she looks at her photocopies, makes a dot in the margin with a pencil.

So, with the assays, what do you see as the options?

Well, I think we have to be very careful to pick the right thing. That's where a lot of people might be going wrong. If we're right at all, the rhythm issue is very important. I've seen enough articles now to suggest to me pretty clearly that anyone doing things like twenty-four-hour totals might be wide of the mark. This is the problem I have with measuring metabolites. I mean, the obvious metabolite to measure is urinary six-sulphatoxy melatonin. That's how it seems.

Yes.

But of course the problem is that doesn't really tell us what we want to know.

Isn't there a study suggesting morning urine six-sulphatoxy melatonin is a good indicator of nocturnal peak?

Yeah. One study that I know of. Six subjects, I think.

Other studies don't show that, and even if it's accurate it tells us nothing about the timing of the peak. There's a study showing no seasonal variation of total twenty-four-hour urinary six-sulphatoxy melatonin, despite an average summer to winter difference in peak time of a hundred minutes in thirty normal subjects.

That's a problem. So what do you need? Plasma? Is plasma validated, as far as what you need goes?

Yes. For any particular time it is. I've got studies that show that the plasma melatonin rhythm reflects pineal production and nothing else. And there's no significant storage mechanism, so it's not like the thyroid. When the melatonin's made, it's released.

Yes. With the levels in blood slightly higher than in CSF due to albumin binding, but predictably so.

Therefore if the CSF melatonin is the active melatonin in terms of depression, we get an accurate reflection of its status at any particular moment by measuring plasma levels.

And urine is just too crude, isn't it? Too far down the track.

I think so.

So we need plasma. And accurate serial measurements over the course of the night. How often do you think?

I think at least every hour and a half. I'd like to do it like that and see how it goes. I'd be happy if there was an easier way, like maybe an eleven p.m. measurement, but I can't see that any shortcut would be reliable enough. Not at this stage.

No. So you'd put in a two-way tap before the person went to bed?

Would we? I don't know.

That'd work. And who'd take the blood?

Probably me. Other people, if they were happy to. I'd probably be putting the tap in. The night nursing staff might take the samples. I don't know. We haven't got that sorted out yet.

You'd have to make sure they knew what they were doing. And obviously you'd be collecting in low-lux light to avoid suppressing the melatonin.

Another good reason to use the tap, rather than having to find a vein.

All right. So what we want is a highly accurate way of measuring plasma melatonin. That's it really, isn't it?

Yeah.

And do you have any preference? RIA or HPLC?

I'd be happy with anything that you thought could do the job. People do seem to use either.

Good. Good. I'll start looking into it then.

She smiles again, and shakes our hands when we go.

You two were cooking in there, Johnno says. *It was like watching tennis, the way you were hitting it round.*

What do you think I've been doing in the library? Napping?

Now that would have been impressive. Stringing this along for a month, just to be the best-slept resident in the hospital. You know, I really didn't think it'd get this far. I didn't necessarily think it wouldn't either, but that was strange in there. It made it all seem suspiciously reasonable.

Yeah, I know. I know what you mean. I was thinking, Joan Shand, you know? Joan Shand will tell us one of two things. She could be way ahead of us, and know the whole idea is crap, and know just why it's crap, and I'm going to come out of there feeling like crap. Or she could say, Sorry boys, can't be done. But she wants to do it.

Can't stop it now, then, can you?

22

And he's right. I can't stop it now. So here I am, suddenly in this life made up of blabbing about blow jobs and romancing the hormone of darkness. It's peculiar, but it's all pretty enticing.

On Wednesday it gets better. I'm in the library chasing the word melatonin around and I find an article on jet lag. It's only when I start making notes that I realise how useful it might be.

Melatonin and jet lag

Jet lag, essentially, is the subjective interpretation of the physical rhythm shifts that arise as a consequence of rapid travel across meridians of longitude. While a number of rhythms have been measured (including those of core temperature, melatonin, cortisol, REM sleep, subjective measures of tiredness and others), evidence suggests that REM sleep normalises and the subjective sensation of jet lag lifts as the melatonin works its way back into line. Cortisol takes weeks, others more time or less, but the righting of the melatonin rhythm is the only good fit.

So jet lag, which seemed to be a good example of chronobiology in disarray, might be more, might also involve melatonin directly.

And I remember jet lag, from trips back to the UK to visit family. Feeling heavy and hungover (before I'd ever been hungover), hungry and not hungry, concentrating poorly, and not feeling good.

Thinking about it now, the symptoms of jet lag seem very like the vegetative features of depression. Just a self-limiting syndrome, with a different label. A syndrome that lifts when melatonin normalises.

I look up jet lag, searching for other articles. I find them, and not just articles about what happens to melatonin levels with transmeridian flight. Articles about administering melatonin, giving it as a drug.

Melatonin as a drug

Eight out of ten well volunteers flying from New York to London suffered jet lag when they were given a placebo. Nine of the same ten did not when they took melatonin at the right time.

Half of a group of non-travelling volunteers were given 2 mg of melatonin at five in the afternoon. It doubled their plasma levels, increased early evening fatigue, brought on sleep and had no effect on mood. There were no undesirable side effects. And their own pineal secretion of melatonin advanced by one to three hours.

So melatonin may be much more than just a marker for depression. It may have a role in treatment.

Depression delays the nocturnal melatonin peak by one to three hours. Melatonin given as a drug advances it by the same, at least in the non-depressed. Perhaps a small, regular dose of melatonin in the evenings could retrain the delayed pineal to secrete normally, and perhaps this would treat depression.

Two rows back, a chair scrapes out from behind a desk, and then in again. A large book thumps open, knuckles start cracking, fat, gifted fingers tap on a hard head (perhaps in the unusual rhythm of the Pink Floyd song 'Money', from the legendary album *Dark Side of the Moon*). A pen clicks in and out, in and out. Marlon's arrival takes my mind from melatonin for a second and I realise I'm late for lunch.

Kelly is on days off and I haven't seen her since the weekend, so we've arranged to meet. *Lunch*, she said, *I'll make you lunch*, and I've tried to stay calm, tried to tell myself I'm not DMO so this is fine, not marinara on a Sunday night and its fearful consequences. Besides, I want to see her, I want to talk to her. I call her and tell her I'm on my way.

We sit on the grass outside the Quarters, the side away from the hospital, facing the hedge that separates the Quarters from the street.

You wouldn't believe what I've found, I tell her.

Try me.

So I do. With vigour and detail and a waving chicken drumstick, I tell her about jet lag, I tell her about melatonin the drug, I tell her how it might fit in with what I've been looking at, how big it might be.

And she gives me coleslaw and a bread roll and says, *Why hasn't anyone worked this out before?*

This is what scares me, all of this. The possibility that I'm adding up two and two to make a very large number. There could be some horrible reason why no-one's worked it out before. But maybe not. Maybe I can fit this all together, maybe this will actually get somewhere. The possibilities are pretty amazing.

Well, yeah.

No, really.

Yeah, I'm not disagreeing.

This is something I could do. I could look into this. I could look into this as a job. I could have a job where I investigate all of this. How would that be?

Instead of the sick people business, you mean?

Whatever. Don't you ever have ideas and want to follow them? Don't you ever sometimes get struck by something you really want to do?

Sure.

Like what?

When?

Whenever. Now. The most recent. The most recent thing you thought of that you really wanted to do.

Okay. My degree, maybe.

What degree?

My nursing degree. I figured my training would only get me so far, so I should do something more. So I thought about doing my degree.

Okay, yeah, that kind of thing. I designed a rocket once. Not a good rocket necessarily, but I've got a card from Edward de Bono about it.

Who's Edward de Bono?

Lateral thinking? You know lateral thinking?

Yeah. Said with a shrug, as though she too might have the capacity to substitute yes for no if it seems helpful.

It's his idea. He came up with it. My father sent my rocket design to him when I was five and he sent a card back and it said, 'I like its elemental simplicity and confidence, both of which so easily get lost later on.'

I'm not completely getting this yet. I think I should tell you that now, because the way it's heading I think I could be about to get it less.

No, it's fine. It's easy. This could be my chance. And maybe the melatonin idea is confounding people because at its heart it's so simple, all the connections make themselves so easily. Like a rocket designed by a five-year-old. See? We've got to come up with these things sometimes, and follow them. Take the chance of following them.

But the rocket designed by the five-year-old didn't work. Did it? I mean, if it did, tell me.

No. That is the concern. I used to be fearless, I used to be happy putting any kind of idea out there in case it had something going for it. Not now. But I still have to try this.

She laughs. *Why do you have to try it? Try it if you want, but why do you have to?*

Because it's there?

So are lots of other things. I don't really get all this lateral thinking. What's wrong with what's straight ahead?

Nothing. That's not what I mean.

I'm sure there are plenty of good things straight ahead, she says, and pushes me over onto my back on the grass, her hair blowing across my face.

She clears it away and kisses me, and beyond her there's blue cloudless sky, poinciana branches, my hand holding the chicken drumstick at arm's length so that I don't wipe it all over her.

She laughs, kisses me again. I want to stop her, just to explain something, but I'm not exactly sure what. Not at all sure how.

23

On Monday in the Sunny Garden Rick says to me, *Just for the moment, not another fucking word about melatonin, okay?*

All right, topic of your choice then. Pick a topic, any topic.

I've invited someone round to dinner this Wednesday.

Good topic. Tell me more.

It's the one who helloed me in the lift. I had to deal with her about a matter late last week and I think it went all right.

So what's all right?

Well, I maintained my composure throughout, so that was a good start. And on her desk she had a photo of a cat. Just a cat. No sign of deep human attachment. I think she could be receptive to an offer.

A cat. That's okay. So what's the offer likely to be?

I'm thinking quiche isn't a good idea.

True. Not everyone likes quiche.

It was bad, wasn't it? The quiche was bad.

I wouldn't say bad.

Not good. You wouldn't say good, would you?

What, like, from the food perspective? I'd say consider the wok. The wok offers all kinds of possibilities, requires no special training, looks pretty good.

I can't. I don't relate to the wok. I trash anything I put in there. I see you with the wok and I feel nothing but envy.

I thought that was girls.

Girls? Nothing but wok substitutes.

That's a very interesting view of woks.

Nonetheless, I think it leaves me with bolognaise.

Don't ever be left with bolognaise.

What's wrong with bolognaise?

Everything's wrong with bolognaise. Bolognaise is far too obvious. You can't have any respect for anyone who sleeps with you after bolognaise.

Respecting her is the least of my worries.

Bolognaise is such a dysfunctional bachelor thing. Cooking bolognaise as a first meal is a signal. It says, You should know now that I can only cook bolognaise. And by extrapolation the interpersonal limitations are quite

189

unacceptable. Women know this. The average man who cooks only one meal, that meal being bolognaise, changes his sheets no more than monthly, thinks khaki is a low-maintenance colour for the inside of toilets and treats his women with contempt. Bolognaise is a ploy of the most transparent kind. Any woman who lets you get away with it is morally obliged to condone the rest. So she won't let you get away with it. Don't do the bolognaise.

I'm over the khaki toilet thing now. Totally over it. You think people never change, don't you? And anyway, Jen cooks bolognaise.

That's totally different. Sure it's a signal, but it's not the same signal. It's a gender thing. It's a deliberate choice *not* to establish serious kitchen credentials.

And do you think they get that? The men, do you think they get that?

I'd be surprised. I imagine entire relationships are conducted with Jen, with the boy involved never quite knowing what's going on. Jen is a conundrum. And her boys can't even spell conundrum.

What is it with her and men? What does she have with men that I don't have with women?

I'm assuming that's rhetorical.

Assume it's not. What is it about her?

Well, she's pretty relaxed for a start.

I'm relaxed. I'm relaxed. I'm fine.

Don't squeak. It doesn't become you.

I'm not relaxed?

Not very.

So Jen's relaxed. That's it. How do you make yourself relaxed?

It's tough. First you have to be prepared to give up the almost physiological aura of desperation.

I thought they liked that. I thought it was interesting.

Not very. Not from the point of view of them actually having sex with you. And then, of course, there's the totally separate issue of the Porky Pig doona.

The Porky Pig doona's a problem? I would never have thought it was a problem. That worries me. I thought it was kind of quirky, engaging. It didn't occur to me that it might be a problem. I'm way off the pace here, aren't I? Way off the pace.

He scoops more Mongolian lamb into his bowl and then just stares at it.

For the right girl, I'm sure it's not a problem. Maybe it's just a question of you and the doona finding the right girl.

Do you think so?

24

Late on Wednesday morning Johnno shamelessly takes all three remaining Monte Carlos, lowers himself into the green vinyl armchair near the tearoom window and says, *Glen, I thought we might talk about the melatonin idea. Jon's getting an application together for the Ethics Committee, and we thought it would be good to get the whole ward involved, if everyone's interested.*

The task of outlining the project, as expected, falls to me. They are more interested in the practicalities than the melatonin, since their main concern seems to be that the project might mean more work. We get bogged down talking about specimen collection, until I move things along by saying I'll be here overnight when we have a patient, in case the cannula needs resiting.

Very noble of you, Johnno says when they're back at work and he's making himself a second cup of tea. *Offering to stay overnight.*

It'll be all right. And I had to do something. It was getting stuck there. When it looked like getting them involved meant they'd actually have to get involved.

Yeah. I think they're very keen to offer in-principle support. Doing something is another matter entirely. Most of them are in Nine, after all, because they find the thought of doing things distasteful. So exactly how does the staying overnight plan work? Have you got that covered?

The Dud'll give me a bed. I can just see myself telling him it's part of this, and him nodding and rustling up a bed from somewhere. Besides, if we left it to the night resident, who knows when it'd happen? My guess is it wouldn't be seen as a high priority. I think it is something we have to cover.

You really think the Dud'll give you a bed?

Sure. I can make it sound like dedication to the project. I'm so committed, I need a bed. Shit, I can look so committed he'll give me a room.

A room.

Yeah. Why not? We need a room. We've got lots of articles. We've got a lot of stuff happening. We've got to have a room. He'll understand that. A room with a custom-made sign on the door. How credible would that be? A room with a lockable door and a sign. Credibility and mystique. Think about it. We're ready for this.

Yeah, I think we are.

A room sends out the right signals. We need more than just a smart hypothesis. It's a little too subtle on its own. A room very clearly says you're up there with the big players. Think of the endocrine research going on in Four A. It's supposed to be a pretty big deal, isn't it? I've been up there, and it's nothing special. It's just like a normal ward, except they've got a couple of rooms with custom-made signs on the door.

But Harry's got a syndrome named after him.

Not a syndrome anyone gets outside Four A. Harry's got rooms, with signs. Harry takes up space. That's what gives him credibility.

Like a dog marking out territory.

Exactly. He's got space, and he's got mystique. Think of what goes on in there.

I don't know. I've never been in there. I've never seen the door open.

So don't tell me Harry hasn't got it worked out. It could be nap time in there. There might be nothing in there but a comfy chair and the biggest big-screen TV you've ever seen, Harry, beer in his right hand missing not a ball of the entire summer of cricket, dozing during the drinks breaks. Harry with his feet on the desk watching *The Bridge on the River Kwai* on video all day long and thinking, Hey, good syndrome. Have you noticed how often he struts around whistling 'Colonel Bogey's March'? Who knows what happens in there? A room, a sign, a lockable door. That's all it takes. Whatever happens behind the door is up to Harry.

And I don't know why I'm handling this the way I handled the bolognaise conversation with Rick. This may not be a good idea, may be a little more complicated. Looking at it another way, perhaps I wasn't being entirely fair to Rick, or even to bolognaise.

Paradise, Johnno says distantly, contemplating the endless possibilities offered by a room in a way that suggests there's no turning back. *And when you say big-screen TV, would it have quadrophonic sound?*

Well, we might not get the big-screen TV straight up.

We work up to that. We could probably get a computer and tea and coffee making facilities, and then maybe a bar fridge, but, you know, one thing at a time.

Monte Carlos? Could we get Monte Carlos?

Monte Carlos?

Sure. They just don't last in the ward. Monte Carlos'd be good. In fact, that'd be enough for me. After the crash of '87 I'm a man of small ambitions, you understand that.

I'll do what I can. I'm sure the Dud'd stretch to Monte Carlos. It's all in the wording really, how we handle it in the application.

A room, he says, obviously thinking it over. *A reasonably prominent room with a sign on the door. Some days you can actually feel this becoming important, can't you? People would laugh at us if we didn't have a room. I can see that now.*

When I call Kelly in the Quarters not long after, she says *I'm not sure how having a room makes it a better theory.*

I tell her that's not the point. I tell her I've talked it over with Johnno and we're both pretty sure a room would be good. A room, a sign, and it's probably only a matter of time before I have a syndrome named after me.

I check that she's still okay to come over for dinner tonight and she says *Sure, but could you make it a nice syndrome? Does it have to be something to do with depression?*

I decide to check the library one more time to see if any new articles have come in before I write the Ethics Committee application. Marlon de Lisle is going in as I'm going out and we nearly collide because he has eyes only for his favourite seat, currently occupied by a med student who has no idea of the form.

Why are you in here all the time? he says, contrary to my theory that he has been completely unaware of my presence. *I keep seeing you here. Are you studying for something?*

It's to do with some research, a research project that we're putting together in psych. To do with melatonin, from the pineal, and a role it might have in depression.

Thank god I'm way past the hamster stage, when my principal objective was to understand the connection between furry animals and the rectums of astronauts.

Melatonin? I thought melatonin wasn't up to much. I thought the whole pineal wasn't up to much. I'm basing my exam preparation on the assumption that there's nothing I have to know about melatonin.

I don't think it's a big issue yet. It's still early. I don't think anyone's got anything really conclusive. We're starting by exploring the possibility that it's a marker for depression. Its nocturnal peak may be delayed and lower in people with depression with vegetative features. It's maybe a bit like hibernation in animals. And then we might give people melatonin, eventually, to see if they respond.

You give it to them? You measure low levels and then you give it to them? You can't just do that, can you? Just because you might be measuring some deficiency doesn't mean that topping it up will produce any clinical benefit. You're not saying the low melatonin is actually the cause of the depression, are you?

I don't know. It might be part of it. And anyway, poorly functioning thyroids and pancreases get topped up all the time. Why not the pineal? Melatonin treats jet lag better than anything else, and jet lag's not unlike depression. But giving it's all a way down the track. First we're just looking at it as a marker.

As if there's not enough endocrinology to get on top of already. Well, as long as you don't come up with anything

I have to know within the next couple of months, you can do what you like. It's amazing what you don't keep up with, when you've got your nose stuck in one of these things, he says, and waves his copy of *Harrison's Principles of Internal Medicine,* careful to keep his thumb between the right two pages. *I'd better get to it.* He glares again in the direction of his already occupied seat.

They should put a sign on it, shouldn't they? I suggest to him. Or let you take it home with you.

I don't get home much, he says, and then realises that he can ease up on the glare, that all this mightn't be quite so serious. *But the sign's not a bad idea. Something discreet, a small plaque maybe.*

Discreet, but clear. I don't think that's too much to expect.

He goes off to stalk the med student, to walk to the vicinity of his usual chair with purpose and to stand there saying nothing until the student picks up on the vaguely menacing sense of seniority, gets the picture, apologises, moves.

I'm surprised melatonin was such a blank for Marlon. I probably shouldn't be. A month ago I knew nothing about it, but I knew nothing about a lot of things and I just assumed other people had them covered. So even though he said nothing to reassure me, he didn't know anything that would put me off, either.

When I meet Kelly at five I want to talk about something else, something other than melatonin, the hospital.

As we're driving away I can see the multistorey filling up the rear-view mirror until we turn, and I say to her, Sometimes don't you want to get away from this?

Often. I even live there, remember.

So where would you go? If you could go anywhere, where would you go?

I don't know. Europe? I've never been to Europe. But somehow I don't see myself getting there in the near future. North maybe. North for the winter.

Yeah.

Far ahead of us, quite by coincidence and a couple of thousand feet up, I can see a plane about to push into cloud. And I don't know what I want. I've got psychiatry all lined up, a project underway, Kelly in the passenger seat. For several of the last few years this would have been some kind of dream, closer to perfect than I had any right to expect.

Sometimes Kelly really matters to me. Sometimes I really want to make the melatonin thing work. It even seems important. But sometimes Kelly's just someone on the passenger seat, way outside my head, someone who probably wants clear signals and doesn't always get them. And the whole issue of melatonin seems too big for me, me and my fearful ignorance. Me and my noble offer to stay back nights, my spontaneous theorising about rooms with signs on their doors. Credibility and mystique. All becoming some dumb dare. And they'll give it to me, I bet they will. And what if I'm totally wrong, totally, embarrassingly wrong?

So where would you go? Kelly says. *Where would you go?*

And I don't really have an answer.

I know where I'd be going from, I tell her. It's the to I don't know.

And I think it's Kelly who works out that there's no-one home when we get there, leads the way to my room, says, *We've got to do something about this, you and this mood, wherever it's come from.*

Her hand takes mine, moves it into her clothes and encourages exploration. She pulls my tie off, and still I haven't told her that I never actually undo ties, but this isn't the moment and later I'll forget again. She pulls my shirt down over my shoulders. It's getting dark outside and I watch her in the fading light, the two of us wearing nothing now, her face shadowed by her hair, her pale body moving on top of mine. Getting into a rhythm, saying my name softly and looking down at me, her hands on my chest.

And I think, just on the brink of orgasm, she nearly tells me she loves me, but she stops herself just in time. This is just what I think, from the way she looks when she says my name. But I could be completely wrong. It could be the angle, the light.

Then she's beside me and I'm looking at her dark eyes, kissing her on the mouth.

You have to let me know what's going on, she says. *If there's a problem you have to tell me.*

Yeah. There's nothing going on. Not really. No problem. I'm okay. I'm just not always sure. The melatonin stuff's a good example. It seems like a great idea, but it might be complete crap. Only now it's crap that more people get caught up in every day, and I can't stop it. And if it's crap, it's crap that I started. I could look very dumb.

I think it'll be okay. If it was going to make you look very dumb it would have done that already. You could still be wrong, but that's not the same thing.

I'm not afraid of being wrong.

Aren't you? It's all right if you aren't right all the time. People make mistakes, you know.

I think I make plenty. But thanks.

It's nice to see you excited about things, anyway. When you find out something new. The way you get really focussed on it, and the real world passes you by.

You make me sound like Kierkegaard walking through a flower bed.

I don't know Kierkegaard. I was thinking Elmer Fudd. That's why you can't help but like Elmer Fudd. The way he's so caught up in his own little world.

Elmer Fudd?

Yeah. He's so detached he could get hurt if he wasn't lucky, or if someone didn't look after him.

Who looks after Elmer Fudd?

I'm not saying anyone looks after Elmer Fudd. I'm just saying that some people are sometimes so detached that they don't know how much they need other people.

She kisses me again and I watch her eyes when our faces stay close after. I want to stay with my arms around her a while, stay lying here next to her doing nothing, stay in the room here with her for a long time, stay with my fingers in the mess of her hair.

Enough fuddling, she says. *We should probably get moving.*

Rick arrives, before we've been able to do anything to make our recent activities a little less obvious.

Thanks, guys, he says. *When I mentioned making a good impression on this girl it wasn't flushed cheeks and pheromones I had in mind.*

Come on, Rick. She has to know this is a place where passionate acts are a genuine option.

Is it safe to sit you two next to each other or would it be better to separate you by a couple of metres? You understand that groping at the table will not create the ambience I require.

I think we'll be fine. For the moment anyway.

Despite our commitment to refrain from groping there is an ambience problem most of the evening. By the time Julie, Rick's target for the night, is five minutes late, he's convinced she isn't coming, pacing up and down and carrying with him a tension that almost smells. And when she tells him, shortly after arriving, that she's lactose intolerant, he nods a little too much, blinks quite excessively and convinces no-one when he goes back into the kitchen saying, *No problem.*

I follow, offering to help him and he's staring down at the stove muttering, *White sauce. I've got a fucking white sauce happening here and try doing one of those without dairy.*

He beats his head softly against the wall, declines all offers of assistance, pours the only perfect white sauce he's ever made down the sink.

This is bad, he says. *This is bad.*

Easy boy. You can save it. We'll stall, you sauce.

Okay. He flicks through a recipe book. *Okay. I can save it.*

He doesn't. And the perfect white sauce is a secret known only to the two of us as he hands out the plates of chicken breast surrounded by small brown lumps.

I ask him what the small brown lumps are and he says, *Sauce. New sauce. I didn't have all the ingredients, but there's no lactose in there. Guaranteed.*

Sorry, Julie says, looking down at her plate and feeling that she drove him to this.

Rick knows he's behind, and he's never good when he's behind. He sits as though he wired his jaw in the kitchen, wired his whole face into a desperate sweaty grin, and he keeps kicking me under the table whenever there's a lull in the conversation. Long periods pass with him saying not a word.

We all try hard. Even Julie tries hard, and I don't think she's got any interest in him at all.

I ask Jen how things are with her thesis and she gives

me a look that seems to say, *Surely the evening's not going so badly that we have to resort to this.* But she knows just how badly the evening's going, and knows we have to resort to anything.

I provoke her to quite a level of detail. I try to draw the others in, and I fail. Rick sweats, grins. Julie nods politely, fiddles with her fork until it arranges the small brown lumps on her plate into a letter J without her even knowing it. And Kelly says, *It sounds a bit too much like post modernism for my liking.*

To which Jen says, *That's a good point. This is exactly what worries me. This is exactly my fear. Looking as though I'm aligned with some discourse, just going through this as an exercise to lead to a degree. It may be post modernist, but I don't want it to get lost in that. I don't want to look as though I'm just fitting in with a trend. Do you think there's merit in the idea though? Do you think something worthwhile can be done using this approach? I want to do a good job with this. I want to get it right.*

Kelly looks at her for a moment, saying nothing. Jen, I think, takes this as a pause for thought. *Sure,* Kelly says eventually. *Yeah. I'm not quite sure what you mean by right, though.*

Well, of course you aren't. You can't be, can you? As if there's any right in a post-modern world. You can't even be right any more. I don't know what I'm going to do. Maybe I could talk to you when I've done a bit more work on it. Could I do that?

Yeah, Kelly says, obviously hoping it never happens. *That'd be good.*

Rick watches this without listening. Sits back hoping Julie will manage to find a good time for herself among it all, and will somehow come to the realisation that he is therefore desirable. He watches our plates and I'm sure sees few signs of enthusiasm for the meal. He drinks wine and begins to laugh inappropriately at times, and to interrupt conversations with long, boring stories about work. And he knows the harm of this, even as he's doing it, but he can't stop himself.

After Julie has gone he just says, as though it's all my fault, *I knew I should have cooked the bolognaise,* and he goes and lies on his bed with his pillow over his face.

Rick . . .

It's too late. It's done now. I can't talk about it any more.

I was just wondering if you wanted any downward pressure on the pillow.

Thank you, but no. If I was planning suicide I'd just be scavenging the sauce from everybody's plates, wouldn't I?

Who would have guessed? Kelly says later in my room. *You aren't even the saddest boy in the house.*

Poor bastard. You don't know how much I want his luck to change.

Yeah, it'd be nice.

It'd be much better than nice. He's really dragging me down.

She laughs.

What? You didn't think I was sorry for him, did you?

She laughs again and hits me with a pillow. *Selfish and proud of it,* she says. *How unattractive.*

No, no. Not selfish. Thoughtless. I'd go for thoughtless. Inconsiderate, even.

She takes another swing at me with the pillow.

Okay, selfish. A bit selfish. But a nice guy at heart. Many desirable qualities and a few forgivable imperfections.

You'll admit to imperfections?

Well, you have to, don't you?

So name them.

Name them?

Okay, name three.

I can't think of any. So there's one. Lack of insight. Lack of insight and not as broad across the shoulders as some. That'd be about it. Frequently misunderstood, but that's an error at the other end. That's not my fault. I mean well.

You mean well?

I never cause harm deliberately.

So does that mean it's okay?

It means it's just thoughtlessness, and I've already admitted to that. I am entirely without malice, and that's got to be a plus. Anyway, what about you?

What about me?

You have no imperfections?

Feel free to name them.

You actually like Elmer Fudd. I think you might actually like him.

That's just a thing. It's not an imperfection.

Where I come from it's pretty close.

Okay, I don't get some things about you. Is that an imperfection? Parts of you are locked in there maybe, and I haven't worked them out yet. We don't think quite the same. You're lateral, and I'm more straight ahead. Now would that be just a thing, or an imperfection?

Just a thing. Surely just a thing. Normal variation. You couldn't be penalised because you didn't design a rocket at the age of five. Besides, you had it happening with the post-modern stuff tonight.

Any more of that and I might begin to think I know what I'm talking about.

But that's how it works. Everyone fakes it, just in slightly different ways, and with varying degrees of comfort. I think that's how post modernism operates. And every now and then you make a new word out of a few old ones. That always impresses.

As if there's any need for new words.

She shivers. With the clear night sky it's quickly getting cooler and we move into bed for the warmth.

I like it here, she says. *And some nights in the Quarters when there's no-one else around and I go to bed early I could just about cry.* Said in a slightly self-mocking tone, as though she caught it on the way out when it was about to sound a little too serious. *I should get out of there. I should share a flat with people, or something. You just shouldn't live where you work. So for me this is getting away, even if it's not exactly Europe. This is good.*

We stay close, stay warm. And I'm still awake a while after she falls asleep, her arm over my chest, her breathing on my neck, her left leg crossed over mine at the ankle.

I move in even closer, put my arm around her, kiss her head.

She doesn't wake.

25

In the morning I go into the bathroom and Rick is rummaging around in the drug-free sample box.

Is there any part of your body you don't dominate pharmacologically?

Is there a problem with that? I thought that's what pharmacology was for. I abhor nature. Look what nature did for me. A glass of red wine and my sinuses close over. All said with two Teldane clamped firmly between his front teeth. *How do you think it went last night, really?*

I think the dose of Teldane is one tablet twice a day.

One doesn't touch me any more, he says almost heroically, as though his body fights it off, as though Teldane is an anaconda rather than an antihistamine. *So how do you think it went?* I can't believe he's revisiting this already. Prepared to give it another go, in case last night's assessment was a little harsh. *I was hoping it would be great, obviously, and I know it wasn't. It wasn't great, I can accept that. But it wasn't too bad, was it? How do you think it went?*

I'm not sure, I tell him.

Not that the words come easily. I'm as sure as I can be that it wasn't good. I should say, Crash and burn. I should say, The foreseeable future holds little for you, save yellow gloves, loneliness and the abuse of expensive prescription drugs.

Instead I say, She didn't really give much away, did she?

He likes this, takes it with him to think over while he slips the cartoon silk around his neck, sings the theme song from 'Gigantor' deep and low, but without the resonance of a man with open sinuses.

By evening he's working it out.

I didn't hear from her today, he says. *Not a thing, not a word, she didn't call. Crash and burn, Jon-boy. Crash and fucking burn. That's what I'm thinking.*

That's a fairly harsh assessment.

It's the way it is. I knew it was bad, and it was bad. You might have thought it was okay, but it was bad. And don't do the plenty more fish in the sea remark. My mother would do that. Give it to me straight.

It was fairly bad.

Oh no, really? I was hoping she just had a busy day today. Oh no, fairly bad. You think it was fairly bad?

Well, let's look to the future, I tell him, figuring that, when it comes to the immediate past, I obviously don't have the right answer. I've got an idea, and I think it's a good one. Don't start with dinner. Dinner makes you tense, and that's not helpful. How about a cup of coffee? How about something like, Do you want to go for coffee sometime? Try it now. Say it now, calmly, as though you do it all the time and your life doesn't depend on it.

It's deceptively simple.

That's perhaps its best feature. That's one of the main things that put it ahead of brown sauce. And what was it that made it brown, anyway?

Fucked if I know. It didn't have any brown ingredients. Combustion? It did combust for a moment. Do you want to go for coffee sometime?

Sure. That was good. I'd go for coffee. It just slipped in there, didn't it? It was easy.

Yeah. I think I'll write it on all my cuffs.

So he still doesn't quite get it. He still manages to be deceived by the deceptively simple, but if I've talked him out of dinner, I've done a good thing. If he doesn't begin with a frontal assault using sorbothane quiche or combustible sauce or his uniquely dire interpretation of bolognaise, maybe he's got a chance. And where did this dinner obsession come from? Is this his mother again?

On Friday the project application is nearly done. I sit with Johnno in his room finalising the details as the dull murmur of the Dubois ward round proceeds on the other side of the wall.

You'd better put the two of us and Joan Shand down as co-researchers, he says, *with you as the contact. We can see if anyone else is interested as we go. I'd like to have at* least one of the registrars in, but I just don't know that either of them'd be right.

We'll manage. We'll probably only have one patient at a time. We can bring them in under you, and I can put them through whatever depression scale we're using on the day of admission and I can site the cannula.

And then retire gracefully to the room. Which, may I say, on reading the application appears to be an essential element of the project.

Absolutely.

You know, reading this through, I think we're actually going to get the room. However vaguely ludicrous that is. I think I wouldn't like to have you trying to sell me aluminium siding.

I don't think I'd like to try to sell you anything.

I drop the application off to the Dud's secretary at lunchtime, make sure it's on the agenda for the next meeting and play half a dozen mediocre games of Galaxion. When I get back to the ward the registrars have each done one of the two admissions that were waiting for me.

Certain remarks were made, Glen says. *Remarks of the Now we don't seem to have a resident kind, but Johnno just told them it'd be good for them, since they have to be able to do a physical examination for the college exams.*

So how did they take it?

Like medicine, he says, and laughs. *Don't worry. It was fine. Helen'll be doing the exam next year so she didn't mind at all. Dean was less than enthusiastic, but then, enthusiasm's not his strong point, is it?*

So how fine was it, really?

Don't worry. It's not like they're overworked. They just took one each after the Dubois round and Helen's off now doing a consult in the multistorey and Dean's at

Outpatients. They did ask if you could order the blood tests. I don't think there was anything special though.

Order the blood tests?

Obviously beneath them.

I decide that, if this is some feeble-minded power play, I'm not buying into it. They can win. I put in a high-quality half-hour of resident work, the blood tests, medication sheets for the weekend, another failed attempt to contact Podiatry. I walk around the ward chatting to people to see that I'm missing nothing, and I am persuaded to play table tennis.

This might seem like a much better deal than doing the admissions, or doing real multistorey resident work with its chronic overload and occasional life-and-death moments, but since I'll be DMO on Sunday it's not hard to persuade myself that guilt is quite unnecessary. Half the multistorey will be mine then. And the table tennis is close, but I get there 21–14 in the third.

The winner and still champion, my gracious opponent declares, and raises my bat hand in the air to scattered applause.

When I get home there's a parcel from my parents from somewhere in France, an Easter parcel, apparently. In my family this means just one thing. Underpants.

Easter, in my family, is traditionally the season of the pant. I don't know if this is some Christian thing, an impossibly baggy, sternly reinforced symbol of newness (On the third day he rose again, changed his underpants, cleaned his teeth and . . .), or if it just evolved in my mother's head. At least it's not Christmas. I'm not sure that the chocolate money would have survived.

Along with the underpants and a cheery Happy Easter!

note from my mother is a postcard from my father, with the undies folded around it as though it's in some way fragile. A scenic view of Banyul-sur-Mer, with a small biro cross over their pension and an arrow pointing to the station.

Arrived in B-s-M last p.m. Thought about going into Spain. Thought better of it. Managed a sleeper gratis from Lyon to Marseilles. Did you know this is one end of the Pyrenees walk? Maybe next year ... Can't work out which way would be best. W->E? E->W? Cheers. Dad.

Managed a sleeper gratis from Lyon to Marseilles is not, of course, merely a piece of news. From my father it is a boast, another in a long line of small triumphs.

My father, who wangles upgrade after upgrade simply by wearing a suit and being middle-aged and British. My father, who approaches the counter this way, has Doctor on his ticket and tells airline after airline about the problem he had last time with a nearby passenger's container of orange juice, the discomfort, the dry cleaning. *And I just wonder if you can assure me that it won't happen this time. I just wonder if there might be any arrangement you might make that might make it less likely.*

So he pays economy and travels business and sometimes first, all because of a story he once made up about orange juice, told with only minor variations.

But this isn't just about travel. It's a lifestyle. He is regularly engaged in unsolicited communication with the CEOs of major organisations, making minor complaints or offering detailed but gratuitous advice. He always gets a reply. He usually receives material benefit. Free bottomless coffee with any muffin purchase, in perpetuity. That kind of deal. One of them visited him at home. Another, after a few letters each way, said a seat on the board wouldn't be out of the question.

He calls these occurrences results, and he likes getting

results. A room for the melatonin project. That would be a result.

So they proceed through Europe, my mother readying herself to talk about fruit flies in London, my father visiting one CEO after another, this time as part of a project assessing their use, or lack of use, of information technology. I just hope he doesn't expect them to be like him.

It's amazing I can cope in the outside world at all, coming from this stock.

26

The DMO Sunday slots into its usual unappealing routine from the start. I spend four and a half hours chronically behind and then I decide it's not worth the anguish, and I give myself twenty minutes for lunch in the dining room with Kelly.

I ladle as much beef stroganoff onto my plate as it can hold and we take a fork each and approach it from opposite sides.

She asks me if I have plans for dinner, which, not surprisingly, I don't, but I tell her the way the day's looking any dinner plan isn't likely to work out.

A surgical procedure comes along and proves this right. Shane Sandercock, buck's party survivor and now happily married surgical registrar, calls me shortly before any dinner plan would have taken effect and says, *Mate, I've got a pretty acute abdomen in Cas and I think we've got to go in and take a look.*

I meet him in theatre and he's already standing at the

sink and scrubbing, yellow iodine-stained water running from his elbows. I ask him what he thinks it's likely to be and he says, *Perforated duodenal ulcer, I reckon. But we'll see, won't we?*

It doesn't take long to work out that he's right and while he's deciding how to handle it I'm making the most of this opportunity to switch my brain off, slipping very easily into a welcome period of mid-procedure vacancy, holding onto a sucker with one hand and a retractor with the other. Thinking about the Black Widow (and whether this might be the very Richardson retractor), my list of things to do, DMO Sundays.

I wonder if Kelly cooks marinara. It wouldn't have felt good if I'd buckled tonight, taken the dinner option and she'd served marinara.

Standing retracting and sucking encourages vacancy in the best of us. Shane, for all his faults, at least acknowledges my right to vacancy, and doesn't expect me to be interested. Doesn't do the Big Surgeon thing and interrupt the noises he's making to accompany 'Smoke on the Water' to ask me to name the immediate anatomical relations of the first part of the duodenum.

There are times, though, when it's a close call, when I'd almost rather go, Look, if I offer to name all the anatomical relations of the first part of the duodenum, will you give us a few seconds of peace?

Shane has a pathological attachment to classic rock and as he's in charge he gets to pick the music. What he doesn't seem to understand is that this does not give him the right to do what he's doing now, something he would probably call singing along. Making noises intended to bear some resemblance to the definitive instrumental breaks of the seventies. It's not words, it's not singing and it's probably good that Marlon de Lisle never has to assist him in theatre. Never has to say, *Listen arsehole, I didn't play it that way so you could murder it in some different key over a perfed ulcer, okay?*

Came within a bee's dick of something important here, he says, leaving the guitar part alone for a moment. *What do you reckon that'd be? Gastroduodenal artery?* And that's the closest we get to discussing anatomy. He's still some way short of being a big surgeon, or a reasonable musical instrument.

'Riders on the Storm' begins and he makes noises in time with the organ parts. In time with them, but not like them, more like a distant misfiring pool filter than a melody. We oversew the perforation and wash out as well as we can.

I'll close and write it up, if you like, he says. *You've probably got a lot of shit building up in the wards.*

I check my beeper when I get back to the change room and I've missed a Code Blue in a medical ward. I call switch and they tell me it was more than half an hour ago, so the medical registrar and resident must have covered it. I grab a handful of sandwiches from the theatre tearoom and eat as many of them as I can while walking slowly back to the multistorey. Four C pages while I'm still in the corridor. Seven pages before I get to Four C.

It takes a couple of hours to catch up with everything the medical DMO hasn't done while supposedly covering for me, and it's after eleven when I'm riding the lift down to ground with the big, brown, vinyl armchairs of the Quarters and bad TV on my mind. Marlon de Lisle gets in at One, looking more sullen than usual.

I ask him how things are going and he says, *Don't ask.*

What was the Code earlier?

He shakes his head. *An old guy, regular respiratory patient, came in yesterday with a load of green pus in his* lungs, which he couldn't clear because of a stroke he had a while back. Which also stops him talking.

He doesn't sound good.

He does the crossword every day, according to the nursing home.

Quick or cryptic?

They didn't say. Anyway, he was started on IV antibiotics but he got worse, so the DMO got me to see him today. I cleared some of the pus with a sucker and he looked a lot better, so I told the sister, If there's any problem with this guy, suction. Okay? Just suction and more suction. We clear the pus, we let him breathe, we give the antibiotics a chance. And if you're worried, call the DMO straight away, don't wait till he goes flat. And call me before you call a Code Blue. So someone called a Code while she was at dinner. I was in Seven. Miles away. And by the time I got there he had an enrolled nurse on his chest, and every one of his ribs was broken. So his chest is just one big flail segment and he can't breathe at all.

He's got no chance, has he?

No. No chance. He's in ICU, but he'll never get out. We might have sorted out the pneumonia, but his ribs'll never heal. He's going to die with that flail segment. He'll never get off the ventilator, will he? They'll give him a few days, and then they'll let him slide. This is not an appropriate death. This is not an unresponsive cardiac arrest. This is not some guy coming in with an advanced malignancy and getting morphine.

27

As usual, at home after a DMO shift, I don't sleep right away. I lie there telling my stupid body about the circadian consequences of staying awake all night, but it takes a while to listen.

Marlon's right. Sure the guy was old and crumbly, but he had a chance till his ribs got broken. This isn't a heart stopping because its time has come. Marlon's right to be pissed off. *He does the crossword every day.* A clear signal from the nursing home not to be deceived by the lack of talk. A clear signal that they wanted him fixed, wanted him back.

I don't know if I can remember seeing this guy during my respiratory term or not. I probably didn't. I should remember a patient who didn't speak, no matter how the term was going.

My problems in respiratory began when the other resident got chicken pox and had to be excluded from contact with anyone with a fragile immune system. When he came back near the end of the term and saw how it had gone he said, *To think I couldn't go near them in case I killed them all. Pretty ironic, really.*

The respiratory ward wasn't the same by then. We had seven patients. We'd peaked at fifty-two at the start of the term. The ward usually had forty-something patients, and they'd never had seven before. Admittedly, we couldn't hold it under ten for long, but most of the time we kept it below fifteen.

One of the reasons for this was Gary Costello. The Wall. Gary was the toughest registrar the world has ever known. He had passed all his exams and was doing his time before taking up a position in America. He had no inclination to work and therefore turned down all possible admissions coming in through Cas, and sloughed patients to other units whenever it was remotely possible. Nothing got by him, people started calling him The Wall, he took it as a sign of respect. Better still, surrender. It only spurred him on.

He'd stride down to Cas, and browbeat someone else into taking the admission. I went with him once, when he got called about a regular respiratory patient who'd come in marginally more short of breath than usual. I made the mistake of saying, This one's going to be pretty hard to slough and he just said, *Oh yeah? Come with me.* By the time we got to Cas I'm sure he was two inches taller, bigger all over, looking dangerous and clearly taking nothing.

He went up to the resident and said, *Are you seriously telling me that you've categorically excluded a cardiac cause for this shortness of breath? Are you guaranteeing me that this patient hasn't had an infarct or isn't in failure? It all looks pretty general medical to me.* And he flipped the patient's X-rays up onto the viewing box and said, had the arrogance to say, *This guy's lungs are so shot I don't know how you can think you can exclude heart failure with X-rays like these. This is what you're going to do. You're going to call the general medical unit of the day. You're going to tell them I've reviewed the patient and I'm not taking him. And you can say we might consider doing a consult in a week or so if they haven't got to the bottom of it. Sound okay?*

And he was laughing before we left Cas.

Often he wouldn't let them in at all. He'd say they were using the place like a hotel, and that was all bullshit as far as he was concerned. *A change of a few per cent in their lung function and in they come. It's a bloody joke.* And he'd bounce them right out the door with adjustments to their medication, saying to them, *You don't really want to be in here, sir. You'll do much better at home.* Sometimes he'd even shut the cab door behind them when they left.

It was like watching evil genius showing off, watching The Wall at work. The day a more junior medical registrar reminded him that he only had nine patients, Gary just stared at him and said, *That's about nine too many.*

But we were never quite going to get to zero. Gary could keep the patients with end-stage emphysema at bay, but cancer wasn't going to be that easy, not primary lung cancer anyway. Gary thought lung cancer should go to oncology, but he was overruled by the respiratory physicians who wanted to retain at least some patients. So he decided instead that cancer was residents' work.

This left us, and then just me, in charge of the chemo, writing up drugs we'd never heard of before. Copying from the protocols in the ward office, working out doses based on body weight, putting in the IV line and getting the consent form signed. Most patients would be out in a day, some in three days, depending on the protocol.

Occasionally one needed something more involved, like a drug that had to be administered directly into the chest cavity. This took an intercostal catheter, a catheter passed between two ribs and fixed in place with a skin suture. The first time I did one I watched my gloves filling with my own sweat, felt the sweat prickling in my hair as I pushed the tube in, drove the firm plastic deeper into the chest. And I was so concerned with the anatomy, so concerned with getting it right and harming nothing, that I inexplicably tied the suture in a bow once the catheter was in.

I should have known better. Sure I wanted it to be easy

to tie off when the catheter came out, but my shoelaces come undone all the time. It was madness to trust a bow.

And about thirty seconds after I'd syringed the drug down it, my first intercostal catheter was loose in the patient's pyjamas, swinging by its one saggy suture, and the drug had poured out into the bed.

Within minutes, men in Hazardous Materials suits arrived to take the mattress away and burn it. It was a learning experience on two counts. I learned that the passage of the tube into the chest is not the end of the task and I also worked out, from the suits, what HAZMAT meant.

HAZMAT was something I'd seen on a building next to the chapel and, until the catheter incident, I'd sincerely believed it was a Yiddish word denoting a small place of worship. Even now, and even though no-one ever found out, a moment's contemplation of this makes me quite uncomfortable. If I ever want to remind myself that I might not know as much about something as I think I do, Hazmat does it for me every time.

Hazmat, a Yiddish word for the learned humility that comes from knowing one has over-reached oneself, but has been fortunate enough to avoid extensive public mockery.

What if someone had said to me, at any time during my first ten months here, *Could you tell me where the chapel is?* And I'd said, Sure, it's up there, next to the Hazmat. And I know I would have done the accent too, starting with a husky middle-eastern H, leaning on the second syllable and making it all as multicultural as possible.

HAZardous MATerials.

So when I think melatonin, I have every reason to be afraid. I could have a great theory, but I might be over-reaching again. And if melatonin itself seems like a hazmat, expecting to be given a room for the project is surely far worse, a greater vanity set to come unstuck.

Of course, on a day-to-day basis, library time spent pondering melatonin feels far better than shoving stiff plastic tubes into frail old chests. Knowing you're causing pain, knowing they won't live long anyway, wondering if you're doing any good. I couldn't do that for forty years. I could hardly do it for two months. Even when I became confident and my knots could be relied upon.

Not that I did many intercostal catheters. Most of the cancer patients weren't coming in for chemo, not even the regular intravenous chemo. They were at the end, in pain. They didn't need a procedure. There wasn't a procedure I could do that would help.

They weren't going to last long and they usually knew it, but they weren't coping. Everything that could be done had been done, and some of them were in a lot of pain. So that's what I focussed on, that's what I worked out I could do something about. They didn't want to die in pain and in fear, and I could make sure they didn't, just about every time. A pattern developed, irresistibly. With practice, it became easy.

We'd talk when they came in. I'd ask them how they were feeling. I'd say to them, This is not the time to be holding back, and I'll hold nothing back. You can trust me with that. I want to get on top of this pain quickly, and I can almost guarantee that we will. We'll use morphine now, since other things aren't working. Morphine beats pain, you just need enough of it. It's usually written up as something you can have every three or four hours, but you can have it whenever you need it. I've explained that to the staff. All you have to do is ask. So you won't be waiting for pain relief. If you want it, it's yours. It's up to you. We'll get on top of this pain, and stay on top of it.

And there are three effects of morphine that you should know about. The first is the pain relief, and it's very good at the pain relief. The second is its ability to induce a mild state of euphoria. The third is that, in high enough doses, it stops you breathing. How do you feel about those effects?

They all said *Good,* and they trusted me, and I relieved their pain.

And they died like I knew they would, like they knew they would. They knew the deal, swapping weeks of pain for perhaps days of comfort. They drifted off, into some kind of peace away from the pain. They took the morphine and the fear went away, and they had lucid days to say goodbye, most of them, and then they were gone.

I got to work it out, how long they'd live, after a while. It all became so familiar. I could predict it.

Their families brought gifts, and thanked me more than I could stand. The use of morphine in the whole hospital increased by thirty per cent late last year, and all of that because it more than tripled in the respiratory ward. And one of the respiratory physicians said to me *This is very good. There is no excuse for pain. Not once they come in here. This is very good.*

That was the other part of the Dud's autopsy talk. The reassurance. His need to confirm that this was good work, and that the death certificates were spot on.

It's the cancer, he said. *It's not appropriate to mention terminal pneumonias or heart failure or any understandable effects of treatment. It's the cancer that's doing it. And it's been a bad month for cancer.*

We called it vitamin M, the morphine. Vitamin M, and we were treating vitamin M deficiency. And it was the best thing we could do, sometimes the only thing we could do. It's strange to be so powerful, and so powerless, both at once.

28

When I get home on Tuesday, Kelly's already there. In the kitchen with Rick. Being calm, reassuring, encouraging a strange kind of domesticity, and gentleness with pastry.

I don't think that I was expecting her to be here. Not that it's anything but fine that she is here, helping Rick through a recipe or two. And not that she has to talk to me about it in advance. So what is the problem then, if there's clearly no problem?

She's helpful, Rick says. *Properly helpful. Not like a lot of people. I have a rapport with pastry now.*

Mind if I watch?

Watch, Kelly says, *but say only nice things.*

Hey Rick, the flour in your hair makes you look quite distinguished.

That's not nice enough. Even when you're being nice you're not actually nice, are you?

She's on to you, says her distinguished flour-dusted apprentice. *And anyway, you're not exactly Mr Perfect in the kitchen, are you? Mr Mushrooms-up-the-extractor-fan.*

You told him about that?

It's only fair.

I hope you told him it was only because you were inter-fering with my genitals at the time.

No, I was keeping that to myself.

Behind her, Rick, in a baffled kind of admiration, gives a hint of an oral sex gesture. I'll have to correct this later. I'm just not that good. Not so good that I could wok with a distraction of that magnitude.

I pour myself a glass of wine, and I put the wok out of

my mind, but the Kelly parts I keep thinking of. The cooking lesson goes on and all I can think of is that I want to be in bed with Kelly. I want Rick and the meal to be gone, and I want it to be just the two of us. It's been days.

Jen comes home, with a boy. A boy who doesn't know he's here solely because the coin fell the right way, and we eat. Minestrone first, and then apple pie.

I told you this'd be good, Kelly says to Rick when we're all going for seconds of the minestrone.

It seemed too easy, he says. *But, you know, I think I could do this. Solo, I mean. I think this could be my best recipe now. I think I never have to win hearts with bolognaise again. I could be a lot less tense with minestrone.*

And the bread rolls, Kelly says. *Nice crusty bread rolls hot from the oven. Remember the bread rolls.*

Girls like bread rolls?

Yeah. It can be those little things that make the difference. This is what worries me. See, I just didn't get that.

You didn't get bolognaise either. The principle is straightforward. You serve bolognaise, you look very limited, and your objectives are questionable. You serve minestrone, things are a bit better. You add the hot crusty bread rolls, and you look like an individual. You look like a man at ease in his kitchen. You're saying, Hey, I thought I might do us up some minestrone tonight, and then out comes the tray with the hot crusty bread rolls.

Credibility, he says, thoughtfully. *Desirability.*

Even in oven mitts, both of the above. And no tension in the air at all. Can you feel that? Minestrone, bread, wine, relaxed conversation. How much better is that?

Later, after the apple pie has also met with modest acclaim and it's just the two of us washing up in the kitchen, he says, *So, do I do the apple pie too?*

My feeling is maybe not. Not that it wasn't a fine apple

pie, but I'm thinking cut down the variables. Keep it simple, but appealing.

Simple, but appealing. That's the bread rolls, isn't it?

Exactly. But still, I think, pace yourself. I'm still thinking coffee to start with, something like that rather than dinner.

Yeah, I don't want to get over-confident.

Round about ten-thirty I wonder how his confidence is going, while Jen's bed is rhythmically squeaking its way to climax and he's alone in his room across the hallway.

I think Rick really appreciated that, I tell Kelly. You coming over, the cooking, all of that.

Yeah. It was probably a change for him, doing anything here without you messing with his head.

What do you mean?

Bolognaise. There was some theory about bolognaise, wasn't there? Something that really didn't sound helpful.

I stand by the bolognaise theory. Besides, Rick's bolognaise could kill a dog and his head's a mess already.

I don't think the theory helped, you know.

It's a good theory. Bolognaise is so ill-considered.

When did it all get to be this strategic? You're telling Rick to relax, but you seem to think the whole thing has to work to a plan.

Well, it does, to some degree. You don't just get naked and happen to bump into each other. You notice someone, you plan. You've got an outcome in mind, and I think that's fine.

I don't like the sound of it. It's pretty clinical.

There's nothing clinical about noticing someone, about noticing some seemliness that you mightn't have noticed before, and then acting on it.

But what do you mean by plan? What do you mean by outcome?

Well, nothing necessarily specific.

You said, You've got an outcome in mind. It sounds specific.

It's not specific. What are you getting at?

For a while she says nothing. *I'm just being dumb. Of course you think about things. Of course outcomes cross your mind. It's just, the way you tell it to Rick, it sounds like a board game. Like it matters as much as a board game. It doesn't sound like there's another person involved at all.*

Well, there isn't, for Rick. For Rick it's all theory at the moment. Theory, a box of tissues, his own two hands and a rapidly fatiguing imagination.

You really aren't very nice, are you?

If I showed him any sympathy he'd give it all away. I have to treat him like a contender, like a player with a run of bad luck. Hell of a long run of bad luck, though.

There's that game thing again.

It's metaphorical. It's the way I have to handle things with Rick. As though it's luck, and it could change any time. And I can't take it too seriously. That'd only depress him. He'd think he was nowhere near it.

I don't get you sometimes.

What's not to get? What do you mean?

I don't know what you feel sometimes. I don't know how you think. I don't know about this plan thing. Are we a plan? Do we have a plan and I don't know about it?

No. There isn't a plan. Please, relax. This is not a planned thing. It's good. I want it to keep being good. The last thing we need is a plan. I mean, if I had some kind of plan when I became aware of your seemliness, it's happening. This is good, you being here, all of this.

So what's it like when I'm not here?

Roomier.

223

Thanks. Probably colder, too. You can't take this seriously, can you?

How seriously do I need to take it? One of the things I like about it is the lack of analysis. The fact that I'm not sweating it out, thinking all the time, What does she really mean by that? It's one of your qualities. You are calm, you are not bizarre, you don't drive me crazy with elliptical remarks that torpedo me with sub-text.

Tell me what that means and I could.

Don't. You don't mess with my head. I can lie here all night with you, thinking that you aren't messing with my head and it makes me feel comfortable. Everything's good, and it doesn't benefit from detailed analysis. It's good as it is, and my head's enough of a mess anyway.

So you want me here?

Of course I want you here. Even earlier this evening, watching you and Rick in that little domestic pastry-making scene, the bit of it that I wanted was you. I wanted to be here with you. I wanted there to be no-one else around.

It's not a big bed. There'd be no room.

If I said that, there'd be trouble. If I interrupted you at a moment of self-disclosure there'd be hell to pay.

Yeah, but I said it, so it's okay. I have no torpedoes, remember?

I have no torpedoes either. You should stop worrying about torpedoes. I'm much more direct than you think.

So get back to the nice bit.

What do you think I am? I can't just switch the nice bit on and off like that.

You're quite a troubled boy, aren't you?

Deeply. Deeply troubled. And that's the way I like it. I'm a great respecter of anguish. If I wasn't deeply troubled, what would I be? I'm not at all sure of the alternatives.

The nice bit. Get back to the nice bit. You could try that more. There are people out there who don't mind nice, you know.

She moves closer to me, up against me. Her skin is warm, smooth. We take it slowly tonight, and it's good. Slowly and quietly, without the odd speed of last time, last week before brown sauce.

And at the end I don't want to let her body go.

In the early morning, not long before dawn, I wake because I'm cold. Somehow the doona has been tossed aside, kicked away in a dream, and the sheet with it. The moon is over the house next door, shining in on Kelly and she's pale and cold and elegant, lying there with nothing on. Lying on her side, facing me with one knee bent, her smooth curves, her crazy hair lit like a veil, hiding her face.

She's breaking out in goosebumps, starting to stir. I pull the doona back up over us and she settles again, reaches out towards me and sticks her index finger in my eye. I shut it just in time, and the yelp doesn't seem to wake her. I go back to sleep, in only minor discomfort.

She stays the next night too. Comes to the hospital with me in the morning and then home again after work. She calls it her weekend, and she says it's nice to go away for most of the weekend, to spend time out of the Quarters.

Wednesday night we have cocktails. I drink too much, and too quickly, but she says she doesn't mind, and she laughs at the idiot things I seem to be saying, even as she puts me to bed and goes back to the others to keep on drinking.

He's hopeless, she says, and Rick says, *Hopeless, I can't understand the attraction,* and she just laughs again. Then I sleep.

29

It's Sunday morning, dark and cold again, when I wake from a dream that became so cold I thought I was only cold bones, lying here. I'm completely uncovered and Kelly's there next to me, breathing calmly. Everything is silent and the bone-cold dream is gone but there's still a chill in the night and there are parts of me that will surely never feel warm again.

She has got to develop better doona habits. When I'm in the bed alone it stays on all night. When it's the two of us it never seems to, and I feel the cold first. But tonight I can't blame it all on her imperfect doona etiquette.

We went out, hours ago, I drank too much. So did she. We played pool somewhere with some people from her ward and we ended up back here.

I remember trying hard to be quiet as we moved through the house, trying so hard that I fell over and pulled the phone out of the wall. And I remember some joke about pool cues, and how her mouth was like strawberries when I kissed her, sweet strawberries, and the joke was her joke and she thought it was very funny.

I slept badly, as I do when I've had too much to drink. I slept badly, dreamed vividly and woke confused, getting my bearings only when I recognised Kelly next to me, and then the pattern of the doona, rolled up in her arms.

I pull some of it free and arrange it over the two of us. She murmurs something, but not words.

When I wake again it's light, and well into morning.

Have a good time last night? she says.

Yeah.

I might be sick soon.

Please don't be. I don't think I'd cope well.

She shakes her head. *Well, that's a good reason not to be sick, isn't it? Oh god, it's all such a blur. Did we win at pool?*

Who knows? I don't usually.

Breakfast is ready, noisy children, Rick says as he thumps on the door. *And what you were doing with the phone last night I don't want to know.*

We go out into the lounge room and the phone is sitting, with its cord wrapped neatly around it, in the pot of the now-dead plant that Jen bought at the fete a few weeks ago. I'm about to ask Rick why he put it in the plant pot when I remember that at around two this morning I thought it constituted putting it away.

What exactly happened here last night? Jen says as she puts jam on a croissant. *What were you two doing? How does the phone come to be in the plant pot? How does this very strange hole come to be in the new jar of jam?*

She shows us the jam, shows us the hole.

And it's Kelly who works it out first. I can tell this, because it's only the horror on her face that reminds me of what actually happened with the jam. Or, more precisely, whose penis is responsible for the hole.

I wouldn't eat that, she says, quite slowly, knowing she's not saying enough but not knowing where to go next.

I have never felt more need to leave Australia than I do at this moment. To just get up from the table, pack my bags and go. And try my luck in one of the world's almost two hundred countries where I have yet to shame myself by fucking food.

And it's no misty-eyed dream about a plane pushing up into cloud now, taking me away from ambivalence to the romance of the unknown. We're all staring at the jam hole, knowing it's the result of some unnatural interference but only two of us aware of the details. Looking down into the hole and thinking, penis. I have to cover this, or I have to leave. Either way, I guess I'll be buying new jam this morning.

Why? Jen says slowly, through a mouthful of heavily jammed croissant. *Why shouldn't I eat it?*

My thumb, I tell her. I stuck my thumb in there.

That's disgusting. Why would you do that? It's food.

Yeah. I'm aware of that. Jack Horner, the Jack Horner thing? I was illustrating a point, I think. I'd had a few drinks and it was some Jack Horner sitting in a corner allusion. Thumb in a pie, you know?

Meanwhile I'm thinking, Does it taste like thumb? I really, really hope the taste of jam is strong enough to swamp any lingering tincture of penis. And just how familiar is Jen with . . . I should focus on the salvage operation, the thumb story.

Next time you drink, do you mind not getting that elaborate? I'm really not sure how I feel about the croissant now, she says, and takes another mouthful. *Anyway, it's your thumb, so I guess it doesn't bother you.* She pushes the jam across. *If you wouldn't mind using a knife this morning that'd be fine.*

I look down into the jar, at the part of the penis hole not disturbed by Jen's knife. I don't really want to eat the jam now. I've never eaten anything I've stuck my penis in first before, and I think that's a pretty good rule to live by.

The oral event, Mark III. I can recall bits of last night when I think about it later. The darkness, Kelly's trip to the kitchen, the joke about chalking the pool cue, and suddenly her mouth again. I wasn't quite getting the joke, and the mouth surprised me. Suddenly it was all happening down there and the last thing I was likely to do was query any of the details.

After breakfast I apologise and I tell the others I'll buy new jam when I'm dropping Kelly back at the hospital.

I refuse to take money from kitty and Rick says, *What is this, remorse? You must have a hell of a dirty thumb.*

I do my utmost to avoid eye contact. There are some things you can never tell people, even long after breakfast and the replacement of the penis jam, and this has to be one of them. The elbow hitting the wall was one thing, this has to be another. I think that confessing would be crossing a line. Even in a house full of intimate sounds and thwarted pheromones, there are limits.

Kelly and I say almost nothing on the way back to the hospital, even though it's only the two of us in the car. It's as though if we talk about it now they still might find out, and we mightn't have got away with it after all.

I buy the new jam at the Night Owl on the way home, and even on the shelves jam doesn't look the same now. I want to tell the guy behind the counter about our jam. That we finished our last jar this morning, used it up, put it on thick on our croissants and finished it off. And that's why I'm here. No-one fucked our jam. Especially me.

I start to feel unwell, last night's drinking making itself known. I feel like I need to eat something, some greasy morning-after thing, so I drive on to Hungry Jack's. And I sit there with a bacon double cheeseburger, just a man and his jam and his headache and his swirling nausea, wanting the next few hours to pass as quickly as possible.

I go home, and there's jam in the bed when I lie down, smeared across the sheets down at groin level. But how can this be any surprise at all? Last night was not a night for precision.

30

On Monday I enter the Ethics Committee meeting feeling less than well prepared.

I expect that I am the only condiment fucker in the room. And if I'm not, I really don't want to know about it.

The only easy part of the meeting is the part where I have to leave while the others discuss my project. I'm not sure what I'm supposed to do apart from leave the room. So I pace. I pace and I try to prepare for questions, but I'm thinking only about Kelly.

Trying not to contemplate her like a project, trying not to see pros and cons, trying not be analytical. I'm feeling good things about her. I'm wondering if I can or will feel great things about her. Wondering how much specific things matter, when it seems that I'm forever telling people that that's not the way to do it.

Kelly, and the warm silences when she's deep asleep and hasn't yet stolen the doona. Kelly, who manages to get away with so little anguish, and that's quite a quality. Who doesn't know what spoonerisms are, who knows just enough of my mind to know she doesn't know how it works.

Will I be falling in love with Kelly? I'm thinking. Is it probable, possible? Is it something I even understand, a concept that I can work with, that doesn't stick in my throat? I wish it was easy.

The Dud opens the door, smiling.

Come on back in, Jonathan, he says, and I'm paying insufficient attention to be sure if the twitch at the side of his face is a wink or not. I hope it's not. *Well,* he says, and no-one seems to take it from there so he goes on, *looks good. Very interesting. Very nice application, very nice.* He taps it softly with his right hand. *Just a few questions. Shouldn't be any problem. Just a few things we wanted to find out about. Not a lot of melatonin experts in the room.*

He lets out a chuckle and a couple of the others smile to be polite. We talk through several aspects of the project, questions about melatonin and the anticipated issue of patient consent. A few amendments are suggested, easy things, and then the Dud pulls out the page where I've listed necessary resources.

Now, let me see, he says, and fiddles with his glasses. *This isn't strictly Ethics Committee business, but I think we're all happy enough with the project for me to address a few of the practical issues, if no-one has any objections.* He lifts the glasses so he can look up, maneuvres them back into reading position to look down at the page again. Where the objections could have fitted in, I don't know. *Now. Staying overnight. Pretty thorough. Don't want to discourage thoroughness. Hot jug's easy. And I'll sign a requisition for the necessary consumables. Tea, coffee, and we'll divert some biscuits from the RMO's Quarters. Any preference? Sweet, savoury, cream or otherwise? It's much easier for catering if you're specific, when you're looking at small numbers.*

In the interests of decency I allow a moment's pause before saying, as though I'm just being helpful, Monte Carlo?

Biscuits, he says, making a note of it, flourishing his pen and writing in big noisy letters, *Arnott's, Monte Carlo, four, daily. Now then, overnight fridge for the keeping of specimens before transfer to biochem. Absolutely necessary. You could keep your milk in there too, couldn't you?*

And he smiles, with a saggy old innocence. *Desk, yes. Chair, certainly, goes with the desk. Computer, no problem with that.*

And I'm trying not to think of the Dud in a shabby red suit in a down-market department store at Christmas, or fronting a brown-setted TV game show completely without pizzazz. The avuncular host roaming among the prizes, the His and Hers bean bags, the bus trip to Melbourne, the juke box already chock-full of hits from the fifties and sixties.

And the idea of your own room for all this. I don't see any problem with that. When we start looking at your quite regular need to use a bed, as well as having all these resources, I can't really see how you could do it without having your own room. And I think we're all happiest with you and the project materials and overnight specimen storage in one place, and the project subject voluntarily in the unlocked seclusion room in the ward. We've got a couple of rooms in the multistorey near the conference room and the library. You can have either of those. Anything else come to mind?

Well, it could be good to have a sign on the door. We should probably let staff know that the room is dedicated to some proper use. That way the work would be less likely to be disturbed.

They all nod at this, and the Dud says, *Good thinking.*

The meeting winds up around six-thirty, and I go to visit Kelly in the Quarters. And maybe Johnno was right. Maybe I shouldn't have left till I'd signed them all up for aluminium siding. Or at least tried for the big-screen TV.

Let's go out and get something to eat, Kelly says.

But it's Monday night. Rick and the Sunny Garden have expectations.

For one Monday they can do without you.

Okay. But don't think I can make a habit of it.

We go to the nearby Pizza Hut.

So how did it go, the Ethics Committee meeting?

Good. Fine. We got approval, without having to change much. Just things like having to specify in writing that we're only using the seclusion room for privacy, and that the subjects can come and go as they please. Of course, if they do they'll expose themselves to so much light they'll bugger up their melatonin levels, but it's not as though I could say no. Not as though the Ethics Committee was going to let me lock people up for the night.

You wanted to lock people up for the night?

No. That's not what I meant. I just need darkness. Don't worry.

So how are things at home? Are we still in the clear?

Yeah. We have new jam now. And I've managed not to put my penis in it so far. You know, the whole thing would've been okay if you hadn't taken it back into the kitchen.

I can't help being tidy.

Tidy? Tidy? You leave a big penis mark in jam and you tell me you're tidy?

I don't think I can leave a penis mark in anything.

The family at the next table moves, grandparents standing first and ushering the children to their feet, shepherding them to safety closer to the salad bar, to other family groups, decent conversation. The grandmother gives me a look over her shoulder, as though I've spoiled Pizza Hut for them, as though I'm the sort of person who would lure children to unnatural acts.

Jam-fucker, Kelly says.

I was flat on my back. I am not responsible. The jam had more say in it than me.

She fetches more pizza, and I demonstrate my usual unhealthy commitment to the All You Can Eat concept.

You know what I was thinking? she says.

What?

I was thinking we should go up north in June.

June?

Well, June or July. When it's winter here. It'd be a great time to go. And you've got the leave entitlement, since you couldn't take holidays last year.

Yeah. But it doesn't mean I'm guaranteed of it then. And, you know, the project might be starting.

I was only thinking a week or two.

I remain non-committal. I eat far too much pizza.

When we leave I tell her I should probably head home. I've got things to do from the Ethics Committee meeting. Things I should sort out tonight while they're fresh in my mind.

Think about it, she says. *Winter. North. Where it's warm.*

Yeah. Warm would be nice.

But June and July seem a while away, I'm thinking in the car on the way home. Sitting here in mid-April, June/July makes pretty big assumptions. The nurses' grad ball was a month ago tonight, and it's not a month I can complain about, but why do I have to be planning things two months away? I can't think that far ahead.

When I get home Rick's sitting alone in front of the TV, eating Sunny Garden Mongolian lamb straight out of the plastic take-away box.

I waited, he says.

Kelly, I tell him.

Figured.

She expected a meal. I told her, Hey it's Monday, but she expected it.

I've been watching a doco.

Yeah?

Wildlife of the Serengeti. Do you know how interesting wildlife of the Serengeti is?

No.

It's not fucking interesting at all. In the Serengeti, the carnivores don't have to hunt because the herbivores die of boredom.

You want some coffee?

I'm still on the mong lamb. You want some mong lamb?

No. I had pizza. Heaps of pizza. She made me.

Once I've made my coffee I watch the last five minutes of the doco. In the Serengeti, life is cheap.

How'd the meeting go? he says when the credits are rolling.

Good. It got up.

They didn't give you a room though, did they?

They did.

Bullshit.

You would've hated it. I got it all, right down to the biscuit ration of four Monte Carlos a day.

He laughs. *The poor bastards,* he says. *Fucked over big time. Four Monte Carlos a day. How can you mock them so?*

They mock themselves. An offer was made, and duly accepted. I asked for nothing that I did not get, and I accepted all with grace.

Four Monte Carlos a day.

Proposed, accepted and signed.

You scam machine. He laughs again. *How can they not be wise to you? I just don't get it.*

I have such an innocent face. Could you deny me biscuits?

I'm sure you're very persuasive.

And besides, it's a good idea, the melatonin thing. I think

it's a good idea. I hope it's a good idea or I could be scoring a lot of biscuits on false pretences.

I'd almost prefer that. I'd almost be more impressed.

It's a good idea. I could do anything with this. I could do an MD in it you know. It could be big.

An MD?

Yeah. An MD or a PhD.

You really liked uni, didn't you?

Uni was fine.

And presumably if girls continued to treat you with this unfathomable post-graduate regard it'd be almost perfect.

Almost. The only thing left to achieve would be world fame.

Just a matter of time, I would have thought.

Yeah. First, credibility. Then fame. Fame, I think, with melatonin administration. Maybe a couple of milligrams at night, a slow-release preparation to replicate the natural cycle. Melatonin in a wax matrix.

You're making it up, aren't you?

Absolutely. But it's good. Slow-release melatonin. Slo-Mel. That's the brand name. Slo-Mel. Hyphenated, no 'w'.

Slo-Mel?

Yeah.

Is that the whiff of rapidly combusting Mokable Rocket fuel?

I doubt it. If it was, your sinuses'd be crazy by now.

At least the Balsa Car was hypoallergenic.

Tonight it's the pepperoni, too much pizza, that stops me sleeping well. Reflux. I should put more thought into All You Can Eat. I should learn to recognise satiety, and to recognise that it's not the same thing as All You Can Possibly Eat.

I sit on the edge of the bed with the doona round me, as warm tonight as I need to be, but with the acid

uncomfortable in my throat. Too tired to go to the bathroom looking for Mylanta, inclined only to wait for
gravity to help me and sleep to come back.

A big pepperoni burp hisses out of my throat.

How can I not know how much pizza is enough?

31

On Thursday Imelda from the library calls with more articles. She is still enthusiastic, and clearly has no idea of the
hazards of over-reaching, no idea that any article could be
the one that brings me down.

But even the sign for the door is under way now, despite
Glen saying we'd have no hope of getting it made for at
least a few weeks because the guy who does that sort of
thing is retiring in August and is away just about every day
using up his sick leave.

I asked if he was taking early retirement because of illness and Glen said, *No, he's in great shape. That's why
he's got so many sick days to use up.*

I called the number anyway and it was answered by a
man who said, *Trev's off sick today, but I'm his off-sider.
Anything I can do?* I told him what I had in mind and he
said *Signs, I like signs.* And he was in the ward the next
morning, checking the spelling of melatonin, checking it
wasn't melanoma, showing me white letters, royal blue
backing, showing me a pigmented skin lesion or two, just
for the hell of it. Telling me *I'll do a beaut job for you, doc.
I could be up for Trev's job when he's gone, you know.*

I go back to the ward with the articles, pick up a leftover

237

patient lunch and sit in one of the registrar's offices reading. A beaut job, a big sign, white letters on blue. Hazmat, hazmat. But the articles do me no harm. A couple add to my case, a couple have such spaces in them they have no bearing at all.

There's a knock on the door and it opens before I can say anything.

Glen said you might have the tuning forks, Dean says.

No. Why would I have the tuning forks?

You might have been doing an admission. But I guess not. The tuning forks, they're for the neurology part of the admission. Remember?

As if he's ever done an admission that thorough in his life. I almost tell him that I usually leave the tuning forks with the Ishihara colour blindness charts, but I let it go. I catch up with him half an hour later, when he's writing it up, and I ask him if there are any tests that need to be ordered.

Nothing special, he says. *I've made a list in the file anyway.* He passes it to me. *There are no big dramas with this guy. He's depressed, pretty profoundly depressed, not coping. So if you could just do the usual that'd be good.*

Five o'clock comes slowly. Too slowly, so at four forty-five I tell Glen I'm off to the library again and I go to the Nurses' Quarters, but Kelly isn't there. The TV is on, 'Brady Bunch' repeats, but no-one's watching. I knock on her door, but there's no answer. I hang around, and five is even slower coming here than it was in the ward.

It would have been good to see her this afternoon, but she's obviously out. I leave for home at exactly the right time to hit peak-hour traffic.

Jen's been working on her thesis, but is clearly craving

distraction. We kick a ball around and when it gets dark we make beef stroganoff. Rick comes home to cooking smells and opens two bottles of red wine before we can tell him that one would be enough.

When we finish the second, in front of the TV after dinner, he says, *I feel like a port. How about you guys?*

Jen says, *Sure,* and he goes into the kitchen and comes back with two unopened bottles.

Which one?

The one on the right, I tell him. I'm saving the other one.

Saving the other one? What do you save port for?

I got it from a patient. Let's just drink the other one. The one in your right hand.

He shrugs, hands me the bottle and says, *Over to you, maestro,* and he goes back into the kitchen to fetch the glasses.

And the port sticks sweet to my teeth and I drink it quickly and I'm ready for bed just as Rick's pouring his second. I find the other bottle again and take it with me, so that I can put it where it won't be opened inadvertently. Not that I have any idea when I plan to open it.

It came from a patient, Jack Ridgeway. Or at least from his family, from Noela his wife. She came back the day after he died to give it to me, to thank me. And she wrote a letter about me to the Dud, and it was such a good letter that he gave me a copy.

Jack Ridgeway, from the short time I knew him, was a great guy. And something of a treatment dilemma. He was looking down the barrel of a very bad death, and he told me he had no pain at all.

He had a mesothelioma constricting his oesophagus, but no pain, tumour filling up the middle of his chest X-ray. And he was wasting away.

239

He hadn't swallowed solids for a long time, and then he couldn't swallow liquids either. He had a nasogastric tube in, but the tumour started clamping down on that as well. I had to replace it once when it came out and he didn't flinch when the tip stopped somewhere in his throat, and I started banging it up against the constriction. I offered to stop, to find someone better at it, but he shook his head, as much as he could, and eventually it went through. He reached for the bowl by the side of bed, spat some blood into it and said, *Wouldn't want to have to go through that too often,* and smiled.

I asked him how he felt about things, and he said, *Well, I'm jiggered, aren't I? What do we do, doc?* And the way he looked at me I knew this wasn't a time for any bullshit at all.

So I thought through the consequences of the biggest mesothelioma I'd ever seen, and I told him frankly how I thought it looked. That without treatment he would starve or dehydrate to death. And the nasogastric tube might do us for a little while longer, and when it was no longer an option we could give him an IV line for fluids. We could even use a more involved kind of IV line, a central line, to give him a calorie input. We could think about an operation, a gastrostomy, that would allow us to feed him through his abdominal wall and directly into his stomach. The problem with all this, obviously, was that the gain would be very short term. That the chest specialist, on looking at his X-rays, felt that in the next few weeks pressure from the tumour would cause his large airways to collapse, or tumour erosion would lead to massive haemorrhage, probably into the airways.

So now give me the bloody bad news, he said, and smiled. I apologised and he said, *Cut that out, doc. What did you think I wanted you to say? That I might get better?*

Realising that these were bad deaths on offer, he told me he didn't particularly want to sit around waiting for his airways to collapse or fill up with his own blood, and he didn't want any more operations, cause he couldn't see the point.

I told him this was a tough one, and that it usually became easier at this stage, at least in some ways, because the person was in pain and pain was something I could do something about.

I told him about morphine, the analgesia, the euphoria, the respiratory depression. Its tendency to move things along. So if there came a time when he had pain, there was something we could do, and while the nasogastric tube was still working he wouldn't starve or dehydrate. He'd be comfortable, and I wanted him to be comfortable. And if any pain developed, he should let me know right away.

He asked me if I could go through all this again with Noela, and it was even harder the second time.

Later that day he had me paged. *I'm in pain, doc,* he said, smiling. *Can you do anything for that?*

He was dead in three days. With an intact airway, no haemorrhage. Noela beside him, and peace as he drifted off with the morphine, holding her hand. Then still. And for Noela, this stillness was the sign that she need match his stoicism no longer. And suddenly, now that he wasn't there to care for, now his hand was slack in hers, it struck her how desperately bad this was, this loss, this opening void. As though she was, temporarily at least, losing everything they'd had, every moment of it. Thanking me, and inconsolable.

And she was back the next day with the bottle of port, and a box of chocolates for the nurses.

The resident gets port? Gary Costello said later when he saw the bottle next to my briefcase. *The resident gets port?*

Don't these people know anything about etiquette? I assume there's at least a single malt whiskey somewhere round here for the registrar.

Months before then, the first time I'd been in a cancer ward as DMO, I was offered chocolates from two different boxes. I asked if it was someone's birthday, but this was before I knew better. The two boxes of chocolates were there because two patients had just died. *For birthdays we have morning tea,* the nurse said, a little confused.

The wind picks up outside. It would be good to have Kelly here tonight, even if it meant waking up cold and uncovered occasionally. I get a strange urge to call her, to talk to her, to see where she was this afternoon, to see that she's okay and just to hear her voice.

Not that her voice would welcome me particularly, since it's the middle of the night. So I lie here, looking up at a few stars and listening to the wind.

I've never been less attractive than I am at the moment and it's like I've got a dog whistle in my pants.

32

On the first of May the melatonin room becomes reality.

The Dud hands me the key as though I've just won a car on his bad, brown game show, and he moves into mock-royal mode and does an inspection. Names each item as though he's ticking it off on a list and at the end he says, *Yes, I think you'll be happy here.*

As soon as he's gone Johnno says, *I thought he'd never leave,* and he peels the Glad Wrap off the plate of four Monte Carlos and eats them all while swivelling in the chair. *Paradise,* he says. *I think you'll be happy here. A bed. I can't believe you have a bed in the multistorey wing. You are perhaps the most successful second-year resident in history. You realise that, don't you?*

It's a lot to live up to.

But they'll talk about this. The second-year resident who got his own room with a bed in the multistorey. Who rooted nurses with his beeper still on, next to the conference room and right beneath One C. Who rooted, and then ate hospital-issue Monte Carlos. The stuff of legends.

Hey. I've been going out with the same person for six weeks now.

But that's not the stuff of legends. Hospital legends, you have surely realised by now, rarely celebrate long-term monogamy. They're much more inclined to celebrate hazardous intercourse. Intercourse with large numbers of the wrong people, in the wrong places, at the wrong times. In

the legend, you will have made the most of the room.
There will be nurses you will have rooted here for the first
and perhaps only time, when you heard them tapping at
the door and let them in and let them give you pleasure.
Who knows? Mrs Liebowitz is close. Who knows how
lucky you might be?

I've never been sure of his claims involving Mrs
Liebowitz, and now I'm wondering if they're part of his
own legend, wondering if she exists at all. Or if Johnno
created her to give him at least some control over the
things said about him, limit the damage. Or if he's just
making it up as he goes along, because he can. It's not as
though I know of any confirmed sightings.

After he's gone, I flick through a few articles, and
I leave the door open so I can see the sign.

I want to do this. I want to call the melatonin legends,
Lewy in Portland, Arendt in Surrey, Vanacek and Illnerova
in Prague, or at least Redman and Armstrong in Melbourne, to tell them I'm on the case. I've got a room, I've
got a sign, I've got a project happening. I'm about ready
to start pulling this together. I'm still motivated even after
I check the computer for games and find that it's only got
Solitaire and Tetris.

I fix my Edward de Bono card to the wall with Blu-
Tack.

On Wednesday, Johnno says we should lunch at the Fed
again, to celebrate the success of the project. I tell him the
project hasn't actually started yet, we've just got ourselves
a room, and he says, *I thought that was the project.*

I give him eight Monte Carlo biscuits, yesterday's and
today's, and he says, *Fuck, why couldn't you give me those*
before I committed myself to paying for lunch? Still,
there's always tomorrow, I suppose.

There'll be twelve by tomorrow.

Jesus, he says, *four biscuits a day, a furnished room, regular intimate attention and such big plans. Why was I never this organised? Do you know how long it took me to work out what I wanted to do?*

He tells me about his time at uni, how in the middle of it he thought medicine might not be for him and he took a year off to keep goats. *It was the seventies, after all. But by the end of the year I had a sneaking suspicion the goats thought I was a fuckwit. And that's it, isn't it? Once you think you've lost respect you have to move on.*

So you decided you wanted to do medicine then, or were you just shamed into it by the goats?

I eventually worked out that what I wanted to do was play jazz sax and make a million on the stockmarket. And, you know, I'm not half the sax player I used to be. Back when I'd never been transiently wealthy, things were so uncomplicated. I was always chronically dysthymic, of course. I just try to take things less seriously now, I try not to get too attached to them. Gold shares. Who would have thought gold shares could stiff so badly, when they were looking so good?

After lunch I find a set of NHMRC grant application forms in my pigeon hole, with a scrawly note that appears to say, *I thought you might be interested in these – FD.*

While I'm looking through them in the room and thinking, So this is how you do it, and starting to become a little less certain of my global melatonin ambitions, Kelly comes to the door and says, *Don't frown. I've got something much better to look at.*

North Queensland holiday brochures, and she deals them out in front of me like a card trick. Pick a holiday, any holiday.

What do you think?

Sure looks warm up there. Nice and warm.

Shall I leave them with you? You look like you're busy.

Yeah. I've got these grant forms to go through.

And when she leaves I make two neat piles on the desk, grant forms in one, holiday brochures in the other, and I lock the door and go back to the ward.

But with the excursion on and no admissions coming in I've done everything I reasonably can by about three, so I decide to give more serious consideration to the grant application.

I sit in the room and think about Kelly, about the holiday. About how I wish she wouldn't push me. I don't know what she's expecting. Or thinking, or feeling. If it was this weekend it'd be fine, but how can I guess about June and July? We look at things in different ways. This could be a problem, and I've got a lot in my head at the moment.

When I get home there's a letter from my sister in the mail box. She tells me it's rained every day in April. She says she would like to get out more, or at least have a room other than the attic room, because there are times when she would like to stand up straight, and even at the highest part of the attic room she still has to bend her knees. She says she has a new theory, a nose-measuring theory. She believes that the standard human is proportioned in such a manner that if the thumb is lined up where it naturally fits next to the base of the index finger, the portion of the index finger protruding beyond this point is exactly the length of the person's nose.

I'm trying to remember if I've written to her yet about my melatonin theory, and I'm wondering if her letter might, in some less than subtle way, suggest that she thinks it isn't brilliant. Or if the weather has been so bad lately that, all over London, people are spending so much time inside that they're having to entertain themselves by discovering new things to do with their own body parts.

The application forms, the brochures, the letter. This hasn't been an easy afternoon for me and paper, and the only thing I'm certain of at the end of it is that if I line my thumb up where it naturally fits next to the base of my index finger, the portion of the index finger protruding beyond this point is exactly the length of my nose.

Rick sees the holiday brochures on the table when he gets home.

Hey, who's going up north?

I don't know if anyone's going up north. Kelly got them. She had an idea about a holiday.

A holiday? Just her or the two of you?

She was thinking the two of us. June or July.

Do I sense reticence?

Sense what you like.

Oh dear. I do sense reticence. June or July a problem for you?

They're a while away. July in particular. And I'm just getting started on the project.

Danger Will Robinson, he says and robots his way around the room. *Danger Kelly McLean. Will the evil doctor be gentle and warn her?*

Just do this, I say to him, making the proposed nose-measuring gesture. Just do this.

And again it works.

33

Is there a problem? Kelly says when I answer her page on Friday.

No. What do you mean?

I just thought you would have got back to me by now. About the trip. The brochures I gave you.

Oh, yeah, sorry. It's the forms that I had. The grant application. There's quite a bit of work involved.

I meet her in the Quarters at five-thirty, and she's dressed as though we might go out.

I've made coffee, she says, and I follow her into the kitchen. She pushes the plunger and pours, says, *One,* as she puts a spoonful of sugar into my cup.

On the TV, the 'Happy Days' theme song begins.

Shall we go to my room? she says.

Does that TV ever go off?

It doesn't seem to. Not during the day.

But there's no-one watching it.

There might be soon. She shrugs. *I'm not turning it off.*

Well, obviously not. Who knows how people might interpret it. Actually turning the TV off.

She shuts the door when we're in her room and she sits on the only chair, leaving me to sit on the bed.

You've been busy this week.

Yeah.

You really need a break.

I'm fine.

I was thinking first or second week in July. I picked up some leave application forms yesterday.

Leave application forms? But I haven't said I'm going.

I was hoping I could persuade you. Is it such a bad idea? The two of us having a holiday in a couple of months?

I can't tell what I'll be doing in a couple of months.

It doesn't matter, does it? The way you're going now another psych term'd be pretty likely, but even if you don't get it, what's the problem? Anyway, it was your idea in the first place. You were the one saying you wanted to get away. What's changed?

Nothing's changed.

I look at her. I watch this mystery afflicting her. Kelly dressed for an autumn evening in her jeans and navy jacket. Making plans, planning easily for some time months away. Looking at me, her coffee steaming away unnoticed.

I don't want to plan this, I tell her. It's too far ahead for me.

What do you mean?

July. It's a long time away.

So you're never going to take a holiday then? They don't just happen. You do have to plan them. I'm not getting this. Is there something really strange about the idea of a holiday?

No.

She shakes her head. *Some days you are such a mystery. You want to get away, you want a holiday, and then you don't. Suddenly it looks like a huge hassle to even think about it.*

I think it was a bit more abstract than that, the idea of getting away, when I first mentioned it. It wasn't meant to be me saying I wanted a holiday. Not that I'm saying I'm completely against the idea of holidays.

An abstract kind of getting away. Well, that'd be heaps of fun, wouldn't it? Lots of post-modern windsurfing

I suppose. Plenty of spoons and Joe Bloggs. Do you try to make me feel stupid?

I'm sorry?

You suggest getting away, I suggest a holiday and I'm made to feel that I'm just too dumb to understand, that I've done something wrong. That I'm putting some terrible pressure on you just by suggesting it. What have I done? What am I doing wrong? Why can't you just tell me what's going on?

Because there's nothing going on. There's nothing particularly wrong. Things are fine as they are.

Nothing particularly wrong? What does nothing particularly wrong mean?

I wish I wasn't making her unhappy. Kelly, trapped in these Quarters. Trapped here with endless repeats on TV, other nurses drifting in and out. No-one she's really close to, and she's so good at being close, so unafraid of it. I can't hurt her. I don't want her to be hurt and I don't want to hurt her.

I wanted to keep this the way it was, but she's not letting me. Not letting it just go day to day. She's talking two months ahead, and I can't do two months ahead. So much can happen in less time than that.

I can't think of what to say to her now. I can't think of anything that will fix this up some way that works for both of us.

I want to reach out to her now, and pull away. Not an easy maneuvre to execute. Sometimes I think I conduct most of my life in an abstract domain, as though it's only a concept. And not a very good concept, either.

I'm the problem here, I tell her. But let's not make it a big problem. I've just got a few things to work out.

What things?

What term I'm doing, the project, stuff like that.

What stuff like that? Why is there never a complete list? Why do you never tell me everything?

Please. I don't know everything. I don't know what's going on.

I don't get this. Why are you shutting me out?

I'm not shutting you out.

What am I supposed to do? It's just a holiday. What's so complicated about a holiday? I can't handle this. This isn't fair. Some days you really get to me. Sometimes I see a glimpse of the real you, the you without the dumb jokes, but the moment you realise I'm looking, you're gone again.

I don't know what you mean. I don't know what you're seeing. I don't know what the problem is with the dumb jokes.

There's no problem with the dumb jokes. That's not what I meant. She slows down. *And they're not dumb. I just, sometimes I just think I hardly know you.*

I don't know what there is to know. I don't know what you don't know. This isn't getting us very far. Could we just relax with this?

You tell everybody to relax. You tell Rick to relax, and does it do him any good? It's your way of telling people to shut up, to stop talking about what matters to them. As though they're stressed about nothing. And you never relax yourself.

Hey, I got so relaxed you stuck my dick in jam and I didn't even know it.

That's drunk. That's not relaxed. That's chemical oblivion.

I don't get this. I just want to have a good time. I want a low-stress life. What's the problem with that?

Having a holiday would obviously be a disaster then, wouldn't it?

Can I think about it? Can I think about it over the

weekend? While I'm not here at work and I can think a bit more clearly, maybe?

She gives this some time. Lets some of her anger fade. Looks at me closely as though I might give something away. *Okay. The weekend. Think over the weekend then. And if you wanted to think about any other things that'd be fine too. If you wanted to think about what's happening with us.*

What do you mean?

Don't give me that What do you mean shit right now. You know what I mean. So go. Please. Go and think. Go while I can still tell you to go. 'Cause I don't want you to go. I just want this to be good. I want you to go now before I start trying to do anything I can to make this good. So go. Think. Two days. Then we'll talk.

She says all this sitting quite still in the chair, staring near me but not at me, starting to blotch red, like the night she asked me to the ball.

I reach out to her. She pulls away, waves me away. Keeps staring ahead at nothing while I leave. Her coffee still untouched but still steaming, this has all been so quick.

I shut her door behind me, walk down the hall and out, past the TV, still 'Happy Days', Ritchie having girl trouble, Penny Frew and someone I don't know, sitting facing the other way, staring at the screen, drinking beer.

In the car on the way home I'm angry, but only with myself. I'm hurting her, and I didn't want to hurt her. This is such a mess. Such a mess for something so simple. I want her, and I don't want her. And I don't know what I want.

We're pulling this in different ways, and the holiday talk just makes it apparent. I can't believe that I'm in this situation again. The idea of a holiday in two months, committing to a holiday in two months, crowds in on me. To agree to it wouldn't be fair to Kelly, in the end. It would imply a level of attachment that I'm not at all sure about. I can't mesh my life with hers the way she wants me to. That only complicates things when it ends, makes it much harder. And any independence I try to keep baffles her, seems like rejection.

I really do wish we could relax. Things are fine as they are, and we pushed it to the brink back there. I've had conversations like that before that have been the end.

But I watched her in the chair, and I knew it wasn't going to be the end. Not today. She looked so lonely. That's the problem with this. That's what she sets herself up for. But maybe it's me. Maybe I'm the problem with this. Or maybe I just know that, in the end, it's not going to work. I'm not sure, not sure about much. Talking in circles without leaving my head.

I go with Jen to the Underground.

I drink, I dance, I drink.

I think, I watch the room move, the well-dressed people. I bug Jen when she's talking to boys. I talk to her and they listen too. Remorse hits me like a fist.

I can't believe I'm doing this to Kelly, I hear myself telling her, telling them, all the time wishing I wasn't.

I am being so bad to Kelly.

And the boys are looking at me now as Jen's saying, *He's my housemate,* making it clear that I'm not some lingering lean-shouldered piece of business that hasn't yet been finalised. And they're looking at me not unkindly so I tell them more.

You wouldn't believe it. You wouldn't. She's fine, right? And I'm fucking killing her, right? Fucking killing her.

Do you want to go home? Jen says. *We could go home now.*

Why? That's the question. Why am I doing this? Or worse still, why am I like this? That's much worse. What am I expecting? But sometimes you've got to work out that you've got to do it to them. It's the best thing really. Better than letting it go on and on. Jen'd back me up on that.

I decide I should dance then. I dance alone and then I'm dancing with someone, in the corner of the dance floor and leaning on a railing and apparently dancing with someone. Near her first and then definitely with her, and in quite a sleazy way. And then I realise she's a nurse from work and I'm still trying to remember her name when she pashes me.

Pashes me with a wet mouth tasting of smoke and for a second I can't breathe 'cause I've been dancing hard and I think I'm going to black out. I've got a throatful of tongue and my nose happens to be blocked but I hadn't realised till now since I was apparently breathing through my mouth. Dancing and mouth-breathing, not very attractive, but obviously okay by her. I'm trying to talk but since I can't make words she thinks it's just arousal, a moan of appreciation. I go a bit saggy and feel hot and strange but I hold onto her, and I wonder for a second if I died on the dance floor and she's resuscitating me. And I hope her record's better than mine.

But no, it's okay. It's a pash.

So we lean against the railing and this goes on a while.

We stop for breath and I tell her I'm glad I'm not dancing. I have no energy left, and I've had far, far, far, too much to drink.

Jen takes me home in a cab then, and she doesn't say much on the way, but I think I'm talking. I still don't know the nurse's name, but I think I covered it. We exchanged very few words.

When I get into my room I notice my fly's undone, and I can't believe I've been going round all day like this. But then I realise I haven't.

What is her name?

Four thirty-eight a.m. I wake face down. Still dressed, fly still undone, cold.

Mouth tasting of refuse and I'm going to be sick now, I could be sick.

Damn the architect who put the toilet outside this house, beyond the complex locks of the back door and in the cold. I sit on the toilet, shivering and trying to decide whether it would be better to be sick, or better not to be. Tough call.

I fall asleep, but I wake again when I hit the side wall with a thump, and empty toilet rolls cascade around me. I jump away instinctively and hit the opposite wall. It's a small room, and presumably not made with jumping in mind.

To avoid further injury I return to bed.

In time, I watch the dawn.

I am, I must admit, not totally impressed with last night. But I am relieved that I stopped when I did.

I am dissolving aspirin and planning a slow day when Rick emerges from his room, pauses at my open door and meets me in the kitchen.

Just you this morning, is there? he says.

Yeah. And today that's probably for the best. I plan to

be bad company, to eat small, bland meals and recline in front of television.

A day of suffering.

No more or less than I deserve.

Jen's door opens.

Jennifer is a liar, I say to Rick. You should know that now, and remember it through all that she will say.

At first she says nothing. She stands in the kitchen doorway shaking her head and smiling sadly.

What have I missed? Rick says. *Please.*

You were just disgusting, Jen says, still looking at me and taking far longer over each word than she needs to.

What? What happened?

Just disgusting. Who was that woman? Where did you get the idea that that was any way to behave in public?

I'd had a few drinks. My mind was on other things. I was grappling with some complex issues and then suddenly there was this mouth.

Disgusting. She turns to Rick. *You should have seen him. She was awful. Comprehensively awful. Smoking and sleazing all over him, groping him in the corner.*

I was a bit saggy. I think she was just trying to inflate me. You're getting this all wrong.

It was so foul the staff even asked her to stop and she just told them to fuck off. Somehow I got him out of there. She turns back to me. *I assume you still have a penis. The way she was yanking something in your pants I thought you must have had a motor mower in there.*

I am a little uncomfortable.

Do you even know her?

Not really. And I don't plan to.

What's not really? Rick says.

I don't really know her. She's from work, I think. I've seen her round.

Nurse?

I guess so.

Oh, you bad, bad man.

Please, it wasn't a good night. It's a night I plan to forget. A night that will have no bearing on my future activities. A learning experience. And I've learned. Do not go about in public like a deflating love toy, or the kindness of others may be misunderstood. And so, this first lesson duly noted, I shall begin an alcohol-free period, a time of fasting and contemplation. A period of reassessment, good sense and much televisual sport.

Kelly's about to get the flick.

I am not about to break up with Kelly.

If you do, could you please not go out with this one. She sounds terrible.

I am not about to break up with Kelly.

One more time before the cock crows.

I am not about to break up with Kelly.

He makes a chicken noise.

They go to the shops. I sit down. I want to call Kelly. I hate soluble aspirin so I swallow it in one mouthful and it fizzes back up into my sinuses.

I want things to be the way they were a month ago. I want to call her, but I don't know what I'd say. Would I mention any of last night? All of it, because I have to, because I can't lie to her? None of it, because she wouldn't understand? It was an accident, the worst kind of accident. It means nothing. I was in such a bad way that I'm sure the only things that stopped me falling over were the grip on my penis and the facial suction. What is her name?

So if I called Kelly now would I be full of apology, but not mention last night? Apologise so much for yesterday afternoon that it would cover for last night too? Would

I end by saying I'd go on the holiday? Would I say things I didn't mean?

Would it all come to an end?

I'm not looking forward to our next conversation. So I'll leave it till Monday. When I won't have this headache, this nausea, this taste of someone else in my mouth, this messed-up perspective of things.

Late morning, when I'm hanging my laundry on the line, Jen shouts to me from the back steps. Kelly's on the phone.

Hi, she says, quite softly, without any of yesterday's edge.

Hi.

I'm sorry about yesterday afternoon.

So am I.

No, you don't have to say that. I didn't handle it well. It looked like it was heading somewhere I didn't want it to go, and I got defensive.

No, I didn't handle it well.

I know that you don't know what term you're doing next, and whatever you're doing you have to fit the pro-ject in. I was just misreading it. I was taking it the wrong way and I felt a bit threatened. So I did your thing. The shutting down thing. The get-the-hell-away-from-me-so-I-won't-get-hurt thing.

I'm not sure that's my thing.

Sorry, I didn't mean to . . . It doesn't matter. Yesterday it was all me, so forget about it. I got worried, and I backed off. And then I drank too much afterwards.

Now that's more my thing. I'm not feeling the best today.

What did you do?

I went to the Underground with Jen. I drank too much and cramped her style. Beyond that, chemical oblivion. You know me. So I'm taking it easy today.

I watched bad TV and drank bourbon, just with a few of the others in the Quarters. And I'm sorry about the chemical oblivion remark.

That's okay. I've never seen you drink bourbon before.

No. Well, it was what I was being offered last night. I drank bourbon and said some very unreasonable things about you and then I went to bed. The others were about to play board games, and I knew I couldn't handle a board game. And now I've got two lates, today and tomorrow. So I blew the only night we could go out this weekend.

Well, it's supposed to be thinking time for me anyway, isn't it?

You've got two days, pal, she says and laughs. I'm sorry about all that deadline stuff. It's not exactly helpful, is it?

It's okay. It wasn't a great conversation from either of our points of view.

Well, I should go. Iron something white and seemly, she says, and pauses. So I'll see you then. Monday, maybe.

Yeah.

Some time after lunch Jen says, *You look like someone who needs coffee. You want coffee?*

She makes some and we sit on the back steps.

You were pretty crazy last night, she says.

I wasn't at my best.

You seemed to be going through quite a struggle. All of that angst about Kelly and then suddenly there you were up in the corner with . . . What was her name?

I don't know. I don't know her name and I will never need to, so it's not a problem. Kelly and I had had a conversation, yesterday afternoon. About the trip.

What's the story with the trip? It's obviously not as straightforward as it seems.

It's exactly as straightforward as it seems. It's just two months away.

And Kelly's making the assumption that it'll all still be on in two months.

Exactly.

She doesn't realise that'd be a personal best for you, that you've never stuck it out that long before?

Strangely enough, that's not the way we've ever discussed it.

And you're having doubts?

I don't know.

Sounds like a yes.

It got pretty close to the brink yesterday. It's like I've got a choice. End it, and I don't like that option, or commit to the holiday. Which means a guaranteed further two months, and who knows what beyond that. That'd be four months nearly. That's a long time, and I can't guess what she'd be thinking at the end of four months. If it ended then, how bad would that be? It'd be a much bigger deal. Sure, it might go four months anyway, who knows how long it might go, but why do we have to lock it in? Why can't people just relax and take it day to day?

So do you tell her about the nameless one?

No. Shit no. I didn't tell her on the phone, so I'm not telling her now. The longer I go without telling her, the less possible it would be. She'd think it was some big deal if I told her on Monday, and it just isn't. The nameless one isn't the issue at all. You are right of course. It was pretty disgusting. And I'm sorry if I got in the way of anything.

Nothing important.

I plan to stay more in control in future, if that's any help.

35

But Monday is a day of surprises, and little control. And it involves the nameless one more than I had hoped.

I've done some thinking, not two completely concentrated days of thinking, but some thinking nonetheless. I realise I could be on the brink of messing things up with Kelly, and it's this that I'm working through while I'm sitting in the melatonin room with the NHMRC forms in front of me.

This, and the numbers that are building up to suggest a pattern. To suggest that I'm much better at starting relationships than I used to be, but not great with what follows. It's like the room. I'm still treating relationships and room plans as though they're sufficiently unlikely to amount to anything, that I don't need to think through their implications.

And now it's too late to think, What if they give me the room, the gear? Will they expect something? Will they expect me to be right?

I have the room and the gear. The forms, the holiday brochures. The implications that weren't apparent in the moment of contemplating the possibilities. Possibilities have always appealed, particularly when I didn't have any. Relationships were easy when no-one wanted one. I could spend months, years even, contemplating the possibilities. And they were never tested. They stayed perfect, my possible relationships. I kept fantasising about their beginnings. I never thought they might have middles, or ends.

Am I being unreasonable now that I've stepped out of

the implication-free zone? Am I expecting something to be perfect, Kelly to be perfect, when I'm far from it myself? Do I go on the holiday? I'm not sure yet. Am I making more of this than I should? Am I the one who should relax, instead of telling people to relax to shut them up? She's harsh when she's angry, but I can't confidently say she's wrong.

I take the NHMRC forms in both hands, tap them on the desk to line their edges up neatly. Should I at least write my name on them? Would that be a start?

I thought I'd find you here, a voice says at the door.

The nameless one, coquettishly arranging herself against the architrave, but managing to do so in a way that is strikingly unappealing.

The blunders of Friday night smack back into me in a wave of nausea.

This woman has sucked my face so hard I swear I have several loose teeth. This woman has held my penis in at least one of her hands. And I don't know her name. I still don't know her name. And when I fantasised about beginnings, it wasn't like this. In the fantasies, any time my penis ended up in a woman's hand it was something that seemed like a great idea to both of us. And I always knew her name. But Friday night was no fantasy, no beginning, just the penis-in-hand part, things on my mind, too much to drink.

Hi, I say to her, but somehow this only emphasises the space after the hi, the bit where the name might go. How are you?

I'm fine.

I'm just filling in these forms, I tell her, as though this is all social, normal.

She nods.

I want her to go away. To vanish completely. I want to

clear this up but I can't. How can I? I am embarrassed by my behaviour on Friday night, embarrassed I don't know her name, embarrassed that I might have misled her at a time when I wasn't really in control. Deeply embarrassed that it meant so close to nothing, was only a mistake. How do you tell someone that? What kind of apology would do? Which part of it do I begin with?

I look at her name tag, as surreptitiously as possible, but it says only D. Ford, RN, and there's none of that I can call her out loud. Why Sister Ford, good afternoon, and many thanks for fiddling with my privates the night of Friday last.

I tell myself to be calm, relax, but this only seems to make me shut up.

Meanwhile she's shutting the door, locking it, saying, *Great room. Hey, you've even got a bed. It'd be dark with the light out.* She flicks the switch off and then on again. *Wow, that was dark. What do you do in here?*

Nothing. Nothing much. Just these forms.

I seem to be thinking the forms will save me, but I don't know how.

She smiles, I smile. My smile is tension, more of the embarrassment. I want to tell her that Friday just wasn't me. That I had things on my mind and I drank too much. I want to clarify, I want to apologise, I want her to go. I stand up to unlock the door, so she can go.

But this is the wrong order. The order was supposed to be clarify, apologise, go, but the first two were harder and I'm realising that starting with the final part leaves me open to misinterpretation again. Leaves me standing, and closer to her since her back is against the locked door.

I want to tell her that I have matters to resolve with Sister McLean. That in my head there are many things that are far from clear. Many things I'm not handling well. I want to tell her these forms are complicated, and I do. I tell her that bit, but nothing else.

You obviously need a break, she says.

And I want to tell her that's where these problems began, and I'm already tossing up a suggestion of a holiday up north, when I realise she's only talking about a couple of minutes.

She moves towards me, takes the forms from my hand, stands on her toes to reach my mouth.

Friday night, I say, and then there's too much tongue for me to get any sensible sound out and that's just like Friday night, too much like Friday night, tasting of old smoke and not easy to deal with. And I'm thinking, If only you were a dentist you'd understand this was a cry for help, an apology, an attempt at explanation, feeble but well-meant.

Was I rough on Friday night? she whispers, easing her hand into my pants. *I didn't mean to be.*

Well, I . . .

Then she's on my mouth again, on my mouth with hers and massaging frantically down lower, doing the lawn-mower thing.

You want me, she says. *You want me, don't you?*

Look, I . . .

And she's pushing towards me and my shoe gets stuck beside the leg of the table, wedged between the leg of the table and the bed, and I start to overbalance. I grab hold of her, grab her round the thighs and I'm trying to tell her about my shoe, about the pain in my ankle. About Kelly, that all this seems unwise, that I'm sorry I've misled her, that in a life of ambivalence the only thing close to certainty is that I don't want her.

But how do I do this? How do I handle it decently? How do you ever tell someone that, particularly when your foot's slipping out of your shoe and you're on the bed and she's on top of you and her skirt is messed up around her waist and your hands happen to be on her skin as a consequence of falling? And your penis is in her hand and functioning in that strictly mechanical way that penises do.

It's ridiculous that things could get this far before I have a chance to stop them, before I really get to address the issue. Ridiculous that my penis is ragingly hard when my entire life is characterised by indecision and a marked lack of confidence.

How can I explain this to Kelly? How can I explain this to Kelly and give her an accurate impression of how D. Ford and I just came to be in this situation? This lying down juxtaposed penis situation, when it wasn't what was on my mind.

And how do I explain it to D. Ford? How do I bring this to a conclusion that doesn't leave her feeling unwanted? I hate hurting people's feelings. I should be able to do this. I should be fine with this. I got a seven in psych at uni. I should have dozens of different strategies for raising contentious issues in uncontentious ways.

I break free from her mouth, just for a second.

Is this a good idea? I say, trying so hard to be tactful that I inadvertently couch my uncontentious statement about the mistake we're making in terms of the wimpiest style of psychotherapy around.

She says *Yeah,* rolls her eyes, reclaims my mouth, moves my hand slightly to the left. *Yeah, just here.*

I'm done for.

I decide that as long as we don't actually have sex, it's okay. That's the rule. Pashing, okay. Rubbing, okay. But no sex. That's where the line would be crossed. If we stop now it'll be okay. Or soon. It's not as though I can just throw her off me. That would be unreasonable. I have to negotiate my way out of this. Pash, rub, ease out with some sense of grace. Apologise and make sure D. Ford realises it's nothing personal.

You can't just go from all this pashing and rubbing to flipping the person onto the floor and expecting that it won't harm their self-esteem. And I can't put the 'good idea' line to her again. Who knows where my hand might go. So it looks like I'm lined up for a few more minutes of the pashing and rubbing and I'm beginning to think that I can live with that, that worse things could happen. That this is fine for a few minutes and then I'll sort it out. In a clear but non-judgemental way, then back to the forms.

At least there aren't any condoms in the room, so there is a limit to this. That's how I'll, in a few minutes, if it looks like . . .

Oh.

I actually hear myself say, Oh, at the moment D. Ford manages the maneuvre that breaches the rules I was deciding to work to. That makes it plain that, while a condom might be good sense, it's not technically a necessity.

She goes from rubbing, rubbing, rubbing me up against her, to rubbing somewhere slightly different as though I'm back at The Naked Lunch and playing the role of the whip handle. And suddenly it's much easier than rubbing, much smoother and it's gone too far to stop now, way too far. The line is crossed and I'll just have to sort it out later.

And the clip of my name tag pushes into my skin uncomfortably and she reaches past me to grab the bed rail, groans into my pillow. And the rubbing is swapped for writhing now, writhing, writhing, and her breaths are shorter, shorter, and I know I'm going with this, and I know I shouldn't, but the line is crossed as much as it can be, so . . .

And there's a Code Blue. Right above us, One C, Code

Blue, in the usual relaxed tone of the head wardsman, giving nothing away but the information. Calling it as though he's announcing correct weight over the rough PA of a country racetrack.

Feet running, the crash trolley, speed but not panic, all right above us and totally surreal. My beeper double-beeping and double-beeping and D. Ford reaching back to turn it off, fumbling, sending it to the floor. Gripping the rail hard, writhing, writhing, pushing herself up and pushing harder against me, her upside-down nurse's watch bobbing away on her left breast.

Code Blue, I say ineffectually, as though it might stop things now, and she says, *Yeah, yeah, yeah,* lets it all go, a long breath out, slumps down over me as I let go too.

And we lie there, the running stopped above us, the back of her head sweaty under my hand.

Wow, she says, pushing herself up onto her elbows. *Wow. I only meant to visit.*

She straightens her skirt when she stands, adjusts everything else through it. Gives me a red-cheeked, sweaty smile.

I've got to work now. I can't believe I've got to work now. She pauses at the door and shakes her head. *I nearly went to the dining room.*

She goes, leaves me sitting on the edge of the bed in a state of some dishevellment. I can't think how to begin the fixing of this situation. I think it will end with me breaking up with Kelly the next time I see her, but right now I'm a long way from being ready to see anyone, sitting here with mess in my lap, my pager on the floor, its back broken off, its two double-A batteries rolled somewhere.

I can't tell Kelly this didn't happen, and I can't tell her it did. She deserves better.

I can't even handle the next five minutes. It's not as

though I have tissues, or running water, and while there's a bathroom nearby it's not exactly en suite. I have sheets, but I don't think that would be smart, or fair on the hospital staff. This leaves me with the choice of using one of the less prominent carpet tiles to clean myself, or the only paper in the room, the NHMRC forms. And the carpet tiles look mighty scratchy.

So, with some reluctance, the paperwork that has already provoked such deliberation (but very little writing) gets used for wiping. And I think of the forms in the Dud's hand, being slotted neatly into my pigeon hole with such good intentions.

And soon he'll ask me how I'm going with them, and what do I tell him? Frank, they mop up semen like you wouldn't believe? Can I possibly say I made a mess of them, in a very generic way, and ask for more?

It's only when I'm standing with the crumpled wad of paper in my hand that I realise I can't put it in the bin. That tomorrow morning the cleaner will empty the bin, and I just don't want this to be there. Oh, look at the mess Doctor Marshall's made of his grant forms. He must get really excited about his research.

I put the paper in my briefcase, close it, lock it and decide I'll sneak it out later.

This really is some kind of personal low point, having sex with someone I don't know and probably don't like, wiping semen all over my grant forms and then filing them away in my briefcase. Not at all the clarity I was seeking at the start of the day.

I go to get the beeper fixed and I explain that it fell off during the Code Blue.

And the technician says, *No worries, doc, these things happen. I'm sure you had plenty on your mind at the time.*

He tests it and tells me it still works. I should have

figured it would still work. He says he'd like to replace it and sort the case out, but beepers are in short supply at the moment so he'll have to just tape it up.

Hope that's okay, he says, handing me a beeper that looks like crap but will probably work forever. *You know, these are in such short supply that we're having to page some people over the PA.*

They can have mine if they want.

Oh no, doc. You're a priority customer. Doctors and wardies, they get priority with pagers. The wardies because their union insists. Any wardie without a two-way gets a pager. Everyone else, if they don't already have one, we've got to get them over the PA at the moment. And of course, with the budget cuts we're having, the PA's pretty much had the dick as well. Have you heard the sound quality lately?

It's not good.

Too right. Of course, some of it's technique, but Ron is the head wardie, so it's his gig. What can you do, hey? He talks right into the mike instead of over it, he spits at it, but what can you do? Take him aside and say to him, Ron, mate, your technique's a bit dicey? He's a proud man. He fought in a war once, you know. For Australia. So you're just lucky you're a priority customer and you get the pager.

For the entire rest of the day, no-one pages me.

Five o'clock comes, I turn the pager off.

I'm going to hate this scene, I'm thinking on my way to the Nurses' Quarters. Do I do it in her room, do I do it in the garden where we've had picnic lunches, do I take her somewhere? And what happens then? This won't be helped by Scrabble with the girls in the Quarters, or fixed in one of the ad breaks during 'Happy Days'.

I should have thought of this long ago. Kelly has come

to have expectations. I've seen them coming, I should have handled it. I wanted to find some way of taking the pressure off, but I couldn't. I thought about breaking up, but I couldn't. But now I have to.

Kelly doesn't know it's coming. She's in her room when I get to the Quarters, wearing her Elmer Fudd T-shirt again. Not that this gives it away that she doesn't know it's coming, but it's obvious she doesn't.

We've got to talk, I tell her.

No, I thought we'd sorted that out. I thought we'd agreed that it all got out of hand.

We have to talk.

It was my fault, remember? I made it get out of hand. I gave you the deadline.

She is now getting an inkling that it's coming.

The holiday, I tell her. I don't think I can go on the holiday.

That's fine.

No, it's not fine.

No, you're busy. You don't know what term you're doing next. You've got the project. I understand.

I don't think so. I've thought about it, and it's just too far away. I don't know that it'd be smart to commit to anything that's not until July.

The inkling of something coming, something approaching rapidly and promising harm, is now surely unmistakable. She doesn't swerve.

Are you saying it'll be over before then, between us? Is that what you're saying?

Who knows? It's a long time. Too long for me to give any guarantees, and that's what the holiday would be.

So what am I supposed to do?

Whatever you have to. But I thought it would only be honest of me to let you know. It's just not me. And I think

272

we have to be clear on that. I don't think I've handled this well and I want to sort that out. I think we might have been looking at this very differently, and I don't want to go on doing that, 'cause it'll only make things worse.

So is that it? Is that what you're telling me?

I'm just trying to clarify things.

Have you been keeping this from me all the time? All the time when you've been keeping nothing from me.

No, I haven't. Really. I've been thinking, I've had two days of thinking, and I think I haven't been fair to you, but it hasn't been clear to me either until now.

Until I pushed it with the holiday. So is that it? Are you being honest with me now? It's not that there's anyone else, or anything like that?

No.

So you'd just walk away from this, then? Right now?

If that's what you want. That's not exactly what I was saying, but if it's what you want.

She thinks about it. Looks at me, but I stop looking at her and I look past her. She's giving me time. Time to pull it back from the brink. Outside, an ambulance thumps slowly over a speed bump on its way out of the hospital.

I can't stand this, she says. *If I said I wanted to keep this going, how long would it be before we'd be having this conversation again?*

With that, it's done. The back of the conversation is broken. From that point, the end assumes inevitability. When it's over I go to the melatonin room. I can't go home. I can't face Rick and the Sunny Garden tonight. He'll work it out too quickly, and drag me through it all again.

When the light's off it's totally dark. I hang my shirt over the back of the chair, as though that'll give it some air, and I lie on the bed.

273

In the morning I shower in the bathroom down the hall and I go to the ward for a patient breakfast. I tell them I've come in early to do a few things with the project, and then I go back to the room.

I can't think what D. Ford's D stands for.

Is there anyone else? Yes, but I don't know her name. We have had sex though.

Is there anyone else? Why, yes. Sister Ford.

Is she my Mrs Liebowitz, the strange formality, the one time only? I don't think so. Mrs Liebowitz was awesome. I think D. Ford scares me, and that's not the same.

There's no-one else. D. Ford is nothing to me. It would have been misleading to mention her, perverse though that sounds. I know we've met before, in some ward in the middle of last year and maybe once or twice on DMO shifts since, and I know we've bumped into each other twice recently, once heavily, but there really is no-one else. I'm not ending it with Kelly to start anything with D. Ford.

But I couldn't tell Kelly that. I couldn't tell Kelly that I happened to have sex with someone because I wasn't concentrating. Because I was thinking about the NHMRC forms and distracted by the state of our association. Or because I couldn't think of the right thing to say. That could imply that I would have nailed anyone who appeared at the door at that moment, and that's just not the case. I hope it's not the case. It would certainly have been a surprising turn for my relationship with Frank Dudgeon to take, a tumble on the bed, a good deal of rubbing, writhing our way to glory while he gripped the rail.

I go for a walk. As I expect anyone, regardless of gender preference, needs to should they accidentally lead themselves to contemplate sex with the Dud. I happen to be passing Seven when there's a Code Blue. I look at my beeper, and it's in Seven.

Why not? What have I got to lose? I'll be the first there for sure and the worst that can happen is that I might extend my strike-out streak to forty-two to zero.

Half an hour later, when my strike-out streak is forty-two to zero, I'm back in the room. What is it that happens with these? Technically I'm sure I've got it covered, but I'm not exactly a lucky charm when someone calls a Code Blue.

I realise now that I'm missing Kelly, or the idea of Kelly. Already. But I really don't think it was going to work, not in the sense of being a longer-term thing. Looking at it objectively, I think it's better that it's sorted out. We could have become too attached, this could have been worse.

I get paged during the Dubois round. Two C. Probably the haematology consult I've been trying to line up sporadically for a week and a half. I excuse myself and go to another office to make the call.

Hi, it's Dawn, the person who answers the phone says. And then she says nothing.

Yeah, it's Jon Marshall from psych. You paged me.

Dawn, she says again, as though she's insisting, as though this is all as clear as a wake-up call to her.

And just when I'm thinking, Surely it's mid-morning, even in Two C, I work it out. Dawn, Sister Dawn Ford. She's assuming that, because I've had sex with her, I know her name already.

How are you? I ask her, in an almost generic way, in case I'm wrong.

I'm fine. I thought maybe we should talk.

Good. That'd be good. That's probably a very good idea.

How about when you finish work today? I live pretty nearby, so, you know, wherever.

We agree on a time and place, six o'clock in the car

275

park of the El Guacamole Mexican Cantina, neutral ground but near her flat (the only place near her flat that I know). I start formulating my approach, my 'What a silly mistake we've made' piece to complement hers.

I'm glad she's called. This had the potential to be very embarrassing if we didn't sort it out quickly. And I've already shown recently how poorly I respond to embarrassment.

At least I know her name now. Even though we're going to be calling this a mistake, putting it behind us, et cetera, I think she would see it as pretty poor form if she found out that I didn't know her name.

This is not the late 1960s. This is not a time when having sex with someone and subsequently asking their name is highly regarded. Is it better to have sex with someone and then not ask their name? I don't know. I think it wasn't long ago that I was stressing to Rick that conversation came first. That a bit of high-quality chat was seen as an important precursor to intercourse in the circles in which we moved. I don't think it would help either of us, Rick's cause or mine, if I took him aside now and told him of this exception to the rule. Rick appreciates clarity more than most of us.

I want to get some work done. I want to feel I'm at least in control of something. There are two admissions. I do them both, before the registrars can even think about looking for tuning forks. I play no table tennis, and I walk out of the ward at five forty-five.

Dawn Ford is waiting in the car park of the El Guacamole Mexican Cantina when I arrive. She flicks her cigarette into the garden, and she waves.

It's BYO, she says, *so I brought rum.*

And I'm thinking, Why are we having a BYO conversation? Why do we need rum for clarity? And isn't it illegal to consume alcohol in car parks? I'm wondering how to begin this, who will begin it, wishing I'd put more thought into the specifics. Even if we both know it was a mistake, it has to be handled tactfully. She walks and I walk beside her, assuming we'll get down to business at any moment. We don't.

Been here before? she says as she swings the door open with her free hand and leads me inside to a booth. Why are we inside? Why are we not talking?

A uni student in a poncho comes up to us and says, *Yep?* Looking at me, looking at Dawn Ford.

Nachos? she says. *What do you think of nachos?*

Well, they're fine, I say, agreeing in principle since that's the way the question was worded. I want to clarify things already. I want to restate our purpose. I want to tell her I have no philosophical objections to nachos, and I want to send the uni student and his poncho away, tell him this'll only take five minutes and we'll be gone.

We'll share a large nachos first, she says. *And could we have a couple of Cokes and an ashtray?*

Any sour cream? Guacamole?

She looks at me and says, *Honey?*

And my instinct is to think that she just doesn't get nachos. Sour cream and guacamole are almost universal nachos options, but honey is perverse. And I'm back-tracking, thinking what are we here for? How did food get involved? What's all this rum and Coke and smoking and nachos? What kind of place has honey as a nachos option? Why not jam?

And it's only when she says, *Both,* that I've tracked forward enough in my back-tracking to get to the Honey part again. And it's my name. It's my name now. In front of the shabbily ponchoed uni student, the far from desirable Dawn Ford is calling me Honey. Right at this second it would be much more applicable if she called me Nausea.

This is a disaster. For the next half hour we role play. I am a rabbit. Dawn Ford is an astoundingly bright light.

I dream of invisibility, but I'm still far too tangible. I dream that the uni student is a sporting shooter, with an insanely large rifle about to take me between the eyes.

Dawn Ford smokes and drinks and chows down on the nachos.

This is pretty cool, you and the room, she says. It's wild that we can, well, you know, pretty much whenever we want right in the middle of the multistorey. I'll probably never go to the dining room again. Still, you've got to eat, I suppose. All said through a soft, blue cloud of smoke and with a piece of shallot the size of the Yucatan Peninsula on one of her front teeth.

So it's on now, me and Dawn Ford. I get no opportunity to move into my 'What a silly mistake we've made' piece. I've actually made a much bigger mistake than I realised, but Dawn Ford is fine with this. Dawn is working on the sex first, conversation after model, and she seems fine with it.

Have you spoken to Kelly? she's saying, and I'm nodding. I hope it wasn't too hard on her.

I shrug. I'm non-verbal now. Rabbits, they don't talk. They just wait for the bullet. I always thought bullets were faster than this, a quick death. Depends where they get you, I suppose.

There is a corn chip in my hand and I'm turning it over and over. It's an isosceles triangle. Dawn's talking about the Code Blue, making double-beeping noises and laughing, as though we're reminiscing already, looking back fondly on first-time awkwardness.

I have to go home now, I tell her. People are expecting me.

This surprises her, but she recovers easily.

Tough with Kelly, hey? she says, and pats my arm. That's okay.

We split the bill and I'm getting the impression she wouldn't say no to a lift home, so I don't offer.

In the car I try to see the positive side. This is something my mother always said I should do when anything really fucked happened when I was tiny.

And I tell myself I'm only one sensible conversation away from straightening things out with Dawn Ford. That's the best I can do. And considering I hardly seem to have the capacity for sensible conversation any more, it's not great.

On the passenger seat, my briefcase begins to disclose its secrets, leaks out an unwelcome smell of old orgasm.

This is one thing I can fix, one thing I probably have to fix before taking it inside when I get home. I head off the freeway and drive around until I find a discreet industrial bin. I open the briefcase and yesterday's misjudgements come back all too clearly. I stuff the forms into the bin, and then it occurs to me that there might be something identifying on them so I pull them out again and take them back to the car to check. Challenging myself to see the positive side to this, but there is no positive side to pulling semen-stained paper from industrial bins. Whether it's your own or not.

Two people walk past, and I have to sit there with the light on as though I'm contemplating every question carefully, thinking only of a great theory, and possibilities, as I uncrumple the pages across my steering wheel, fiddle with a pen.

And as soon as they've gone, and as soon as I'm sure that there's no serial number, no hospital stamp and no-one's name anywhere, I run back to the bin and push the forms in as far as I can.

Rick and Jen are eating at the table when I get home, finishing some takeaway. The moment I walk in Rick says, *I smell something.*

Smoke, Jen says, picking the better of two bad options. *Tell me it's not that awful woman from Friday night.*

And I have to admit it's over with Kelly. They ask me why and I tell them it's just over.

And it's on with the nameless one? Jen says as I'm putting my briefcase in my room, leaving it and the window open, shutting the door behind me as I come out again.

Dawn Ford. Her name's Dawn Ford.

And the answer to the question?

Fuck, I don't know. It's not supposed to be.

It must be special, what she's doing for you, Rick says and makes the standard hollow-hand, tongue-in-cheek oral sex gesture and laughs.

What's so special about that? Jen says and takes her plate into the kitchen.

Rick's tongue stays stuck in his cheek. He flicks a glance to the kitchen, then looks back at me.

I mean, what's the big deal? she says as she runs water into the sink. *Why wouldn't you? Doesn't everyone?*

Rick's expression turns to pain. As though he's just found out he's much further off the pace than he thought. As though everyone else in the world is lining up for the oral event, but no-one invited him. He slides back in the chair, lowers his head, takes the edge of the pine table between his teeth, and bites.

It's okay, fella, I tell him. She's messing with you.

You'll never know, will you? she says and sticks her head round the corner. *Strange boy.*

He unclenches his teeth, sighs in a seriously melancholy way.

Teeth marks on the landlord's table, I say to him, pointing.

Before our time. He wipes the saliva away. *What's he going to do? Check dental records?*

Jen goes to her room to do some work on her thesis. Rick makes coffee and we drink it at the table.

When she drops them, he says, *shit, they land hard.* He sits looking down in the direction of the teeth marks, muttering, *Why wouldn't you?* and, *Doesn't everyone?*

I'm about to give him Johnno's reading of it, the phenomenology, the demographics, north of Townsville, Sydney, major metropolitan hospitals, when Jen walks back in to pick up a couple of biscuits and says, as though it's continuing her previous sentence, *And I'm sure Jon's more than happy to return the favour.*

Yeah. What do you mean?

I'm sure it's not just something you arrange to have done to you.

What?

I think we've got to get some balance into this. I think Rick needs to know that this doesn't just work one way.

Oh, yeah.

And that you're giving as good as you get.

Yeah, sure. You mean, in principle.

No. I mean with your mouth. Orally.

It's about to be my turn to bite the edge of the table. They're both looking at me and I'm realising it could be something I've arranged to have done to me, and right now that seems very shabby. Ungenerous, inconsiderate, worse. I'm even more thoughtless than I realised. I may not have returned the requisite number of favours lately, three perhaps, and it's not as though I can call Kelly now and offer to make it up to her. Why did no-one explain this to me before? And would it have changed my view of the whole event, and its uncomplicated (selfish) pleasure?

But I've broken up with her now, I say, as though this begins some kind of answer, and Jen's about to challenge when a cat screeches behind her. Hisses, and another cat hisses back.

Fuck, Rick says, and jumps. *Is that in the house?*

There's a thump as a cat hits the floor, more hissing. And just as I'm starting to laugh because I think it's in Rick's room, I realise it's in mine.

Rick gets there first, opens the door just as Jean-Paul vanishes out the window, chasing some other cat. There's nothing in the room now. Nothing but a briefcase open on the bed, and a smell.

He screws up his face. *I think they fucked in your brief-case, Jon-boy.* And he backs out laughing.

And just when I'm laughing too and thinking I might have got away with it, I realise that the smell is truly awful, and not the same, not the same as a small amount of yesterday's semen on paper.

And I realise that the cats almost certainly did fuck in my briefcase. And I don't like that at all. My briefcase has been there plenty of nights, back when it just smelled like a briefcase, and cats had no inclination to fuck in it then.

This is bad chemistry.

And across town, I imagine the cats are circling the industrial bin right at this moment and realising that, whether or not it's a good idea, biology's about to get the better of them. And that's just how it is.

Bad chemistry.

36

There's a lot they don't teach you at Med School. Most semen tastes grassy and mine, at least, appears to be a cat aphrodisiac. If I had to begin a list of things I didn't need to know, these would be two.

The next night, on a DMO shift, I bump into Kelly.

She's calmer now and I tell her I'm sorry for being such a dickhead.

It doesn't seem to be anything you've got much control over.

We talk, and I apologise for several minor inconsiderate acts, two or three times each, as though this compensates for not dealing with the Dawn Ford incident, or the fact that I'm up three–nil in the oral event.

She's still far from impressed but she says, *At least it's sorted out. I don't know what's going on with you, but I think my life could be a bit easier if you're not a part of it.*

Yeah, I think mine could be easier if I wasn't a part of it as well.

Still the jokes, she says. *Irrepressible, aren't we?* And she reminds me about the social club dinner dance this Saturday, and asks if we're still going. *Just as friends,* she says. *That's what I was thinking. If we're still going.*

Sure. That'd be good.

And I can't say anything else, because she's being more generous than I deserve. And because I'd totally forgotten about the dinner dance, so I didn't have an excuse ready. I couldn't trash her twice in the same week, end the relationship and say no to the friend idea. Not that being friends ever works. Not that there's ever really anything between you but a wall once you've stopped having sex. But you have to try. You can't say no to trying, if it's suggested.

The next day I'm wondering how I'll explain this to Dawn Ford. If I have to explain it to Dawn Ford. I shouldn't, but I'm guessing I will.

And where did Kelly get irrepressible from? How could someone use the word 'irrepressible' in conversation, and never have heard of spoonerisms? Knowledge is so inconsistent. But I have to admit I'm not hanging out for anything gloriously polysyllabic from Dawn Ford.

Why do I keep doing this, turning this into a comparison? And anyway, isn't *irrepressible as always* slightly tautological? Is there any need for the always?

None of this, not any part of it, is worth the trouble.

I should be thinking of work now, melatonin. Replacement grant application forms. I should write myself a note and Blu-Tack it to the wall next to the Edward de Bono card. 1: Get grant application forms. 2: Fill in grant application forms. 3: With ink this time, black or blue, doesn't matter which.

The door next to the melatonin room is open when I get down there. I'd heard that Marlon de Lisle had claimed the room, apparently because he assumed he was entitled, since someone else already had one. He's on his way out, and in the interests of neighbourliness I tell him I've got a couple of dozen Monte Carlos, should he ever feel the need.

Shit. They give you a room and biscuits? He shakes his head. *And a sign on the door? I wonder what I should get on my sign?*

Dawn Ford turns up not long after. She locks the door, and in my anxiety to frame my Saturday night arrangements the right way, we seem to end up on the bed again, before I've offered any worthwhile contribution to the conversation.

I prise her face away and I clap my hand over her mouth when she's saying, *I want . . .* and I tell her about my conversation with Kelly, Saturday night, just as friends. Just in case she had anything else in mind. And she says, *I want it like last time,* and I'm saying Saturday night, Kelly, just as friends, and she's crouching over me, saying, *I didn't wear any underwear today,* and I'm saying Saturday night, okay by you? And she's grabbing the bed rail with one hand and yanking at my pants with the other, saying, *Okay, okay, I get it. You're letting her down gently. Fine. Shut up. I want it like last time.*

And my pager goes off, like last time (but earlier), and she whips it from my belt like a gunslinger and I shout, No, just before she drops it onto the floor. The tone surprises both of us, freezes her in the middle of her frenzied pant-work, her other hand still grappling with my belt buckle.

Expecting an important call, are we?

Yeah.

It's a lie (of course it's a lie), but it might slow things down, give me a chance. She presses the button. The lie won't last long.

Who's 7939?

Frank Dudgeon.

Oh. It is important, she says, just as I'm thinking I should have kept lying, come up with something better. *Can't have you keeping Doctor Dudgeon waiting, I suppose. Bugger.* She swings herself onto the floor. *Some other time then.* She pats my thigh, gives it a squeeze. *Some other time very soon.* She pulls me to a sitting position using my tie, kisses me on the lips, quick and hard. *If I don't go right now you're going to have to fight me off. Bloody Doctor Dudgeon.*

Yeah. I'd better call.

285

Yeah. She doesn't move. *Shame you don't have a phone on your desk. You could call him from here. Get it over with in a second.* She puts my pager down, but not quickly, giving me plenty of time to reassess the urgency of the call. She notices my Edward de Bono card. *What's this?*

It's just a card I once got.

And when she's reading it, I swear I see her lips move.

'Elemental simplicity and confidence both of which so easily get lost later on.' You haven't lost your confidence have you?

It's the elemental simplicity that I miss. Things get complicated far too easily when you aren't five. He's a smart man.

Really? Complicated?

On the inside. Way complicated.

I've got something very simple in mind right now.

I'd better call Doctor Dudgeon. He doesn't like to be kept waiting.

Who does? You call me soon, okay? And she gives me her version of an impish smile (not a good version), blows me a kiss from the door, and she's gone.

It's some effort not to thank the Dud profusely when I call, but I manage to hold back.

Just checking to see that you got the NHMRC forms, not that the deadline's for a while yet.

Yeah. Yeah, thanks. I did.

I decide not to mention that I've used them already, but for a slightly different project than we'd discussed. It's enough that I'm aware that my semen may be a cat aphrodisiac. I don't think I need to share it with the Dud. He'd probably see it as another research opportunity (*Well, goodness me, I wonder how other mammalian species would . . .*).

He tells me he and Johnno have talked about the rosters

for Term Three and I'm too important to be moved. *Staff numbers'll be down because a couple of people are leaving, and you're probably aware that in the past that's sometimes meant that psych has gone without a resident, but we think we can manage it this time if the registrars take up a bit more of the load and you're prepared to do Staff Health for part of two mornings a week.*

All this and biscuits, I'm thinking as I go back to the room. Who could ask for anything more? New NHMRC forms maybe.

37

Saturday night turns ugly far too quickly.

Dawn watches us arrive, and keeps watching us. Is there no subtlety about her? I'm hoping it's obvious only to me. Hoping that, to Kelly, Dawn is just another background face in the crowded dining room.

Kelly goes for drinks when we haven't been there long, when I still haven't adjusted to the 1940s theme that no-one warned me about, or the mock-Andrews Sisters doing something bad on the small temporary stage. Then I remember it was all made clear on the poster, and the tickets, but I stopped remembering this about two weeks ago, when we decided to go and I realised that two weeks was around the commitment perimeter for me and I was more comfortable if I didn't think about it.

So I just said, Sure, sure. Telling myself, two weeks is fine. Probably suggesting to Kelly that a holiday in two months wasn't out of the question.

I involve myself in a nearby inane conversation and offer my views on the Broncos' chances this season when asked. There's a crowd around the bar and Kelly's somewhere in the middle.

The Broncos aren't finishers, I tell everyone around me. They'll get to September and choke.

Kelly is talking to some nurses now, nurses from Two C who are in the queue next to her. She looks back this way, and then looks back at them.

My Broncos remarks are challenged.

Two C is Dawn's ward, but I hope that's not a problem. I hope Dawn's been discreet. Kelly gets to the front, gets served. Comes back.

Not quite back. At a distance of about two metres, she says, *Catch*, throws me my beer, and walks out.

I do not catch beer well. It's not something you ever get to practise, and she sends it to me like a knife thrower, end over end. The spray catches several people in the vicinity, and the stubbie hits my hands upside down, glugging beer onto my shoes while I'm trying to work out which way is up.

I apologise to everyone around me, both wet and dry. I apologise because I can't explain, and they're all looking at me as though I can.

You should be more careful what you say about the Broncos, someone says. *Some of their supporters are pretty committed.*

The beer soaks through my shirt to my skin. The singers are beginning 'Boogie Woogie Bugle Boy' as I leave. I shower and I rinse the beer out of my shirt. I leave it hanging from the shower rail to drip and I go to the melatonin room. The stage backs onto the wall and the singing is loud in here, loud and unwelcome, but I can't think where else to go. Topless, dateless and damp, backing onto music I hate.

I hadn't had high hopes for tonight, but I'd had higher hopes than this. I should just go home.

There's a knock at the door. I don't know if it's Dawn Ford or Kelly, or someone else, and I'm not at all sure who I want it to be. The mythical Mrs Liebowitz maybe?

I know you're in there, the voice of Dawn Ford says.

Hey, no shirt, she says when I open the door. *I've never seen you with no shirt before.*

And she turns the light out.

And just as I'm thinking, That's a hell of a way to tell a guy his body's not the best, she lunges at me, knocks me onto the bed and winds me.

I'm not good at judging things in the dark, she says. *But I thought this'd be fun.*

I'm still trying to catch my breath as she's whipping my pants off like it's an Olympic event, grabbing my penis in both hands. As though it ever needed both hands.

Wow, she says, and I realise she really isn't good at judging things in the dark, even tactile things.

You must have very small hands, I say, and then it's mouth down there, warm, wet mouth and, sure, I don't really like Dawn Ford, but this could be a very bad time to tell her.

She works away as though she's pneumatic, faster and faster, as though there are lives at stake with this penis. On the other side of the wall it's all aboard the 'Chattanooga Choo-choo'. In the melatonin room, Dawn Ford switches to express. And I'm thinking everybody does it, and sometimes you just can't stop them. We'll talk later, we will have the necessary conversation, but just not now.

And I'm seeing nothing but I'm sure my eyes are wide open. Wide open. Closer, closer, danger in the tunnel. I can't believe the speed of this. The breath leaves me like a rush of steam. I derail.

Dawn recoils, spits, coughs, starts making wordless oral noises and interrupts these only to vomit. I jump up and turn the light on, wondering what's gone wrong. She's sitting on the edge of the bed, with her head between her knees and a mess on the floor.

How the fuck did I ever get diced carrot through there? I say, in case it lightens the mood.

Big mistake.

What made you think you could do that?

I guess I just thought it's what people did.

Did we talk about it?

No. How do you talk about that stuff? And I don't think we've had a conversation yet.

Oh, fine. Well, at least it's not really your fault then.

One of my housemates said everyone did it. She said, Why wouldn't you?

Why wouldn't I? You talked to your housemates about me doing this?

No, no. I don't do that sort of thing. She meant, Why wouldn't you? Why wouldn't one? General, not specific.

Why wouldn't one? Have you ever tasted it? I don't care if Kelly McLean did it to you all the time.

Hey, I didn't mention Kelly McLean. I want to be clear on that. I might do some crappy things, but one thing I don't do is blab about stuff like this. Okay?

And I can't even take it up with Jen later, much as I'd like to. Much as I've been misled by her advice.

The evening ends, as it can only end, with me apologising again. Driving home with my wet shirt in a ball on the passenger seat. Knowing that I needed to raise the 'relationship' issue, but completely unable to do so.

I'm trying to explain it to Rick the next day when we're watching the football on TV. Trying to tell him how it can be that I haven't had the chance to be clear with Dawn

Ford yet, even though we might have managed several sexual incidents.

But since almost all of the details are appalling, I can only speak in generalities. I tell him there can be problems with this business. That the conversation part's okay. It's just that once you've actually had sex with someone it can be hard to stop.

Jen seems to find it easy enough.

It could be a gender thing. There are certain expectations placed on a male. It's expected that you will want sex, and if you try to resist any sexual overture, it's not well received. It means you get into this pattern where you just keep having sex.

Bad pattern.

The problem with Dawn was the conversation part. We haven't really managed that yet, and I have a feeling that if we'd started with that we could have avoided a lot of this. The whole thing, in fact. I think, if we'd started with talk, we could have exhausted all possibilities in about five minutes. The only common ground we've got is that we had sex in the same room at the same time about a week ago. Imagine if we'd talked instead. Imagine how clear it would have become. What would we have talked about? The Broncos' prospects this season?

They'll choke. For sure.

That's what I figured.

38

On Monday I play Tetris, but I'm getting no better.

I am left surprisingly alone. By the ward, by cats, by Dawn Ford. I take patient sandwiches to the melatonin room for lunch, and I actually prepare for the Ethics Committee meeting.

In the Sunny Garden Rick says, *Trash anyone today?*

No.

Bugger. I thought it'd be today.

Why?

You usually trash people early in the week, and she's really due. You've already pretty much decided. Besides, I've got five bucks on this with Jen. I said it'd be today and she said it wouldn't be till at least later in the week.

Why not?

She said you'd probably decide to have sex with her again first, and you'd probably only get round to trashing her when you found the next one.

It's remarks like this that suggest that I might be developing an image problem. How can I make it clear that the last thing I want at the moment is a next one? I'd really love to be left alone for a while. I could do with a holiday, up north perhaps.

When my Tuesday plate of four Monte Carlos arrives, it's the ninth since Johnno last ate any. I now keep them in a pile in the corner, nine plates each with four biscuits, all with the Glad Wrap still on to avoid encouraging rodents.

The Dud drops in. *I thought I might find you here.* Said

as though it's a good thing, as though being here means work, rather than work avoidance.

He tells me that my submission to the Ethics Committee was very well written and that I should present a paper at Hospital Week next month. My pleading that it's all still conceptual does me no good. He's already got me pencilled in for a session time.

I've got a bit of an interest in writing myself, he says. *Medical history mainly. I've been wanting to write a* Life of Paracelsus *for a while. A monograph for the quincentenary of his birth perhaps, in 1993.*

Sounds interesting.

You think so? Good. Not everyone's cup of tea, but I thought you might go for it.

And when he leaves, he's absent-mindedly whistling 'How do you solve a problem like Maria?' from *The Sound of Music,* probably because his brain has made some loose Tyrolean connection with the ancient Swiss physician. And what does it mean, that I'm the sort of person who might go for it?

In the next room, Marlon de Lisle, having studied most of the night, rolls heavily around in the bed, reciting something over and over in his sleep in a blurry kind of way, rolls again, muffles his voice down into the pillow.

I call the Dud's secretary to ask for another set of grant forms. I tell her that I thought it would be smart to have one for a draft and another for the final version. *Good idea,* she says, in a way that suggests the Dud will think it's smart, too.

On Wednesday Johnno decides we'll have lunch again.

Presenting a paper will look good when it comes to applying for a position on the training program in a few months, he says, just when I'd relaxed and thought we'd never have one of those lunches where your future gets discussed.

Today, the thought of my future on the training pro-gram sinks in me like a stone, so it's good I've got a mouthful of potato salad and I can only nod.

But anyway, he says, either picking up on the sinking feeling or deciding by himself that there are more interest-ing topics, *you seem to be involved with a different nurse now.*

It wasn't my plan.

But didn't I tell you? Didn't I tell you when you had the room they'd all want you? It's the Monte Carlos, isn't it? You lure them to the room on the pretext of a biscuit or two and then you root them. Oh god, those were the days, when someone'd root you for just a couple of biscuits.

Speaking of which, not the rooting part, the biscuit part, I've got a few for you. Forty, as of this morning.

Why don't you send them to me internal mail? I never get anything good in the internal mail. You should be appreciating this, you know. This time comes to an end.

I certainly hope so. I'm very tired.

At least you're making the most of it. I'm not sure I made the most of it. Not sure if I shouldn't have fol-lowed up with Mrs Liebowitz, but what do you do? Anyway, I'm out of the game now. Now they're just sorry for me. Even the rumour I started years ago about my penis being very large has died out. That's the problem with the high staff turn-over in places like this. You lose so much of that collective memory. The only things people remember are quite unkind.

So now you've moved on to singers.

Well, you have to, really.

It occurs to me later that I'd be quite happy if the col-lective memory after I leave here had me as nerdy, pleasant, cooperative. A skinny guy who slept nights, and deserved to. Who did little harm, wronged nobody.

I work in the ward. I am as nerdy, pleasant and cooperative as I can be. And in the ward, no-one seems to notice the difference. Maybe it's still me after all. The Reliable Marshall. The unspectacular almost-high achiever no-one used to have sex with. Those were the days. Desperate days admittedly, but in retrospect there's a great honesty in desperation. And very little collateral damage.

I should have got out more, broadened my horizons. My mother told me that, and she was right. My whole time at uni I hung around with the people in my year, and its three or four desirable girls decided pretty quickly that we were going to be just friends. But I persisted. I became very good at hanging around. I didn't take No for an answer, I took it on as a lifestyle.

I graduated, and I seemed to go straight from pariah to commodity with no period of adjustment in between. From unnoticed to available and meeting people, single young females in numbers, ward after ward of opportunities to change my luck. And still, I thought, it would take some changing. I had always expected to be in a position where it would take weeks to persuade anyone to have sex with me (or to find out that they weren't going to be persuaded), so I couldn't be ready for the present arrangement, where the sex comes before I've had any chance to work out how persuasive I might want to be. You really are in a much better position if you get to know them first.

I take a large cardboard box down to the melatonin room to collect the biscuits for Johnno. I'm there for about five seconds before Dawn Ford appears.

When you didn't call I wondered if there was a problem.

But I've never called you.

Look, I want to try again.

What do you mean?

I'm telling myself, Be nerdy, be pleasant, be cooperative. Through this there will be long-term survival.

I think we may have a misunderstanding here, I tell her.

I know. I've thought about it. I think I can do it.

I'm not sure that's the answer. I'm not even sure that that's the misunderstanding.

Please, at least let me try. Reaching for my fly.

I should be clear on a few things, I tell her.

I'm being nerdy, I'm being pleasant, but I'm not sure if this is the right time for cooperative.

Please, she says as she kneels. As though this needs silence. What is this? Prayer?

Look, I . . . We've really got to talk, Dawn. We've never even had a conversation, and I have a policy of starting with a conversation.

Honey, she says, chastising me. *I'm trying here. I'm trying to give you what you want.*

But not even I know what I want.

I think I do, she says, and takes my penis in her mouth.

And it's just not possible to have a serious conversation with a head that's in your groin and on the end of your member like a lamprey. That's what I would have figured, and it's true. And what happened to nerdy, pleasant, co-operative? Why aren't these things working, making everything like it used to be? Before graduating, before respiratory, before mouths started attaching themselves to my middle parts.

I actually want her to stop, that's what I want, despite the fact that she thinks my wants are this uncomplicated. I want her to stop, I want her to go away, I want to start this year all over again, but the only way I could get my penis out of her mouth would be to apply direct pressure to her eyeballs until she let go, and that's just not on.

I haven't worked out how I feel about reciprocating, I tell her, but she just waves one hand to shut me up.

No, listen. Returning the favour. I don't know how I feel.

Another wave, a full-mouthed angry noise. As though I'm distracting her.

And I'm doing my utmost to be uncooperative, but it's not easy. Nerdy, pleasant, totally uncooperative, and we all get out of here alive. That's my new plan. I'm working on diversionary activities, but she's working harder. She's a terrier down there. I imagine her as a terrier, an actual little brown dog, and this stalls the progress for a while. I say the word flaccid over and over like a mantra. I wonder at length why it has two Cs and no S, but that doesn't help much. Two Cs instead of one, as in placid. Placido Domingo, Flaccido Domingo. I'm running out of strategies, other then eye-gouging. I'm starting to hyperventilate.

Suddenly, she coughs, jerks her head aside and squeezes. I take little breaths, little breaths, as though I'm having a baby and the head's just through. Why is she squeezing? What did I do to deserve the squeeze technique?

I'm sorry, she says, still on her knees, still squeezing and looking down at the floor. *I can't. I was nearly there, but I can't.*

No big deal.

I was okay till it touched the back of my throat.

It's all right. It's really not a big issue. Maybe we should talk . . .

I wanted to do it, but I even gag if the toothbrush touches my soft palate.

It's okay. Forget it. And any time you want to release the emergency brake . . .

So things are okay, even if I don't?

This is not, of course, the time to tell her that I was again giving an in-principle answer. That I had her long-term self-esteem in mind, and not even a short-term relationship.

So I can't end it at the moment, even though I can't understand how I can be in a position where it's an option, where there's anything to end. I tell her I need to work a lot, right now and for the foreseeable future. I have a presentation to do at Hospital Week, so I'll need to spend a lot of time on that.

That's okay, she says. *If you don't call me I'll understand why.*

Which she won't, of course, but today isn't the day to get into that. Several more times she makes me tell her that her revulsion to swallowing is no big deal, and only when she's sure things are okay with the two of us is she prepared to go.

When I get home Jen says she's cooking dinner, nachos. Nachos with everything. Sour cream, guacamole.

El grande, Rick says. *It's the only way.*

And I want to say to him, You should try it with honey. Rum and Coke and cigarettes and honey. El diablo.

I can't believe the predicament I'm in, I tell them. I appear to be deeply embedded in the second week of a relationship that totally baffles me. I didn't start it, I'm not keeping it going, but it's going anyway. I'm a complete passenger here. I've never been less attractive than I am at the moment and it's like I've got a dog whistle in my pants. I even tried to be nerdy, pleasant and cooperative, but I think the damage is done.

I think you're meat out there, Jon-boy, Rick says helpfully. *You're just meat to them.*

Not that you don't have nerdy nailed down, though, Jen adds.

Nerdy, reckless, thoughtless and meat. And any time anything thirty-seven degrees and soft comes near me I end up deep in trouble of the worst kind.

Is it always framed in such a passive way? Jen says. *Are you always the victim of flesh?*

Yeah. Isn't everybody? Doesn't flesh make us all victims?

Not fucking lately, Rick says, with feeling.

Rick, you realise when I die, and I must die soon, someone's going to have to handle my responsibilities. And it's you I've got in mind.

Could you trash the present one first?

Do you know how hard I'm trying? And when she's gone, I'm shutting the door and I'm not coming out. What do I do? What do I do to sort this out?

You've always managed to squirm your way out of things before.

Yeah, but squirming needs talk. How can we have any kind of discussion when she's always got something in her mouth? She initiates sex faster than I can possibly initiate conversation. She beats me every time. And how can I talk then, when she's on me down there? I've tried. It doesn't work. Do cows chat while they're being milked? I don't think so. I've got to have a plan. I've got to get in early, before anyone reaches for anyone's genitals, and I've got to have something ready. Something with impact, but that doesn't reflect negatively on her.

That's nice, Jen says. *Not exactly definite, but nice. Nerdy, and that other stuff.*

What? Rick says. *Like a bad disease, or being gay, or something?*

Thanks, Rick. Thanks. That ought to do it. I know I haven't handled this particularly well, but I'd like to try to insult her intelligence just a little less than that.

The next day, since an answer doesn't seem forthcoming, I start working on my Hospital Week paper. When I'm taking a break for a few games of Galaxion in the Quarters, I check my pigeon hole. I pull out the usual handful of pointless circulars, and a more substantial document.

Substantial enough to have a title page.

Which reads *Philippus Aureolus Theophrastus Bombastus von Hohenheim (Paracelsus): The Early Years.* Clipped onto it is a note. *This is just the beginning. Any comments? FD.*

39

I'm DMO again on Sunday, and I decide to stay the night at the hospital afterwards.

Around midnight I find myself with Marlon de Lisle, all studied out and standing in his undone black shirt and his boxer shorts at the sink in the bathroom near our rooms. Cleaning his teeth slowly, hogging the sink and gazing into the mirror. Watching himself as though he has to, as though his teeth might have moved since last time.

I didn't think you were on tonight, I say to him. Did you swap?

No. I'm not on. I'm just, he shrugs, *here.*

It must be twelve-thirty, or nearly one, when I'm lying in the dark thinking of dozens of ways of sorting out the Dawn Ford situation (and each of them doomed to failure), and I hear Marlon creak out of bed, his door open, his bare feet on the lino and, shortly after that, music from the piano in the dining room. Music I don't know, complex, strangely shaped. I can only assume it's Marlon, but it's nothing from the Floyd canon, not as far as I can tell.

In the morning we hit the showers at the same time.

This is getting like boarding school, he says, and I wonder if he means I'm getting in the way, if I should be rescheduling my bathroom visits to give him space, give him the latitude due the head prefect.

I dress quickly, so I can be in the dining room first (and in a corner and facing the other way) but we open our doors at the same time and it then seems impossible, probably to both of us, not to sit together. He sighs. I feel I should apologise. I manage not to.

Since there is a rule that a DMO who is held back after midnight is entitled to a bed and a meal, I sign on for a free breakfast. Marlon stands next to me, signing nothing. His right to a free breakfast goes unquestioned.

We sit at a table and he stares down at his cereal, moves his spoon around in it in slow, sullen circles. I pretend my toast is really interesting and I leave him alone. I'd like to mention last night's music, but it doesn't seem like the right time.

Sometimes I think my brain is too old for this, he says, and I figure I should say something, something that leads into conversation, but I'm not sure what.

Study, piano, the limited fine-motor demands of cereal? What's his brain too old for? The moment passes, and nothing seems to have been the right thing to say.

He looks at me, looks down again, shovels cereal.

I just want to get this all sorted out and get back to my life, you know?

Yeah. I've got a few things to sort out myself.

He nods.

I begin to wonder if I'm really pissing him off in some way, if I should qualify the nature and extent of the things

I have to sort out, make it clear that I wasn't trying to compete, and that they're probably pretty minor things really. I wonder if I should try a new subject. I wonder if he's got any views on the Broncos.

You should eat that toast, he says. *It'll get cold.*

It was already cold. They make it cold. They have some special institutional totally non-thermal way of browning it.

He smiles and scoops the last of the cereal into his mouth. *Well, I'm off. I've got some scope driving to do.*

Now this is the kind of enigma Rick would like to be. He'd love to be able to take cereal, add only a few of the most mundane remarks possible, and invest it all with such mysterious intensity. Rather than being the person who rattles off twelve not very funny remarks about toast, just to stop a silence. But the stories Rick doesn't tell about being in bands probably aren't quite as legendary as Marlon's.

Once I've dispensed with the toast I call Dawn Ford, for the first and only spontaneous time. This should have her worried, but it doesn't. Everything else did, but this doesn't. I tell myself it's not Dawn Ford's fault that she's far from clever. As the relatively smart person in this troubled liaison, I should have handled it better. So the sorting out is up to me, and today has got to be the day.

We meet when she finishes work at three, and this time I'm taking no chances. I suggest a place outside, near the multistorey. It is therefore apparent that we are not meeting to give her another chance at overcoming her difficulties with a particular event.

I tell her it's over, because if I start by telling her it never began, this just won't work. I say we've had a few good times, her and me, but it has to come to an end. And the blame lies with me, my work commitments, and so on, and I can't commit to a relationship. Not right now. Everything's getting too complicated.

She says it's fine, that I don't need to commit any more than I have. Everything's perfect as far as she's concerned, apart from her difficulties with a particular event, and that's sorted out. I seem to expect nothing now that she's not more than prepared to give.

I explain that this isn't a good time for me. I present her with a long list of my personal inadequacies, many of which are quite genuine.

She says they're not important (but she doesn't dispute any of them).

I tell her she shouldn't expect these things to change.

She quotes Billy Joel (or, in fact, misquotes, but I know what she means).

I lie to her about her many qualities. I lie even more extensively about my many commitments.

She says she'll fit in around them. She has so far. No problem.

I tell her my track record speaks for itself, that I'm not to be trusted, that I'm the world's worst choice in any kind of relationship.

And when she says, *Not this kind of relationship*, I tell her about a bad disease that runs in my family and kills people young.

And this time she at least pauses before saying, *I'm a nurse, I can help you.*

And for one perverse moment I'm about to tell her that the disease is so bad that for the last few years of my father's life he was blind and deaf and in so many ways dysfunctional that my mother could communicate with him only by sucking his penis. But I just can't do that to my parents. I can't even think it.

And this doesn't leave me with much room to move.

I'm confronting some identity issues at the moment, I tell her. Some things about who I am as a person. Sexuality issues. I'm really not totally sure where I stand, who's team I should be batting for, if you get what I mean. All I'm sure about is that some of the guys round here look pretty good to me. Great in fact.

Which ones? she says. *Maybe we could come to some arrangement.*

I don't even know what that means, I tell her. And nor do I want to. I will practise a celibate life until I've worked through these things, or at least until there's a screening test for the disease that runs in my family and kills people young.

I continue this line, not that it's much of a line, trying to make myself sad and noble (devotion to work, the solitude of the room), but ending up somehow with a restatement of my inadequacies. They're getting easier to believe now, for me at least. I try to work my way back into sad and noble and . . .

Look, shut up, all right?

What?

You talk far too much. All you are is talk. And it's worse when it's this whinging. I'm sorry about the disease, I really am, and I'm sorry if you're worried about getting involved, when that's obviously what you want. Yet again, Dawn Ford takes me completely by surprise. *I'm sorry if you think you aren't good enough. And, to be honest, you weren't great.*

It hasn't been a good time for me lately, I begin to tell her, before realising that this is the worst time for excuses and my mediocrity could be my ticket out of here.

Maybe if you just relaxed a bit . . . God, I want to drop you, but how can I after all that disease talk? Did you put that on Kelly? Why can't you just take it easy? Why do you get so committed? You are completely messed up. Of course, you're studying depression. You don't know what fun is.

I'm obviously totally wrong for you, I tell her, taking it slowly and carefully, not wanting to blow it.

I'm sorry, but, yeah. I'm looking for something that's not such a big deal. A day-to-day thing. Fun, without all this crap. I really hope you don't get the disease, but, you know, don't call me again. Okay?

Yeah.

Except if that guy thing happens.

What?

The thing with you and another guy. That could be interesting. But not if he's a talker.

Sure.

And with that it's over. Several times I nearly blew it, but we got there. Not exactly the way I expected, but we got there.

In the evening I tell Rick I managed it. I broke up with her.

You broke up with her? he says. *You actually dropped her?*

Yeah. I just laid it on the line.

You just laid it on the line?

Laid it on the line.

Just the facts?

Pretty much. I've got a new respect for the direct approach. It's better for all concerned. At some point, someone has to tell someone, Sorry, but don't call me again.

That's pretty direct. And you didn't have sex with her first?

No.

305

He smiles. *Hey Jen,* he shouts. *You have to give me my five bucks back.*

Did he have sex with her first? Jen shouts from her room.

No sex, and it's a Monday.

No sex, including orogenital?

He looks at me.

Including orogenital.

Jen comes pounding out of her room and up the corridor and hands him a five-dollar note. *Fuck, you're hopeless,* she says to me.

She should talk to Dawn Ford. What did Dawn mean? To be honest I wasn't that great. Completely messed up. That's a little harsh. Messed up I'd probably have to settle for, but completely?

Incompletely messed up. More than partially messed up, but not completely. That's what I'd settle for.

Worried about getting involved, honestly not great, completely messed up, forgetting what fun is. Studying depression as a matter of course.

A blistering moment of truth. She really wanted out.

And how did I get it so wrong? All Dawn Ford wanted was more of the same (but of a slightly higher standard). Which is the way I was supposed to be. Day to day, relax, enjoy.

And if it hadn't been Dawn Ford would it have been different? If it had been someone I'd actually wanted in the room? No. I'm incompletely messed up. I would have worried about getting involved. Fretted about whether they were right or not, fought about holidays. Kelly wasn't right, not quite. But if she had been, would I have handled it any better?

The Dud pages me to see if I've had the chance to take a look at his Paracelsus. How did I end up in this position? Does he have no friends?

I think I manage to cover it, but only just, by telling him I want to give it my undivided attention, so I was planning to stay back tonight.

And he says he hopes that I'm claiming meals in the dining room, all these nights I'm staying back working on the project. *Just tell them I approved it if they've got any queries. Special DMO, that's what we'll call it.*

Not special enough to stay awake, I find out later. Around three a.m. when the last of his Paracelsus slides off my face and suddenly I'm sitting up, A4 pages tossed onto the floor and crumpled in the bed. I get up to turn the light out, and I take my shirt off and shake it, as though this will give it some kind of freshness. Paracelsus I can tidy up in the morning.

In the morning after breakfast, I decide when I get up.

I'm already eating when Marlon walks into the dining room, up to the breakfast bar. The staff watch and say nothing, the same staff who intercepted me as I was picking up my tray, who treated the term Special DMO with some scepticism, who said they would check with Doctor Dudgeon when I mentioned his name. Who wrote down 'Special DMO' and made me spell it.

Marlon stands at the breakfast bar without enthusiasm, like a man being worn away by the hardness of study. Scowling at the food as though he's just worked out it can give no satisfaction, tipping some cereal into a bowl.

He sees me, nods, comes over.

Sits down, nods, swirls sugar round in his Nutri-grain, even though Nutri-grain's already more than sweet enough.

The piano, he says. *It's not bothering you? Last night? It didn't bother you?*

No, not at all.

I think of telling him, truthfully, that I didn't hear it, but as much as he doesn't want it to have bothered me it doesn't feel right to tell him I was totally unaware of it. Sleeping soundly with the childhood of a fifteenth-century Swiss physician on my face.

I noticed your light was still on and it was pretty late. Figured you were probably working. I just, you know, I didn't want to be disturbing you.

No. It's fine. It's not disturbing music anyway. Not that I've got anything against bands that play disturbing music. I mean . . .

Debussy, he says. *Yeah. Pretty good stuff really, Debussy. Amazingly put together some of it, as though it's, you know, almost spatial rather than auditory.*

As I start to nod at this, to give a look of genuine concentration while I'm trying to work out what it means, I put my coffee cup down on my toast. Marlon, still away with Debussy, away somewhere in a spatial but non-auditory domain, notices nothing.

He cracks his knuckles, eats a mouthful of cereal, looks back at me and says, *Anyway, it's Harrison's I should be worried about at the moment, isn't it?*

Probably.

So I should get on with it. Well, good talking with you.

This, of course, is the strangest observation of all. If this has been good, he really can't get to do much talking. I understood my relationship with Marlon when he treated me with contempt and ignored me. I understood it less when he seemed sullen and I thought I was pissing him off, but I could live with that. This, I don't get.

The next afternoon I'm sitting at my desk in the room, thinking about the way I might structure my Hospital Week talk, thinking more than occasionally about the quiet disarray of my personal life, when he sticks his head round the door and says, *Got any of those biscuits?*

Sure, plenty, I tell him. You understand you have to eat them four at a time?

I hand him a Glad Wrapped plate and I ask him if he'd like tea or coffee.

You got tea and coffee making facilities as well as biscuits? I just got the room.

It took a lot of paperwork. And I think you might have to undertake to read the Dud's treatise on the life of Paracelsus if you're expecting the whole deal.

I think I'll stick to Harrison's.

I make us both tea and he sits on the bed with his back to the wall, a couple of biscuit plates beside him.

So you live somewhere else? he says. *As well as this?*

Yeah. This is just my town house. I have a property in the country. I fly back there on weekends.

This, naturally, is a joke, but I'd forgotten Marlon had his own plane. So rather than laughing he gives me an uncertain nod, as though a country property and an aircraft aren't completely out of the question. We really have nothing in common at all. This could be easier for both of us if we breakfasted at separate times and I occasionally slipped a few biscuits under his door.

I share a house with two people in Toowong, I tell him. A rented house. One-sixty a week for the three of us.

One-sixty a week. That's not bad. Probably gives you plenty of spare cash to spend on the plane then.

Yeah. So what about you?

Me? I'm focussing on the exam at the moment, so I'll be hanging around here for another few weeks I guess. I really want to pass it, get it out of the way. Then get back to everything else.

Debussy, things like that?

Debussy I seem to be fitting in. I tell myself it clears my mind.

I think I used to tell myself TV was good for that, at exam times.

Have you ever played Debussy?

And just as I think he didn't quite get my TV remark, he's off and talking about Debussy, and I realise he never heard my TV remark.

He tells me about how it feels to play, how it took him years to get there, to work it out, but when you do it's something your hands start to go with, almost automatically. He says it's amazing the different feelings that are in this stuff, and I must admit I haven't seen much suggestion of a great emotional repertoire from Marlon. And his right hand fiddles with the biscuit plate, taps at it in a way that might be Debussy, but might be anything. It's not as though I'd know.

And he tells me about his work with bands, leaving for London when he was nineteen, the touring, the sessions. And he dismisses the Floyd legend as *just a couple of gigs.* Big gigs, but just gigs, years ago, when Richard Wright cracked a metacarpal, something like that. *Sure it was fifty thousand people, but it's not like you get to meet them all. When you're out there it's all just noise.*

He tells me about meeting Sue in London. Sue from Adelaide whose parents didn't want to hear of her hanging around with a musician. Giving up London when she was homesick and the touring was driving them both crazy, coming back here.

And I'm thinking, What did I say? What did I do to burst this dam? Mention Debussy? Surely not.

And I didn't care, he says. I was ready to leave. And I wanted to be in one place. I wanted to be with her. I wanted things to stay that way. So I went for the long-term plan. I thought medicine looked good and I studied, I passed, I lined up for the training program. But somewhere it's come unstuck. I didn't think it could. I've had to put in a lot of time here, and I think she wasn't expecting that. I think there was some idea that when I finished uni things would take up less time. And it's so obvious to you and me that they take more, that it never occurred to me to say that. So I worked hard, and I studied hard, and I thought this is the rest of my life, you know? Get through these exams, get out there and work, put in more time with the kids, if I could. But it's all taken too long, too bloody long, so that's why I'm here.

In the evening he finishes the chapter on connective tissue diseases, and we play pool to celebrate. I was planning to go home, but at around four he paged me and said, *Maybe we could play pool later, when I finish the chapter,* so I stayed. Special DMO again.

He beats me two games to one and I'm beginning to wonder if I was ever good at this. I can't have won a game this year.

The next afternoon he's back for more biscuits, tea, white with none, concerned he might be a bad father, carrying this like a sack. Not the same guy Sue fell in love with.

And he says that it's great to talk, great to have someone to talk to, but that I don't have to let him win at pool again. And he says not a lot of people talk to him, not really.

People think I'm aloof, he says, staring at the opposite wall. But I think that's just because I'm tall. You'd think they could get beyond that.

311

I'm not quite sure of my role in this, other than providing the biscuits and tea, but the process seems important to him. Even if it's not as interactive, not quite as close to a conversation as he thinks. I don't think the legend thing has done him good. No-one ever treats him normally.

But he's back on track already, telling me, *It took a while to get there, but it got there. And I thought it'd be easier on the kids if I moved out for a while. And suddenly it's permanent. How does it happen? How does that shit happen?*

And he tells me he really thought it would last. He never thought that it wouldn't last. He changed his life for this, completely, but somewhere it had gone wrong. He would have changed his plans any time if he'd worked out it was all such a big deal.

I can't believe it'd end up like this, he says. *But you know how it is. You've got to do it. I'd do it again. When it's good it's so much better than anything else. It's just in a different league. I mean, think of the big stars who die young. They're all just lonely, really. Rich and famous and scared they'll end up alone. There's no point in that, not if you've got an alternative. So you've got to do it, even if it kills you.*

And I don't know how it is, not really. I don't know what it is you've got to do. And I can't tell Marlon, the long-term planner, that I refuse to plan for holidays two months ahead. All I can do is listen, feel somewhat relieved that it's not my guts being spilled, and think that the long term he has in mind has the potential to be very, very long, seems to put a lot at stake.

My parents had their twenty-fifth wedding anniversary two years ago. I had to make a speech, so I strung together anecdotes. My mother customising underpants for my father by re-elasticising them just the way he prefers (however that is, and I don't want to know). My mother, at a very tedious function, concerned about his well-being and taking me aside and saying, *I hope he's getting to do some talking, 'cause that's the bit he likes.*

I hadn't realised that this was two people adjusting to each other, and continuing to adjust over a long period of time. Each of them, of course, takes some adjusting to, so maybe they had to be more prepared for this process than most. My father, who by Rick's quite reasonable reckoning is *at least passing strange.* My mother, who is normal only by comparison.

When I saw your mother behind the wheel, my father once said to me, recalling their first meeting when she was an amateur racing driver, *when I saw how quickly she could go round Brand's Hatch, what could I think but that's the girl for me?*

So if she'd been ten seconds slower would he have walked away? If Deidre Phelps hadn't, as he said, *had champion written all over her,* would she have missed out on the enigmatic privilege of a long-term partnership with James Alexander Marshall, his Norton named Bucephalus after the winged steed of mythology, his father's handed-down handmade best shoes and his own yen for speed?

James and Deidre. Jimmy and Dreary, as they fondly call each other. It's just not like Dawn Ford calling you Honey, filling you with fear, reaching for your trousers and making you wish you'd locked the door to your room and hidden under the bed. It's not even like Kelly McLean. It's unlike anything I've ever had.

I stay in the room for most of the next few days, working on my paper. Making the case for melatonin and an association with depression. Outlining the biology, hibernation, jet lag. Outlining the project, speculating about melatonin the drug. Johnno, it turns out, will be away most of Hospital Week, interstate examining registrars, and I want to make sure before he goes that he's happy with what I'm planning to say.

It's the new term now, so I have staff health twice a week. This means there are several places I could be, working productively, at any given time. The ward, the library, staff health, the room. And people are generous enough to assume that, when I'm not with them, I'm working somewhere else, doing some good.

I eat with Marlon sometimes, and we talk. Marlon revisits the crumbling down of his relationship in several different ways, talks in circles, drags himself off periodically for another chapter of Harrison's. And sometimes, when he's tired of the circles, we talk about other things. We have conversations. About whatever subset of human disease he's studying ineffectively at the moment, about melatonin, about my own present lack of attachment, about music.

Debussy, he tells me, is like a pebble in water, waves moving out. I tell him that sounds more like Confucius and he thinks about it and says it could be Confucius as well, but it's certainly Debussy.

I try to put my lack of attachment into perspective, a lifestyle choice, a better option than the problematic attachments that preceded it. I try to explain it in a way I think he'll understand, and I tell him it's pretty risky, all this attachment stuff, getting really attached to someone. And he says, *Yeah, but what are you going to do, live on a mountain somewhere? Anyway, try stopping it.*

I didn't expect to convince him. I wasn't even convincing myself. I think about mentioning the Dawn Ford perspective, and that I'm beginning to have some admiration for its clarity. Dawn Ford knows what she wants. Dawn Ford's head is not incompletely messed up. Dawn Ford doesn't know the meaning of ambivalence. (Actually, she probably *doesn't* know the meaning of ambivalence, but that's another issue.)

I thought things would be okay when I graduated. No exams, fortnightly pay, doing good. I thought I'd do more good. I lived in fear of making mistakes, mistakes with consequences. But it's the good that's had consequences. My best work, in respiratory. And I'd do it again. I'd handle it that way again any time. Any time I was in that situation. I believe it was the best I could do. But how do people detach themselves from it, accept the bottle of port graciously and walk away? Somehow they do, most of them. And some become shits who care about nothing. And one or two get incompletely messed up, develop a personal interest in studying depression.

Sometimes the project looks like a way out, sometimes it makes it look as though I'm stuck here. Maybe the lack of attachment does make sense at the moment. Maybe there'll be better times to contemplate attachment than this. Maybe Marlon's undervalued the mountain, crappy metaphor that it is.

I finally talk to the Dud about Paracelsus and he calls him a restless spirit, as though he admires that and would like to be more restless himself. I want to tell the Dud that, even if he's a completely sedentary spirit, that's not all bad. I want to tell him I've talked to Marlon de Lisle who believes that, in the long term, restlessness does no good.

Sure it's a generalisation. It's probably fine for some people. But it's clearly not for Marlon and, according to the Dud, Paracelsus died destitute and alcoholic in his mid-forties. Maybe he should have settled down. There are worse jobs than town physician in Basel, even if the authorities do keep hassling you because you reject Galen's theory of the four humours.

Later, when I'm doing staff health, the Dud calls me back. *I'm just not sure,* he says, *whether to go for the definite article or the indefinite article. In the title.* Paracelsus,

colon, The Restless Spirit *or* Paracelsus, *colon,* A Restless
Spirit.

Or even *Paracelsus,* colon, *Restless Spirit,* I suggest, but
that only makes things worse.

41

On Wednesday, just as I'm looking at my watch and thinking that I'll be giving this paper in exactly a week and five
minutes, there's a Code Blue in One C. Right above me
again, and this time I'm not having sex with anyone, so
I figure I'm free. The head wardie's voice crackles over the
PA. *Code Blue. Ward One C. Code Blue.* Any less coher-
ent and he could sell newspapers on street corners.

My pager doesn't go off this time, and I wonder if it's
finally broken. But somehow the Dud still manages to get
through whenever he wants to, so I shouldn't get my hopes
up. This is just one of those Code Blues where the system
isn't working quite as well as it should, and the paging
part of the protocol hasn't happened.

I'm the first there, the first out of the stairwell, the first
to run into a nurse who's saying, *I don't know where it is.
I didn't call it.* We run together, a half lap of the ward,
gathering numerous other people who haven't called a
Code Blue, but are willing to do their bit. There's no bit to
do. No Code Blue.

All present and accounted for, the charge sister says,
joking, shaking her head. *And I didn't call it either.*

Was it a drill?

She shrugs. *If it was they didn't tell me.*

So we're all in a clump, nothing to do. Half a dozen medical staff, maybe twice as many nurses and an OT I've never seen before. And I can't believe that my first thought is that she's pretty impressive, and that my second is that there's a price to pay for losing touch with the multistorey.

Not a big price, I decide. The best indicator of the success of my new non-sexual lifestyle is that, not only will I not be winning on to her, I won't even think of her again. Her short dark hair, her long elegant nose that's not quite too long, her red glasses. Her surprising ability to survive the fashion cruelty of green OT culottes unscathed.

We haven't seen much of you here in a while, the charge sister says. *What are you doing now?*

Psych actually. And when I'm DMO I'm surgical, for some unfathomable reason. So I hardly get to visit some of my favourite wards at all.

She laughs at the overt crapulousness of this and sets out to match it by saying, *We miss you, of course.*

That's good. It's nice to be missed, just a little.

Some of the other residents, they just don't know who's in charge here.

Thanks, Luisa. It's good to know I've got what it takes.

So is psych by choice or just a fluke of rostering?

I'm still working that out. No, it's pretty good. And I'm setting up a research project there so I must be serious about it.

Really? Or is it just a way of staying in a cushy job?

You would be amazed how few people have thought to ask that.

And that's your answer?

Yeah.

Later, back in the room, I'm thinking that Luisa Cooper is too smart for her own good. And maybe it's possible to be serious about a research project that also happens to

317

come with a relatively cushy job. That's pretty close to per-fect, surely.

I think Luisa knows me better than most people here, in the way a slightly older sister might work out a few things about her slightly pathetic, slightly younger brother – might see that he craves both glory and slackness, but plods along somewhere competent in between. Might shake her head occasionally at his misjudgments, but assume that he means no harm and will grow out of them one day.

Just you leave my nurses alone, she said to me once, waggling her finger at me. *Don't even think about it. At least until you're out of the ward.*

And I didn't. She never had great nurses.

It occurs to me, though, to give a passing thought to the new OT. This is probably okay, since it doesn't break Luisa's code of conduct (she's not a nurse, and I am out of the ward), and it doesn't break mine, as long as I limit it to thinking. To giving her just this one passing thought. Thinking's nothing, and my non-sexual lifestyle is safe in here as long as I lock the door.

Pressure's totally off in the thinking department then, and anything else isn't on since I'm unlikely to be going back to One C. Even if it is very nearby. Even if I can hear feet on the floor. Her neat, soft-shoed OT feet, perhaps. I bet she's got great arches.

This is not a sexual thing, just an observation about arches. It's more an envy issue, because my arches are quite poor. No-one's ever likely to be attracted to me because of my arches, that's for sure.

And when would a nose be too long to be elegant? Not hers, certainly, but when? I've never really thought about noses before. Other than my sister's theory. Maybe the new OT just has a really long index finger. I'm not sure if that's good or bad, either.

I work on my paper, work on putting something productive into my head, some science, something worthwhile and clever and complex.

Relationships are complex things, I say to Rick as we share a pizza later.

So it seems.

No, I mean relationships, not the recent stuff.

So do I.

Like today, for example. Now, we both know that relationships, even of the liaison kind, are out for me at the moment, but I saw this very attractive new OT today, and I just thought, Wow, you know?

Wow. Wasn't that what Dawn Ford said whenever she confronted your penis?

I've obviously been very indiscreet. But you're right. Wow could be a bad habit to get into. It was, however, what I thought when I saw this new OT, but you'd be amazed how strong I was in putting her completely out of my mind. I don't think I've thought of her since. Not more than once, in passing.

Till now.

And I'm only mentioning her now to tell you how my perspective's changed on these things. There was a time, and not long ago, when I might have thought of her almost obsessively and pursued her in some calamitous way that led to harm for all concerned. But I'm not even thinking about her, not this time.

That's obvious. But you are not thinking about her quite a lot.

That's just 'cause I'm a very not thoughtful person. I'm also thinking how ridiculous it is to take an interest in someone just because of the visual side of things. I'm against that.

319

So the wow was based strictly on the visual? he says, perhaps trying to provoke me to new depths of shallowness. *Just the visual?*

Well, it's not that simple, is it? And I'm against objectification. Even for people who are open to the relationship thing, which I'm not. And even if it's not stereotypical, even if it's more like noticing a few things that suggest a person might be interesting. Short dark hair, elegant nose of probably close to perfect length, red glasses.

You like red glasses, or is that just an observation?

Observation. This is all just observation. But, you know, if it came down to it, I'd probably go for like. But be that as it may, I'm presenting it as interesting. It's a controversial choice. It suggests personality. And it'd surprise me if you saw a lot of stupid people in red glasses. Females anyway. Males it's a different story, a totally different syndrome. Braces, diurnal bow ties, premature male-pattern baldness, a really ugly scene, the sort of thing that could give red-framed glasses a bad name. I don't want to suggest that there's any kind of gender divide with this, but on this OT the red-framed glasses suggested something dynamic. Smart. Smart and confident, yet sensitive.

You must have got a good look at her.

Not really.

You're not giving any thought . . .

No.

Not thinking you might . . .

No. I'm just using her as a case study. Presenting her to you as a case study. An example of how I can notice things, and not interfere. I expect I'll never see her again.

So what were you saying about relationships?

Nothing. I didn't mention relationships. Certainly not in this context.

42

I'm not thinking about the OT while I'm hanging out my laundry on Saturday morning. I'm hanging out undergarment after undergarment that hasn't been near a woman in a while and I'm thinking, this is good. Hassle-free. This is what the OT represents, the choice not to pursue.

I hear the back door swing open. Rick's at the top of the steps, pulling his doona behind him.

Jon-boy, he shouts. *I adopted a new strategy. Last night at the firm ball. I drank too much, put my tie around my head, kept reasonably quiet about the doona and danced like a fool.* He comes down into the yard, the doona flopping step by step behind him. *And you know what? I think it's increased my credibility considerably. I think I'm a commodity now, maybe. And I'm thinking, girls are pretty good, you know? You've got to admit. They're pretty good.*

They're trouble, Ricky. Look at them, talk to them, take them to coffee, just don't let them near your genitals.

Hey, my genitals are just waiting for girl trouble.

And your new strategy, does it have anything to do with the fact that you seem to have pulled your bedding into the garden?

Oh yeah. And he starts popping the press-studs open, pulling off the Porky Pig cover. *I've done some thinking. And I looked at my doona cover, and your doona cover, and Jen's doona cover. And suddenly, the pig looked foolish. I looked like the only loser in a house full of fuck-me doona covers. So this is it. Time to change. Time to get me a fuck-me doona cover.*

I'm not totally sure it's just the doona cover.

Hey, I'm aware of that. I've got to get them in there too. But I'm working on it. And the time has come to kill the pig. Even if I don't know where I'm headed after that. It's just that time. And I'd rather go nude-doona than let my mother choose again. I'm striking a blow for freedom, Jon-boy. Are you with me?

Sure.

Good.

I'm assuming I don't actually have to do anything.

No. Just watch and be supportive.

So what am I watching? I mean, I'm watching, whatever, but what am I watching?

He pulls the last of the doona cover free with a flourish and disappears under the house. I'm about to remind him of the low beam when I hear his head hit it, seriously hard. *Don't worry,* he shouts, *just the low beam,* and he emerges again, with a bottle of metho, most of which he tips over the doona cover.

Smell the freedom, Jon-boy? he says, in a curiously southern and evangelistic accent.

Only metho so far. You didn't get any of that on you, did you?

Just get me the matches.

Can I get Jen, too? I think this is an important household moment.

Sure.

I knock on her door and she makes the none-too-happy incoherent noises of someone not ready to wake.

Come out, I tell her. There's something you've got to see.

What?

Just come out.

It'd better be good, she says as she opens the door and pulls a tracksuit top over her baggy flannel pyjamas.

It's Rick. A defining moment. I didn't think you'd want to miss it.

I pick up the matches in the kitchen and she says, *What? He's started smoking?*

The defining moment has, of course, slipped back a notch by the time we reach the steps. Rick is stuffing the doona cover into the washing machine and squawking, *Get the hell away from me with those matches.*

When he's got the lid down and a really heavy cycle started and he's washed the metho splashes from his legs so he doesn't get a rash, he says, *Don't think I'm backing out of this. It's not going back on that bed. My mother'd kill me if it came to grief, but there's no way, no way, it's going back on the bed.* He makes coffee for all of us, without asking if we want any, and he says, *I've got to tell you about this girl. She's quite small, she's got dark curly hair, she's got big eyes, her name's Elizabeth and she asked for my number. My number.*

And it sounds an awful lot to me as though he met Betty Boop last night. Maybe it's just how he sees girls. Or maybe he always did want Betty Boop.

I suppose we should be glad to see the cartoon fetish realised this way. It could have been awful if Porky Pig had asked for his number (with the sound of desperate squealing from his bedroom suddenly explaining why he'd been single for so long).

Are you ready for this? I ask him, leaving the whole cartoon issue well alone.

I'm ready for this.

No, I mean, are you ready for this? For the possibility that she might not call. For the possibility that it might not work out even if she does. You're sounding pretty optimistic.

I'm not optimistic. I'm just hopeful. I'm maybe getting a chance, and I'm ready to take it. And any week I don't take the chance is another week alone under the pig doona. Bored as all shit and reliving the sickly childhood of Robert Louis Stevenson and his counterpane, lying there making mountain ranges with his knees to stop going totally insane. Don't tell me you never did that poem at school.

Yeah, I did it.

Then you should know better. You should know that when there's nothing left but bedspread topography, a fatiguing imagination and the noises of adjacent inter-course, of course you take the chance.

Today, he even makes toast decisively. Toast for all of us, and plenty of it, even though I've already had break-fast. And then he says, Hey, we forgot to buy croissants.

I'm trying to talk him out of his third or fourth cup of coffee, reminding him that too much caffeine makes him talk quickly and has been known to affect his judgement, when Jen says, I've got a dilemma.

Yeah?

Tonight. The wedding I'm going to? I don't have a part-ner, and I RSVP'd for two.

But there was that guy. The one where you tossed the coin and then picked the other one.

The Devo guy, Rick says.

Well, I should have gone with the coin.

What happened?

He just kept calling me.

Calling you?

Yeah, quite often. You know, here, at home, during the day when he was at work. Calling me. Not about any-thing, just calling me.

Loser.

Well, yeah. So who's coming to the wedding? Bearing in mind that the gift is taken care of and I'm prepared to cover transportation there and back. What I'm saying is, who's prepared to sit through some boring speeches for a free meal?

That'd probably be me. Rick? Are you in this? Do we have to go for the coin again?

I should probably stay here. Chicks might call.

The wedding's at five, Jen says. *So I thought we'd leave about four-thirty, okay?*

Sure.

Good. Thanks. Well, I'd better get to Toowong. Put in a few good hours at the shiny surfaces.

She's tough, Rick says when she's gone. *I'd call. I'd call about nothing pretty regularly. I think I'd like that.*

And you know what? For some of them that might be okay, so don't take Jen as necessarily representative. And they don't all swallow. They're not all tough, and they don't all swallow, okay? I don't know this Elizabeth, but some of them probably like to be called. So don't assume.

So how do you work it out?

I don't know. Trial and error. It's all you've got.

They don't all swallow?

Not all of them. And I understand it's polite to check first.

To check first? How do you do that?

Fucked if I know.

And this is where error can creep in.

Correct. And it's a bad error, a really unpopular error, in case you're wondering.

No, I would've figured that. So this is how you ended things with Dawn Ford? You blew her brains out with the smallest gun in the world?

Surprisingly, no. That made her try harder. And that's when I knew I had to end things with Dawn Ford.

I think I'll just stick to the calling. For now. If she calls. Betty, Elizabeth.

325

Betty?

Elizabeth.

And if she doesn't call, that's okay.

Yeah, I know.

You've still skinned the doona. You've still got just a hint of the commodity about you.

Do I walk differently now? I always thought I'd walk differently at this point.

Yeah. It's almost a swagger.

But she hasn't called by late morning, or by lunchtime, and it's some effort to persuade him that this is okay, a respectable choice on her part. That she mightn't call for days.

And by mid-afternoon, when he's fussing round telling me I have no idea about bow ties, I know he's only thinking about the phone, the call she isn't making.

I've never been to a wedding where I've met neither of the couple before. The bride is an Expo friend of Jen's and we end up sitting at an Expo-friend table, people I don't know reminiscing about a pavilion I never went to. And our place cards have our names written on both sides, so people keep addressing me as Garry, as though I'm some guy who calls too much, and that's never been me.

But even I think it's pretty harsh to trash a guy for calling. Maybe I haven't got the whole story.

The best man begins his speech by saying that he thinks best-man speeches based on giving the groom a hard time are in pretty poor taste, and he wants Andrew to know how much he values his friendship. And I'm really glad I only came for the free meal.

And he's saying how he knows it'll work out with these two, how sometimes you just know.

I wonder if Marlon de Lisle's best man made the same speech. I wonder how much you can just know. Of course, even if you knew you couldn't stand there and say I know it'll work out with these two, until a misunderstanding arises when he's a gastro registrar, but they won't fix it in time, and he'll end up moving out and confessing all to the guy in the next room at the hospital, who doesn't quite know where his own life is heading. Who just knows that hospital medicine isn't quite what he expected, that he's worse in relationships than he thought he'd be, and that an obscure hormone might be really important in depression.

Did my parents' best man make the same speech? Did he say, *If you think they're idiosyncratic now, wait twenty-five years and see how they are?* See what it's like when they emigrate, see how their children cope when they bring friends home from school, how in their mid-fifties they take up back-packing with fervour, scam upgrade after upgrade, walk the Pyrenees.

What if something happened to one of them? Have they thought of that? How would my father ever get the right underpants? How would he ever work out how to prepare a meal? Who would fix my mother's burned-out clutches without a word of complaint, do all her ironing exactly the way she likes it, cut her fringe? And that's just the practicalities.

I know it amounts to much more than that. I know Marlon de Lisle, after all, so I know that far too well. But does it really get down to this or living on a mountain somewhere? Marlon's throw-away image that says that in the end it's not a choice at all for him. That he'd put everything on the line, chance it all again rather than be alone.

I think I've been hoping for something in between, but I don't know if that works. Other than Jen, perhaps, not a lot of people are aiming for in between, someone to go out

327

with on a predictable basis, but without the complications of attachment. Jen and Dawn Ford, maybe, though Dawn Ford doesn't require much going out.

Jen never offers anything but the in between, lures her men with this promise, the promise of fun till it runs out. But they get attached. Call too much. How many calls would have been the right number? How many calls is the appropriate in-between number? It doesn't stay in between. In between isn't a homeostatic point. Someone either wants more, or less. Rick, who has nothing, wants as much as possible. Jen, who has an almost permanent supply of as much as she could want, wants control. Marlon wants what he had.

Should I really have come to this wedding? Damn this best man for this worst speech. How can you *just know*?

Jen turns her place card over and over in her hand, shrugs her shoulders minimally when I make eye contact, puts a tired look on her face. My wine glass is empty, as is the bottle in front of me, and the trousers of my cheap suit are gripping my meal in a way that feels like the onset of a partial gut obstruction.

After the speech, the table talk resumes, all of us now feeling a bond through having endured the last forty minutes together. I give up trying to correct the Garry problem, and I just go with it. I become Garry, but a confident mildly intoxicated kind of Garry, the kind of Garry who would probably know exactly how much to call, who loves life in an uncomplicated way, who has never known a moment's uncertainty, who has no inclination to study depression. I tell many lies, I fake *joie de vivre*, I have a reasonably good time.

It's nice to be out, I persuade myself, out with a few new people. Even if, being Garry, I am one in a way. But I don't mind Garry. He hasn't a care in the world, and he's only drinking a lot because he appreciates wine.

And now, the MC says, *a special tribute to the bride and groom. 'Moscow, Moscow'.*

And he claps his hands twice, the lights dim, the theme music of the 1980 Olympics begins, and the staff perform a very brisk but rigid kind of march among the tables, a bottle with a sparkler in each hand.

For those of us already uncertain about weddings, this is bewildering indeed.

No-one at our whole table gets it. I'm hoping this is because they're all Expo people and they didn't meet the bride until two Olympiads after 'Moscow, Moscow'. I'm hoping this means something to someone, because it looks seriously rehearsed and unbearably sincere, far from a trivial moment. The groom, overtaken by the strangeness of the evening and probably more than a little disappointed by his best man, shrugs his shoulders, leaps up, folds his arms like a cossack, starts to dance and falls over. The bride holds her head in her hands.

Jen laughs. *Don't look at me, Gaz. Your guess is as good as mine.* And in the cab on the way home she says, *When my turn comes, there won't be any Olympic theme songs. Just because I know these people, slightly, doesn't mean I think that was reasonable. I've always thought there were some wedding things I was really against. No doves, no arch, you know? It never occurred to me that I'd have to be against choreographed sparkler marches to Olympic theme songs.*

Yeah. It could be a tough moment. You've paid the deposit on the function, sorted out what you think are all the necessary details and then, at the final meeting a couple of days before, the manager says, *At this point in the proceedings we usually do 'Moscow, Moscow', with sparklers. Trust me, it's a highlight.*

It'd have to be a real moment of weakness before you'd

agree to it. Imagine looking back years later and going, There's only one thing I remember about my wedding . . .

Rick's in bed when we get home.

There's a note on the table. *She called. We talked for thirty-three minutes. Not about anything. Just thought you should know.*

43

On Monday, around lunchtime, I finish my Hospital Week paper. I go up to the ward to give it to Johnno to check before he goes away, but he's in with a patient.

I drop in on Hospital Week, so that I can see how it all works before I get up and talk on Wednesday. I arrive just in time for a trade display on wound closure techniques, and I leave shortly after with two small cucumber sandwiches and a stapling gun, having accomplished a surprisingly neat hose-to-hose anastomosis.

Back in the room, I'm thinking Jen has misled me. She obviously hasn't planned any kind of attachment with the men we've seen her bring home, but she's assuming marriage at some point. Talking about it as though it's inevitable, just a matter of sorting out details. Who the groom will be, for example. That'd be a good one to start with. So when will this happen? Is it a question of the right time, or the right boy? And what if he really likes doves, arches and Olympic theme songs? Has she left any room for negotiation? Is the right boy, perhaps, the one who doesn't quite toe the line, but whose appeal isn't diminished by this? Jen wouldn't be easy.

Well, I'm done, Marlon says, standing in the doorway. *Whatever happens, happens. Harrison's is shut.*

How does it feel?

Shutting Harrison's? Good. Of course it's hard to shake the feeling that I've forgotten most of it already, but it's good that it's shut.

I make him tea. He eats my biscuits. Stares into the distance contemplating the exam in two days time. Probably wondering how he can get through it without a daily Monte Carlo four-pack.

How's your paper?

Finished, I think. Up with Johnno for checking.

You happy with it?

Happy enough. It makes sense to me, anyway. I live in fear of someone shooting a large hole in it on Wednesday, but we'll see.

You're obviously ready for them, he says, looking at my stapling gun.

Later, when a mild crisis of confidence has kept me back well into the evening and I'm rummaging through my references one more time, Debussy begins again in the dining room. The quiet late-night concert of Marlon de Lisle.

He plays for about half an hour and then comes back to his room. Through my open door he looks more relaxed than usual. Still in the study wardrobe of boxer shorts and unbuttoned black shirt, but relaxed.

How's it going? he says, noticing me noticing him. *I thought everything was done.*

Yeah.

It's not easy to leave it alone, is it?

No, it isn't.

Always in fear of the thing we don't know, he says, as though quoting a fortune cookie that's come to mean something to him. *You wouldn't believe the number of times I've stopped myself from starting Harrison's again this evening. Just in case I learn one more thing. So I figured it'd be better to go and play. Have a go at something I know. I've decided I can't ever know enough for the exams. And you won't ever know enough to feel comfortable about standing up and talking about melatonin. There are just too many facts. You can't know them all. Which is where Debussy comes in.*

Very philosophical, I say to him, feeling less than comfortable that he could detect my knowledge crisis through the wall.

Hey, I wasn't the one who mentioned Confucius.

That's true.

You don't get Debussy at all, do you?

Well, I've never really had the chance. To be honest, I'm more familiar with some of your other work. Debussy I've only ever heard in an adjacent room. The knowledge crisis I get. This would all have been much easier five hundred years ago, you know. Galen's theory of the four humours, a few herbs.

Yeah, there probably wasn't as much to know, but I think the standard of medical care left a bit to be desired.

That's a very twentieth-century outlook.

Come and listen to some Debussy. And as we walk along the corridor he adds, with a hint of something that seems like admiration, *Galen's theory of the four humours. You know a lot of shit, don't you?*

Yeah.

I reach for the light switch when we walk into the dining room and he says, *No, don't bother about the light.*

You play in the dark?

Yeah.

I never knew you played in the dark.

Should I have mentioned it? I know the music. I know where I'm sitting. Besides, what do you need to see? You think this comes with a floor show?

He plays, and I stand nearby, listening.

Do you get it? he says. *Reflets dans l'eau. This is the one like the pebble falling into water.*

Yeah. It's quite a small pebble, isn't it?

Yeah, and small waves, and they're all different. And you can hear them all moving out. And you can hear order, he pauses, *and chaos. The notes don't seem complicated, but it's the spaces between them that are harder to play. That's what it took me a long time to work out. And in there you don't think of Harrison's at all. Or anything. And at the end it's still and you have about five seconds of peace before you realise you can't remember the cranial nerves in the right order any more, something fundamental like that.*

But it's nice to have the five seconds of peace though.

Exactly.

He plays on, starts again or starts another piece. I can't work it out straight away. I can't hear the pebble yet, so maybe it's another piece.

Is this the Marlon that Sue hasn't seen enough of lately? The one who appreciates the small spaces between notes and just after them, rather than the big, remote, black-shirted gastro registrar, desperately trying to know enough to pass the exam first time so he can stop his life falling down around him. But somehow forgetting to make it clear to her that she is, in fact, what the desperation's about.

The pedal's sticking. Can you hear that? Listen. Listen

to how it slurs it around. He keeps playing, says, *Shit,* quietly, becomes more frustrated.

Can I do anything?

I don't know, maybe. Maybe you could unstick it. You could have a go, anyway.

I get down on my knees. I feel around for the pedal, and I realise I have no idea of what I should do when I find it. Marlon plays a few chords.

Is it just stiff, or is there something jamming it?

I'm still reaching for it, maneuvering myself between his feet to get closer. And just as I take hold of it, and Marlon's trying to lift his legs and saying, *Yeah, yeah, that's it, yeah,* a security guard's torch flicks onto us from the doorway.

I jump, hit my head on the underside of the keyboard, and then my right cheek on one of Marlon's knees.

Jesus, sorry, the security guard says as I groan involuntarily and realise that my head is between Marlon's knees and he's wearing only boxer shorts (lifting his legs, offering me verbal encouragement).

I suspect that only two of the three people in this interaction are aware that it's a matter of piano mechanics, a dodgy pedal, a point needing to be made about Debussy.

The security guard starts to back out and Marlon shouts, *No, come back,* clearly concerned about the likelihood of misinterpretation. *Come back in here a second.*

I'm a married man, the security guard says hesitantly, flicking his torch from Marlon's face to mine.

So am I, Marlon says. *Well, sort of . . .*

I want to explain. I want to clarify this now, but I'm not sure where to start. I want to make it clear that this is not my sixth misadventure with a blow job.

The security guard stands in the doorway, watching us. Leans against the doorway, flicking his torch around, checking there's no-one else in the dining room, checking our faces again. His expression changes, softens. *You know, I don't mind a bit of piano. And stuff. With the right blokes. You know. Just quietly.*

Um, that's fine, Marlon says. *But maybe I could explain.*

Oh yeah? Leaning casually in the doorway with the corridor light falling across the side of his smile.

The pedal was stuck. That's pretty much all that was happening. Just an attempt to unstick the pedal.

Oh, okay. The smile now looking less sure of itself.

And that was it, really. I was just trying to explain something about a piece of music, so we came in here a couple of minutes ago to play it, and then the pedal got stuck. End of story, really.

Oh, right. And you've got it sorted out then? Regular security guard face coming back. *The pedal? It's unstuck then?*

Think so. Marlon plays a few notes, and the pedal is quite obviously still stuck. *Yeah. That'll be fine.*

Righto. Well, that's that then. It probably doesn't get used enough, the piano. And like I said, I like a bit of piano. Probably needs oiling, or something. The pedal. I'll make a note of it.

Good. Thanks.

And he goes. We listen to him walk away down the corridor, perhaps faster than he usually would, his shoes clicking on the lino until he turns the corner past the library.

So now do you get Debussy? Marlon says, and lets out a long sigh.

44

Johnno pages me on Tuesday morning, while I'm in staff health.

I've read the paper, he says. *Pretty impressive. It could do with a few more jokes, but other than that . . .*

So you think it'll be okay tomorrow?

You're obviously not aware of the Hospital Week standard.

My pager goes off again, and again I'm almost afraid to look at it, still not confident about how we left things with the security guard, but it's another number in the ward. This time it's Dean.

You know I'm going to be away Thursday and Friday? he says.

Not till now. It sounds like everyone's going to be away.

I'm sure you'll cope. I've got to be best man at a wedding in Melbourne.

And I want to ask him if it's regular or Olympic, but I don't think our relationship is ready for many cryptic remarks.

Since you're relieving me I thought we could do a hand-over before I go.

Yeah, that sounds good. How about in the ward tomorrow, after I do my talk?

Yeah, fine.

And I think he likes this, as he's supposed to, since it lets him know that I don't expect him to be in the audience.

When I get back to the melatonin room Marlon is just leaving, a bag in one hand, a suit carrier over his other shoulder. I never knew he had a suit. He tells me he's going on the same flight to Sydney as the other two Mount Stevens registrars who are sitting the exam, and they've just called a cab.

I thought Sue might've called, he says. *To wish me luck. But she didn't.*

Well, good luck anyway. Go and put all this Harrison's time to good use.

I must know nearly everything by now, surely.

So all you have to do is remember the right bits at the right time.

Yeah. Good advice. Thanks. And avoid having a resident's head between my thighs when I'm not fully dressed. That'd be good too. Maybe I should steer clear of Debussy entirely till I get back.

People do tend to make assumptions.

That security guard . . . I guess it's something we'll all keep to ourselves, isn't it?

When he's gone I sit in the room reading over my talk. In the room it looks good. Maybe, instead of standing up in front of dozens of people reading it, I could get them in here one at a time, sitting down at the desk and browsing through it themselves.

A Code Blue is called. One C. Again my pager doesn't go off. Is this a change in protocol or just another slip-up? Is my record so bad that I'm out of the Code Blue loop?

And I really believe that, with my head cluttered with misunderstandings and performance anxiety, I run for the stairwell because I'm nearby, and it's what I'm supposed to do. And thoughts of the OT don't occur to me until I'm nearly there.

A nurse is pushing the crash trolley out of the treatment room when I arrive.

So where are we going?

Don't know.

We check beds one to four, five to eight, nine to twelve. And by then people are realising that no-one's called it. No-one in the ward rang switch to call a Code Blue.

I don't know what's going on, Luisa says, probably to no-one in particular, but happening to face me while she says it. *Do other wards have this?*

I don't know. I only come to your Code Blues. I've got a room directly beneath here. Besides, your Code Blues have got a reputation for attracting an altogether better kind of crowd.

This is a private joke, one Luisa isn't supposed to get, but its privacy is not helped by the fact that it coincides with the arrival of the new OT, just as I'm looking at the door. And then looking away too quickly.

Luisa turns, sees the OT, looks back at me and smiles. *Any kind of crowd in particular?*

No, not particular. Very general.

I wouldn't have picked you as a person who liked crowds, she says, both of us unable to stop paying at least some attention to the OT, who is now flicking through the pages of a file, talking to a nurse.

Great hands, I'm thinking, and I've never even noticed hands before. Long fingers, precise without trying to be. Maybe my sister's nose-measuring theory is right.

No, I love crowds, I tell Luisa. I only went to the Springsteen concert a few years ago so I could be with fifty thousand people.

Attractive people, most of them?

No.

The OT puts the file under her arm and walks off in a way that I'd describe as both relaxed and commanding.

That's Kate, our new OT. In case you're wondering.

Well, I know most people round here. So when there's one you haven't seen before, you notice.

It's a shame she's just a locum. She's only here till the end of next week.

That's not long.

Yeah. So I'll be seeing you at our next arrest then?

Well, I am nearby. And I'm about to be a relieving registrar, so if there are any psych consults, just call me.

It's the first time for some years that I've been sprung looking at a girl.

Kate. I like her name. Kate is nice. Clear, decisive. Great hands. Probably with someone. Probably going far away the weekend after next. And she certainly wasn't noticing me. My undergraduate undesirability returns in a rush.

I imagine conversations with her, when I'm back in my room. While she's probably talking through the stages of cardiac rehab with one of the post-infarct crowd in One C. Week six, resume lawn mowing and intercourse.

One conversation, some time in the next eight working days, that would be good. To shatter my expectations, teach me not to place undue emphasis on red-framed glasses, noses, hands, names. To let me know her lack of interest. To clear my head. Whatever.

45

By morning, seven working days. Seven working days to be sensible, leave well alone. Today, the talk. And if I bump into her, I bump into her. If I don't, I don't. And it's probably better if I don't. Better if I just stay here up my mountain, and ponder occasionally the possibilities. The things that might have happened in a world where

I was clear headed and fearless and an object of desire among women of quality.

I read through my talk and become over-involved with clearing my throat. Mucus is normal, I tell myself, mucus is normal, as it starts to well up and gag me.

Mucus is normal, these people are nice people, melatonin is good.

I lock the door, walk to the conference room. Not enough jokes, not enough jokes. Months of theory, eighty-five references (available from the author on request), out in public for the first time and no jokes at all.

Morning tea is on before the session. Free food, but I can't eat. I go browsing among the drug company stands and I pick up a year's supply of Triquilar ED for Jen, twelve starter packs in Ken Done-style designer boxes, and some Tobispray for Rick. He's never had it before, but it's expensive, new, glamorous, nasal and definitely non-NHS, so my guess is he'll love it.

My talk is the third of three in the session, following 'The measurement of carotid and peripheral vascular disease in diabetics using doppler techniques' and 'Proposed protocols for early mobilisation following total hip replacement – modifications to the Toronto model'.

My mouth is going dry. I am suddenly very aware of my own tongue. I'm not sure if that's normal. It takes up a great deal of space in there. I'm not sure if that's normal either.

I've never heard of the Toronto model, and they had slides, crumbly old people, mobilising early, grimacing. I don't have slides. I have twelve sheets of paper, double spaced. I don't have slides, or overheads, or any use for the laser pointer at all. Twelve sheets of paper, no props, no jokes, and I left the staple gun back in the room, along with the eighty-five references. So they'd better not ask.

The questions are benign and unenthusiastic, just as I'd hoped, and they run out quickly. It's my turn. The Dud introduces me, says he's been lucky enough to have kept up with this project since the day it began. That it took a bit of persuading to get me up here in the first place. *I think the group wanted to keep it to themselves until they'd analysed their data, but a lot of us probably walk past that door often enough and think What's this melatonin about? What the hell's going on in there? And I'm sure you'll all find it as fascinating as I did.*

At the lectern I check my pages. Twelve, all in the right order. Twelve pages and I think they'll find it pretty boring. Not a mention, fortunately, of what the hell actually goes on in or near the melatonin room.

In the audience Joan Shand smiles, but in a nonpredatory, almost pleasant, way. Half a dozen people from the ward sit in a clump, including Dean, despite the fact that I gave him an out yesterday. Maybe he didn't understand. Maybe I should be more reasonable, and appreciate the fact that he's turned up. There are no locum OTs in the audience, not that I'm checking.

I read, and having read it through many times, it goes easily. I am probably not interesting, and I'm certainly not fascinating, but at least I'm not paranoid about my tongue or thinking too much about the locum OT, who doesn't come in at any stage during the talk. When I finish, people applaud, perhaps more than they applauded the doppler group, certainly more than they applauded the hip mobilisers. Why I'm reducing this to a clapometer competition I don't know.

There are questions, but manageable questions. Exaptation, the site of action of melatonin, my feelings on the biology behind the symptom of depressed mood. Some I can answer, the others I can at least say something about.

The Dud, in game-show-host mode again, wraps the session up by telling us how proud the hospital should be of all three groups, calling for another round of applause.

That went well, he says to me as people start to leave. *Very well,* I thought.

Glen and two other nurses from the ward come up and ask when we're going to start collecting, and Joan Shand says, *I've actually been meaning to talk to Jonathan about that. I'm waiting to hear back from a few people about assays, and I could hear something any time. I'll let you know.*

Thanks.

It's taken longer than I thought. It's the precision that's the issue. Soon, hopefully.

She leaves, obviously not quite satisfied with herself, and Glen raises his eyebrows at the credibility with which she's treated me.

Kind of strange isn't it? I say to him, watching her go, striding off in her long white coat.

Well, he says, *yeah.*

Dean hangs around, near the back of the conversation, comes up to me when the others have gone. *There's not much really, about the patients,* he says. *Not a lot of handing over to do.* We walk outside and he gives me a list. *These are mine. The first eight are Dubois's, the rest are Johnno's.* And he tells me about them from memory, more than I'd expected Dean could do, and then he says, *I didn't want to raise this in front of everybody, but there's an article you should probably know about. Before anything goes much further. I just happened to be looking up something else in an old issue of the* American Journal of Psychiatry, *from the mid-1970s, and I saw a study where they gave melatonin to depressed people and it made them worse. More depressed.*

And this is what he leaves me with. This and a shrug and his list and details about patients I've forgotten already. Having sat through the talk and not raised it, not asked a question, waited till he'd be telling only me and telling me without any expression on his face, just the last of a number of things he thought I needed to know before he left town.

It probably is something I needed to know. And I don't know if it gave him any pleasure, if he went looking for it, if he wanted to mention it in question time but didn't, or if he told me now because it really seemed the best time to tell me.

I can't believe it made them worse. I can't see how.

I lock the door to the melatonin room. I lie on the bed.

There's more to it than this. This is only part of the project. But I can't see how it made them worse. It could explain a lot though. Why I'm making a connection no-one's been making during the last few years. Because everyone who's been around more than five minutes is sure it was disproved long ago.

This is the article I dreaded, but never found. I always knew it might be there. Suddenly I feel very attached to my theory, and spiralling down with it. I don't know where to go now. The whole room makes me look foolish. The room, the computer, the notes, the eighty-five references. A shrine full of hazardous materials, collapsing around me, all ready to be dragged off by men in space suits. But they never come, and the quiet of the room is intruded upon only occasionally by trolleys passing, people in conversation, Ron, the head wardie, calling the names of the beeperless masses over the PA, and the wards that want them.

I should have known, the moment Dawn Ford jumped me here. The room was false hope, a bad joke biding its time. How do I sort this out? Who do I have to tell? How dumb will I look? Five o'clock takes a long time coming.

At home, I give Jen and Rick their presents.

Wow, a whole year, Jen says. *Excellent.*

But don't think it gets you out of any of those women's things.

Rick looks at the Tobispray and says, *Is it expensive? It looks expensive.*

Oh, yeah. Brand new and totally non-NHS. And designed with the really bad cases in mind.

He runs into his room and there is an immediate and disgraceful snorting sound, followed quickly by another that's at least as bad.

I can feel it already, he says when he comes out, scrunching up his face and blinking, making me wish I'd tried him with a placebo. *Can I have more? Can I do it a couple of times?*

Rick, this is strong stuff, I tell him. A pretty serious drug. You don't want to mess with this. You could maybe use it again in the morning. Maybe.

And I tell them someone stuck a knife in my theory today. I've got problems. I don't know what kind of problems. I haven't seen the article, but it doesn't sound good.

A night of cocktails is declared, even though the kitty surplus is only marginal.

We drink too much and run out into the cold, broom-spinning. And if it's difficult sober, it's almost impossible drunk. I hold the broom at arms' length, pointing up to the sky. I look up at the top of it and spin, I don't know how many rotations before they shout, *Now.* And I throw it to the ground, try to jump forward over it. But I stagger backwards and it gets further and further away, bouncing on the lawn and stopping as I hit the ground and roll. Seeing the sky and the ground pass me in a blur, Jen and Rick near the lights of the house. Cocktails churning inside me.

I smell grass, when I stop face down.

I'm next, Jen says.

46

So how bad is it? Rick says in the car on the way into town. *How big a problem could this new article be?*

I don't know. It could unravel the whole thing. Or just most of it. What a dickhead. As if it was going to work out. As if I could sit in the library of the least significant hospital in the world with a word stuck in my head and find the answer to anything. What a fucked idea. Why didn't you stop me?

Have you read the article yet? How do you know they didn't make the mistake?

It's in one of the world's leading refereed journals in the field. I'm pretty sure it put off a lot of people who actually knew what they were doing, back when I was still a child. But did they tell me? They just went, Hey, this is the Mokable Rocket kid. He comes out with shit like that all the time. He doesn't actually know about anything, but he's got that confidence happening. He's got that simplicity. The idiot savant of psychoendocrinology. But now just the idiot.

At least you're not letting it get to you. So what next? Back to girls? Back to the swinging single resident lifestyle?

I don't think so. Not a lot of vigour in the swing at the moment.

What about that OT?

Well, I have seen her twice now, so I assume we'll be having sex very shortly. She'll be gone by the end of next week. And who knows, she's probably taken. Anyway, what would I do? Just call her, go the big ask? You've never seen me in your life but I've noticed you in the distance twice and take it from me I'm as desirable as buggery, so let's do something Friday?

If only she was a nurse. Or desirous of buggery.

Life's not that easy. So, no girls, no theory, what next? I've cleared the decks pretty effectively now. I'm completely open to inspiration. But it's got to be good. Right at the moment, the psych training program doesn't look like it. It just looks like a way of shackling myself to a place where I'm in the process of making myself look like a dickhead.

I've got a Porky Pig doona cover I can lend you.

Thanks.

And you know, I think it might have been the problem.

Really?

We're up to the coffee stage. We had coffee yesterday, and I surprised myself with my own competence. And you know what's next?

Don't rush things.

More coffee.

Really?

We should do this again sometime, she said. Soon. And then she said, How about Friday? And I said, Fine. And she liked my Snow White tie. She worked out that it had to be Grumpy and Sneezy round the back. I think that stuff's okay in a tie. Bad in a doona cover. Okay in a tie. That was my problem.

Sometimes it's a much more subtle world than either of us realises.

I devote the entire morning to an attempt to be a competent acting registrar (an attempt to get back to my recent but temporarily forgotten philosophy of nerdy, pleasant and cooperative). I make contact with every patient, I make a note in every file.

I buy Pink Lady food and have lunch in the Quarters. I allow people to beat me at pool, twice.

I check in the library and the bound issues of the *American Journal of Psychiatry* are there for every year of the 1970s, other than 1976. The abstract of the article, the particular article from the missing volume, is in *Excerpta Medica*. Eight depressed males, all given melatonin. Self-reports of lethargy in all and a worsening of mood in five. Evidence of impaired concentration on psychometric testing. One subject withdrawn from the study when he became suicidal.

Tetris is not a game, I decide when I'm back in the room and sitting at the computer. It's barely even a prototype for a game. It's very hard to care about Tetris.

The head wardie calls a Code Blue in One C. Nothing comes through on my pager but I'm used to that now. Damn them, I'm as entitled to be part of the One C Code Blues as anyone.

An L-shaped Tetris piece chugs down the screen, and there's no way I'll move it left in time.

I should go. I should go to One C. Just as I'm telling myself, Don't be an OT-chasing dickhead, I realise I should actually go. It's possible that no-one's been paged, and I'm close. And it might be real. One day it will be. And Tetris is so dull I could die playing it and never know.

The crash trolley is already rattling up and down the corridor in search of someone in the act of demising.

You'd think you were doing cardiology, the amount we're seeing of you at the moment, Luisa says when I get round to the Nurses' Station.

I'm nearby. Nearby and aware of my responsibilities. Code Blue, if you're near, you go.

Well, yet again there's no arrest. And I don't know how you do it, but I've just paged . . .

The OT walks in.

What's happening? she says to Luisa, and therefore right next to me. *You seem to be in a perpetual state of alert. Do you really have that many arrests here?*

No more than anywhere else. I don't know where these calls are coming from. And it's not as though they happen all the time. They just seem to happen when you're on your way in. Usually it's a very peaceful ward.

The OT looks thoughtful. *So when you page me, what do you do? After you've tried the OT Department and I'm not there.*

Well, like anyone whose pager number I haven't got in front of me, I call switch and get them to page you.

Could we try that now?

If you want. You are here though.

The OT nods. Luisa calls, says, *It's sister in One C here. Could you please page Kate Blue, our locum OT?* She puts the phone down. *So what's this about? What's going to happen?*

I don't have a pager.

The PA crackles into life. *Code Blue, One C, Code Blue.*

Or is that Kate Blue, One C, Kate Blue? Kate Blue says as the crash trolley lurches out of the treatment room and down the corridor, someone's voice saying, with determination, *We're going to find it this time.*

Luisa laughs. *That is just the dumbest thing.* And then

she tries it head-wardie style, crackling from the side of her mouth into a mock microphone, *Kate Blue, One C, Kate Blue,* and laughs again.

Thanks very much, Kate Blue says. *Around here my name means death. How do you think that makes me feel?*

I, of course, have some idea of how it feels, and it's not good. But I keep this to myself, and I watch her feign exasperation.

So is the Kate short for anything? Is there any way around this?

Of course there's a way around it. Giving me a pager.

I'm sure there'd be plenty of people happy to give up their pager to somebody who actually wanted one, I tell her.

But if you gave up your pager, Luisa says, *how would we get you up here all the time on these Kate Blue calls?*

Somehow I think it's Kate Blue you're after, not me. And Kate Blue calls don't double-beep anyway. They're strictly PA jobs.

Kate, have you met Jon before? Jon Marshall, the psych resident?

No, she says, and reaches out to shake my hand. *Hi. Kate Blue, Angel of Death.*

That's a big job.

Somebody's got to do it.

She shrugs, just a hint of a shrug, and smiles. Lifts one eyebrow. And I hate the fact that the *Kate Blue, One C, Kate Blue* problem is being so easily solved.

Switch aren't always good with these things, I say. One night last year, when someone swapped a DMO shift with Marcia Hall, switch thought they said Doctor Marshall, so they kept paging me for two hours. When I didn't answer they even called me at home. Meanwhile Marcia was sitting in the Quarters having the quietest DMO shift of her life, and then she was suddenly fourteen calls behind. The problem with these things is people just keep trying. They're too busy to work it out.

Kate Blue smiles, somewhere near the end of this, but in a way that suggests I've been trying to win her with boredom, and should know better. I feel so adolescent. I just didn't want her to go yet. Why couldn't I think of something witty and engaging, rather than merely pertinent? No-one ever fell for pertinent. No-one ever said I want that guy because of his great facility with the pertinent example. If I get any more off the pace I'll be offering to make her brown sauce.

She's coming to the cocktail party tomorrow night in the RMOs' Quarters, Luisa says when Kate Blue has gone to meet her new patient.

Really?

Have you got a ticket?

Not yet.

There's someone in each ward selling them. In this ward it's me. They're twenty dollars.

Okay.

I take twenty dollars out of my wallet and give it to her.

Just the one?

Just the one.

That's interesting. That's how many Kate bought.

Well, they are twenty bucks. You wouldn't be buying dozens, would you? So, do you think I did myself harm with the anecdote? The Marcia Hall story?

I don't think so. It was, you know . . .

Pertinent.

Yeah, pertinent.

But not much more than that.

Not much.

Shit. Shit.

And you did seem to get very tense at one point.

Probably the point when I realised I shouldn't be telling it. That was obvious? I'm twenty-five this year. I should be way better at this.

Well, I noticed it, but that doesn't mean it was obvious. She might think it's just you.

Shit. Nerdy, bad stories, chronic tension problem. How do I do this to myself?

Relax, she says, and laughs.

Relax? I only tell people to relax when I want them to shut up.

She laughs again. *I only tell people to relax when I think they should relax. Now, why don't you run off and carve your initials in a tree? JM and KB and a nice big heart.*

I retire to the room. I carve nothing. I tell myself this is not hiding, and I didn't fuck up. But I did, and it was going to be worse. That was only my first unfunny funny paging story. I had a bagful of them, and my plan was to tell them all. And that's such a Rick plan, such a mummifying, stultifying, pillow-over-the-face-of-opportunity Rick plan. When did we swap? Did he sneak the Porky Pig cover onto my doona before we left for work this morning?

Now he's having coffee several times, starting with conversation and proceeding slowly, and I'm out there boring them, about to put them off in droves.

I was so close to telling her about the old med student prank of getting switch to page Sister Scope or Sister Circosis, and if I got that far I would have been certain to have told her about the time in fifth year at the Royal when we thought we were hilarious because we got them to page Mike Hunt. And even if she was comfortable with the H word, which a lot of people aren't, I don't think I would have got a great result with the story. She would

have been ducking and weaving to steer clear of me at the
cocktail party. Thinking, *That guy thinks I just became his
fifth funny story about paging.*

How does she get to be so cool, even in green OT
culottes? The hinted shrug, the lift of one eyebrow, the
small, neat smile. Why can I never show such restraint?

On Friday, a letter arrives in the internal mail.

To: The Director, Melatonin Project

Dear Doctor,
As part of the requirement to streamline in order to gain
second-tier wage rises, hospital RMOs have elected to give
up their biscuits. We regret that, as a consequence, we are
no longer empowered to supply you with Arnott's Monte
Carlo x 4 daily. Cream biscuits will henceforth be in lim-
ited supply generally, and available stocks will be diverted
to the psychiatric ward, due to their special needs. We
apologise for any inconvenience.

J.J. Liebowitz (Mrs), Catering Manager

So perhaps Johnno isn't badly thought of by everyone
around here. A single night of passion could become a life-
time supply of cream biscuits. Mrs Liebowitz has not

forgotten. Maybe I should show this to him on Monday. Or maybe I shouldn't, maybe this is how she wants it.

Or maybe it's all Johnno, keeping his made-up Mrs Liebowitz going, dropping this in the internal mail before leaving town. Another reason to say nothing.

Since I'm being Dean Kruger at the moment, I do a shortened staff health session and get back to the ward at about ten-thirty for my half of the Dubois round.

The first couple of patients have been in for weeks, and Dubois despatches them with little interest and less empathy. It's been a while since I sat in on his ward rounds.

Are you still feeling as though your bowels are rotting inside you? he says to the third patient, and then turns to me. *Or was that someone else?*

Someone else, the patient says. *As far as I know. Should I have a test? I mean, can you be sure? I went this morning and it seemed okay. What would you notice with rotting bowels?*

You'd be very sick, I tell him. Sick in a whole range of ways. Your bowels are fine.

Good, Dubois says. *Well, everything's all right then. I'll see you on Tuesday.*

And with this neat maneuvre we move on to patient number four.

After the round, I swerve the Hospital Week Friday lunch (traditionally a seafood smorgasbord, and therefore well attended) and pick up a couple of Pink Lady sandwiches before catching up with a few patients, the ones I think got a particularly raw deal earlier. I talk about adjusted medication doses, I explain why things take time, I offer further reassurance about bowels.

And I wonder how Marlon's going in the exams. If he's got far enough to still be a contender this afternoon. At least half of the candidates will already know they've failed by now. I'm not sure how Marlon would be if he failed, but I don't know how he'd take success either.

For some reason I decide to try to fix the piano pedal. There is nothing in my past that should make me think I might be any fixer of piano pedals, but maybe it's something simple, something I couldn't see in darkness the other night. Or by inquisitive torchlight, but by then all that mattered was making it clear that we weren't having a go at Debussy's Concerto No. 1 for Piano and Pink Oboe.

The dining room is empty. Afternoon tea is over and the start of dinner is half an hour away. I move the stool aside and squat under the piano. I try to move the pedal, first with one hand and then with both. Nothing happens. I strain, and still it seems stuck down. I lean back to pull hard, and just as I jerk at it someone says, *Excuse me*.

This is the second time in a few days I've been startled under this piano, the second time I don't respond well. My hands let go of the pedal and it's as though I'm spring-loaded, launching up from the floor while trying to turn, trying to maintain dignity, getting halfway through a thought about explaining this to the *Excuse me* person as I flail out from under the piano like a bad backstroker just missing the start, but somehow managing to meet the edge of the underside of the keyboard with my left eyebrow.

My momentum carries me on, turning (now more like a hammer thrower, and even good hammer throwers look very silly), rising, with my head ringing with discordant notes from the jolt I gave the keyboard. Turning and rising and hitting a large bosom like a crash test dummy hitting an airbag. Glimpsing a name tag, a longish name ending in Z, the word Manager, just before impact.

The owner of the bosom, who may or may not be Mrs Liebowitz, takes this well. The impact (clearly involuntary), the blood on her front, the disconnected statements I find myself making about Debussy, as though I'm leading up to an explanation for my behaviour but deciding to approach it from a long way off.

But before I can even start to explain my explanation I'm on a chair and a tea towel is being clamped firmly to the front of my head, held right across the front of my whole head, I'm sure by one large hand, like a hand guarding the head of a baby on the way out of the birth canal.

I can see nothing, nothing from under the tea towel, but I'm sure this must be the awesome Mrs Liebowitz. I try to lift up the edge, to get a look out with my right eye, but she pushes me back in the chair, continues the pressure. She's in charge, and she knows how to handle bleeding.

I'll get someone to help you down to Casualty, love. You'll be right.

A smaller hand takes over, a smaller voice says, *What's happened?*

Hit his forehead, just above his left eye. And then quieter, but in fact not at all quiet, *I think I saw bone.*

And I think it's the idea that some of my bone is now exposed that stops me feeling good.

I'm helped to my feet, and it's only when I'm out in the corridor that I manage to lift the tea towel from my right eye. The person who might be Mrs Liebowitz is no longer there, and this remains, at best, an unconfirmed sighting.

In Cas they page the plastic surgery registrar who checks me out and says, *A really good knock on the eyebrow's going to give you a look at bone, and that's the way it goes.* With the kind of nonchalance a person can only have about another person's eyebrow.

It's my eyebrow, my skull we're dealing with here in Cas. All my careful childhood I showed no-one the bones of my skull, and now I'm head butting the undersides of

355

pianos. My theory is fucked, I'm fighting cravings for an OT I don't even know, I haven't come to grips with Debussy at all and one of the Cas sisters is asking me if I want the forms for a Workers' Comp claim, while she's shaving off my eyebrow. I don't really like this week.

And the local anaesthetic hits like a bee sting. I lie patiently in the dull green light under the drape while the plastic surgery registrar counts the sutures out loud as he does them. I wonder if this is for his benefit or mine, or if he's simply the father of small children and now does it automatically.

When he's finished he lets me look in a mirror, and it's as though he's renovated my left eyebrow and added a verandah.

Swells a bit with the local, doesn't it? he says.

But it does at least give me off-street parking.

The RN who shaved my eyebrow fixes a dressing over the suture line and says, *There you go, spunk.* And she brings me a green surgical top to wear and I rinse most of the blood out of my shirt and tie. She insists on checking my orientation in time, place and person, even though I try to tell her this should be seen as a high facial bump rather than a head injury, and she says, *You're not driving home till I'm satisfied you've got binocular vision.*

When we're both happy that I'm orientated and binocular, I call the ward, since it's almost five. Everything's fine there, apart from the fact that they've already heard that I'm in Cas because I split my eyebrow on a piano. And it used to be just my relationship indiscretions that got around this quickly.

I tell them they can see it on Monday, I'll explain on Monday. I tell them no-one else was involved, that I only harm myself now. I tell them not to get too near pianos over the weekend because they just can't be trusted, and

356

I drive home. Still wearing the green surgical top, with my wet shirt and tie in a bag on the passenger seat. And this time actually feels slightly better than the last time I drove home with my shirt wet on the front seat, even though this time it was my own blood that was responsible, and I'm driving home with half the number of eyebrows I left with.

In the mirror, later, when I'm dressed for the cocktail party and seeking to appear attractive, eyebrows come right back into fashion, and facial verandahs are out.

You don't have to go, Rick says.

I've paid for my ticket.

I'm sure they'd give you the money back.

People are expecting me to go.

People?

Yeah.

Is the OT going?

I can't get the bow tie straight.

He insists on driving me, and as we're looping round onto the freeway he says *I'm still not sure how a door did this to you. I don't know how you didn't see it.*

I can't really explain it myself, I tell him, and leave it at that.

Rick knows I have no feeling for piano, no inclination towards pedal fixing. And I can't find the right way to tell him that Marlon just needed to demonstrate something about Debussy. In the search for the simplicity between notes, this week has all become a little complicated.

I had my second coffee thing today, with Elizabeth, he says.

And?

It was good, still good. I don't think either of us was exactly rushing to go back to work. So, what do you think happens next?

Next? What happens next?

Yeah, after coffee twice.

I don't know. I've never actually done coffee twice before. It's all very much part of the town paradigm. Coffee's so easy in town.

But I thought you had it all mapped out for me.

I can't even keep my own eyebrows. It would be bold in the extreme to try mapping for other people. What I meant was, coffee rather than dinner as an opening gambit.

What next though? Coffee's great, but I can't let it stagnate this early. I have this feeling that if we get to coffee four times we'll be stuck, coffee friends, no pash. Somehow I've got to find some very respectable, irresistible way of upping the ante. I need more of a structure to this.

Rick, this is good. Coffee twice is such a calm way to open. You've done well. I wish I could do so well. And now you only need a little imagination, a different venue, remote from crowds and business hours, and if it's working you'll find the distance between you diminishing, a bit of leaning happening, and away you go. No structure. Some things are science, Ricky, but not all things.

So tonight, what about you? Any science planned? Anything of the rocket variety?

Tonight? I don't think so. Worsening upper facial pain, brow asymmetry, a sense only of impending disaster. But a day of great peculiarity in a long line of days of peculiarity, so who knows?

And the OT, does she have a chance, if she throws herself your way?

What am I going to do? Live on a mountain somewhere? But it does seems somewhat academic, just at the moment. I seem to be preoccupied with bringing harm to myself, and I'm not sure that that's a particularly attractive attribute.

Oh, I don't know. It lends a certain complexity. You were hardly interesting at all when you had two eyebrows and you looked like you had your shit together.

When did I have my shit together?

I said you looked like you had your shit together.

And the pain pulses in my eyebrow, pulses down across my face like a warm bright light. My body feels heavy and unwilling, my shit far from together. And Kate Blue will be gone in a week. Rain starts to flick across the windscreen as we drive into the hospital grounds.

Don't be easy, Rick says as I get out of the car. *Make her earn it.*

No sooner am I handed a Strawberry Daiquiri than the plastic surgery registrar wobbles towards me and says, in one long breath out, *What the fuck are you doing here, Marshall?* And then his tongue seems to move independently until it meets the Brandy Alexander he's lifting towards his mouth, like a pink creamy slug leaning into milk. He laps at the edge of the cocktail and says, *You're post-op. You should be taking it easy.*

Well, what does this look like? Contact sport?

Who knows? The night is young. And he gives his eyebrows such a lift he starts to fall backwards, and he ends up talking to someone else.

Some people really want their twenty bucks' worth, don't they? Luisa from One C says. *Nice to see you made it. I heard about your little accident this afternoon, and it struck me as particularly bad timing.*

Only for my beauty. It wasn't going to stop me being here. I want my twenty bucks' worth too.

I don't think she's here yet.

Luisa, could we be subtle about this? Could we at least pretend that I've got an interest in cocktails, or something?

Sure. You want to give me your views on the daiquiri?

It's good.

You're not trying very hard. And anyway, she's been talking about you.

What?

Yeah, saying that she can't wait to see that guy with the funny paging stories again. And she laughs.

That's not very nice. She hasn't mentioned me, has she?

Not really.

I go to the bar for another cocktail. It's getting crowded now and I find myself behind Kelly McLean. She, too, laughs at me.

What did you do to deserve that? she says, looking at the bandage on my head.

Just the usual.

It's been a while coming.

Thank you.

So how's everything going? The melatonin project and things.

Oh, fine. I did my paper on Wednesday and it seemed to go okay. One or two things to clear up with it. Other than that, there's no other than that.

It's good it went well, then.

Yeah.

I talked with Dawn. She says you might be gay now, or maybe bi.

More a nonpractising heterosexual, really.

Me too. Maybe that's what happens after the Dawn Ford phase.

You had a Dawn Ford equivalent?

A physical relationship on a day-to-day basis, with a guaranteed lack of commitment? Think about it. You and Dawn should have been perfect for each other.

But I didn't even like her. It was all a big mistake. Dawn's awful.

Dawn's okay. She knows what she wants. I don't have a problem with Dawn. I can't believe she's okay with Dawn. More than that, I can't believe that she's thinking of me as her Dawn Ford phase. She laughs. *I have lunch with Dawn sometimes.*

And she leaves with as many drinks as she can carry. It now seems likely that, when I leave here, the collective memory of me will not be good. I'll be filed somewhere in the hopeless bastard category, that is, someone who managed to be both hopeless and a bastard. Even Dawn Ford's *completely messed up* seems better than this, and closer to the truth. But that's too subtle, a state of mind, and it's the actions that will be remembered, the conduct. They didn't know me at uni, they won't know me next year, they can't know that I'm already trying to be different, to make this a passing phase. Particularly now that Kelly's looking on it as her Dawn Ford phase. Dawn, but without the directness, the honesty.

Maybe Penny Frew should join them for lunch, and the others who came before her. The Better Off Without You Club. But I hope not. I hope I don't matter that much. I certainly didn't treat them as though they did.

I flagellate my way to the front of the queue, where several cream-splashed RMOs are pouring as fast as they can. I catch the attention of Marco Cassimatis, whom I haven't seen for ages, and I demand the cocktail of the hour, one for each hand.

Fluffy Duck, he says. *One for the piano tuner, one for the piano tuner's imaginary friend.*

I wasn't tuning the piano.

That's kind of a relief. You are aware that that's the story going round, aren't you? That you did that on the piano in the dining room.

Where do these things begin?

Hey, did you hear about the med regs who went to the exam?

No, what happened?

Kenny failed. The other two passed.

Marlon passed?

Yeah.

I turn to get away from the bar, to let him serve some-one else. I turn, and I almost push a cocktail into each of Kate Blue's breasts. I'd really prefer to get to know her first.

Two, she says, just as I'm telling myself it would be counterproductive right at this moment to imagine her bathing up to her neck in Fluffy Duck. *I didn't know you could get two.*

You can't, really. I'm just well connected. I'm very important around here. But I should probably give one to someone else, someone who's had to endure me standing there, hogging the front of the queue. I'm sure that one of these is actually yours.

Yes, but which one? She takes the cocktail from my right hand, tastes it, shakes her head. *No, the other one's mine.* She tastes it, too. *That's better. Much better.* And she hands me my glass back with a fat, red, lipstick mark on it. *Did we meet yesterday? In One C?*

Yeah. And in case you're wondering, no, I didn't have the bandage then.

So is this a costume event and no-one told me?

No, there's a small wound under there. A bit of a bump.

A bit of a bump? I'm sure there's more to it than that, some story behind it.

Obviously I've had an impact with paging stories, and one deserving of subtle mockery, so I just say, A minor incident with a piano.

A minor incident with a piano?

Yes. And that, I can assure you, is the last you'll hear of it. Not one single boring detail.

But a minor incident with a piano sounds quite interesting, or at least as though it could be quite interesting.

Not this one. This could be a tedious incident, tediously told. A simple moment of collision. The piano and I happened to be attempting to occupy the same space at the same time.

Mysterious.

Hardly. Nothing more than physics really.

I stop, already teetering on the brink of tedious, and for once self-monitoring effectively. She smiles, raises her eyebrows in a way that only one of us can, sips at her cocktail. And she doesn't have the red glasses on tonight and her eyes are a quite surreal blue.

She finishes the cocktail, hands me the glass in a way that suggests I'm to get another. *I'm told you're very important around here,* she says. *And I assume it would therefore be easy for you to come across two more of these.*

When I get back, three other people from One C are with her and I'm suddenly aware of the room again. Still watching her, trying to handle this reasonably, trying to stop one boring story about a piano and several about paging from lurching out, trying not to over-analyse a minute's conversation. And she's saying that she's explained her situation to the technician and he said he thought it made her a priority customer, but he didn't have any pagers free at the moment. And that the reason for the PA system being the way it is is something to do with the head wardsman having fought in a war.

I didn't quite get that, she says. *But you don't like to ask.*

And the end of her nose moves up and down when she

talks, just slightly. I wonder if she knows. Watching it now, I think it's a good thing. But then I would.

The other people from the ward want to take her to meet someone, and she turns as they lead her away and says, *I'll see you later.*

The plastic surgery registrar is dancing on top of the piano while another drunk person plays, despite the CD that's already turned up loud. And I can't work out which one he's dancing to, but my guess is he's doing his best to dance to both. I want to tell him pianos are dangerous, he should know that by now.

As though to prove my point, he falls gracelessly in a distracted moment (maybe between notes) and lands face first on the edge of a table. He pulls himself to his feet, as I move to help him, and he grips onto my arm and says, *You're really just post-op, you know. If anything happens to you tonight it's my responsibility. My responsibility.*

And then he moves sideways, his nose quite brutally misshapen, and he starts dancing like John Travolta in *Saturday Night Fever,* even though we're several minutes into the extended mix of Joy Division's 'Love Will Tear Us Apart'.

I wonder how Marlon is, how he's feeling now. I wonder if the exam matters to him at the moment. If passing feels good, or if it's just a hurdle crossed, allowing him to get back to something more important.

I'm finding it hard not to watch Kate Blue. I want to talk to her, I really want to talk to her. I want to get out of here with her, but I haven't thought this through. My head is sore with the impact, thick with creamy cocktails.

I'm drinking too much. I'm not growing up enough, or I'm drinking too much.

So, it turns out, is Kate Blue. She's on her way past to the bar some time that must be midnightish, and I'm doing some stupidly obvious looking when she comes over to me.

And before I get to tell her that I was actually looking just beyond her, at something on the wall, she says, *I think I owe you a drink. Stay there.*

She comes back with four drinks, sloshing them down over her hands and onto the floor.

Two actually. I remembered it was two. Therefore I ordered four. I mentioned your name, bearing in mind your influence. Well actually I didn't, because I forgot your name. But I was planning not to tell you that because that kind of thing's disgraceful.

Well, you did bring me two drinks. I can't complain.

Just returning the favour. She shrugs, licks the spillage from her fingers. I am a bit upset that she forgot my name, but it really isn't something I can complain about. *I'm only here for another week. What do you think of that?*

It's not long enough. It's a beautiful part of town.

So you'll be staying then?

I don't know. I do have a job here till the end of the year. Beyond that I don't know. I might travel, I suppose. Bit of a restless spirit. But you've got to watch out with that stuff. You've got to call somewhere home.

Very philosophical.

I wouldn't say that.

It's noisy in here.

What?

Noisy in here.

Yes.

We'll talk outside.

So we take our four cocktails onto the balcony, just as it starts to rain again, to drizzle down through the poinciana trees and across Kate Blue's face, making her blink. She seems unaware of the rain, and the blinking.

I don't know about all this.

What exactly?

Well, restlessness. I don't know if it's an answer, or just a question. And you shouldn't think I'm tied up with this OT stuff.

They say very good things about you in the ward, you know.

Do they? Why? Why are you saying that?

They do. Plain and simple.

Well, I don't know, you know. I don't know about that, or where I stand with that. I've got a few things to work out. And she thinks hard, counts with her wet, elegant fingers, loses count because it's that or lose at least one cocktail glass. *About six things. About six things to work out. And that's a bugger. I don't really know what happens next. And that's all I'm saying.*

Six things.

Approximately. And that's all I'm saying.

I understand that. And it's not my business, you know. I understand that.

I don't mean to be rude. I'm being rude to you now. Again. Rude with the name, rude with this.

No, not at all. I don't want you to tell me anything you don't want to tell me. And I hope it works out.

Thank you. You're very understanding.

No, I mean it. It matters to me.

She looks down into one of her empty cocktail glasses. The water that has matted her dark hair dribbles from it and down her face. Her clothes stick to her, her bare shoulders shine and shiver. She looks up at me again, with a slightly puzzled smile.

Thank you, she says, quite formally.

Can I just ask a question?

She nods, looks down again.

It's not a personal question. You wouldn't be put off anyone because of an eyebrow, would you? Temporary lack thereof.

I've never been much on eyebrows. I'm really not the right person to ask.

Okay.

Anyway, I have no idea why I'm telling you all this, why I'm telling all this to someone I've just met. Now you have to tell me something about you. You have to tell me something that matters to you at the moment. Not gruesomely personal, but quite important. Then we're even.

Something about me? I don't want you to get cold. That's quite an important thing about me at the moment. I heard this story, when I was young, and I now think there must be more to it . . . Do you like cricket?

It's okay.

Yes. Two brothers, I think, called Bannerman, played in the first test team for Australia, 1877, you know the one. Well, I heard that one of them got wet and cold and died of a fever. Young, healthy man. And I know there must be more to it than that, but I don't want you to get cold. You understand?

Yes.

And this, this is difficult, of course. I don't want to mess up with the gender stuff here. I'm not going to be opening doors or anything. But I'd be interested in perhaps getting you a towel.

Yes.

Now, you see, that's okay, 'cause I could have offered my jacket. And while, in a lot of ways, I'd rather offer the jacket, so we could stay out here, even though it's wet and probably practically freezing, I think we should get towels. And towels are inside.

Yes.

367

She wraps her arms around herself and shudders, flicks the last creamy residue of one of her cocktails up her right arm. Doesn't notice this, or the intensifying rain sweeping it away.

Inside we find an unlocked room, with towels and a bar heater. She sits on the edge of the bed with the towel draped over her head. Looking, with her long, elegant nose, more like Peter O'Toole in *Lawrence of Arabia* than I'd like her to. His nose, I assure myself, is stationary when he talks. I have not erred and brought Peter O'Toole to the room. Besides, he is much older. Despite the similarities I'm sure I could tell them apart.

I've had too much to drink, she says sadly.

Water drips from the end of her nose. She wraps herself in a blanket, but still shivers. I want to hold her, to make her warm. But I can't move. All that crap I said to Rick in the car. All that crap about leaning, and away you go. She's on the bed, I'm on the chair, and she's got six things on her mind. I'm not one of them. So I'm sitting nearby, watching her needing warmth and wishing the bar heater would come through, knowing I can get no closer. I've had no signal that I should be over there, next to her.

This isn't a tactic you know, I tell her.

What? she says, as though I've caught her by surprise, as though she was far away. Six things away, or maybe just increasingly unwell.

Getting you wet, getting you in here, asking the eyebrow question. I don't do tactics. And anyway, whatever I might be feeling right at the moment I know I shouldn't be. It's none of my business. Just ask people. Ask anyone round here and they'll tell you how smart it is to avoid me. That's all I'm saying.

What?

It's not a tactic. It's good advice. I could have six things

myself you know. This hasn't been a good year. I have conducted myself poorly. I've become a little depressed. I have
no idea, no idea what I want to do with my life. That's all
I'm saying, okay?

*I'm sorry, I don't understand. I'm very tired. I should
call a cab.*

Smart move.

I take her to the phone and she calls. We stand at the
door, at the edge of the rain, Kate Blue with the blanket
around her shoulders and starting to shiver less perhaps.
Headlights appear on the wet road, a cab drives slowly
into the hospital.

I walk with her out into the rain, and I open the door
as she fumbles with the blanket, drops it in a puddle.

Fuck.

Leave it to me.

Her foot slips on a pizza box and she falls onto the bitu-
men, limbs going everywhere.

It's just a balance problem, she says dismissively as
I help her up. *But thanks anyway. It's been a lovely night.
And I hope you're okay, you know?*

Yeah. You too.

Inside, people are concerned about the plastic surgery
registrar. Apparently he danced on the piano again,
against advice and unperturbed by either the largeness or
the blueness of his nose. He fell and was then noted to be
more subdued, and later seen lying across the bonnet of
his car, throwing up. Now he and his car have gone.

I go back into the room where we found the towels,
since it's the only warm place I can think of. I turn off the
bar heater. I remember my mother telling me you never go
to sleep with a bar heater on because of the fire risk.
I watch the glow of its element fade, and then I realise
I must have turned it off so that I could go to sleep now.

I start counting my six things and I only get to three, but I do hold two almost opposite views about each. My career, the project, relationships.

I dream of cricket, of slatted pads and the majestic driving of Victor Trumper.

And I wake stiff and cold, with the sun angling through the windows and pointing into my eyes.

I drink water in the kitchen, and I go over to Cas for some Panadol, B group vitamins and Maxolon. I don't feel too bad. Far from perfect, but not too bad. At least I'm not one of the people lying in Bays One and Two with drips in their arms, running the vitamins and Maxolon in IV and still throwing up.

Good cocktail party, one of the RNs says, and leads me round the corner to the cubicle where the orthopaedic registrar is examining X-rays, and the plastic surgery registrar lies looking totally white (other than his nose), with a piece of his right tibia poking through the skin just above the ankle.

Good cocktail party, he says to me. *Hey?*

48

When I walk out of staff health on Monday, the early morning coldness has gone and it's a perfect, warm winter's day.

I could go up to Nine and catch up with the last part of Johnno's round, but I don't. I'll go after morning tea and be given my list of mundane medical tasks, and I'll face the conversation about Dean's article later. And no-one will notice that they haven't done journal club, not since it died the death of a thousand yawns at least a couple of months ago. I probably spoiled it by getting excited, by putting pressure on everyone to come up with an article that would get them a room.

It's still cold in the Quarters when I walk in to make coffee. The sink is full of dirty mugs and the only one left in the cupboard has 'Help me' on it in bold black letters. I don't know whose it is but I can't be bothered washing another, so I use it.

And I'm thinking, How do I do this? How do I discreetly ease my way out of melatonin? I don't think I can. I think there'll be some time, and quite soon, when I have to tell not just Johnno, but also the Dud, Joan Shand, Imelda in the library, anyone who asks.

I go outside, out the back way, away from the crowd of people at morning tea complaining about the lack of biscuits.

My face still hurts. I never realised how expressive I was facially until the last couple of days, when any twitch of my eyebrow has felt like a jump start. My eye is open, enough to drive, enough to claim competent binocular vision, but not much more, and I'm peeping out between two purple flaps of eyelids. It's quite a sight, my big, ugly, black eye looking like a fat, black patch stitched onto me by the bristling line of sutures.

I take off my jumper and sit on it on the steps to drink my coffee. I take off my tie and put it beside me, roll up my sleeves. And the sun soaks into my thick purple eyebrow, throbs away in there.

So what did I do with Kate Blue on Friday night? And what made me warn her off? She was confident and she was cool, and then she was trapped by her six unresolved issues, wet and cold. I liked her both ways. I'd take either,

371

I'd take both. I'd take the bits I do understand, and the bits I don't. Given the chance.

Despite the obvious danger in the open confession of the six unresolved issues. At least one of them's a male, surely. Or a female. Or maybe that's one of the issues.

And I'm trying not to tick them off, count them off on my fingers, as though that might allow me to know her better, formulate a strategy. It's easy sitting here, looking down into the empty 'Help me' coffee mug. I can want her as much as I like without making a mess of it. It's better, probably, that I leaned the way I did on Friday night. Away and not towards. Better for both of us.

And I want to have words with Marlon about putting that mountain shit in my head, and whoever it was who told me the story of the younger Bannerman brother, and thereby made Kate Blue's wellbeing a matter of critical importance to me on Friday night. I can remember it going through my head at the time, but I think I managed to keep it to myself. And a good thing too, since it occurs to me now that it was actually the youngest Grace brother. So I could have blown it all then, if she's got any significant knowledge of nineteenth-century cricket.

And she really did look a lot like Peter O'Toole. Is that my problem? I haven't yet come to terms with my feelings for Peter O'Toole, and that's why my life sometimes seems confusing?

I shuffle aside to let an old couple walk past me up the stairs. A twenty-cent piece hits the bottom of the empty 'Help me' coffee mug.

By the time I've worked out what's going on, it's too late to chase them and give it back, so I end up shouting, Thanks, and hoping no-one else hears. It doesn't hurt for them to think they've done some good. And it covers me for Galaxion for this week.

I must be looking great today if old people think they should give me money. And what do I do if someone pages me now? Tell them I'm sorry, I'm just on a begging break? Sitting here, looking like crap, looking like I'm just coming to terms with some clumsy neurosurgery, probably looking as though beggar is one of my better career options. Did Paracelsus face this moment, in the last days of a life of angry science, sitting on the steps of a Strasbourg almshouse, pondering, the morning sun taking the cold from his bony limbs, a centime or two dropped into his borrowed 'Help me' mug?

I rinse the mug and the twenty-cent piece in the Quarters' kitchen and check my pigeon hole.

There's a photocopy of an article, a note from Dean saying, *In case you're interested.*

I don't want to read it, but I can't not read it. I don't want it to exist, but it does. Eight depressed men given melatonin. And I'm very aware of how little I knew and how far I pushed it, of the Hazardous Materials building up near the chapel. But in the outline of the method I start to notice things. The dose is higher, much higher than I would have expected. I was thinking two milligrams, maybe up to five, given in the evening. This is fifty, 50 mg four times a day. This is just wrong.

This is a circadian nightmare. Melatonin is all about rhythms. I'm convinced it's all about rhythms, making the small changes necessary to restore a normal rhythm. This is huge doses, four times a day. There's no rhythm here. Any rhythm these men had, any readable signal, is completely obliterated by this noise. Any receptor that picks up fluctuations in melatonin levels and signals action would be blown away by this, and continue to be blown away every minute of every day this treatment went on.

And if I'm right, the only way a mood could go with this is down.

How many people have been misled by this, led away from something that might work? How could it have looked like the right thing to do?

Johnno and Dean and some nurses are in the tearoom when I get to the ward.

Dean, this article, it's really interesting, I say rather loudly, hoping they'll stop staring at my eye. Did you see the doses they used and how often they gave it?

No.

I explain, Johnno nods. Dean smiles, says, *Glad I could help. I was worried for a while there. I thought it might be a problem. But you've obviously got it covered.*

Yeah, and I think it's actually better than that. This could be the reason no-one's pursued it.

And one more thing, Johnno says. *You seem not to have noticed that you've got quite an impressive facial injury there. I heard it was a lively cocktail party but . . .*

It was something to do with a piano, wasn't it? Glen says.

Yeah, setting up for the party. I surfaced at the wrong moment.

Somehow this, this shorthand version of not quite the truth, seems the best way to head off a long explanation in which no-one is really interested, particularly when meal trolleys can now be heard in the distance. I page Marlon de Lisle to congratulate him, and he offers to buy me lunch.

We meet at the Pink Ladies at one and he buys me sandwiches and a cream bun. And again I have to explain the eyebrow.

Setting up for the party, I tell him. The cocktail party on Friday.

I like this story, and as long as I don't try it with any-one who actually set up for the party it should continue to serve me well. And I couldn't tell Marlon it happened while I was trying to fix the pedal for him.

We sit in the sun, but at a table rather than on the begging steps. He tells me about his exam, but what he really wants to tell me is that he's tried to call Sue a few times since, but she's screening him out.

But I've got a plan. You'll like this. I want to let her know how much things mean to me, okay? How much what she needs matters to me. So my plan is that, with another couple of years of advanced trainee time to put in, I offer to pull out now. I write her a letter and I tell her that even though I've passed the exam I'll drop out of the training program and we'll work out something else. Change whatever we have to.

That's making it pretty clear.

It's got to. Nothing against your tea-making ability, but I just can't stay in that room, lying on that single bed in that grey-walled room not even knowing if it's day or night. Saying to myself, forty years and this is all you've got, this suspended animation.

And I don't want to get into a discussion with Marlon about his plans, and their chances. I can't guess how she'll deal with the letter, and he needs his optimism badly, needs me simply to nod along, temper this hope with nothing. As he works out Debussy can't save him in the end, works out just how much he'll put on the line for this.

49

By the next morning, my feelings about melatonin are changing again. I am a prisoner of oscillation.

Today's feeling is that Dean's article was a warning. That if he could, quite by chance, pluck an article from a decade I hadn't even considered and nearly trash the whole thing, there may be many articles out there that would do the job properly.

I think there may not be, as well, but it's quite a risk. I feel good about the model, I can still see the sense in it, and the possibilities, it would just be a lot easier if I wasn't in it too. I'm sure there are plenty of theories that looked great, but were only one convincing piece of contrary evidence away from looking very bad, and dragging someone down with them.

In the late-twentieth century, Galen's theory of the four humours, which ruled the world for longer than a thousand years, looks more than slightly ill-informed. Few contemporary citizens of Basel would hold to the idea that good health is achieved through balancing one's phlegm, blood, black bile and yellow bile. And around the same number would, I suspect, maintain confidence in Phil von Hohenheim's replacement theory, that of the three elements, in which all disease arises from an imbalance of sulfur, mercury and salt. Or his model of the four principles of medical practice: philosophy, astronomy, alchemy and virtue, with the greatest of these being virtue.

This, of course, may simply reflect my own shortcomings, and some troubles I've had with the virtue. And perhaps the astronomy points to a more significant role for the butt-wired astronauts than I'd first realised.

I'm being a bit hard on Paracelsus. He was never going to replace the four humours with a working model of a DNA molecule, and he did come up with ether, laudanum, a treatment for syphilis and some very reasonable theories about silicosis, goitre and St Vitus's dance.

This is where we differ. The restless spirit had no fear of the hit and miss. *How about we poke a bit of mercury around that chancre, Gustav?* A risk some of us, me included, would never take, but the invention of a cure that lasted centuries.

I tell Glen I've got a lot of consult requests to take to the multistorey and a few other things to do and he says, *Doctor Dubois will just have to do without you then,* as though he knows I have only three consult requests and little else.

I go anyway and it takes about five minutes to drop them off. Or perhaps a few more, as I keep taking short-cuts through One C.

I'm sitting in the melatonin room with the door open when Kate Blue walks past. I hear her feet stop. She comes back.

I heard you had a room here, she says.

Yeah, well this is it.

She's wearing the red glasses again today, curling her long fingers round the door frame, keeping her culotted parts outside.

I asked around, she says. *About you and tactics, about you being a smart person to avoid, like you said. And you were right. People did back you up.*

They backed me up?

She shrugs, as though I can take it or leave it. *You mean they shouldn't have?*

I guess I hoped they wouldn't have.

So it was a tactic?

No, not at all. Well, maybe. I don't know. It's not a night I can account for well. They probably should have backed me up, to be honest. There have been some things that I haven't handled very well. I've been . . . thoughtless, to put it mildly. But I'm much more aware of other people's needs now. I regularly make cups of tea for the guy next door, and I'm putting in quite an effort to help him through a personal crisis. And all altruistically.

And you were worried about me getting cold on Friday night.

I was, wasn't I? Very worried. You look warm now though, so that's good.

Yeah.

Friday wasn't my best day, you have to understand that. I'd had the minor facial injury that afternoon, and I thought that my great theory about the aetiology of depression had come unstuck.

Now, you see, a lot of people could get confused at this point, and think this was a tactic. The sympathy vote.

No, it's true. And my theory's okay now anyway, for the moment.

And she gives me a look, as though simply claiming to have a theory might be some feeble shot at a tactic. I think she's decided I'm a science nerd. This only makes me decide to try again.

If I had a tactic it'd be much better than that. If I had a tactic I'd be dangerous. So what if I had one? What if I actually had a very persuasive tactic that I was interested in trying out?

Do you?

I don't know.

Then you won't know, will you?

How are the six issues going?

Six issues?

The six issues that needed to be resolved. I'm not meaning to push for inappropriate disclosure here, I'm just wondering how they're going.

Six issues. I can't think of more than five. I don't think there were ever more than five, so if I've overstated my case, I'm sorry.

Yeah, sure. Six issues, dripping wet, freezing. Sympathy vote. Cheap tactic.

No tactic. Five issues, dripping wet, freezing. Simply a twenty per cent issue overcount. Quite forgivable in the circumstances. And even though it wasn't a tactic I think you were going for it anyway.

Come on. Dripping wet, freezing. I could be just a decent human being who can recognise someone in need of a towel and a bar heater.

Altruism, then.

Yeah. So tell me, you'd find altruism pretty attractive wouldn't you? As far as tactics go I mean, objectively.

As far as tactics go, more subtle than most. And I hope you and the guy in the next room are happy together. He's obviously dozens of cups of tea ahead of anyone else.

Hey, I never gave Marlon de Lisle a towel. I never gave anyone a towel before.

I'll remember that. I'd better get to the ward. I've got patients to see. If I don't get there within the next minute they'll be paging me, and we all know what that means.

And she gives a hint of a wave with her long fingers, and her feet move quickly away along the corridor, faster than walking. The stairwell door creaks open, slaps shut.

50

Is it any surprise that I spend much of the next several days thinking of Kate Blue? Wanting to call her, thinking I shouldn't. Seeing her in my doorway, seeing her doing her wet Lawrence of Arabia look. Seeing the puzzle find its way onto her face when she let slip more than she meant to on Friday night, but still told me nothing.

This is dangerous. I could get attached to the idea of Kate Blue. I could miss her when she leaves, and I don't even know her.

I check the OT Department number so often that I don't need to check it any more. I think about paging her, but of course that'd only end up with me flat on my back with some big enrolled nurse jumping on my chest, and that's not what I've got in mind right now.

I can't seem to call. I can't call without a reason. On Wednesday and Thursday I can't call to ask Kate Blue out. I play it through in my mind, and it works well, other than two points. One is that I can't see why she'd say yes, and the other is that I really want her to. Some more time would have been good. Time to take it slowly, get to know where things stand, but I'm not going to get that.

She doesn't call, I don't call.

By Friday, I know it's today or not at all. I've had the stitches out, but this seems to have failed to make me suddenly more attractive. I'm just going to have to go with what I've got, some time between now and five p.m. Or not at all.

Rick and Elizabeth are going to a movie tonight. He sang in the car on the way to work this morning, even when the radio was between songs. He said she was more than ready for a good deal of leaning, and that she'd even suggested a film that was conducive to it. I tried to tell him that once people are over eighteen, they tend to avoid going the lean actually during the film, and he just said, *What if she can't stop herself? Do I tell her it's inappropriate? I don't think so.*

And I asked him if he could at least please wait until there was a song before singing, and he pushed the tape in, sang along to The Go Betweens, loudly and in the vicinity of the tune.

Be nice to her, I told him, and he said, *Of course, what else would I be?*

In the ward I write up medication sheets for the weekend, discuss conjunctivitis with one patient and constipation with another, and I work so efficiently I'm on my way to staff health early. I decide I might as well go to the Quarters and check my pigeon hole and, while I'm scrunching up two circulars about parking area designation and the slipperiness of the new tiles outside Cas, I see a notice that I haven't seen before, pinned next to the DMO roster.

It says, *Kittens anyone? Five kittens of uncertain parentage (half tabby), free to anyone who'll give them a kind home. Call Kate Blue in OT or One C by 5 p.m. 23 June, or at home any time.* The bottom of the sheet is cut into tabs that each say, *Kate Blue, Kittens,* and a home phone number. How could I resist? How could anyone resist kittens? Kate Blue's big looping writing and bold invitation of *Kittens anyone?* I have to persuade myself not to take the whole page, to limit myself to the first of the tabs at the bottom.

And when the number's in my pocket, I take some convincing that she didn't give it to me, that I just happened to find it on a public noticeboard, regarding a matter of five kittens.

I also have to tell myself that Kate Blue's five things that need sorting out are not likely all to be kittens, even if this is a very good explanation. The kittens are, at most, one of the things, and possibly none.

And there's no point in being excited because I have her number in my pocket. I've had the OT Department number within easy reach all week, and it helps you not at all if you don't call it.

How would Jen and Rick feel about a kitten?

Fortunately, I arrive at staff health and I have to discontinue this internal monologue. My first hour is booked up with pre-employment medicals and hepatitis B vaccinations. And then it's a sore ear and a cough, and a wardie with a very nasty rash that's been neglected despite previous visits to staff health.

He's just pulling his pants up and I'm writing a prescription when something thumps heavily against the door. I open it, in case I should, forgetting that the wardie's pants are around his knees, and the top half of a fallen man flops into the room, his bent legs kicked out into the corridor.

A patient from Dermatology Outpatients, grey and still in my doorway.

I shake and shout, he does nothing. He's not breathing, there's no pulse.

Could we call a Code Blue? I say to the receptionist. And could we get the crash trolley here right now?

And already I'm on my knees, working his chest alone, figuring that until the gear arrives, until we have other people, I'm going to be giving him one-operator CPR, mouth to actual mouth.

We've never had a crash trolley down here, she says, standing still, doing nothing.

Okay. Call the Code. Get me help. Let's move. Get me a bag, get a trolley and we'll get him to ICU.

And I'm stopping for breaths in the middle of this, losing count by having to give instructions, on my knees in a four-hundred bed hospital with a man dying and not a single piece of helpful equipment.

There's just my handbag.

What?

My handbag. You wanted a bag?

Sorry. Bag and mask. Emergency equipment. Call the Code. Do that now.

She goes to the phone. An enrolled nurse kneels down beside me with a bag and mask, and a plastic Guedel's airway that may not be the right size.

Tell me what you want, he says, as I slip the airway into place and prove myself wrong.

Take the chest. And go easy. He's already on a hard floor.

I'll be fine. And he is. His hands well controlled, his timing good. He counts to five out loud, one to five, one to five, so I can get my timing right with the ventilations.

The Code Blue sounds, and even now it sounds just a bit like Kate Blue.

I look around between squeezes of the bag, and there's no trolley yet, nothing coming along the corridor. Still just the two of us.

The dermatology registrar opens his door. *Shit.*

He's just gone down, we got on him right away. What's his story? Anything I should know?

Just really bad dermatitis.

The wardie with the rash is trying to move past on his way out of my room.

Now you see what happens if you don't use the cream? I say to him, because I'll never get another chance like this. Could you get things moving for us?

He gets on his two-way and gives directions to who-ever's bringing the trolley and says, *We need it right bloody now, okay?* And he says to me, *ICU doc, is that where we're going?* and he reaches over the desk for the phone and calls ahead to warn them.

Could you get a lift held?

Done.

The trolley arrives and we're pumping, pumping and bagging. I keep thinking I should be getting a line in, rolling out the emergency drugs, but there's none of that, no defib down here, however much there should be. Just us and the bag.

The wardies and the EN hoist the patient onto the trol-ley and it's too high to give reliable compressions.

There's only one way to do this, I say to them, and I can't help but smile.

Residents and registrars are starting to arrive in num-bers, and I swing my leg over the rail, move myself over the top of the patient and crouch, working on the chest, counting out loud.

Go, go, go, I tell them after five, when I'm stable.

The wardie pushes, and we move, all of us. And some-how I'm in charge here and I don't know why. Maybe because I'm tall now.

We run along, through the long corridors of Outpatients, past urology, past general surgery, past nurs-ing admin, doorway after doorway with fifteen people shouting duck at just the right time for me to get down close to the patient's chest and avoid losing my head. And the wardie runs long after he's out of breath, puffing and pushing, running like a red-faced old cowboy, thighs well apart at all times to stop chafing.

And my beeper gets flicked off in a doorway, hits the unforgiving lino floor, and this time smashes to pieces.

I'm eight feet up, my head eight feet above the ground, counting to five and five and five, working the chest with an unbroken rhythm. And I can see over the heads of the people packed around me. I can see visitors stopping, turning, watching this chariot ride, appalled by the apparent frivolity and then realising what's going on. Kate Blue with a file under her arm as we hit the lifts.

I want to talk to you, I shout to her, past everyone else as we start crowding in.

Fine, she says. *I think you're busy. Call me.*

She smiles. The doors shut.

What was that? someone says. *Who was that you were talking to?*

I think it was personal, the dermatology registrar says. *Could it have been personal?*

How can I keep counting to five with all this speculation?

It's personal.

We leave the lift, turn left, turn left again, crash through the plastic doors of ICU, and the guy working the bag has to move aside.

The patient coughs, chokes on the Guedel's airway and lifts his hand to try to pull it from his mouth. He opens his eyes. Comes round with me hovering over him. Me and my one eyebrow and my yellowing bruise, kneeling over his body, hands overlapped on his chest. He startles, as though I'm a vision from hell. Certainly not a vision from Dermatology Outpatients.

He struggles to sit up as I dismount, looks around at the crowd, sees the dermatology registrar, a face he knows. And he says, with a little embarrassment, *Is there a problem?*

Somebody connects him to a monitor and the cardiology registrar takes over.

That looked good up there, the dermatology registrar says on the long walk back down to our end of Outpatients.

Yeah. Beats staff health.

And the guy lived. I revise my CPR stats to a quite respectable forty-two to one. He hit the door a dead man, grey and gone, and now he's up in ICU, being told about it all.

A dustpan with my beeper parts is waiting at the desk when I get back to staff health, and the receptionist says she cancelled the rest of the clinic and sent everyone down to Cas because she didn't know how long I'd be.

I call switch to let them know my pager's temporarily inoperative and I'm told, *Doctor Shand from Biochemical Pathology paged you a few minutes ago.*

I call her back and she says we may have a problem. We've got some choices to make about the assay, and would I be free to come up and see her? I wrap my beeper parts in a paper towel and walk back through Outpatients, not sure I can talk about melatonin right now, make assay choices.

She has a pile of documents on her desk. Two manuals, a number of letters, pages of photocopied graphs.

I've been waiting to hear back from a few people for a while, she says. *And now I have. And I think, particularly after listening to your paper last week, that the options available to us at the moment may not be quite good enough.* Telling me slowly, watching me nod as though I'm concentrating, as though I can get any of this into my head at the moment. *Part of the problem with this area of research is that the things that are easy to measure, and cheap to measure, are the ones that you've worked out are less worth measuring. Morning urine six-sulfatoxy melatonin, for example. If we wanted to measure that, I think we could do it.* She puts it to me as though it's a question, as though it's my call.

But should we? Would it give us anything worthwhile?

386

From somewhere deep down, my melatonin knowledge surfaces.

Maybe not. Your plan, and I understand the case you're making, needs serum melatonin to be measured down to the picogram level. It's the precision that's the challenge. That's what costs the money. At this stage. People are working on other methods that would perhaps give the accuracy we need, but they're some way off being available for us to use. You understand the position?

Yeah. We can't afford to measure what we need to measure at the moment.

We could try to set up something that would measure melatonin itself, rather than metabolites, but I think this is how it would end up. She turns a graph round to face me. *This is the one I was hoping would work. The problem, as you can see, is that when you look at the measurements compared to the gold standard test, they're plus or minus up to forty per cent in some cases. If we were looking for presence or absence that'd be fine, or if we were looking at ten-fold changes in order of magnitude, but we aren't. For our purposes, I can't see that this test can be made reliable enough.*

And I could push it, perhaps. It occurs to me as I'm looking at the graph that we could look at the possibility of getting enough funding to pay for someone who does have the right equipment to do it for us. We could add that to our NHMRC application. But I don't say this, not today at least. My head's still crowded with the dash through Outpatients, the gagging man waking, wondering, pink again.

I tell her we'll wait. She looks at me as though she's not able to break it to me that the wait might be a very long time, and we leave it at that.

I'll let you know, she says, *if anything comes up. It's still a good idea, and I know this is disheartening.*

And I could feel the life come back into the man's chest, his own breathing begin, the muscles in his arms as they started to act against me. And I don't know what the problem was, or what his long-term outlook is like, but I know he's got a chance. A better chance than he had when he fell against my door. And I'll never again get such a good excuse to behave that way, to take on the murmuring quiet of Outpatients at such a charge, to wake up the whole length of it and be eight feet tall. To look so irresponsible, so out of control, when I was indisputably doing nothing but the best I could.

This is my out. This assay problem will leave my theory untested, at least by me. Someone will look at it again, sometime. Someone will work out that 50 mg four times a day simply had to make people depressed. Someone who understands rhythms will fight to get an assay good enough and will test this, somewhere. And the answer will be theirs, not mine, whatever the answer is. And that's okay. I don't know what I'll be doing then, where I'll be, but that's okay too. It's a great theory, but I'm better off out.

I walk into One C as Kate Blue is walking to the stairwell.

Hi, she says. *And can I just say, if you were looking for an impressive tactic, that was pretty good. Very noticeable at least.*

I didn't have any choice. There's no crash trolley in Outpatients. It was fun, though. And the guy lived.

The guy lived?

He's up in ICU. He's conscious, he's pink, all the things a guy bringing a rash to Dermatology Outpatients should be.

That's what he was here for?

Yeah. So death would have been seen as a very inappropriate outcome.

Lucky you were there, then. Now, we were going to talk, I think.

Yeah.

How about we grab some lunch? Is that okay?

Yeah. Sure.

So we walk down to the Pink Ladies, Kate Blue next to me in her green culottes, talking about her last day, about how it hasn't been bad here. And I want to tell her I don't think she's got CPR worked out. I want to put today's result in context, eighteen months as resident, forty-two to one. This is a big moment, not an automatic outcome. Not even a likely outcome.

I'm beginning to realise how much I sweated during the arrest, and hoping she won't take me for someone who is habitually casual with body odour. If all of this was looking good, and then I put her off with the smell, I think I'd have to kill myself. But how do you deal with this? Point out the odour and try to explain it? Look, I'm aware that I'm putting out a bit of a stink at the moment, but you have to understand, all that CPR is pretty invigorating, and I'm just one shower away from smelling like green apple shampoo again, the regular me.

We buy sandwiches and sit in the sun, coincidentally at the same table I sat at with Marlon de Lisle earlier in the week. This must be where I bring my altruism dates.

So, she says, *we were going to talk.*

I should have prepared for this. I should be much better prepared. I wasted all the time on the way down here listening to her and thinking about stink. All week thinking I was never going to be brave enough to call her.

I know some people who might like a kitten, I tell her, the very bad best I can do.

Really, who?

I don't know. I hadn't thought that far. What kind of a question is that? What does it matter who?

Of course it matters. Some people are completely inappropriate for kittens. A kitten's not a toy. You've got to want it. You've got to be prepared to put time in, treat it responsibly, take it to the vet when it's sick. So you know some people who might like a kitten, but you're not sure who yet?

Yeah. That's right. Pretty shitty tactic, really.

The shittiest. You'll have to do better than that.

She laughs, and this one I can't save, can't hide. I'm out in the open now as someone who might have an interest and that wasn't the plan at all. And I can't avoid her eyes, can't stop myself looking at their surreal blue, being quietly dazzled by them, and thinking that's such a crappy idea.

There's something wrong with my lenses, isn't there? she says. *Something wrong and you're not telling me. I've got a blue tint on one side and a plain one on the other, is that it?*

No, I think they might both be the blue tint.

Thank god I thought it was crappy to fall for her eyes. Thank god I'm enthusiastic about the whole Kate Blue.

I liked the red glasses anyway, I tell her.

They were my mother's idea. A bit of a trick really. I didn't want to get glasses at all, and she said, If you're getting them, go all the way. Make a statement. We chose them together. People think it equates with personality. That it signals a certain zaniness, a capacity to take risks, something dynamic. Which it doesn't, of course. But as my mother said, if you're getting glasses, use them to your advantage.

Well, I fell for it. I was impressed. I thought, pretty cool. Impressively incongruous with the OT uniform.

I'll have to give up the OT business, then, because I plan to keep the glasses. Lucky I started that MBA.

You started an MBA? Or was that just a joke?

I started an MBA. What's the joke in an MBA? I've been going for months now and it hasn't been funny at all.

Why would you, and if this is one of the five things that aren't to be disclosed feel free to let me know, why would you do OT and then do an MBA?

Why not? Why would you stop at OT? I mean, pardon me for not loving this, but I don't know what I'm going to do with my life.

Is this one of the five things?

It might be. But they might all have been kittens, mightn't they? Will you get over the five things?

Only when I think I've worked them out. So you don't really like OT?

Not really. You're not going to tell me you're exactly addicted to this? And she indicates with a sweep of one arm the concrete tower of the multistorey, the old stone wards.

Well, maybe not as much as I thought I should be.

And suddenly I don't have to be. Suddenly, it would be okay if I'm not. I may not be cut out for this. Some people aren't. I don't know yet. And I've never been able to accept that I mightn't be cut out for something. Until far too recently I still hoped I'd play test cricket some day. Of course, I've got no idea what else I'd do. Without a good assay, a higher batting average or a better understanding of rocket science at least.

But don't think I know what I want to do in the end, she says, as though she's picked up some of what I'm thinking. But hopefully only some of it. *At least I'm not going around inventing people who might like kittens.*

Lots of people like kittens.

Don't even try. Anyway, I'm assuming you have my number, in case you're planning to call. About the kittens.

Of course, they won't be around for ever. They're being advertised in the paper tomorrow.

Tomorrow?

Yeah. My father's coming over to spend the day with me. He says you can never be too sure about the sort of people who come to take kittens. Presumably he thinks they're all rapists who use them to train greyhounds.

That's very much a father way of looking at the prospective kitten buyer. He's going to come and spend all day with you?

All day, or until the last kitten. And then he'll make me owe him for going to the trouble.

I've got an idea, depending on how much you want to be in debt to your father.

Not much.

He could take the day off. I'm not doing anything, and I think I can pick a greyhound-training rapist as well as the next guy.

Okay, she says. *My father was going to bring lunch though.*

I can cover that, too. You'd be surprised how wide-ranging my skills are.

Okay. I'll tell him. I don't know how he'll take it, but he'll have to live with it, I guess. And she eats her last mouthful of sandwich. *Shit. I just remembered they're having lunch for me in OT.* She looks at her watch. *Starting fifteen minutes ago. Not a great way to finish the locum. I'd better go. Are you serious about tomorrow?*

Completely. I've got your number. I'll call you.

Before ten, she says. *That's when the greyhound trainers'll start calling, if they go by the ad.*

Okay. Have a nice lunch.

Thanks.

And these have become the strangest of days, these

unspecial days just after the solstice, the day lengths imperceptibly growing now, Kate Blue casting an angular mid-winter middle-of-the-day shadow as she walks and then runs away. Across the pavers, beside the multistorey, up the hill to OT.

I pick up the wrappers on the table, drop them in a bin and go to the ward.

It's dark just after five when I'm driving away from the hospital. And Kate Blue's gone from here for good but I'm seeing her tomorrow.

I think about lunch. Fresh bread from the bakery for a start. And probably my second-best bottle of wine.

What if I really like her? What if I crash and burn? What if? What am I going to do with my life?

So many questions. So many pointless questions. In six months, I won't be a second-year resident and that's no answer, but it's a start.

I want to call her now, but I'll wait till morning.

The peak hour traffic closes in around me.

The tape plays, and I sing along.

ACKNOWLEDGEMENTS, AND MORE

This story is fiction, as are the characters in it. With a small number of exceptions.

The layout of Mount Stevens Hospital is not unlike that of the hospital where I did my residency, but other than that Mount Stevens is completely fictional. Terminology such as charge sister, rather than unit manager, is consistent with the time in which the novel is set.

The Director of Psychiatry has some of the characteristics of the present Director of Psychiatry of the above hospital at the time of writing (the beard, the Honda 100, the melancholy brilliance), but Gil Johnson is, ultimately, not John Gibson.

I was a co-researcher on a melatonin project not unlike that outlined in the novel (very like it, in fact, since I used all the references), but despite our similarities in work and suburb of residence, I am not Jon Marshall and his dilemmas should not be seen to be mine. His various partners in the novel, and other hospital characters, are made up, but I do now realise there were some situations (and people) I should have handled better.

Admittedly I borrowed a few things from family and friends, but if they're going to come up with Balsa Cars and nose-measuring theories, it's probably what they deserve.

I also borrowed the entire contents of the card Edward de Bono sent to my father in 1969, and I'd like to thank Edward de Bono for taking the trouble to write it, and for giving me permission to pass it on to Jon Marshall.

And thanks to The Go Betweens, whose album *Spring Hill Fair* was the first sign for me that things could happen here.

Finally, for their support, advice (much of which I took) and perspectives on particular aspects of interpersonal relationships, I'd like to thank Fiona Inglis at Curtis Brown; Clare Forster and Rachel Scully at Penguin Books; and of course Sarah.

I'd like to thank the Queensland Office of Arts and Cultural Development for the grant that assisted the writing of this novel.

QUEENSLAND GOVERNMENT

Sing to Me   Penny Flanagan

'When the silence had struck, some five years before, Margaret hadn't cared to dwell on what exactly had caused it. All she had known was that one day she had opened her mouth to sing, and what poured forth was not a pure golden sound that filled empty rooms but the deepest, widest, most aching silence she had ever known in her life.'

Once a singer of great promise, Margaret has turned her back on music in an attempt to control a wilful, damaged heart. She exists in a blank cocoon of silence, untouched by passion, until Adrian brings music crashing through the barrier and with it joy and danger . . .

A story about how music makes us fall in love.

Left, Right and Centre Tim Ferguson

Ten seconds into the future . . .

Luther Langbene is a man with a plan. Luther Langbene is a human juggernaut. Luther Langbene is a trained killer. Luther Langbene is a very charming bastard. Luther Langbene is running for election.

Armed with a gotta-love-me smile and a wicked sense of humour, Luther Langbene hits the campaign trail. But will the lovely Lorelei and the dazzling Tallulah Lowe get him over the line? And is his plan to save the nation all that it seems?